"From the opening [...] r senses, coaxing you [...] bridged over a cent [...] tion long after you've finished the last page."

D. J. Williams, author of King of the Night

Past Praise for Jaime Jo Wright

"Wright is in a class by herself, writing her own twists into the classic gothic mystery trope and exploring how people from all centuries face fear. Readers will want to read this novel in the light of day or commit to finishing the creepy tale in one sitting."

Library Journal

"Wright is an expert in her element. She elevates the classic haunted-house tale with this exceptional story of fear, unexamined grief, and hope through faith. Wright's white-knuckled suspense and thrilling plot twists frame the novel's beautifully tragic theme of reclaiming life within loss."

Booklist

"The twisting, fast-moving plot is loaded with secrets. Readers won't want to put this down."

Publishers Weekly

"Wright entertains with fast pacing, great writing, deep spiritual truths and just the right amount of spookiness."

BookPage

"Dark, suspenseful, and decadently atmospheric . . . an exceptionally satisfying read that weaves together past and present, light and dark, love and death."

Hester Fox, author of A Lullaby for Witches

"A bit of Stephen King, Rod Serling, and Alfred Hitchcock, this novel kept me guessing to the very end. It is scary, wonderfully crafted, and ultimately inspiring. Recommended."

Historical Novels Review

"A deeply felt novel that mixes suspense with the heartfelt need for healing."

Foreword Reviews

"A wonderfully layered mystery with a deep sense of place and well-drawn characters. Jaime Jo Wright is one of the best writers out there and an automatic buy for me."

Colleen Coble, *USA Today* bestselling author

"Wright pens an imaginative and mysterious tale that is both haunting and heartwarming."

Rachel Hauck, *New York Times* bestselling author

"Jaime Jo Wright takes readers on a journey that leaves them with a renewed sense of hope. Jaime masterfully weaves a narrative that demonstrates the resilience of the human spirit in the face of adversity. . . . Read this story. You won't be sorry."

Lynette Eason, award-winning and bestselling author

"An eerie multilayered novel that kept me guessing . . . a novel so atmospheric and gothic that it will delight the most discerning reader. . . . The twists will leave you gasping and deeply satisfied when you reach the magical words *the end*."

Cara Putman, award-winning and bestselling author

"Whenever I need a novel that will cause me to pay attention, to care and to be transfixed by an excitingly unique fictional world, I pick up a novel by Jaime Jo Wright. Jaime does not disappoint."

Tricia Goyer, *USA Today* bestselling author

"It's rare when a book carries me so deep inside its world that I forget I'm reading. Buy this book. Now. You'll absolutely love it."

James L. Rubart, Christy Hall of Fame author

SPECTERS
IN THE
GLASS
HOUSE

Books by Jaime Jo Wright

SPECTERS
IN THE
GLASS
HOUSE

JAIME JO WRIGHT

BETHANYHOUSE
a division of Baker Publishing Group
Minneapolis, Minnesota

Published by Bethany House Publishers
Minneapolis, Minnesota
BethanyHouse.com

Bethany House Publishers is a division of
Baker Publishing Group, Grand Rapids, Michigan

Printed in the United States of America

Library of Congress Cataloging-in-Publication Data
Names: Wright, Jaime Jo, author.
Title: Specters in the glass house / Jaime Jo Wright.
Description: Minneapolis, Minnesota : Bethany House, a division of Baker
    Publishing Group, 2024.
Identifiers: LCCN 2024002309 | ISBN 9780764241468 (paperback) | ISBN
    9780764244094 (casebound) | ISBN 9781493448197 (ebook)
Subjects: LCGFT: Christian fiction. | Detective and mystery fiction. | Novels.
Classification: LCC PS3623.R5388 S74 2024 | DDC 813/.6—dc23/eng/20240129
LC record available at https://lccn.loc.gov/2024002309

Unless otherwise indicated, Scripture quotations are from the King James Version
of the Bible.

Scripture quotations identified NIV are taken from the Holy Bible, New International Version®, NIV®. Copyright © 1973, 1978, 1984, 2011 by Biblica, Inc.® Used
by permission of Zondervan. All rights reserved worldwide. www.zondervan .com.
The "NIV" and "New International Version" are trademarks registered in the United
States Patent and Trademark Office by Biblica, Inc.®

Cover design by Jennifer Parker
Cover image of conservatory © James Kerwin / Trevillion Images

Author is represented by Books & Such Literary Agency.

Baker Publishing Group publications use paper produced from sustainable forestry
practices and postconsumer waste whenever possible.

24 25 26 27 28 29 30   7 6 5 4 3 2 1

This is for the warriors who have gone ahead and paved the trails of fear and faith so that we can follow in their footsteps and not trip. This is for you who have left legacies behind so that we can be sure our faith is not in vain.

To Dale Finger, who in my humble opinion was and is one of the strongest men I know. Thank you for the legacy you left behind so I could write you into my story as a permanent reminder of your faith, your courage, your fearlessness in the face of fear, and your remarkable will to never stop.

And to Mom, who, the same weekend as Dale, went along with him in your move to Heaven. Thank you for the legacy you left behind for my children—for me. One of faith, of invincible hope, though you lived daily with unfaltering fear and crippling anxiety. You never faltered in your faith either, and, Momma, fear did not win! That is your legacy.

In His grip.
See you both in the morning.

In peace I will lie down and sleep,
for you alone, Lord, make me dwell in safety.

Psalm 4:8 NIV

1

Marian Arnold

MÜLLERIAN MANOR
THE COUNTRYSIDE NEAR MILWAUKEE, WISCONSIN
OCTOBER 1921—ONE YEAR INTO PROHIBITION

DEATH HAD ALWAYS been fashionable. Women celebrated it by donning black silks and feathers and shawls and lace. Men acknowledged it with a band on their hat or a mourning ring on their finger. Of course, that was more to announce their eligibility than anything else. For what man could continue to flourish in life without a wife to manage his household and rear the children?

But what did a daughter do when in mourning? An adult daughter whose marriageable prospects had withered to almost nil, and who was just dull enough not to try to lean on her personality to charm a man?

The motorcar rumbled and jolted across the country road with the tenacity of a horse that was almost dead but determined to make it one last time around the racetrack. The vehicle wasn't the sleek and shiny kind that Marian Arnold was accustomed to. It was dusty and brilliantly held together by pieces of metal welded to various joints and hinges. Oh, Marian didn't understand cars any more than she'd ever cared to understand her liquor baron father's brewery business. Neither mattered anyway. They were both dead. Father, in his grave, and Arnold Brewery belly-up in the bankruptcy that Prohibition had ushered in.

"I will not become a soda manufacturer, and I've no interest in cheese!" Marian could still hear her father's irate words ringing through the hallways of their ostentatious mansion in the elite corner of Milwaukee. That had been two years ago with the threat of the federal government listening to all the "pearl-clutching mothers" who thought liquor was "the devil's brew." Father had created monikers for everyone he disagreed with, and neither the government nor the female population was spared his derision.

Marian bit back a yelp as the motorcar connected with a pothole and sent her rear off the seat. She wildly reached for something to hold on to, but her gloved hand found only the edge of the seat.

Father was dead now. He'd followed Mother into the otherworld after his fury had culminated in a stroke. Could she blame him? Marian couldn't. Not really. Their entire livelihood was Milwaukee, its breweries and their powerful influence. The family's social patterns lay in the beer gardens, enjoying the magnificence of the homes that lined the shores of Lake Michigan, reveling in Germanic roots declaring Milwaukee a new "Little Germany" instead of disconnecting from the homeland. That Father wasn't German didn't matter—Mother had been. Richly and lusciously German, who was also distantly related—though Marian could never repeat how—to the Pabst family. A rival brewery to be sure, but a relation Father capitalized on nonetheless.

"We're almost there, miss!"

The shout from her chauffeur brought Marian's attention back to the present. To the summer home she was being shuffled to. The one that Father had built for Mother over thirty years ago. The only remaining portion of his estate that her lawyers had been able to retain on her behalf.

Milwaukee was no longer her home.

Müllerian Manor was.

A bit of a lofty name, Marian concluded as it came into view, considering it was a summer home. But the name was also apt. On the one hand, it was a thing of beauty, while on the other it mimicked the noxious nature of a house a soul could get lost in. Mother's certainly had. And Marian? She'd spent summers here growing up, attempting to see past the warning signs to the beauty beneath. Now, as she surveyed the sprawling brick, three-story home with its angular gables, multiple chimneys, and maple-studded lawns, Marian knew she could have done far worse with bankruptcy. At the same time, she wished she had never returned to this place of confusion.

The motorcar backfired, and this time Marian couldn't squelch her cry. A cloud of dust, a flurry of blackbirds clearing the way, and the rust-colored foliage waving in greeting proceeded to welcome her to her now-permanent home.

Marian's muscles relaxed as she caught sight of Frederick, who had managed Müllerian Manor since before she'd been born. This time he was alone instead of having a footman by his side. Father had attempted to maintain his English roots by employing a litany of household staff that would imitate an English estate. Apparently, that too had been affected by the recent fall of the Arnold Empire.

The car door was wrenched open with a protesting groan. Marian palmed the hand of her chauffeur and crawled from the innards like a butterfly from its cocoon. A rush of fresh air filled her nostrils, the crispness ripe with the scent of dying leaves and the out-of-doors. Her shoes connected with the brick drive, and she held on to her turban-wrapped hair as the wind picked up and threatened to undo it.

"Miss Arnold." The warmth in Frederick's voice was accompanied by the shaky vibrato of age. His smile was oh so familiar, and without thought Marian hurtled herself into the older man's arms.

Frederick stiffened, unaccustomed to such displays by Marian or anyone of the upper class, but within a moment he'd returned her embrace with a grandfatherly one of his own.

Marian pulled away, her hands holding either side of Frederick's shoulders. "Oh, I'm so thankful you're still here!"

"Of course." He gave a nod. "Where else would I go?"

"Can I afford you?" Marian looked to her side as though the lawyer who had attended to her for the last six weeks would still be there.

"Don't fret on that." Frederick waved her off. "All has been handled."

"Who is left?" Marian inquired of the household staff as her chauffeur took on the task of dumping her trunk at the door since no one else had come to assist him.

Frederick's wince wasn't disguised, but he smiled anyway. "Felix is home from the front, missing a leg and a large part of his soul, I'd say. War took a toll on the boy."

Marian offered an appropriate nod. She'd heard Felix—who had worked in the gardens with his father as a boy and grown up alongside of Marian—had gone to France not more than three or so years prior. She'd never inquired as to his welfare. "And his mother?"

"Still here, thank the good Lord, or we'd all be starving." Frederick chuckled and offered Marian his arm. She slipped her hand into his elbow, and they took the rounded stone stairs up to the veranda together.

"I do love Mrs. Dale's cooking."

"Mm." Frederick nodded, but a strange look crossed his face, and Marian was quick to notice it.

"Frederick?"

He patted her hand even as she extricated it from his elbow as Frederick stood to the side to allow Marian passageway into the manor. "Don't worry, Miss Arnold. I was only thinking how little Mrs. Dale and Felix are appreciated these days. I'm glad that we are here—in the countryside."

The war. Mrs. Dale's German roots in spite of her married English name.

Marian cringed internally. The war had done awful things to many people, and for certain had created a new sentiment toward the German population in Wisconsin that was unwelcome and yet more real than imagined.

"Thankfully, the war is over. Feelings will die away, and it will all go back to normal," she reassured Frederick. Well, as normal as it could.

For a moment, Marian was lost in the memory of a brown-haired, brown-eyed lad in suspenders and trousers. Felix Dale had never held still, always darting here and there, and dropping his eyelid in the most mischievous winks at the most unexpected moments. She had always smiled shyly in return. It was difficult now to picture that same boy grown into a man and donning a helmet and uniform. It was even more difficult to picture Felix Dale without a leg. A consequence of a war that made little sense beyond regimes' quests for power and dominance. Marian didn't understand war, but that was because Father had said it wasn't something she should bother trying to understand, with her being a woman and all.

Marian had accepted her father's stifling dominance, because in a way, there was security there. She could pretend all was well with the world. Until it wasn't. Nothing was right with her world anymore, and from the way Frederick spoke of Felix Dale, home from the war front, it seemed his was also quite ruined.

". . . nonetheless," Frederick said, still speaking, drawing Marian back to the conversation, "we may be running on a pittance of what once was, but we are your loyal and faithful employees, Miss Arnold."

Marian offered a smile to the older man, noticing new creases by his eyes. The clock was a friend to no one, in the same way the world was a friend to no one. It seemed, Marian decided, that there were more forces out to destroy versus save.

Movement caught Marian's eye, and she noticed a maid glide through a doorway at the back of the hall. The maid met her curious gaze with a pointed look, and then she slipped away through another door and out of view.

"Who was that?" Marian turned questioning eyes to Frederick. She'd not seen that servant before, and it seemed odd— especially in light of the conversation they'd just shared—that new staff would have been hired after releasing others due to lack of funds.

"Who was who, miss?" Frederick inquired.

"The maid." Marian pointed to the now-empty hall.

"There's no maid, miss." Frederick gave a confused smile, and Marian frowned before shaking her head.

"Never mind then. I was sure I saw—" She bit her tongue. It had happened before. The *seeing*. It happened more frequently of late, as a matter of fact, especially since her father's passing and the upheaval of the brewery's bankruptcy. She preferred not to dwell on it. None of the faces she ever saw were ones she recognized, and though no one else ever seemed to see them, Marian knew they were there.

"You've always been a sharp child," her mother used to observe. *"You see and read people in a way no one else can."*

Mother had recognized it as a gift. Father had avoided it altogether—perhaps afraid she would become more like her mother as she grew?

Marian followed Frederick toward the broad flight of stairs that led to the next floor and the wing of bedrooms. The carpet snuffed out the sounds of her footsteps, but she heard footsteps regardless. Not hers. The ones of the maid who had disappeared, but who Marian was certain followed her now. A wisp of invisibility that wanted to be seen but demanded to be kept a secret.

She was good at secrets, Marian determined, even if they terrified her.

"Please," she implored in a whisper to the unseeable soul beside her on the stairs, "leave me alone."

"What's that, miss?" Frederick spoke over his shoulder as he ascended before her.

"Nothing, Frederick." Marian smiled gently in spite of herself. "All is well."

Though it probably wouldn't stay that way. It never did. Not in a house that had become a sanctuary for the ghosts invited to hide away here. Ghosts that had no care of Prohibition, or Germany, or even financial instability. Just ghosts who attempted to find a place to continue, long after their lives had been snuffed by death.

Yes. Death was a fashionable thing. But admitting to others that you saw the dead regularly? That was not.

REMY CRENSHAW

MÜLLERIAN MANOR
THE COUNTRYSIDE NEAR MILWAUKEE, WISCONSIN
OCTOBER, PRESENT DAY

One dead butterfly lay flattened on the stone step at the front door. A monarch. Its wing tilted precariously from its body like the wind, or someone crueler, had attempted an amputation. Its orange-and-black body slowly dried into a crisp corpse. This cool autumn was not a friend of butterflies, and this particular one must have missed the memo that it was time to migrate to Mexico.

Remy stared down at the butterfly. She had been here at Müllerian Manor for a week now. She craned her neck to see through the study window. It was like looking at a chalet from the Black Forest, only it wasn't, and she wasn't in Germany. Which was a shame. She'd always wanted to visit the Black Forest and Neuschwanstein Castle. Germany was a land of rich culture, layered history, strength, and brutality. Germans were often misaligned, Remy concluded, but then the world wars hadn't raised friendly memories either. Come to think of it— she turned her attention back to the manor—Müllerian Manor wasn't particularly inviting. Not with its ignored gardens, collapsing outbuildings, and worse, its eccentric occupant.

Elton Floyd. The infamous biographer of famous persons from history, such as Martin Luther King Jr., General George Custer, and Pope John XII. A motley crew of people, and then his more obscure biographies that highlighted the controversial lives of the lesser known, such as Kimball Brey, the serial killer of San Antonio in 1867; Lisa Cummings, the female spy during the 1962 Cuban Missile Crisis; and now Marian Arnold. Floyd's latest foray was into the life of the Milwaukee socialite and daughter of a brewery baron—and her interludes with the Butterfly Butcher of Pickeral County during the Prohibition era. The story of a killer, a disturbed young heiress, and the eventual disintegration into history that left only unanswered questions and unfinished tales.

Who wouldn't want to be Elton's research assistant? More qualified people had to have applied. People clamoring to bear the weight of the elderly man's investigations. They all wanted to live at Müllerian Manor. What greater place to research a biography but the location where the story actually occurred? It was a coveted position . . . for everyone except Remy.

Remy preferred the familiarity of the Twin Cities. She could get lost there, downtown or in the parks that encircled the sibling populations. But here? In the southeastern corner of Wisconsin, in the woods, without the luxury of being able to merge with the masses and become a nameless face? She missed that. She missed the sounds of an indie band playing in the park, children squealing and laughing at a splash pad, bicycles cycling by with no heed to her. Being anonymous was important to Remy because she had always been *seen*. From the moment her mother had died, and her dad had overdosed, she'd been seen. Social services saw her for what she didn't have, foster parents saw her for what she could bring to them by means of government aid, and schoolteachers saw her for all the trouble she *might* make—the stereotype slapped onto every kid in foster care.

She'll be a problem.

She'll murder her foster parents in their sleep.

She'll have behavioral issues and learning disabilities.

Frankly, Remy had been none of that, focusing instead on flying as under the radar as possible. Which, back to her original thought, was far easier to do when one could get lost in the city.

But here at Müllerian Manor? Not so much.

Elton was his own sort of eagle-eyed host. Then there was Aimee Prentiss, Elton's nurse, Flora Flemming the housekeeper, and Charleton Boggart, who was a haggard and wrinkly version of Kermit the Frog. If Kermit turned into a zombie, that was Charleton. Remy had fast learned to avoid the ancient groundskeeper. But that left her with the other three for company, of which Elton was probably the most normal. "Normal" being a term frowned upon these days as classifying people as "better," which wasn't Remy's intent. She just didn't have any other word for it.

She pushed open the arched wooden door that gave way with a groan, just like a haunted house should—only she'd not seen an apparition yet, even though Elton had promised she would.

"There you are." The crisp voice of Flora cut through the still-ness in the front hall, which wasn't magnificent but also wasn't demure. It had dark wood beams spanning the vaulted ceiling, and a chandelier of antlers that hung and lit the wood floor. A staircase, open on one side with a thick balustrade, was bordered on the other by floor-to-ceiling bookshelves. There was one window, and from it a beam of daylight cast its path down the stairs with dust particles dancing within it.

"Remy." It was a sharp jolt back to reality, not a question. A command from the pinched-face housekeeper who looked as though she'd never been allowed to leave Müllerian Manor. Only she did. Every night at seven, once dinner was cleaned up and the cook—whom Remy never met—was also ready to depart. "I am speaking to you."

Remy finally latched gazes with the older woman. She didn't answer.

"Mr. Floyd has been calling for you for the past twenty minutes. Aimee is on her break, and I certainly don't have time to entertain his whims. Go, do what you're supposed to be doing, and *aid* him." With a flick of her bony wrist, Flora pointed toward the stairs, her black eyes skewering Remy. "I don't know what you were doing outside anyway."

Getting fresh air? Remy squeezed a polite smile and edged past the woman, taking the stairs with soft footsteps. She ran her fingertips along the book spines as the stairs curved and then, on reaching the top, she hesitated. Müllerian Manor was a confusion of illogical halls and doors. In fact, there was a door directly ahead of her, but Remy had already opened that on her arrival at the manor to find that it went nowhere. Literally. There were four feet of empty space and then a wall. It wasn't large enough to be a closet, but it was tall enough to appear as though it were a hallway begun in error during construction. To fix it, they'd attached a door and forgotten about it.

Go right. Then take the second door on the left. Staircase up to the attic level. Right at the top of the stairs. Up the final three steps to the left. Open the first door on the left—not the right. The right is Mr. Floyd's living quarters, and it's not to be disturbed.

Remy heard Aimee the nurse giving instructions in her head as her body followed them. She ducked through a doorway with an *Alice in Wonderland* feel because anyone over five and a half feet would have to stoop to go through it. The stairs to the attic were narrow and unbalanced at different heights. There was an elevator, she'd been informed, but that went to Mr. Floyd's living quarters and was reserved only for the rare times he left the attic. Otherwise it was not to be used. By anyone. Ever.

At last, Remy reached the doors: Elton's study to the left, with the one on the right leading to his mysterious living quarters.

"Remy!" The shake was evident in the old man's voice, but his volume didn't suffer.

She twisted the copper knob, the etchings of a snake curving around it, and pushed inward. A rush of musty air, mixed with the smells of old books and ink and a whiff of fresh air from the cracked window, met Remy's senses.

Elton Floyd squinted up at her through gold, wire-framed glasses. His eyes were magnified, making them appear exaggerated. His wispy white hair was sparse and feathered from either side of his head, with a bald scalp dotted with age spots and, as Aimee had informed Remy needlessly, patches of melanoma that Elton refused to treat with the prescribed chemotherapy cream.

"Well?" His tone was warm, laced with expectation. He twiddled his thumbs that were oddly bent due to arthritis.

"Well what?" Remy seemed to find her voice and her sass only around Elton. Which was strange, considering anyone in their right mind would find the intellectual elderly man intimidating if for no other reason than his huge analytical eyes.

"Did you find it?"

"The butterfly house?" Remy pushed Jupiter, the fluffy gray

cat, from the chair opposite Elton. He leapt down and slunk to the corner of the room where he stared at her from his yellow orbs that communicated the depth of his feline emotions.

"What else would I wonder if you found? The garden rake?" Elton's eyes twinkled. He was teasing her.

Remy smiled in a way that told the man he wasn't going to one-up her, that she could match wits with him. "Actually, I did find a garden rake. Quite old. The handle dates back to the turn of the century," she quipped.

"Ah, yes." A gnarled finger tapped the arm of his wheelchair. "I believe it was circa 2001, from Home Depot."

"Menards," Remy corrected.

"By what evidence?"

"The sticker on the handle that somehow has never worn off."

"Is it Menards green?" he asked, a bushy eyebrow raised.

Remy sat with a plop into the chair Jupiter had abandoned by her shove. "No."

"Then how do you know for certain the rake was purchased at Menards?" Elton's other eyebrow joined the first in an upward thrust.

"Because oddly"—Remy cracked her knuckles—"it says *Menards* on it. A clue, yes?"

Elton nodded. "Ah. You got me!" A crooked grin revealed aged teeth set nicely in a row that, according to Aimee, were one hundred percent his own. "Now . . ." Elton tapped his finger on the thick journal lying open on his lap. "You have work to do."

Remy leaned forward, propping her elbows on her knees. She knew she didn't look the part of research assistant, and even now wondered if that was doubt she saw flicker in Elton's eyes. He'd given her a quick once-over like older men were wont to do. That assessment between appreciating young beauty and reminding themselves they were too old to be allowed to care too much—that is, without coming across as creepy. Yet Remy knew she'd probably failed his assessment. Elton would have gone after classic beauty in his younger years. Not her straight, chin-length, dark blond hair with strawberry-striped sections of it framing her face. The nose ring in her left nostril couldn't have helped either.

"Marian Arnold." Elton Floyd's finger thudded on the journal again. "I like to imagine she was a bit like you."

"Me?" Remy raised her eyebrows. She could never raise just one—she wasn't that talented.

"Of course." Elton closed one eye and assessed her through the other. "It's why I decided you were the best to assist me with this project."

Remy wasn't sure she was keen on where the old man was going with this. But he didn't seem to care, nor did he possess a tact filter.

"You're mysterious. I can see it in your eyes. Secrets to tell, just like Marian Arnold's ghost."

"Thanks." Remy's response was flat, even to her own ears.

"Don't get miffed." Elton waved his hand at her, his gnarly fingers callused where his pen rubbed against the knuckle. "Nothing was as it seemed at Müllerian Manor back in the twenties. Everything was *trying* to be normal after the First World War. The *Roaring* Twenties were a cacophony of ideologies and postwar culture and individualism that sent young minds into rebellious flares of independence. And then we meet Marian Arnold. Traditional, polite and cultured, shy and unassuming." Elton rubbed his nose with his thumb and forefinger, sniffing in thought. "While young women her age flirted with feminism in its early years, Miss Arnold hid away here at the manor, spending her spare time you-know-where."

"The butterfly house," Remy provided rhetorically. Her recent jaunt outside had brought her only to its border. The skeletal remains of a building shrouded in the spirit of Marian.

Elton gave a curt nod and drew his bushy brows together as

he closed his eyes and steepled his fingers beneath his clean-shaven chin. "The butterfly house, the house made of glass—or the glass house, as some call it." His voice dropped in pitch, and he sounded as if he were narrating a novel when he continued. "Marian Arnold was never the same after what happened there. The darkness . . . the hauntings."

"The Butcher?" Remy added.

Elton's eyes snapped open, a sharp blue, colliding with Remy's. "Yes, the Butcher," he said in a hoarse whisper. It was a drawn-out declaration as he hung on the word's last syllable. He stared at her, unblinking.

Remy shrank back into her chair.

Elton leaned toward her. "The Butterfly Butcher. He is as much a mystery as Marian Arnold. As Müllerian Manor. And why is that? Why is he a mystery? There must be archives, newspapers, more than just conjecture and legend. Yes? And yet no one seems to know what happened to the Butcher—or to poor Marian. The story is like a road that vanishes into the fog. No one knows where it leads, and where it ends."

Remy couldn't respond. She didn't care for the way her throat constricted at Elton's words or that her skin rose in tiny bumps. Her intrigue awakened, but with it came trepidation.

Elton brought his palm down on the book in his lap with a sudden slap that jolted through Remy. She jumped, her foot kicking out and striking the leg of the coffee table between them.

A thin smile stretched Elton's mouth. A gargled chuckle collected in his throat. He laughed and coughed simultaneously, in that old-man way that made death seem as though it were clutching at his breath and trying to get him to slow down to the point he would finally die.

"You're here because of her, Remy Crenshaw. She said you would come, and you did."

Remy frowned. "Who said I would come?" These were the moments she was quickly coming to learn that she disliked sharing with Elton. When his banter and wit turned to subtlety, insinuation.

Elton sagged backward, his shoulders slumping. His eyes were still sharp as they rested on Remy. "Why, Marian Arnold, of course. She is as alive in this place as she was a century ago." The old biographer's eyes narrowed. "You need only listen and you will hear her whispering."

MARIAN

"Y OU'VE RECEIVED a telephone call, miss."
Frederick's announcement cut through the silent morning breakfast that Marian was dutifully partaking in. Dawn had broken over the horizon but was hidden by the trees, and only now did the sunlight stretch through the clean, crystal windows that spanned the east wall of the dining room.

"Oh, you startled me, Frederick!" Marian's teaspoon fell with a clatter onto its saucer.

The man bent slightly at his waist. "My apologies, miss."

"A telephone? When did we get a telephone here at Müllerian Manor?" Marian dabbed at her mouth with her linen napkin and laid it to the side of her mostly uneaten breakfast. She rose from her chair, not at all sorry to leave the lonely dining room behind. The lace on the table, coupled with the dried floral bouquet in the crystal vase in the table's center, had left Marian feeling as though it were the parlor for a wake rather than the sunlit sparkle of a fresh new morning's nourishment.

"Your father had one installed a year ago, miss." Frederick extended his arm toward the main hall.

Marian preceded Frederick, her low-heeled shoes echoing on the wood floor. She tucked her chin-length hair behind one ear as she reached the telephone that was in the alcove behind the main stairs.

"Did they say who it was?" she whispered over her shoulder at Frederick.

"A Mr. Lott, I believe he said."

Her heart rate quickened. Marian pressed her lips together and lifted the earpiece to her head, leaning forward to speak into the candlestick telephone. "Hello?"

The other end of the line crackled. "Annie? Is that you?"

The exuberant tone of Marian's cousin carried across the line. She hadn't heard from Ivo in a few years. "It's me, Ivo." She shouted into the line, glancing at Frederick as he left her to her privacy. She wasn't accustomed to speaking on the telephone, let alone to a cousin she'd not seen for some time but was probably closer to her than anyone in her family.

"It's the berries to hear your voice, Annie!"

More crackling on the line.

Marian winced and pressed the receiver harder against her ear. "Ivo, I can hardly hear you!"

"You're at the manor?" he asked.

She nodded, then realizing her cousin—who in truth was her second cousin—couldn't see her, answered, "Yes."

"Wonderful! I'll be there by tomorrow!"

"Excuse me?" She couldn't help the surprise that squeaked into her voice.

"I know! Six years too long! Haven't seen you since all the boys left for the front. But don't fret, Annie. I heard about Uncle

Ralph's and Aunt Verdine's passing. You're not to think you're all alone in the world."

The mention of her parents' deaths brought a pang to Marian even as she tried to deal with the sudden reappearance of Ivo. His mother was Marian's mother's cousin and the only other German relation in America. She had grown up with Ivo, spending time at family reunions and summertime outings. Ivo's mother had been the only woman Marian could recall her own mother ever tolerating. But still . . .

"I heard you got the bum's rush from your father's estate. But I'll be there as quick as a wink. You're not alone, Annie, and we can pull you out of financial ruin if I have any say-so!" He repeated his reassurance, but Marian wasn't certain how comforting it was. "I'm already in Milwaukee. I'll be there tomorrow. So don't keep all your father's juice hidden, all right? We'll have a real reunion when I arrive!" He shouted out a few more words she could barely make out, and then Ivo ended the telephone call.

She stared at the earpiece as she pulled it away and slowly hooked it back onto its stand.

Ivo. Coming here. To Müllerian Manor? A swirl of excitement coiled in her stomach, and then tears sprang to her eyes. The comfort of Ivo! The *intelligence* of Ivo! He would know what to do. The brother she had never had, the boy who had always included her no matter how timid or shy she was. And he had never judged her when she was jumpy or nervous. The last time she had seen Ivo, she was seventeen and he nineteen. All the young women adored him for his dark German good looks that made some think he wasn't German at all but of different ancestry. But his sleek black hair, his piercing blue eyes, his chiseled jawline—the girls all tripped over themselves in hopes he would court them. To Marian, he was just Ivo. Her comfort. Her rock. But he had grown up. He had gone away. A few letters were exchanged, yet Marian had felt all but abandoned by him.

A surge of excitement flooded her. Marian couldn't stifle the smile that stretched across her face. Ivo was . . . *brave.*

Yes, he was brave. He had rescued her when she was a small girl who fell into the park's pond only to come up crying with a lily pad perched on her curls. He had taught her how to play hide-and-seek and escorted her into the mischievous ranks of childhood. He was everything Marian was not. Exciting. Adventuresome. Daring. Charming. Oh, the list could go on and on.

Marian sank against the wall and drew in a steadying breath. She glanced around, hoping no one was watching her.

Because they'll hate you for it.

The words reverberated in Marian's mind. She was not worthy of Ivo Lott's brotherly devotion. She never would be. She was merely the homely, thin, morose little girl he had once taken a mind to making his pet. And it worked. But only when Ivo was near to give her inspiration. Without Ivo, Marian fell back into the shadows beneath her father's looming personality and her mother's unpredictable self.

Mother.

Marian pushed from the wall, snapping back into the moment. She glanced around, the dark wood walls making the alcove in the foyer feel like a cave. She left the telephone behind. Frederick would need to be informed that Ivo was coming tomorrow. Mrs. Dale would need to plan for one more at the table. A suite would need to be prepared.

And Mother hated visitors. Even dead, Mother hated visitors.

Marian could sense her mother's anxiety in the pit of her stomach, her mother's chilling breath on her neck.

Ivo shouldn't come here.

This is our place.

You and me. The two of us.

Mother had wanted Marian, had been devoted to her, but she had not tolerated many others—Ivo included.

Ignoring the need to inform Frederick of Ivo's impending arrival, Marian hurried up the stairs that curved to the right as they rose. On the left were shelves ladened with keepsakes and books, all collected on the whims of her mother. As the stairs turned, Marian saw the door ahead but ignored it. That too was the whimsy of her mother. A pointless dead end in the house—and not the only one.

At the top of the stairs, Marian turned left and hurried down a corridor that was dimly lit because of its lack of windows. Instead, the walls were the backdrop for various paintings that Marian's mother had collected. Landscapes of English moors and German mountains. At the end of the corridor, a deer head stared at her with its glass eyes, its antlers with enough points to hang Christmas ornaments from.

"Never mock the stag."

Her mother's voice reverberated in Marian's mind as she reached the door at the end of the hall, just to the right of the deer. A buck was what they called it in Wisconsin. *Stag* was so very English, a carry-over from Father.

Marian pushed open the door, and once again the room's musty air filled her nostrils. A lonely room. It was an anomaly in the manor, barely large enough for a small bed. No windows whatsoever. And the room was barren of furniture. None of this surprised Marian. Instead, she moved across the familiar and odd little room to the lone painting on the far wall.

A monarch butterfly, its orange wings outlined in black, its painted feet perched on the leaf of a milkweed. It wasn't a beautiful painting. Mother had painted it, and for the butterfly's eye she had brushed two thin lines in the shape of a crucifix. When Marian was a child, the butterfly had frightened her. Its beauty was obscured by the dagger-like eyes and the claws that tipped its feet.

Marian took down the painting and set it on the floor, leaning the frame against the wall. She preferred to ignore the butterfly and instead focus on the tiny latch hidden behind it. When she pulled it toward her, there was a creak, followed by a small plume of dust as the wall gave way to a secret room behind it.

Mother's room.

Marian hadn't been here since Mother had died. That was over a year ago. This manor had been Mother's playhouse, her escape from Milwaukee, from the breweries, from Father. Mother was so much healthier when she was alone.

Alone with her paintings.

Alone with her butterflies.

Marian stepped into the secret room. A shaft of daylight snuck its way in because of a lone, narrow window. If anyone took the time to study the window from the outside of the manor, they would realize it did not match up with any of the obvious rooms inside.

Drop cloths covered the sparse furniture in the room. Not a large room, but larger than the decoy room she'd just left. A room, Mother had said, that was designed to keep people from looking further inward. To the heart of Müllerian Manor.

Mother's room.

Not her bedroom suite, but a room that reflected the chaotic nature of her soul.

An easel stood in the center, a canvas resting on its ledge. A few swaths of rose-red swept across it, long dried, the painting otherwise unfinished. Next to the easel was a table, and Marian carefully pulled the drop cloth from it to reveal rows of paints, bins of brushes, and a few smaller canvases.

She stared down at these canvases. Butterflies. Always butterflies. Ones that didn't even exist except in her mother's mind. Purple and yellow, brilliant red, and another dull brown with white spots in the tips of its wings to mimic eyes.

Marian stared at them for a long moment, dreading what was to come next. What must come next. Before Ivo arrived.

The butterfly house.

Mother had always insisted that it be locked when guests arrived but left accessible when Müllerian Manor was private to only her. It was Mother's sanctuary, where the creatures from her paintings took flight.

But what would it be now? Now that Mother was dead?

The butterfly house *had* to have been spared the decaying, crumbling bodies of Mother's unattended monarchs and tiger butterflies! Surely, Frederick would have seen to its care if no one else had. He could have hired a caretaker for the butterflies. The milkweed patches would need tending. The green-leafed plants that Marian couldn't identify if she tried would need watering. And the conservatory's glass would need regular cleaning.

Fear that none of that had happened paralyzed her. Marian had hoped to avoid the butterfly house, to avoid this room entirely. The essence of her mother, who her mother had been, and what she had left behind.

But now with Ivo coming . . . it could not be avoided. He would want to roam the estate, poke his nose into every corner. That was Ivo. Curious and adventurous and completely unaware of boundaries.

Marian replaced the drop cloth over the table of paints and brushes and disconcerting, nonexistent butterfly species.

No wonder Müllerian Manor was still hers to own and inhabit after the Arnold Brewery went under due to intolerance of liquor. No one had wanted Müllerian Manor because no one wanted its mistress, Verdine Arnold.

The butterfly house was not only her mother's forgotten world, it was her tomb. A crypt. Mother had never left the manor. She was still here. Encased in stone with a butterfly carved into its lid and the hovering aura of the creatures she had all but worshiped.

Butterflies that weren't as beautiful and promising as so many believed but instead were omens. Omens of trouble. Omens of horror. Omens of death.

3

REMY

Y OU'RE GOING TO FIND that you hear things at night."
Aimee Prentiss had told Remy more than she'd ever
wanted to know about Müllerian Manor the first day
she had arrived here. "It's just Marian Arnold roaming about.
She's harmless. Really, she is."

Elton's nurse wasn't far from Remy's own age. She was of
medium height and a tad overweight, with pretty blue eyes that
were intense and never seemed to blink. Her friendliness was
a bit suffocating, and Remy learned very quickly that Aimee
did not understand social cues. Nor did she keep information
to herself. The woman thrived on being the keeper of inside
information and distributing it liberally on her own terms.

Now, Remy flicked the light switch on her bedroom wall, and
sconces around the room lit up with a yellow glow. The room
was in fact a suite. A big bed took up the right side, a wardrobe
stood against the wall on the left, and large windows ran parallel

to the door. Off the left side of the room was the bathroom with its black-and-white tile, claw-foot tub, and toilet with one of those chains that hung from a tank overhead and made it flush when pulled. The place had been updated only to the point that was necessary for current-day living.

Remy glanced at her phone she'd dug from the pocket of her jeans. There was no Wi-Fi to go along with the spotty cell service. How Elton planned for her to get any research done without good internet was a mystery she hadn't solved in the week she'd been here. She'd mentioned this a few times, and Elton had only responded with "Have you not heard of books?" She couldn't tell if he was serious or not. As acclaimed a writer as he was, Remy had to believe he was messing with her. Which meant visits to the town's library and courthouse archives were more than likely in her future.

Remy tossed her phone onto the bed as she approached a door to the right. This was another part of her suite and weird enough to keep her unnerved. She went to open the door, which stuck and then scraped against the doorframe. Beyond it was, what, a sitting room? Hardly. She stepped inside and scanned the space.

The only furniture in the room was a table in its center. On the table was a lone item. A glass dome mounted on a gold-plated base. Inside the dome was a small piece of wood, and on its end perched the perfect specimen of a monarch butterfly. However it was preserved, Remy had no clue, and the fact it sat on a table in the middle of an otherwise empty room creeped her out. But each night she still came in here to stand before the thing and stare down at it.

There was no way this butterfly could be preserved from the 1920s. Could it? It mystified her. If she wasn't respectful of the belongings of others, Remy would have figured out how to remove the glass dome and touch the butterfly to see if it was actually real. As it was, she studied it again, remembering what Aimee had said when she'd given Remy the tour that first night.

The nurse had entered the room first and waved her arm with a "ta-da" toward the butterfly shrine. "Marian Arnold's preserved butterfly—made infamous in story and lore."

Remy had stared blankly at Aimee, whose mouth had turned down slightly in disappointment.

"You really don't know, do you?" she'd asked. It seemed Aimee adored being the first to share a good story. After Remy shook her head, Aimee clicked her tongue and said, "Why did Elton think you were fit for the job as research assistant?"

Remy didn't think Aimee had meant it to be demeaning, but she stuffed the hurt away just as she always did. No one felt Remy belonged anywhere she'd been, so this was nothing she hadn't heard before. It still stung.

Aimee had spun with a new smile and pointed at the butterfly. "Anyway! You'll find out soon enough the stories behind this and all the other butterflies." Aimee had given Remy a stern look at that point. One that speared Remy with enough force to instigate an insatiable curiosity going forward and an awful sense of wariness as well. "But for now, this is where you'll hear Marian most nights. In this room. Because this is the only furniture, her footsteps echo a lot." Aimee nodded then, as if Remy had asked a question—which she hadn't. "Yes. I've heard it. Many times." She frowned. "I'm surprised Mrs. Flemming put you in this suite."

"Why?" Remy took the bait.

Aimee's eyebrows had wagged as she informed Remy conspiratorially, "Because these were Marian's rooms. When she was alive and until she died. They say a servant found her right there on the floor by this very table, dead and lying in a pool of blood."

"She was murdered?" Remy had her suspicions.

Aimee shrugged. "That's the question. Was it the Butterfly Butcher? No one knows."

But it seemed, Remy determined as she left the odd room and latched the door behind her, that Marian wanted someone to know. Because Aimee was right about one thing. Remy *had* heard the footsteps. Every night since she'd arrived. Hollow, methodical, someone wearing heeled shoes. She'd even mustered the courage to fling open the door. To confront the ghost, or whoever, behind it. But all Remy had found was the table and the glass-domed butterfly, undisturbed, and the lingering scent of lavender.

Marian *was* here.

Visiting.

Every night.

Every night she taunted Remy with her aimless wandering across the wood floor. And when Remy had returned to her bed, covered herself with the sheet and blankets, it was only then she would hear it. Barely audible, the whisper that filtered through the crack between the bottom of the door and the floor.

Death comes in a day or two.

Death comes in a day or two.

The revving of a car engine was the first sign that today was going to be a mess.

"Who is tearing up the drive?" Elton craned his neck from his position in his wheelchair, pen poised over his journal where he was composing his thoughts.

Remy, thankful for the distraction from the hardcover book with about eighty appendixes, shut it with a thud and moved to look out the window.

Sure enough, a sports car with an attitude was flying up the drive, a cloud of dust swirling behind as it spun onto the circular part and skidded to a halt under the portico.

"Who is it?" Elton's tone indicated he was annoyed that their first full day of research and writing Marian Arnold's story had been interrupted, the peace of the manor disturbed.

Remy pushed her hair behind her ear as she eyed the car. The driver's door flung open, followed by the emergence of long legs in jeans, shoulders clothed in proper Wisconsin flannel, and a head wearing a baseball cap bearing the logo of Milwaukee's top baseball franchise. She didn't recognize what she could see of the man's face. A trimmed goatee drew attention to his square jawline. Dark hair curled on the back of his neck.

"Who is it?" Elton demanded again, a tremor in his voice.

Remy gave him a reassuring look. "Some guy who thinks he's all that. But I've no clue who he is, Elton. He's driving a four-door something or other with flashy rims."

"I knew it." Elton grimaced and tapped his pen against the journal.

"You did?" Remy stepped back from the window.

"Mm." Elton's nod turned conspiratorial, and he looked both ways as if to be sure they were alone. He coughed old-person phlegm from his throat and nodded. "I knew he'd show up. I'm surprised it took this long."

"So who is he?" Remy returned to her chair.

"Don't make yourself comfortable, Remy. You've work to do!" Elton's mouth quirked with a bit of mischief and a lot of ire. "*You* need to make sure our visitor doesn't make *himself* comfortable. You're my assistant, remember?"

"I'm your *research* assistant. Mrs. Flemming is your house-keeper."

"Yes, but it's you I trust," Elton said. "And trust will be needed to handle this."

He didn't trust Mrs. Flemming?

"Elton." Remy was growing impatient. "Who is this guy?"

Elton dropped his pen into the spine of the journal. "Tate Arnold would be my bet, and I would put money on that. He's the last remaining Arnold, and I expected him to catch wind that I'd moved into his ancestral estate last year. Only he never showed. But after the paper printed that article about my work on Marian's biography, well"—Elton chuckled—"that was enough to get our man out of hiding."

"Hiding?"

Elton waved his hand toward the door. "Never mind that. Go see what he wants, and tell him I'm not available. Not for argument or for conversation. I'm at work, as are you. Respectfully ask him to leave."

"But if it's his family history—"

"Blech!" Elton stuck out his tongue and shook his head like he'd tasted something disgusting. "The Arnolds forfeited their privacy when their company became the second-largest brewery in Milwaukee before Prohibition and went belly-up after. And that was only the beginning. So send the man on his way and then come right back here. We've work to do."

Remy let out a heavy sigh. "Fine."

"You're a good girl," Elton said, patronizing her as she headed for the door.

Not to be outdone, Remy shot him a glance over her shoulder and quipped back, "And you're an old coot."

His congested chuckle followed her as she left the room and closed the door behind her.

After Remy had figured her way through the maze to the main corridor, she heard voices echoing in the front hall and rising to meet her. Mrs. Flemming was talking, and she sounded shaky and unsure, which was unlike her. Regardless of her annoyance with the crotchety housekeeper, Remy increased her pace. The man's voice was raised and held a commanding, confident tone that bounced off the wood-paneled walls.

"I came to see Elton Floyd, and I *will* see Elton Floyd."

"Mr. Arnold, I must insist that—"

"No, *I* insist. And I—"

Remy reached the top of the stairs and cleared her throat loudly. Tate Arnold halted and lifted his chin to look up the stairs at her. Mrs. Flemming backed away a few steps, appearing to want to make her exit.

Okay, so the man wasn't bad-looking, but then Remy wasn't

a swooner. She could come face-to-face with Mr. Darcy himself and not be swayed. If growing up in foster care had taught her anything, it was to be scrappy and always present herself with confidence—even if inside she wanted to run back to Elton's study and the hardbound book with its endless appendixes.

"Maybe *you* can help me," Tate said, his eyes focused on her now.

"Doubtful," Remy replied and skipped down the stairs, her shoulder brushing the bookshelves. "Mrs. Flemming has already told you that Mr. Floyd isn't to be disturbed, so that's that." She sounded cavalier to her own ears and applauded herself for it. Especially when she saw a flicker of doubt in the man's eyes. Sky-blue eyes with indigo rings around the irises and long black lashes. Men always had the best eyelashes. It was totally unfair.

"Miss—"

"Remy."

"Miss Remy," he echoed.

"Just Remy. No *miss*. We're both of the generation that has dispensed with formalities. So let's not pretend we're in the upper echelons of society." Remy crossed her arms over her chest.

Mrs. Flemming gave her an incredulous look and, at Remy's nod, made a quick exit, her back ramrod-straight.

Tate Arnold had taken his ball cap off when speaking to Mrs. Flemming. At Remy's words he smashed it back onto his head, no longer concerned with protocol. His stance relaxed only to the point of matching her casual defiance. He didn't bother to extend a hand as he introduced himself. "I'm Tate—"

"Arnold. Yeah, I know." Remy waited. She really shouldn't take such satisfaction in goading the man, but she couldn't help but enjoy it. Maybe Elton was having an influence on her after a week of conversation and stagnant afternoons matching wits in an attempt to entertain themselves over games of chess.

Tate Arnold's chest heaved in annoyance. "Listen, I *really* need to talk to Mr. Floyd."

"So does the *New York Times*, but he's a busy man and isn't cool with being interrupted. Especially without calling first."

Tate was chewing gum, and he snapped it between his teeth. His eyes were icy. "This is my family home."

"Which you don't own," Remy countered.

He drew a steadying breath through his nose. "My great-great-grandfather built this house."

"And?" Remy wrapped an arm around the banister.

Tate Arnold weighed his words, his jaw working back and forth.

Remy knew she should say something more. If she was going to be Elton's publicist as well as his research assistant, then she probably shouldn't be a complete irritant to the man. She tried to affix a small smile and soften her features.

"Mr. Floyd is truly busy." Remy even gentled her tone to sound somewhat apologetic. "He doesn't take appointments when he's working on a new book."

"Which is about my *great-grandmother*."

Remy conceded with a nod.

Tate adjusted the brim of his cap. "Look, I know I don't have any right to push my way in, but you've got to understand. The Arnold family has not given Mr. Floyd permission to publish Marian Arnold's story."

Remy listened.

Tate took license from her silence. "Elton Floyd may have bought my family's manor, but he can't buy the rights to my family's story."

Remy considered his words. She didn't think he could stop Elton from writing and publishing the story, but what did she know? Then again, didn't authors write unauthorized biographies all the time?

"She's a vital part of Milwaukee history." Remy's statement drew a dark look from Tate. "And she's central to the Butterfly Butcher case."

"And what do you know about the Butterfly Butcher?" he tossed back at her.

Not much—not yet. "I've been researching a lot about the Butterfly Butcher," Remy lied.

Tate assessed her for a long moment, then gave a little laugh. "No, you haven't."

It was Remy's turn to be offended. "Excuse me?"

"You've never been a research assistant before. Your last job was as an administrative assistant at a car dealership. You have an associate's degree in library science that you've never used."

Remy found herself holding on to the banister tighter. A nervous squiggle disturbed her stomach. He'd done a background check on her? Tate Arnold had made sure to know Elton Floyd's business *and* that of his assistant.

"Before that, you worked at a fast-food joint." Tate shrugged. "Which means you aren't at all qualified to help with research. So the magnanimous Elton Floyd has hired someone green to research my great-grandmother's story. Aside from the myriad of questions that raises as to the man's reasoning, I'm not *cool* with your researching for him any more than I'm cool with Floyd writing her biography."

Remy struggled to steady her nerves. Under the man's icy stare, she was caving and losing her confidence. She'd give anything not to be the center of his attention right now. Conflict didn't frighten her, but when people started nosing into her background . . . Though she'd aged out of the foster-care system and had nothing to hide, the stigma of it all followed her into adulthood. She herself had avoided looking into her own past, and she certainly didn't want some stranger doing it for her.

"You can leave now." Her voice faltered, which annoyed her.

Tate Arnold stiffened, but then something shifted. His dark brows drew together, and he lifted his left hand as if to rub the back of his neck. Dropping it to his side, he tried again.

"Maybe we should . . . start over?"

Remy wasn't sure if the apologetic expression that crossed his face was contrived or genuine.

"I'm Tate Arnold." He extended his hand.

Remy eyed it.

Tate dropped his hand. "This place used to be in my family's trust. Then it was sold to other owners, then sold again two years ago to Elton Floyd. I'd really appreciate a chance to speak with him. I know he's working on writing the biography of my ancestor Marian, who is associated with the serial killer of the twenties, the Butterfly Butcher. I'd . . . appreciate a chance to discuss that with Mr. Floyd." He finished, fixed a polite but thin smile on his face, and waited for Remy's response.

She could toy with him, but she'd had enough of that, seeing how quickly it could backfire. "Mr. Floyd is not taking appointments at this time." Remy reiterated what Elton had told her.

Tate sniffed and nodded. He ducked his head for a moment, then lifted his summer-sky eyes and peeked at her from the brim of his cap. "Even if I can give him information about the Butterfly Butcher?"

Remy stilled. Okay, that could make life easier. Nothing better to help with research than a descendant of the woman she was researching. "But you don't want Elton writing your great-grandmother's story," Remy concluded out loud.

"No." Tate shook his head. "I don't. But if I can give you enough information on the Butterfly Butcher, maybe Mr. Floyd would be willing to emphasize the killer's story and make Marian a secondary character."

"This isn't fiction," Remy stated.

Tate locked eyes with her. "No. It's not. That's why, if it's going to be written, it needs to be written right."

"Which is what we intend to do. I mean to explore the mysteries of Marian Arnold, this manor, the Butcher—"

"The Butcher," Tate cut her off. His eyes were steely again. "Lost to the annals of history and time. A secret. That should be interesting enough without dragging my family name into it. Who was the killer? Where did he kill? What weapon did he use? Go that route and you'll have the reader's attention.

"Like a game of Clue," Remy whispered.

"An unfinished game of Clue, with my great-grandmother its primary victim." Tate paused. "Haven't you ever wanted to be left alone, Remy?"

The question stung. Remy bit her lip. She was beginning to understand his point of view but wished she wasn't. She wouldn't want anyone writing a story about her history—it wasn't for other people to know. And even if one didn't have secrets, they just . . . well, a person was owed their privacy.

"Fine." She blew out a breath, her shoulders sagging. "C'mon. I'll take you to Elton."

Tate Arnold had won this round, and Remy decided then and there that she'd let Elton Floyd fight his own battles. Who was she to disturb the ghost of a disturbed woman whose encounter with a serial killer had resulted in her dark mystery?

Maybe Marian Arnold deserved her privacy. Maybe that was why she wouldn't let Remy sleep but instead paced the floor invisibly stained with the memory of her own blood.

4

MARIAN

OCTOBER 1921

THE WIND WAS BRUSQUE with a biting chill to it. Marian wrapped her scarf around her neck and pulled her overcoat together with its large buttons. Her bobbed hair blew across her face, and she pushed it back, pulling her cloche hat as low as she could.

October was a wicked month. Though clothed in the beautiful colors of autumn, the wind picked up and blew an ominous chill, a precursor to winter's icy days and dark nights that were to follow and soon.

Mother's butterflies never flew through fall and winter. They lived their short lives, then fell into the conservatory's greenery without agony of death. They just fluttered and then plummeted. When winter set in, gas piping helped keep the butterfly house warm and the plants alive. A humid setting insulated by snowdrifts just outside the glass. But no butterflies. Not during the winter months.

Mother had hated winter for that.

Marian had slipped out through the back door of the servants' hall of the manor. Her low-heeled shoes clicked as she hurried along the brick walk, a flurry of leaves rustling across it in front of her. She stuffed her hands into the pockets of her wool coat and gave the lawn a cursory sweep of her gaze. It was sloping and expansive, bordered by woods that dotted yellow and orange and rust and red with the leaves of oaks and maples. Two outbuildings were on her left. The garden shed and carriage house. Cultivated gardens wrapped around the manor, including shrubbery turned flaming red from autumn's kiss, as well as potted chrysanthemums.

She traversed the walkway as it wound beneath a cedarwood pergola with the vines of morning glories curling downward. Beyond it, Marian caught glimpses of glass through the maples and sumac. Mother had instructed that the butterfly house be built set off from the rest of the property in seclusion. The trees surrounding the glass house had been trimmed to keep an adequate distance from it so as not to block the sun's rays with their branches.

Marian emerged into the clearing, and there it was before her. Muted glass, foggy from the humidity inside and clouded due to the large panes not being regularly cleaned. The iron framework between the panes was spotted with rust, the copper cupola on the domed roof tarnished green.

Marian hesitated, staring at her mother's shrine to the butterfly. To nature. Her place of peace and now her crypt. Father hadn't argued when Mother's last wishes were read following her death: *Bury me with the butterflies.*

And so he had. A granite sarcophagus, whose heavy lid slid with a grinding echo until into position, shut forever. The carved butterfly on its top was accompanied by Mother's name, her birth and death dates, and the words *May she fly forever*.

Marian hadn't been back to the butterfly house since the day they buried Mother here. That was a year ago. It wasn't that grief had choked from her the courage to return. It was instead the sinister peal that had rung through Marian at the sound of the granite lid sliding into place. A scraping sound that was so final, so dark and morbid that she never wished to return.

But now here she was, orphaned, though she was in her twenties and a permanent resident of the manor now. And with Ivo coming tomorrow . . .

Marian started forward. She needed to be sure the butterfly house hadn't been neglected—and that it was locked, otherwise Ivo might attempt to explore it. Not that he was unworthy to visit her mother's grave, but it had been Mother's wish to keep outsiders away. Even in death, Marian could not defy her.

The door to the butterfly house had an iron handle that pushed up to release its latch. Marian did so now. There was a click, then the door gave way, and along with it a puff of moist air.

The shock of it stifled Marian's breath. The beauty inside that greeted her ended all her fears of withering vines and empty cocoons. It was luscious, the air filled with the almost smothering scent of plant life and earth freshly tended. She was instantly warm, and not a little overwhelmed by the sight before her. Vines grew along the sides of the butterfly house, around framework, and hung from the ceiling. Tall, large-leafed plants mimicked the larger trees outside, only they waved feathery branches at her, some with flowers blooming like white blossoms of hope. A walkway curved through the butterfly house with foliage on both sides, leading toward the back of the house where her mother's stone sarcophagus kept vigil.

Marian pulled her hat from her head and shrugged from her woolen coat, suddenly warm and sweaty from the welcome she'd received. To her delight, a butterfly—how was it possible in October?—fluttered across her path. A monarch with vivid orange wings outlined in a daring black.

"Oh, Mother," Marian whispered to no one but the spirit that seemed to hover there. This was a fairy-tale garden. Her mother's soul must tend it somehow, and yet Marian knew that wasn't possible. Felix Dale perhaps, the groundskeeper's son? Frederick?

Marian took slow, awed steps along the walkway. Another butterfly, this one white, winged its way in front of her, dancing on invisible air until it diverted into the foliage.

If God existed anywhere on earth, it had to be here. Marian believed it firmly now, and she understood why Mother had wanted this place locked to outsiders. It was as though her mother's very spirit had nurtured her butterfly house.

Marian breathed deep, inhaling the earthy perfume. She closed her eyes as she took a few methodical steps forward. She had entered a dreamlike place, one she didn't wish to awaken from. The butterfly house had emptied the world from its insides and retained only the beautiful. Only the living. Only the hopeful joy of—

A choked scream curdled in Marian's throat as she opened her eyes. She clapped her hands over her mouth as a second scream gained momentum and volume. Her eyes fixed on the sight before her, and every shroud of ethereal pleasantry dissipated with the onslaught of terror.

Her mother's stone grave was in its place, plants on either side, butterflies dancing amid the leaves. But above it? Above it, swaying left to right in a slow rhythmic dance with death, hung a man. The rope creaked beneath his weight. His face bulged from suffocation, his neck angled in a way that made him more monster than human. His mouth drooped open, and his arms hung limply at his sides. His legs, his feet—

Marian averted her gaze, squeezing her eyes shut. A vision. It had to be a vision. But when she opened them, he was still there, staring down at her with lifeless, bloodshot eyes. She dropped her gaze to her mother's stone coffin below the man's dangling feet. There was something there. It was . . . Against her better judgment, she tiptoed closer.

It was a pile of dead butterflies lying on top of her mother's stone coffin, directly beneath the swaying body of the man. Orange monarchs, wings broken, thoraxes crushed.

Marian's cry ripped from her throat. An agonizing cry of horror and loss. It wasn't true. None of it. The beauty maintained in the butterfly house was merely a facade. Death came in all costumes, and as Marian stood frozen below the creaking rope, staring at the dead butterflies, she knew that being reborn was impossible. Death shrouded itself with the deceit of hope, but truly, death was the end purpose to every life.

Marian stumbled from the butterfly house, her scarf hanging haphazardly around her neck, her hat lost somewhere in the greenery, and her coat open to welcome the burst of cool October breeze. She gasped, clutching at her throat as she gagged on bile that rose there, choking her.

The thumping of footsteps down the walk alerted Marian that she wasn't alone—not for much longer. But even in her shock, the steps sounded abnormal.

Step, *thunk*. Step, *thunk* . . .

Regardless, there was an urgency in them that relieved her. She buckled at the waist, holding on to her legs, fighting for air. A hand thudded against her back as if to dislodge something she was choking on, but Marian choked on the appalling nature of death itself.

"Miss Arnold!" The male voice broke through her panic and brought her back to a standing position. She spun toward the man, grabbing at his arms.

"In the butterfly house—" Marian sucked in another breath— "there's a dead man."

"What?" The very alive man in front of her was familiar, but it was his eyes that reintroduced her to him. His dark brown eyes, burrowing into her soul. She need only look at his one leg, the other missing from the knee down, to confirm it was Felix

Dale. He leaned on a crutch to support himself and her wild clutching at his sleeves.

Marian dropped her hands to her sides and took a quick step backward. "I'm so sorry," she muttered, eyeing his missing limb.

A sweep of impatience flashed in his dark eyes and then dissipated. "What do you mean 'there's a dead man'?" he asked.

Marian struggled to collect herself. "In . . . in there." She pointed to the glass house door that was open and allowing the cool outside air to mix with the warm humid air inside.

She watched as he limped toward the butterfly house, his crutch tapping on the walk. As the man disappeared into the greenery, the butterfly house door shut behind him, and Marian looked for a place to sit down. An iron bench was just off the path, and she stumbled to it, collapsing onto its cold seat that awakened her senses as her legs brushed against it.

A dead man.

Hanging.

The creaking of the rope.

His face, the suffocation frozen in place on his death mask.

Marian startled as Felix appeared in front of her. She'd lost herself in the terror of it all, in the image imprinted in her memory.

"Are you all right, Miss Arnold? Marian?"

Her name on his lips made the years since she had seen the groundskeeper's son fall away. The last time she'd seen him, he'd been nineteen and she only fourteen. He had aged significantly in the last six years. War did that to a man, she supposed. Her gaze drifted to the empty spot beneath his knee. So did barely surviving.

Felix was not clean-shaven. The lower half of his face was covered in a short, dark beard. His dark hair curled from his head in tousled waves.

"I'm not going to faint," she assured him, although she wasn't sure herself.

Felix gave a quick nod. "Good." He shot a glance at the butterfly house. "Let me see you inside the manor. And with your permission, we can use your telephone to ring the police."

"Of course." Marian tried to stand and was surprised when her legs wobbled.

Felix's hand gripped her upper arm to steady her.

"Thank you," she mumbled.

He dropped her arm as she retained her footing.

"D-do you know who he was?" Marian hesitated. Did she want to know? Did she want to put a name to the face of the grotesque image hanging in the beautiful retreat of her dead mother's butterfly garden?

"Percy Hahn," Felix provided. "He delivers our milk."

"The milkman?" Marian's perplexity was matched by the expression on Felix's face. "Why the milkman?"

Felix didn't answer, only motioned for Marian to move forward. She followed his lead, questioning why he didn't answer and what the milkman had done to deserve such a fate. Worst of all—and this she felt most guilty for—she bothered over why whoever had hung Percy Hahn had decided to annihilate the butterflies as well and place them in a little pile of broken bodies below Percy and atop her mother's grave. Or had Percy done it all? Hung himself over a memorial of butterflies?

Butterflies that would never fly again.

Not unlike her mother, or the dead man who now swayed from the rafters of the butterfly house.

5

MÜLLERIAN MANOR would never be the haven that Marian had hoped it would be. She'd assumed this only because it had always been shrouded in the unpredictability of her mother. But she'd not expected it to be cloaked in the fearsome elements of death.

As the police roamed the property, Marian huddled in the sitting room while Frederick took the bulk of the questioning on her behalf.

No, they hadn't seen the milkman, Percy Hahn, this morning.

Yes, milk had been delivered, just as it was every Tuesday morning. Mrs. Dale had retrieved it from the back kitchen entrance.

Yes, they could interview Mrs. Dale.

Frederick had led the sheriff through the maze of hallways, crooked and making no sense, toward the kitchen. Marian was thankful to be left alone in the sitting room. It was a dark space with walnut trim and floors, stone fireplace, and windows with dusky violet-colored draperies. The furnishings—which Marian's mother had purchased years prior—were love seats of lavender, vases, knickknacks of purple and lavender tones, and dried lavender bunches tied with purple ribbons.

Marian drew her legs up beneath her on the chaise lounge that abutted the floor-to-ceiling window. She stared out across the front lawn, thankful she could not see the rear of the property toward the butterfly house. Her skin crawled at the idea that sometime this very morning the milkman had delivered their milk and then ended up hanging over her mother's stone-encased resting place. She had been eating her breakfast, taking the phone call from Ivo . . .

Ivo! A flood of emotion coursed through her. Relief because she longed for the familiar, the familial. Apprehension because—well, it was Ivo. Her revered and long-admired distant cousin. She wanted to throw herself into his arms, weep with abandonment over the loss of her father and mother. But now she would have to offer an explanation for the death that had just occurred on her property. Ivo would want to know—*demand* to know. As he should. As the only remaining male influence in Marian's life.

Confident footsteps marched across the floor just outside of the sitting room. Marian swung her feet to the floor and adjusted her dress as the sheriff strode in, Frederick behind him, another officer, and Felix Dale.

With a nod toward Marian and no introduction other than "Sheriff Fletcher, and this is Officer Petey," the detective motioned for Felix to take a seat opposite Marian. He held a notepad and pencil, eyeing them both.

Marian shrank back onto the lounge.

Sheriff Fletcher jotted something in his notepad, then lifted his eyes to level them on Marian. His dark bow tie did nothing but formalize the black stripes on his shoulders, his ironed uniform, the patch on his left arm, and the star on his chest. His hat was tipped back from a broad forehead and a round face.

"You were the first one to discover Mr. Hahn?" His words skewered Marian.

"Yes." She nodded, nibbling at her index fingernail with a nervous energy she wished she could hide.

"And did you see anyone in the vicinity when you approached the building?"

Marian shook her head. See anyone? The idea curdled her insides. Had she been watched? Goodness, how long had it been between when the killer left, Percy Hahn had died, and she had arrived?

"And, Mr. Dale, you came upon Miss Arnold when?"

Felix directed his attention to Sheriff Fletcher with a confidence Marian both admired and envied. "I heard Miss Arnold cry out and came as quickly as I could to her aid."

The sheriff glanced at Felix's missing leg. "France?" He pointed rather uncouthly at it.

"Château-Thierry—second battle of Marne."

"Ah." Sheriff Fletcher grimaced. "Several Wisconsin boys in that one."

Felix didn't reply.

"All right." The sheriff shot a look at his fellow officer as the air grew awkward in the room. "So you came upon Miss Arnold. Then what?"

Felix remained expressionless. "She stated there was a man hanging in the old butterfly house, so I went to check. He was already dead."

"And you didn't witness anyone in the area either?"

"No," Felix affirmed.

Sherriff Fletcher tapped his pencil impatiently on the notepad and then sucked in a heavy breath. "Well then. We've cut Mr. Hahn down. I'll have my men clean up the remaining rope. Obviously we'll be investigating this, but there's not a lot to go on right now."

"But we're safe here?" Marian straightened, unable to keep the question from escaping her lips.

Sheriff Fletcher shrugged. "Let's hope, Miss Arnold. The fact is, any one of you could be a killer. You were all here at the time Mr. Hahn died, and you were all, for the most part, alone. With the exception of you, Miss Arnold, who apparently had taken a call?"

"Yes," Marian assured him quickly.

"Fact is, Mr. Hahn hadn't been in the big sleep for long when you found him. A half hour earlier and he might've been saved."

Was she supposed to feel guilty that she'd not gone to her mother's butterfly house sooner? Marian drew away from the sheriff's pointed stare.

"What else do you need from us?" Felix pushed himself off the chair on which he sat, leaning on his crutch.

"Nothing at the moment." Sheriff Fletcher looked between them. "But don't plan on leaving town or anything."

Felix dipped his head in silent acquiescence.

Marian found herself nodding more exuberantly than she needed to. She wanted the sheriff and his men to leave. She wanted Felix Dale to go back to groundskeeping and staying out of sight. She wanted everything at Müllerian Manor to go back to the way it had been only hours before. Marian knew how to maneuver the oddities her mother had built in her years of solitary existence at the manor. Yet she didn't know how to manage when the place was teeming with strangers, childhood acquaintances were irreparably injured in the war, and butlers like Frederick were growing old and white-haired.

Too much had changed already. The Arnold name was tarnished in Milwaukee. A brewery gone under because of Prohibition, and now a man was hanged in what remained of the estate?

Sheriff Fletcher caught her eye, and for a brief moment Marian was certain he read her thoughts. His ruddy face was stern as he concluded the conversation.

"We'll be looking into Percy Hahn and his connections to the Arnold estate." A warning laced his words. "These days nothing is off-limits, and I don't mince my words when I tell you *nothin'* gets by me."

The long pause. The deep stare. The pointed words. Marian was sure Sheriff Fletcher was insinuating something more nefarious at play than even she understood.

She caught movement behind him and diverted her attention to the figure in the doorway. The maid from yesterday when she'd arrived at Müllerian Manor hovered in the doorway. Her expression was wary. She looked at Marian, and Marian noticed how empty her eyes were. Devoid of emotion, staring right through the sheriff at Marian, as though the sheriff didn't even exist.

The maid held her finger up to her lips and shook her head. *Shhhh.*

Marian knew she was the only one who heard the young woman's whisper, the only one who saw the warning in her eyes.

She was the only one who saw the specter at all.

"Here you are." Mrs. Dale's words held a hint of vibrato as she entered the room with a tray of tea and cookies. The woman who had held various roles and responsibilities through the years—not the least of which was being Felix's mother—set the tray on the table. "Best head outside now." She patted her son on the arm.

The sheriff and his officer had just departed the sitting room by Frederick's leave. A few other coppers were getting into their vehicles. Dust rose from the drive as they rounded the circle and headed away from the manor.

Felix gave Marian a side-eye and then nodded at his mother. Marian didn't miss how his hand squeezed on his crutch, his fingers massaging it in an absent gesture of anxiety.

"Miss Arnold." Felix's farewell was formal, familiarity carefully capped due to convention.

Marian met his eyes and even held her breath. But there was no mischievous wink from him as he'd been apt to do when they were children. There was a seriousness in his expression, one that had memories hiding just out of her sight but that must play like a motion picture in his mind. War memories. Death wasn't new to Felix Dale, but that didn't mean he was immune to its horror.

"Th-thank you, Felix," Marian said. There was something in the way he looked at her that made her feel safe and nervous simultaneously.

He nodded, issued his mother a small but tight smile, and then moved toward the door. Marian watched him exit the room, his limp pronounced but his back and shoulders straight and proud. Then she realized his mother, Mrs. Dale, was watching her. Marian managed a smile.

Mrs. Dale matched the expression, although there was empathy on her face and hinted at by the wrinkles at the corners of her eyes that the years had deepened. Her graying brown hair was pulled back into a bun. She hadn't adopted the current short hair trend but instead stuck with the age-appropriate style that matched her clean-cut, practical dress.

"It's already been a long day and it's only two in the afternoon." Her words brought Marian a semblance of normalcy.

"Mrs. Dale," Marian greeted. "I'm sorry I hadn't the opportunity to say hello yesterday or this morning."

The employee of Müllerian Manor offered an understanding smile. "And today has not gone as expected." She held up a hand. "It is quite all right, Miss Arnold. I hope the tea and cookies will help calm your nerves. I've not experienced anything so unsettling since—" She bit off her words and made quick work of pouring tea for Marian.

Marian frowned, not used to Mrs. Dale pouring the tea. She also noted Mrs. Dale's cut-off sentence and could only assume she was referring to something about Marian's mother. Only Verdine Arnold had the reputation of upsetting things at Müllerian Manor.

"And you've been reunited with my Felix?" Mrs. Dale spoke as the tea poured into a delicate teacup painted with tiny pink roses. She didn't wait for Marian to respond. Instead, she babbled a bit too brightly for the circumstances—not to mention her station. "He's such a brave man, my son. So brave."

Marian nodded as Mrs. Dale handed her the teacup and saucer. "The war was difficult for many mothers," she acknowledged.

Mrs. Dale's eyes bespoke stories she would never tell. Stories of tears shed at night over letters. Nerves fraught with tension and expectation that Felix would not return home. And now? The tenuous hazards of being German. Not much had lessened since the war. It felt as though pieces of it still hung in the air. Ghosts from the front that whispered harbingers of trouble still to come.

"I'm glad Felix is all right," Marian muttered and then sipped her tea.

Mrs. Dale nodded. "Yes. The Lord blesses."

Marian didn't answer. Did He, though? She took another sip of tea. Father had been a Christian man with a patriarchal sense of religion. Mother had been free-spirited. Marian wasn't sure what all her mother had believed. In God? Yes. As to sin and damnation? She didn't know. Mother was unpredictable. What she believed one day could change the next day.

Mrs. Dale was speaking, a tremor in her voice. ". . . I prayed many a night for my boy. If the good Lord had chosen to take him to glory, well, I would have relinquished Felix into His care. I am so grateful—" she choked up for a moment—"so grateful the Lord saw fit to give us more time on this earth together." Mrs. Dale swiped at her eyes, then gave Marian a kind look. "Your dear mother, now your father . . . my girl, if you're ever in need of a listening ear, I know I'm just your employee, but maybe I can be one of God's blessings to you."

Marian offered a small smile.

Mrs. Dale nodded and turned to leave. Marian stared after her employee as the woman exited the room quietly. "God also curses," Marian whispered. She had experienced that side of the Almighty more than the one Mrs. Dale spoke of. And blessings were subjective. Marian wondered if Felix felt blessed, hobbling around with one leg, armpits bruised from utilizing crutches, being stared at and ignored, or worse, pandered to as if he were no longer useful.

No. Blessings to one could be curses to another.

But one could get used to curses.

Marian took a sip of tea and attempted to steady her nerves. She was, after all, living proof of that.

6

REMY

WELL, THAT HAD NOT gone well.

Remy avoided the frown directed at her from Nurse Aimee and left Elton's study. Her employer was in a state, and she had overstepped and offended by allowing someone other than herself access to his inner sanctum. Still, Elton had not shooed Tate Arnold from his study. Rather, he sent her away with a flick of his wrist and a promise in his eyes that he'd deal with her later.

The men's voices were intense, their sentences short. Both had their opinions and points to be made and apparently were equally passionate about them. Tate, that the world never again put his great-grandmother Marian Arnold in the spotlight, with Elton determined the world deserved to know the truth about Marian and the Butterfly Butcher—whatever that ended up being.

Aimee hurried after Remy. "You've upset Mr. Floyd."

A quip would be ineffective in getting Aimee off her heels, so Remy bit her tongue. She turned the wrong way down a corridor and found herself at a dead end of sorts. The door at the end stood open, the room beyond revealing sheet-covered furniture and dust motes in the air.

"That's one of the guest bedrooms." The lofty know-it-all in Aimee's voice slid under Remy's skin and tried her already frayed patience.

Remy spun back the way she'd come and brushed past Aimee, who followed like a yapping little dog.

"You know this will probably raise Mr. Floyd's blood pressure."

And her own. Remy rounded a corner, thankful to see the flight of stairs to the ground floor ahead of her. Whoever had designed this maze of a house must have intended to bring a level of lunacy to architecture that no one would ever comprehend.

"The Arnold family gave up their rights to this home years ago." Aimee moved down the stairs behind Remy. "Tate Arnold is the only heir left. In fact, he's not even Marian Arnold's direct descendant."

Remy stilled, her hand on the front door leading to the outside and her escape. She turned and eyed Aimee. "What do you mean?"

Aimee offered a smug expression that indicated Remy should have given her full attention sooner. "Tate Arnold is the great-grandson of Marian Arnold's brother."

"There's no record of Marian Arnold having a brother," Remy said. Aimee was either living in her own wonderland or she should retire from nursing and take Remy's job as research assistant.

"There's no record of Marian Arnold ever marrying or having children, either," Aimee quipped back. She folded her arms across her chest. "As convoluted as the Arnold family history is, one can only wonder why so little has been said about Marian's brother."

Remy stared at Aimee for a moment, musing. Was she insinuating something more sinister about Tate's ancestral grandfather? Butterfly Butcher sinister? "Wait." Remy locked eyes with the nurse. "Why would Tate call Marian his great-grandmother? Wouldn't your claim mean she was actually his great-aunt times two?"

"I suppose. Something like that." Apparently, Aimee hadn't bothered to write out the family tree and count the number of *greats*.

"What was Marian's brother's name, and why the supposition that Tate doesn't know his own ancestry?"

Aimee raised her palms. "No clue. *You're* the research assistant." She gave Remy a pointed look. "I just know rumors have always swirled that Marian Arnold had a brother. How else would Tate's last name be Arnold? If Marian had married, she'd have adopted a married name. Tate's would be completely different."

There were more *ifs* to Aimee's claims than Remy was comfortable with. Still, it was worth researching to find out if there was any factual basis for them. Besides, that was what she did now—research.

"Where are you going?" Aimee took a step forward as if to follow, but Remy gave her a sharp look that made the nurse stop in her tracks.

"I'm going to catch some air," Remy stated. "Then I may go into town where there's a good internet connection and do some research."

"Elton prefers book research," Aimee snapped.

"Have at it!" Remy's patience ran out, and she swung the door open, stepping into the crisp autumn air, the orange glow of the trees, and the blessed relief from all that was entombed within Müllerian Manor.

Her shoes crunched the dead leaves on the path that ran around the back of the manor. Maples and oaks loomed overhead like witnesses to history that had been bought off to not say anything about what they'd seen. Remy stuffed her hands into the pockets of her cozy fisherman's sweater with its big leather buttons.

She scanned the vast lawn flattened by a few frosty nights and a blanket of fallen leaves. This place was like traveling back in time. It was untouched by the hustle that was mere miles away, a quick jog to the interstate and the plethora of cars and trucks speeding toward Milwaukee's innards. Even here, Lake Michigan saturated the air with its humidity, for although Müllerian Manor wasn't on the lake, folks often underestimated the Great Lakes' influence on the towns and residents surrounding the huge bodies of water.

Remy glanced around for Charleton Boggart, the grounds-keeper. Through the trees she could make out the butterfly house—or what remained of it. Elton had told her on her arrival a week ago that she needed to pay it a visit. It was pivotal to Marian Arnold's story, the setting of the Butterfly Butcher's first known victim. She had yet to approach the place.

Butterflies. They were Remy's earliest memory. Had she been three, maybe four? All she recalled was a green station wagon and her little fingers trying to rescue a monarch butterfly from the radiator grille.

"No, no. It's already dead." A woman's voice. Her mother's, most likely. Remy had been placed into the system before she was five, so the memories prior were mostly shadowed.

She remembered fighting off the adult hand that tried to discourage her butterfly rescue. Remy had pulled at a wing and then actually felt pain as it ripped from the butterfly, tearing her little girl's heart along with it. It was the first time Remy felt empathy, that she recognized another's feelings and sensed their anguish. As she held the butterfly's wing in her hand, she experienced the insect's mortality.

"I said *no!*"

A hand slap. The wing had fallen to the ground, leaving behind a powdery color on Remy's fingers.

Butterflies were a painful memory. For multiple reasons.

Remy stood in front of the butterfly house, built at the turn of the last century, now a broken-down greenhouse. The doorway was wide open, missing its door altogether, and the glass panels to the right of the door were gone, the iron frame having since rusted.

She stepped inside, her breath stealing away as the former butterfly house took on an aura of the past. Her shoes connected with debris scattered about on the stone floor: sticks and leaves, old fast-food wrappers, and those infernal big-box store plastic bags. Old stone planters, probably original, with long-decayed foliage outlined gardens with knee-high brick walls. Rotting, wet boxes were piled against the remaining walls.

The glass house had become Müllerian Manor's dumping ground. Remy sensed the sadness in the air. The loss of the beautiful that once flourished here with greenery, flowers, butterflies—a haven of serenity and warmth. She moved forward, dodging piles of moldy newspapers and a blue plastic barrel stuffed with glass bottles and jars and other items that could have been recycled had they not been stored here in the manor's private trash bin.

Some of the plants still remained but were dead. Winding limbs and vines that tangled with her feet also hung from the framework where they'd once grown yet now drooped, brittle and expired.

Remy stilled as her breath caught again. This time with emotion —something she never let anyone see. The cavalier, confident Remy, or the quiet, bookish Remy—she could turn either of those personas on in a pinch. But the *real* Remy? The real Remy could hear the butterfly house speaking to her soul, reaching out through the decades. Its untold stories and heartbreak so thick and so saturated in their remains that Remy's heart almost physically hurt.

"God, this is awful." A prayer? Maybe. An exclamation, absolutely. Either way, Remy was fine if God heard it because He should. He should see all that was here in the butterfly house. A place where horror had visited and, as far as Remy could see and even feel, had never really left.

She trailed her fingers along a planter with its stone scrollwork. It was empty, minus a pile of cigarette butts in its basin. Remy averted her eyes and looked toward the vaulted roof. No butterflies flitting here and there. No fine mist of spray wetting the plants as she'd witnessed at the butterfly conservatory she visited in Colorado a few years ago.

Her gaze fell on a large rectangular box made of stone. It sat on a pedestal base also made of stone, with intricate carvings of roses and vines along the edges. Perplexed, Remy stepped closer, eyeing the thick vines that wrapped around the box and pedestal, covering it with arms like a hundred skeletons that clung to the last fragments of memories lost.

She saw words carved into the stone and shoved at a couple of vines as thick as her wrist to get a better look. At first the vines resisted her attempt at moving them, but with more force, Remy was able to push them aside enough to make out the words they had fought to conceal.

Verdine Biedermann Arnold
b. November 12, 1877 – d. March 2, 1919
May she fly forever.

A stone sarcophagus . . . in the butterfly house?

She'd been right to feel as she did—surrounded by the unheard voices of prior inhabitants whose invisible footprints she now walked in.

Remy pulled her cardigan tighter around herself, staring

down at the name on the grave. If only the bones inside could speak, could rise from the dead and tell Remy this one's story of pain. She could feel the agony seeping into her being just standing here—

"She was the mistress of Müllerian Manor."

Remy yelped, pirouetting to face the intruder.

Charleton Boggart.

The crooked, angular groundskeeper reminded Remy of a man in the fast lane headed toward death. His nose was hooked, his cheekbones were razor-sharp, his eyes yellowed—either from age or liquor or both. His head appeared bald with the exception of gray wisps over his ears, which he covered with a brown stocking cap that made him look like a chimney sweep from *Mary Poppins*. His jeans were held up at his narrow waist with a wide leather belt, and he had tucked in his green flannel shirt. The shirtsleeves were rolled up to his elbows, the hair on his forearms white, the skin spotted from age.

Enough. Remy shook her head to release herself from the hypnotic spell the strange older man placed on her.

They eyed each other, Remy disappointed that Boggart had interrupted the sacredness of her emotional dance with the dead.

"The mistress." He pointed at the sarcophagus.

"She was Marian's mother." Remy recognized the name from the family tree. She had done her own cursory overview before arriving at the manor. The Arnold family was relatively straightforward—at least it had been until Aimee upset it with a rumored mystery sibling to Marian. Regardless, Remy still hadn't been aware that Verdine had been buried in the old glass house. "Did you know her?" she asked, shifting her attention back to the carved epitaph on the stone.

"How *old* do you think I am?" Boggart snapped.

Remy hurried to respond. "No, I meant did you know Marian?"

"No," he said curtly. In a way that made Remy question if Boggart was being honest.

She looked around at the ruins of the butterfly house. "Why is this place in such a state? Especially when it's home to a grave?"

"Why are there so many weeds in the gardens?" Boggart gritted out. "Why is there garbage lying around? Why are there holes in the roof?" He swore. "Why are shutters falling from the manor's windows? Why is the sidewalk crumbling? Why do the doors stick?"

Remy's eyes widened. She hadn't expected such a defensive response.

Boggart scratched his ear as he glowered down at her. "I'm an old man, missy, and my knees are as useless as a rusty pair of scissors. So if you want this place restored to the magnificence of its golden days, then do it yourself."

"I didn't mean—"

Boggart waved her off, his face darkening. "I came with the place. Same as Mrs. Flemming. Years with no one here, and then *he* bought it." A stream of spit hit the floor by Remy's feet. She stepped back from the groundskeeper. "Elton Floyd. Mr. Uppity Author and his bestsellers' list."

"You don't want him to write the story of Marian Arnold?" Remy dared to ask.

Boggart sniffed. "*Marian* doesn't want him to write the story. That's all that matters, missy. What Marian wants. And he doesn't respect that."

Remy wanted to argue it was apparent no one had respected Marian's mother's grave either, not for decades. Or the property. And Boggart's excuse of age didn't mean diddly. She'd seen him just yesterday raking leaves and hauling wheelbarrow loads of them to the woods, his lean frame moving fluidly.

"But Marian is dead. She won't even know—" Remy wasn't sure she believed the words herself, but once again she was interrupted.

"Is she?" he challenged. Boggart leaned toward her.

Remy could smell garlic on his breath that wafted in the air between them. "Is she what?" she whispered as she shrank under the man's intense stare.

"Dead. Is Marian Arnold really dead?"

"She has to be," Remy replied instinctively. "She'd be over a hundred and twenty years old otherwise."

Boggart shook his head. "Look around you, missy," he growled, then spread his arms wide as if to encompass the entire length and breadth of the butterfly house. "She is speaking to us even now. Only you can't hear it." Then he dropped his stare back to Remy and added, "Yet."

That last word carried a finality with it that made Remy shiver.

7

THE DRIVE TO THE SMALL TOWN fifteen minutes from the manor was an escape. Remy found herself glancing in the rearview mirror, wondering if she'd see Boggart chasing after her like the bogeyman, or perhaps she'd glimpse the wispy-white silhouette of Marian Arnold's ghost, beckoning her to flee before the manor ate her alive.

Remy did the first thing any good research assistant would do. She pulled into the drive-through of a coffee shack for a quick fix.

"What'll it be?"

The woman in the window wasn't far off from Remy's own twenty-eight years. They exchanged smiles.

"Dark, hot, and smooth," Remy ordered.

The ash-colored blonde laughed. "Sounds like my perfect man. I'm assuming no cream in that? A large?"

"Please." Remy nodded. "And I wouldn't be upset if you added a shot of espresso."

"Ooh!" The barista's eyebrows rose in unison. "You are hard core. I like you." With another shared laugh, the barista set to work brewing an espresso. "You're not a regular here. Are you new to Coldwater Valley?"

"No, I'm from the Twin Cities," Remy said. "But I've been here a week now."

The woman smiled as she twisted the portafilter into the espresso machine. "I was born and raised here. Abigail Todd."

"Remy," she introduced herself.

"Let me guess," Abigail started. "You're in Coldwater Valley for one of two reasons: to sight-see the fall colors within distance of Milwaukee's beer gardens and the baseball field, or you're here to drink in the local charm and pretend Milwaukee doesn't exist."

Remy had a feeling Wisconsinites were as proud of their small towns as they were of Milwaukee's guts and glory.

"Small-town charm," Remy answered.

"Good call." Abigail knocked espresso grounds into the garbage. "You don't want to do Milwaukee solo anyway. I mean, the city has its old-world charm, but if you're not a local . . . well, it's wise to be careful. Milwaukee has a bleak side."

"Most cities do." Remy was okay with small talk. It was safe.

Abigail poured the shot of espresso into a to-go cup, then pumped dark coffee over it from a carafe. "Are you in the area for a while?"

Remy hesitated. It wasn't a secret that Elton Floyd lived at the manor, and she hadn't signed a confidentiality agreement . . . "For a while. I'm living at Müllerian Manor. I'm Mr. Floyd's research assistant."

Abigail's eyes widened as she reached through the window to give Remy her cup of coffee. "Ooh. Well. That has to be interesting."

Remy wasn't sure if this was still small talk or a moment of honest hesitation on Abigail's part. The woman's expression was hard to read. "It's a beautiful house," she finally replied.

Abigail rested her arms on the windowsill and leaned forward, her gray eyes alive. She glanced behind Remy's car. Checking for other java-thirsty customers needing her attention? Or making sure no one would overhear what she was about to reveal?

Remy checked the rearview mirror. No one there.

Abigail must have been satisfied with what she saw because she returned her attention to Remy. "The house is gorgeous. Odd, though. Years ago, when it was still in the Arnold trust, they gave tours of the place. It legit makes no sense—the layout? Dead-end hallways. Doors that lead to spaces too big for closets but too small for usable rooms. And there's always been rumors of secret places because the square footage of the published blueprints doesn't equate to the actual size of the manor."

Remy took a sip of her coffee, resting her elbow on the steering wheel as she pivoted to face Abigail in the drive-through. "What do you know about the house itself?"

Abigail gave a small laugh. "Oh, just what everyone in Coldwater Valley knows. It was the Arnold family's summer home before their brewery in Milwaukee went bankrupt during Prohibition. Mrs. Arnold, the mother, supervised its construction for whatever reason, and she was not particularly . . . well, her mental health was in question, they said. And the way the house turned out? Most say it was because Mrs. Arnold was the way she was. An artist. Whimsical. They say Verdine Arnold got bored easily and would just decide to end the construction where it was and go in a different direction. And then there's the tales of secret places inside."

"Like secret passages and hideaways?" Remy hadn't heard that theory.

Abigail shrugged. "Supposedly. Some say, after everything with Marian Arnold and the Butterfly Butcher was over, that the place was used to smuggle liquor during Prohibition. John Dillinger supposedly hid out there. Some have said Al Capone hid at Müllerian Manor too." Abigail laughed and waved two index fingers in the air. "And that is how fact mixes with fiction and you get a history of legends and lore."

Remy had several more questions—her interest had been piqued having spoken to someone local—but a car had pulled up behind her. So she put her coffee in a cup holder and shifted the vehicle into drive. "I'd better let you go. It was nice meeting you."

Abigail gave a perky nod. "Stop in again! We can chat more if you want."

Remy was about to pull away when Abigail's voice stopped her. She glanced up at the woman and saw a slight frown between Abigail's brows.

"Hey, can I ask you something?"

"Sure." Remy waited.

Abigail glanced at the waiting car and then back to Remy. "Whatever happened to Jack?"

"Jack?" Remy shook her head. "I don't know a Jack."

"Oh!" The surprise on Abigail's face was more than evident. She looked embarrassed, and a flush crept up her neck. "He . . . uh, used to come by here almost daily until about a month ago."

"Who is he?" Remy questioned.

Abigail's expression had turned almost wistful now. "He was Mr. Floyd's research assistant. We went out a few times, but then I stopped getting texts from him, and he stopped coming by the coffee shack here. I just—well, never mind. I'm guessing he must have moved on." Abigail switched back to her perky self. "It's all right. He was just a super nice guy and, well, you know how it is. Hard to find nice ones these days!" She gave Remy a little wave.

Remy returned it, but the pit that hadn't left her stomach for some time now felt like it grew even harder. Jack. Elton's research assistant? No one had mentioned Elton had a prior assistant. Not even know-it-all Nurse Aimee, and that seemed like something she wouldn't have kept to herself.

She guessed it was silly to think she was Elton's first ever research assistant. But he certainly hadn't implied that she was there to replace someone. Not someone so recent.

Jack. Remy should have asked for his last name. It was growing more apparent that her research into Marian Arnold was going to take her into areas she hadn't expected. It was probably nothing, but then, in Remy's experience, nothing often equated to everything. And that was never a good thing.

"He's lost his ever-loving mind." Mrs. Flemming hustled past Remy as Remy entered the manor. Her perturbed glance was enough to give Remy pause. Mrs. Flemming wasn't one for explanations, and she disappeared through a double-wide doorway that led into the library, which led into a short hallway, a strangely located set of five stairs, and then another corridor that led to the kitchen and utility rooms.

Footsteps thudding down the main flight of stairs stole Remy's attention off Mrs. Flemming and on to the next occupant of the manor. Only this wasn't an occupant. It was Tate Arnold.

He was still here?

Remy had hoped her jaunt to town for coffee after her unsettling experience in the butterfly house would have given the man time enough to argue it out with Elton and then leave.

His icy eyes caught Remy's, but they weren't as self-confident as she'd first noticed on his arrival. He hesitated a step, then continued his downward journey. "Do you know which room Mrs. Flemming has for me?"

"Room?" Remy eyed him.

Tate had the decency to look apologetic. "They didn't tell you." It was an observation, not a question.

Remy shook her head.

He descended the final stairs, shoving his hands into the pockets of his jeans. "I'm staying here. At Müllerian Manor. Elton hired me to read his manuscript for accuracy. I'll be able to get his take on my family's history and will provide input as needed, plus remove anything my family would find offensive."

Remy blinked. Three times. She counted. Because that was about all she could do as incredulity flooded her. "Check for accuracy?" That was a direct hit on her ability to research correctly. And Remy was, as Tate had so emphatically stated earlier, new to this position. Not to mention, did Elton realize that Tate Arnold was literally the last of the Arnold line? The family tree would die with him, unless of course he married and had kids. So then who was out there to offend with potential erroneous representation in the biography? And wasn't that what many biographies were? Interpretive history according to the author?

"Sorry if that upsets you." There was a defeatist tone to Tate's voice. Remy hadn't expected that. It was almost as if the man had used up his self-confidence at his arrival and insistence on seeing Elton and was now second-guessing his existence.

"I'm not upset," Remy assured him. "Just surprised. Surprised Elton hired you, and surprised you're staying here."

"Mr. Floyd offered, and it makes sense after all." Tate sniffed and cleared his throat. "So I'll just . . . find Mrs. Flemming and see where she wants me to put my stuff."

"Your stuff," Remy repeated.

Tate blinked. "Yeah, my stuff."

Remy pursed her lips and couldn't help but give him a doubtful scowl. "You came prepared to stay, huh?" It didn't match up with his story earlier that he was here merely to meet with Elton about the manuscript.

Tate cleared his throat. "I—"

"No, no." Remy held up her hands. "You don't have to explain. I'll probably get it wrong anyway. After all, you're the fact-checker."

"I knew I offended you." Tate's voice deepened.

Remy didn't break his stare. "Don't underestimate me, Mr. Arnold. Before I even came here, I did research on the Arnold family and this place."

"And yet you didn't know who I was?" Tate challenged.

Remy flushed. "And you brought your *things*?" She diverted from his accusation.

Tate withdrew his hands from his pockets and edged past Remy, heading through the library as though he'd lived here before and knew his way around the twisty manor. He turned at the doorway and studied her for a moment. "I live out of my car half the time, so I have my *stuff* with me." His smile was crooked and patronizing. "You can do a background check on me. I mean, that's what researchers do, right?"

He left her behind, and Remy stared after him. The nerve! The audacity to—to—okay fine. Remy sagged against the wall. She wasn't cocky enough not to have questioned why she got the job as Elton's research assistant from a pool of hungry researchers far more qualified. It nagged at her from the moment she got the job offer. Why her? No qualifications, an unused associate's degree? To any good biographer worth their salt, taking a chance on a rookie researcher when you're a bestselling author wasn't the most logical of moves. Tate Arnold was right to question her. *She* questioned herself—and she questioned Elton Floyd's reasoning. But not enough to ask Elton about it. Why talk herself out of a job?

Remy sucked in a deep breath and shook her head to clear her thoughts. If Tate Arnold left her alone, then she could leave him alone with his *stuff*.

She jogged up the stairs toward Elton's study. When she reached it, she twisted the knob and entered without knocking.

Elton was slouched in his cozy chair, a wool blanket stretched over his lap, glasses perched on the end of his nose, and his writing desk positioned in front of him. He didn't bother to look up when she closed the door.

"I suppose you're annoyed with me," he stated, his pen scratching across the page. He wrote longhand, a habit Remy could not comprehend.

"Just shocked." Remy plopped into her usual chair opposite him. "I didn't think you wanted input from an Arnold."

Elton lifted his eyes. "Whyever not? Firsthand insight? I'd be a fool to pass that up."

"Sure, but—"

"Anyway," Elton said, waving her off, "we've lots to do, and there's something intriguing about having an Arnold roaming the halls while we write, yes?"

"Maybe?" Remy was hard-pressed to understand Elton's sudden change of heart.

"What have you found?" Elton set his pen down and drew back in his chair, an expectant look in his blue eyes.

Remy worried she was supposed to have uncovered some scandalous secret in the Arnold family to make his next chapter work for him. "I found out you had an assistant before me." Remy hadn't meant to say it, but it popped out, so she owned it and held Elton's stare.

He didn't flinch. "Yes. I did. He moved on to another position, and that's when I found you."

A plausible answer.

"No one ever said anything about it." Remy felt like she should apologize for some reason.

Elton stretched his face into a look of bewilderment. "And so there you have it. Now you know. It was never a secret, Remy. Jack was with me for over a year. A restless sort anyway. He moved out west to sow his oats, and that's all right with me. Even I did that once upon a time."

Remy didn't want to hear about Elton's "sowing oats" days, but she accepted his response. She was probably unnerved by Boggart's weirdness in the butterfly house and interpreted Abigail's inquiry at the coffee shack as if Jack had disappeared, not just resigned.

"Now." Elton cleared his throat. "If we're finished talking about Jack, may we move on to the research portion of today?"

Remy nodded and adjusted her position in the chair.

Elton reached for a book on his writing desk and held it up for Remy to see. "This is a volume specifically about the Butterfly Butcher—and other serial killers from Wisconsin. It's a good place to start. Now, I know enough to know he—or she—was credited with several murders, but I need you to dig deeper into the lives of the victims. Who were they specifically? Not just their names and general statistics, but what can we learn of them? Their secrets, their families, what tied them together as victims of the Butcher. Why the dead butterflies at each of their corpses? Back in the day, investigations could go only so far. I'm not looking to *solve* the cold case, mind you, but gather enough information to speculate and theorize as I wind it around the life and death of Marian Arnold."

Remy nodded. It was going to be a monumental task, trying to find out information on unknown people in history. "I will need the internet." Elton needed to understand that first and foremost.

"Of course, I know that," he grunted. "I should get internet here, but there's something about being disconnected from the outside world that soothes my old soul. That's why I have you. You can be connected to the big wide world for me—and you can do it at the library." The old man smirked. "Just be sure you don't use that Wiki-whatever site as your main source. It's been debunked by scholars as untrustworthy."

Remy chuckled at the disdain on Elton's face. "I'll be sure to use only those sources that are reliable."

Elton studied her for a long moment and then nodded. "I want you to start with the Butcher's first victim."

"Percy Hahn, the milkman?" Remy supplied.

"Mm, not exactly." Elton picked up his pen and tapped his pad of paper. "There were butterflies found beneath his hanging body, yes, but I question this. None of the Butcher's other victims were hanged."

Remy leaned forward. "You think someone else besides the Butterfly Butcher was responsible for Hahn's murder?"

Elton gave her a nonplussed look. "I'm not convinced Percy Hahn was murdered. He may have hanged himself, you know, and why some jumped to the theory of murder, I've no idea. No. I believe the Butcher's first victim was someone else entirely, and Hahn was merely someone who interrupted a killer's vendetta by showing up unexpectedly as a corpse—a surprise not only to Marian Arnold when she discovered his body but to the Butcher himself."

"So if not Percy Hahn, who do you want me to research as victim number one?" Remy had already determined she wasn't going to ignore Percy Hahn any more than whoever's name Elton tossed at her as the real first victim. Elton's theories may or may not be right, but research required he have as much information as possible.

Elton raised his brows. "Have you heard of Loretta Habington?"

Remy nodded. In her overview of the history, she'd run across the name, but she couldn't quite recall how Loretta Habington was related to the manor.

Elton's smile reached his eyes, and there was a hint of a twisted thrill at what must be the story of the woman's murder. "The poor creature. But I can tell you can't recall exactly how she fits into the story, so I won't influence your research with my suppositions. Take this book"—he held out the volume—"and read it. Then go do your surfing through the pixelated world of electronics or what-have-you and let me know what you find."

"Loretta Habington," Remy repeated to confirm.

"Yes. She was a beautiful woman, they say." Elton was almost wistful, but then his eyes took on a strange glint. "And she is still here." He looked around the room and drew in a deep breath as if intoxicated with the imaginary soul of this Loretta Habington.

Elton's voice shook a bit as he added, "I can smell her perfume at night when I sleep. She vies with Marian for my attention. Two souls twisted together by the fate of a thousand butterflies." Elton met Remy's gaze. "Such is the fate of everyone who comes to live at Müllerian Manor."

8

MARIAN

"Cousin!" Ivo swept into the front hall of the manor with a flourish and a grin that split his clean-shaven face. His cologne filled Marian's senses with its intoxicating spice, and she didn't resist when he pulled her into his strong embrace. After a moment, Ivo held her at arm's length. "You're a real dish, Marian. Look at you! It's been too long." He dropped his hold on her, and before Marian could say a word, he'd spun around and stretched out his hand toward the door. "Come, doll!"

A beautiful woman entered, her lithe form clothed in a chic dress of deep violet. Her kohl-lined eyes highlighted unusual purple irises, and her dark bobbed hair waved perfectly beneath her beret.

Marian quailed beneath the woman's exotic beauty and instantly knew a deep sinking feeling as she saw the enamored expression on Ivo's face. She had been a fool to think she would be

Ivo's sole attention. That he would arrive here to fill the shoes of a beloved cousin who would take care of her and her problems.

"This is Loretta." Ivo grinned. "I should've given you notice I was bringing her, but I wanted to surprise you!"

Marian mustered a gracious smile. It had been difficult enough to fathom trying to explain the events of yesterday to Ivo. But to a woman of this ilk? Her beauty belied the ugly facts of a hanging body in the butterfly house. It was improbable this woman would want to entertain the thought of remaining at the manor in the shadow of such violence.

"Welcome" was all Marian could think to say.

Loretta smiled in return, her eyes twinkling, and to Marian's dismay the woman seemed friendly. It was so much easier to dislike a beautiful woman, but there was an allure about Loretta that pulled Marian to her in an instant. "You're such a dear to have me! I told Ivo that we mustn't take you by surprise, but he insisted!"

"It's quite all right," Marian said.

"No, it's not." Loretta rested her hand on Ivo's arm. "Don't you see, Ivo? I told you. The poor dear is practically in shock."

Marian hadn't the nerve to explain that her demeanor was not only surprise at Loretta's arrival with Ivo but due to a dreadful hangover from the prior day's events.

Ivo interrupted Marian's scattered thoughts. "I trust you'll forgive me, Cousin. I know this is unexpected, but you see, Loretta and I are engaged!"

And there it was. It wasn't a complete surprise now that Marian was adjusting to the second guest, but a surprise nonetheless. And if she was being honest, not a pleasant one. Her hopes for security beneath the protective wing of family evaporated. Ivo was already distracted—and little wonder why!

"Congratulations," she said softly, then managed to collect herself. "Let me retrieve Mrs. Dale. My . . . staff is rather limited at the moment, but she will see you to your rooms."

Marian took the escape she needed and hurried into the library just off the main entrance, ducking through a doorway and sprinting up the few stairs to the next corridor. She fell against the wall, catching her breath. She needed to be grateful for Ivo. For his affection and loyalty. He was, after all, some of the only family she had left, and thankfully he'd said nothing of the demise of the Arnold Brewery, nor the fact that the lack of household staff meant Marian was running on financial fumes.

And if Loretta was worthy of Ivo, then she too would be kind and loyal, which should be a breath of fresh air to Marian. And God knew that Marian needed fresh air. A new start and something to distract her from the unnerving aura that permeated the manor.

Please, God . . . Marian wasn't sure if her prayer had been heard. Her roots told her God heard and saw everything. But Marian's heart was so tender and raw, she wasn't sure that if He did hear her, He would care enough to do anything about it.

Ivo crossed his leg over his knee and with a wink pulled a flask from his inside vest pocket.

"Ivo!" Loretta mockingly scolded, then held out her glass for a spot of whatever golden liquid he poured.

Marian shifted uncomfortably in her chair. They sat around the fireplace in the library, darkness having set in. She had hoped to inform Ivo privately of the events of yesterday, but he'd never been far from Loretta's side. She debated how to broach the subject, and the inclusion of liquor only heightened her anxiety.

"Don't worry, Cousin." Ivo laughed good-naturedly. "We're not going to be out on the roof, but a little won't hurt, and it won't bring the coppers swarming either."

Marian had been raised around liquor. It was a part of their culture, their society. But it was illegal now, and while Marian wouldn't admit it aloud, there was a fundamental point of reason behind the act to do away with liquor—many abused it. This caused a moral dilemma inside of Marian, and she was grateful she'd not inherited the brewery and the responsibility that came with it. She watched Ivo, grateful to know that he wasn't one of the abusers of alcohol, although he didn't appear to be concerned about the law at the moment.

Loretta looked between them and motioned with her hand. "Put it away, Ivo. You're making your cousin uncomfortable." She turned to Marian. "Ivo is *such* a beast."

"Hey now, I'd take the fall for it if it came to that." Ivo winked again in Marian's direction. "But it won't. The Arnold name isn't much under surveillance anymore, is it?"

"No," Marian admitted softly. It was embarrassing really. A few years ago, she was just past her sweet-sixteen birthday, looking forward to garden parties and a social future . . . and now she was retreating within herself. Hiding at the manor, but not from authorities. No. The brewery was gone. It had hung by a thread while Father was alive. But once he died, it all happened so quickly. The brewery was shut down, the equipment liquidated, inventory dumped into the proverbial gutters. She didn't even understand it all. Marian had been told her father was dead, and his people handled the rest. Her mother had already passed away, not to mention she'd long been away from Milwaukee society . . .

No. No, she couldn't think about Mother. Marian's heart ached at the thought. Her mother's absence from her life when she had lived in Milwaukee at their main residence. Her mother's eccentricities when she had finally visited the manor in the summers.

"You're alone now." Loretta's expression took on a genteel look, but one that hinted at empathy. She was curled up in her chair, her legs tucked beneath her in an altogether inappropriate style, and yet she made it appear almost elegant.

Marian was having a difficult time not liking Loretta—along with admiring her beauty.

"Is it hard?" Loretta asked gently. "I mean, with your father passing and with all that occurred in Milwaukee?"

"Of course it's hard!" Ivo answered on Marian's behalf. He didn't bother to tuck his flask away but instead set it on a table beside his chair. "Marian is an orphan, and her father didn't have the foresight to plan ahead. We all knew the ban on liquor was inevitable. The long-suffering Christian women of our culture have had enough of drunken husbands, I suppose, but regardless." Ivo took a drink from his crystal tumbler. "With a place like this?" He lifted the glass as if giving a toast. "He could have stayed in business if he'd wanted to. He just needed to be crafty. To plan ahead."

The fire crackled in the fireplace, bringing a welcome warmth to the drafty room. But Marian felt sweat beading on her forehead. Ivo was tiptoeing around a sensitive subject. Not only her father's memories, but his ethics. He might have owned a brewery, but he had prided himself on being law-abiding, a man of morals. He would never seek to profit by illicit means and subterfuge. Of this, Marian was sure. The fact that Müllerian Manor was all that had been left to her was evidence enough.

"There are still ways to make a living, Cousin." Ivo lowered his voice. "I'm willing to help you."

"Ivo!" Loretta scolded.

"What?" He acted as if surprised. "I'm just saying there are ways to make a living that won't leave Marian destitute."

"My lawyers assured me I would be taken care of financially," Marian said. "I have no desire to dabble in anything illegal."

Ivo let out a laugh. "I would never suggest you do that! No, you misunderstand me. I was merely stating that dames these days have options. It's not like in the past when, if marriage passed you by, you had no prospects. You can take control of your own destiny—your financial future. That is, with a few nudges and endorsements from men like myself," he added sheepishly. Perhaps he realized the truth of the limitations imposed on women in a man's world of business.

"I've only recently lost my father and mother, and I haven't yet given much thought beyond settling in here." Marian glanced at the door—toward her escape. This visit, this reunion, was not as she'd envisioned.

"Of course you haven't!" Loretta interjected. "Ivo, leave your cousin alone. You're being a cad."

"You know I care, Marian," Ivo said, attempting to reassure her.

And he had. His handsome face gentled, and his eyes crinkled in an apology that melted her defenses. She'd always been putty under Ivo's strong influence.

He smiled softly. "I *do* care," he repeated, "and so do my mother and father. If you need anything, we're here for you. My mother was always keen on yours, being related and all, and family needs to stick to each other, don't you think?"

Marian nodded, feeling better, but also as though her future had already been decided when it hadn't.

"Do tell me what you enjoy doing for fun!" Loretta said with a bright smile. She sipped her illegal drink as though it were water, and yet her energy was infectious.

"I enjoy reading and . . ." She broke off her words and locked eyes with Ivo. She had to tell him. Perhaps Ivo could lend a sort of balance to the tempestuous whirling in her mind. "We had a bit of an incident yesterday."

"An incident?" Ivo shifted in his seat.

"Yes. Our milkman . . ." Marian began. How did a person say they'd discovered a dead body? The truth, she supposed. So she provided it to her cousin. "I found him hanging in Mother's butterfly house."

Loretta's gasp was accompanied by Ivo's stunned expression. "Are you being serious?"

"Unfortunately, I am." Marian nodded. The vision of Percy Hahn's bulging eyes would never leave her memory. Ever.

"Did he off himself?" Ivo moved to the edge of his chair, holding his glass between his palms.

"The police are investigating. They don't know yet."

"Or was it murder?" Loretta had turned pale. Instead of clasping her own glass tighter, she set it on a table. "That gives me the heebie-jeebies! I always thought it would be fascinating to have an unusual sort of death—like being mauled by a lion on safari or something."

Marian couldn't fathom romanticizing being mauled by a lion, and yet she could almost envision Loretta's glamorous smile as she was being eaten. A wave of her fine fingers and a cinematic scream for the ages . . . Marian shook the vision from her mind. The facts. She mustn't let her mind wander—nothing good ever happened when it did. "The police don't know much. I-I found Mr. Hahn, and then Felix came to assist me and—"

"Felix?" Ivo frowned.

"You remember Felix," Marian prompted Ivo. "He was the groundskeeper's son—Mrs. Dale's son—only now he is the groundskeeper."

"Oh, him! I quite forgot about Felix! He's still around?" Ivo seemed more interested in Felix than the body Marian had discovered.

"Yes, but he was overseas in the war for a while and . . ." Marian suddenly realized it wasn't her business to gossip about Felix Dale or his absent limb.

"Was he injured?" Loretta asked.

Marian nodded.

Loretta gave her eyes a pretty roll. "So many boys were injured. It's absolutely appalling! I'm so relieved it's over, and I'm relieved we'll never have to experience something that horrendous again! A world war? Whoever thought that was a good idea?"

"Except now there's a body hanging in the butterfly house," Ivo inserted with a playful smile. He leaned back in his chair and crossed his leg over his knee again. "Truly, Cousin, you kept this to yourself all day? From here on out, allow me to work with the police on your behalf, yes? You needn't be subjected to that. You and Loretta enjoy rest and relaxation, and let a man lead the charge for you."

Marian didn't miss that his statement was in contradiction with his earlier remarks in favor of her independence as a woman.

"You're such a hero," said Loretta.

"I try to be," Ivo responded.

Marian had the intrusive thought that Ivo was remarkably put together in comparison to Felix, whose haunted expression made him seem so much older. What was heroism after all if it didn't invite the risk of sacrifice? Marian realized Felix Dale had more than proven himself. She realized this the same moment she realized that Ivo had never enlisted and gone to the war front. In fact, if she recalled correctly, rumor had it he'd spent most of his time during the war at university and had engaged in gaming and the like on the side.

But perhaps that was because they were from two completely different worlds: the working class and the social elite.

It was enough to make Marian's head spin, for she wasn't sure what to make of it all. For a brief moment, however, she saw Felix Dale as the stronger one. Stronger than Ivo. Even with a missing limb.

9

HOW COULD ONE be terrified in one's own home? Marian wrapped her housecoat around herself, tying it at the waist, her ears straining to hear.

She'd awakened from a restless sleep, certain she heard a muffled voice outside her bedroom door.

It's not right. Not good. Not here.

She couldn't tell if it was a man or a woman. Ivo? Marian gripped the corner post at the foot of her four-poster bed. It was a whispered voice.

Go away. It's not safe. You need to leave here.

Marian forced herself to move toward the voice. It wasn't coming from the door into the hallway as she'd first thought. It came from behind a different door, one that opened into an empty room. Perhaps the room was originally intended to be a sitting room off the bedroom, Marian wasn't sure. All she knew was that she was no longer alone.

You're not safe!

The urgency in the person's tone made a shiver race down Marian's back. The curtain at her window blew inward, the gust of air chilling the room. Marian startled, leaping to the side as if to avoid an actual being. Only no one was there. Just her bed. She didn't recall opening the window. It was a cold autumn night, and the curtain swayed like a ghost mocking her.

You're not safe!

Again the voice beckoned to Marian. She stepped toward the door that connected her bedroom to the empty room beyond.

No, no. Don't.

Marian grabbed the doorknob, twisted, and yanked it open. Humidity had swollen the frame, causing the door to scrape as she tugged it toward herself.

"Who's there?" she called, her voice a frightened whimper, not the strong and fearsome one she imagined it should be. The sweet scent of perfume wafted in the air, but otherwise the room was like a tomb, musty and closed off. Quietly, Marian stepped deeper into the darkened room. "Hello?" she managed.

Silence met her. No one was there. Whoever had been there had since fled. But where to?

Marian pushed the button on the wall surrounded by a brass plate. The dull yellow electric light in the single fixture that hung from the ceiling revealed more of the room. The windows, missing their drapes, were latched shut. The floor looked polished, and a small round table sat in its center—empty, nothing on its top. She had been in this room before. It shouldn't seem as though a strange place to her, but tonight it felt foreign.

She roved the room slowly, bordering it and dragging her fingertips along the cream brocade wall covering. It dawned on her then. There was no other entrance to the room. No way for someone to enter except through the same door she'd come. The intruder would have to push past her and exit through her bedroom.

She could taste the fear as its metallic bitterness bit her tongue. Marian fled for her bedroom, slamming the door behind her. But even in her own room, by her bed, she felt unsafe. The tentacles of danger slithered along the edges of the room, invisible black vines creeping up the walls like a vineyard of omens around her. Omens of something unpredictable, dark, and invasive.

Unable to find any respite here, Marian flung open the door to the corridor. She hurried to the end of the hall where she curved right, leading toward the bookish staircase and the front entrance. Though steeped in nighttime, the world outside seemed safer to her than the confines of the manor.

As her bedroom grew more distant behind her, Marian had the impulsive thought to flee to her mother's secret room with her butterfly collection. The ones on mats with bloodred paints, preserved there by the woman who revered them. Loved them. Created them even when they existed only in her imagination.

But monarchs existed. They were real. They were alive and a remnant of her mother.

Marian fled down the stairs. The butterfly house. In spite of recent events, it beckoned her, and she didn't want to stop to question why.

A shadowy figure shot toward her from the unlit alcove behind the stairs that housed the telephone. Marian fell back, her knee colliding with the banister. The figure disintegrated. Had it been a figment of her imagination? She clutched at her throat, struggling to catch her breath, squeezing her eyes shut to clear her vision from more erroneous displays of nonexistent specters.

Marian unlatched the lock on the front door, opening it without concern as to noise or the possibility of waking Ivo or Loretta. But they were on the second floor in the other wing. Mrs. Dale would be at home in her cottage with Felix, Frederick asleep in the servants' quarters at the back of the house.

So there was no one to awaken. No one to protect her.

Marian's bare feet met the cold ground as she descended the porch steps onto the stone drive beneath the portico. She hurried toward the back lawn, intent on one place and one place only.

No milkman's body would hang there tonight. They had taken it away. Instead, it would be her mother only. A corpse encased in a stone grave, but her mother nonetheless. And the butterflies. Always the butterflies that attempted to prove life could be renewed if only one prayed, hoped, tried hard enough. Couldn't it? Couldn't she break free from the prison of the horrific cocoon in which she was encased to find hope somewhere?

Marian paid no attention to the trees that towered above her, swaying to night's breath. Her feet flew along the path until nothing but the door to the butterfly house stood between her and her dead mother.

She pulled open the door, a rush of humid warm air pummeling her senses. The thick earthen smell of greenery, the deep emerald shadows of the plants, and then, yes! The winged images of butterflies as their tiny bodies fluttered in the air around her, leading her to the far end of the glass house, around the curving brick forms of the gardens. Monarchs that in the darkness looked bluer than their vibrant hues of daytime yellow.

Rounding a patch of greenery that rose to shoulder height, welcoming the flutter of wings against her unbound hair, Marian stumbled to a halt as her mother's grave came into view. A looming rectangular form in the night, the glass roof and walls of the butterfly house allowing the sliver of moonlight to bounce off its reflections.

"You're finally here."

A breathy, feminine voice met Marian's senses. Marian froze, narrowing her eyes, desperate to see where it had come from.

"Mother?" she whispered in return, knowing it couldn't be her mother.

And it wasn't.

On the edges of the plants, with butterflies fluttering around her, stood the form of a woman in shadow. Her face was difficult to interpret, and Marian couldn't make out her features, much less her eyes. But she could see through the darkness that the woman wore a high-collared dress, her hair was swept in a loose chignon, and she was delicate and tall.

"Mother?" Marian tried again, taking a tentative step toward the shadow. Then she saw it. The similarities in the woman to the visions of the maid in the manor. The maid no one knew of, and no one saw.

"I'm glad you've come," the maid murmured. "I'm Violet."

Marian stilled, staring into the shadows. Mesmerized and terrified by the vision before her. Violet. She knew of no Violet. No spirit that should linger or be associated with the manor that had any ties to the name Violet. And yet here she was. Not Mother, but an unknown.

A specter that reached from beyond, not alive and yet just alive enough.

"I'm glad you've come," Violet repeated in a soft whisper.

A specter that shouldn't speak but somehow did.

"Miss?"

Fingers touched her cheek. They were cold. *She* was cold.

"Marian?"

The voice beckoned her to open her eyes, but her eyes were so heavy. Marian thought the world was spinning and her body felt heavy, swirling between sleep and wakefulness.

"Marian." This time the voice was firm. Commanding.

She struggled to open her eyes. She lay on something hard but warm. So different in temperature from the fingers that poked at her shoulder. She could feel the chill of them through her housecoat.

Marian moaned, squinting and moving her hand to brush damp hair from her face. She blinked as she gained her bearings. She noted the hard stone floor. Plants. Butterflies. A wall of stone by her head . . . her mother's grave.

She scrambled into a sitting position. She had fallen asleep in the butterfly house! "W-where's Violet?" Marian asked, her eyes scanning the butterfly house.

Felix Dale crouched beside her, his hand braced against her mother's tomb, balancing on his one good foot, a crutch under his left arm. He looked confused as he followed her frantic gaze. "I don't know who you're talking about."

His declaration returned Marian to the reality that was this moment. Morning sunlight glistened off the domed glass roof. Butterflies fluttered overhead, and Marian allowed herself to smile at them. "They're so beautiful," she breathed.

Felix frowned and then shifted to maintain his balance. "Miss—"

"Marian," she corrected, meeting his eyes. "You never called me 'miss' when we were children."

"When we were children, I never called you anything."

It dawned on Marian that he was correct. Felix Dale had never used her name, nor bothered with the etiquette practiced between a servant and his mistress. Instead, he had call her "girl."

Felix seemed to struggle to find his smile as her remembrance splayed across her face. "You recall now? My youthful rudeness?"

"I thought it was endearing," Marian answered honestly and then flushed, wishing she hadn't admitted it.

Felix winced, then made a move to stand. "I'm sorry I can't help you to your feet." His crutch scraped against the floor as he pushed off the stone grave with his right hand and grabbed at his other crutch that leaned against it.

Marian shook her head as she got to her feet. "No, no, I'm fine."

Concern flickered across Felix's face. "I found you here—I don't know . . ." His words trailed, and as Marian awakened further, she realized how ridiculous and odd it must appear to have found her in the butterfly house. Her clothes were damp from the humidity. Her hair hung around her shoulders. Her housecoat had come untied.

Felix's eyes dropped downward as Marian realized her state of dress. She grappled for the edges of her coat and wrapped it around herself, daring him to stare now that her damp, white nightgown was covered.

He had the decency to flush and look away.

Marian cleared her throat. "I know you're wondering why I'm in here."

Felix shook his head. "It's none of my business."

"I needed to be near my mother," Marian explained anyway. She felt as though she owed it to him. Not to mention just two days before, a man had been hanging in this very spot.

"But you're all right?" Felix asked, concern not having left his expressive eyes.

Was she? Marian wasn't certain. She still felt disoriented. Still wondered who had been in the room and whispering, and even more, how they had fled without her seeing. And a deep part of her wished to see Violet once more—in the daylight. Why was Violet here in the middle of the night? Who was she, and why did she slip in and out of the manor like a wraith if she wasn't one? Which meant she had to be a spirit, a ghost. And how did Marian reconcile the fact that she saw these shadows and visions from time to time? Reconcile that with reality? With God? Did God allow souls to come from the beyond to visit the living?

"Do you believe in ghosts?" Marian asked, then bit down on her tongue in regret.

Felix adjusted his position as he leaned on his crutch. His dark eyes deepened, and he eyed her for a moment. "I believe there are answers to those questions, but we may not be party to them."

"So you *do* believe there are spirits?"

"Spirits?" A faraway expression fluttered over his strong features. "It depends on what you mean. Lost souls? No. Departing souls? Perhaps. Spirits of another world—another realm—angels and demons? Oh, there are plenty of demons, girl."

Marian didn't miss his slip into using the old nickname. She ignored it. "You've seen them?"

"Demons?" Felix's eyes hardened. "Of course. One need only go to war to see demons."

Marian knew he wasn't speaking of proverbial demons at this point. He had drifted to memories she could not share. Horrors he would not speak of.

She toyed with her housecoat's ribbons at her waist. "I-I'm not sure what I believe. Ghosts, specters and the like. I just know that—" She bit her tongue again. Admitting Violet's presence would be premature until she knew who or *what* exactly Violet was.

Felix seemed sensitive to her fumbling, and he rescued her. "Let me help you back to the manor." He tipped his head toward his elbow, his hand gripping his crutch.

Marian frowned. "I'll be fine. I can walk."

A tiny smile toyed at the corner of Felix's mouth. "I don't break, girl, and you look like the wind will push you over. Hold on to my arm. I can support us both."

She followed his prompt and was surprised by the way the warmth of his skin through his shirtsleeve sent a ripple of energy through her.

Marian walked beside him, Felix efficiently making his way with his crutch. She was grateful. The security of his arm helped her regain her equilibrium. Her feet felt heavy, her mind muddled, and the sunlight that broke through the morning clouds hurt her eyes.

"Does it pain you?" she asked, then wished she hadn't.

"My leg?" Felix gave her a sideways glance as they made their way toward the manor.

Marian nodded.

"There's discomfort, yes."

"That was insensitive of me," Marian mumbled.

"It's all right. We all get curious from time to time." Another sideways glance from him and then the familiar wink was sent her way. "Even about ghosts and spirits."

Marian felt she owed Felix another apology. "I really am sorry."

A flicker of something crossed his face. "It's the price of war."

His words cut off any further comments or questions Marian had been considering. There was a tightness to Felix's words, yet he didn't seem angry. It was a quaver. Emotions suppressed and trying to remain hidden.

Fear.

When she realized it, Marian drew in a deep breath, and it was noticeable enough for Felix to pause. He furrowed his brow as he looked down at her. For a moment, they communicated silently it seemed. Neither one admitting it aloud, but both recognizing it.

Fear.

Marian knew then that Felix was not perfectly brave. Nightmares lingered in the depths of his eyes. She wondered if he saw shadows too. Or if his shadows were different from hers. If his were the kind that awakened one in the night with screams of remembrance instead of whispered warnings. Ladened with memories of terror instead of premonitions of violence.

Felix broke their gaze and cleared his throat, moving ahead with his limping. Marian let go of his arm. If their fears were different, it seemed neither of them wished to infect the other with their mysteries. Their brokenness was misunderstood, and they couldn't risk another gaping chasm. It was better to remain separate. Where they belonged. Alone in the secret places of their minds.

10

REMY

OCTOBER, PRESENT DAY

ER EYE MUSCLES HURT. The dim light of the bedside lamp wasn't helping. Remy closed the book with a thud, pinching the bridge of her nose and pushing her reading glasses up to her forehead.

Elton wanted her to research the Butterfly Butcher's victims, but she felt inadequate in her knowledge of the case. How had a century gone by with such a mystery hanging over a place like this? A Jack the Ripper–style story of a killer who had never been identified? There was a woeful lack of public records of the crimes committed. Newspaper coverage in the 1920s had been pathetically absent it seemed. Which was strange, considering there had been three murders attributed to the Butcher.

Remy looked down at the hardback book in her grasp. She had taken it to bed with her, intent on learning whatever had been recorded about the Butterfly Butcher of southeastern Wisconsin.

It was two o'clock in the morning. Thankfully, Marian Arnold's spirit had been quiet tonight and not made any noises in the other room. Remy could do without a night of ghosts. This place was creepy enough in the dark.

Her stomach rumbled, and she didn't bother to squelch her sigh. A snack would be great, but the idea of roaming the corridors of the manor at this time of night seemed like a horror movie scene waiting to happen.

She'd read too much about the Butterfly Butcher tonight. Studying serial killers before bed? A bad idea. She knew that now. Regardless, Remy swung her legs from under the covers and set her glasses on the nightstand. She tugged her T-shirt down over her oversized men's pajama bottoms in a lime-green plaid, then slid her feet into a pair of moccasin slippers. Too bad the kitchen didn't have GPS coordinates. In a building this architecturally nonsensical, Remy wasn't convinced she wouldn't wind up stuck in some secret passageway or room with no way to get out.

Holding her phone out in front of her, its flashlight turned on, she began hurrying through the manor's labyrinth, being careful to avoid the odd steps that led to Elton's study, twisting around a hall that had a strange corner that pointed to a dead end. Finally she spotted the main staircase ahead. There was probably a faster way to the kitchen, but Remy wasn't about to explore new trails in a place that boasted ghosts and murder victims.

Remy reached the main floor, slipped through the library, found the hallway Mrs. Flemming used when she wanted to fetch something from the kitchen, and then at last the door. Turning its brass knob, relief swept through Remy. The kitchen!

Wasting no time, she went straight to the refrigerator and pulled open the door. Supper's leftovers were in glass containers, but Remy wasn't in the mood for more chicken and rice. She pushed them to the side and grinned. Nacho cheese! Within seconds, she had found the pantry and an unopened bag of corn chips. She dove into the snack with fervor, not caring that it was cold.

Remy thumbed through senseless Reels on her phone, watching people dance to silly tunes. It was a fine distraction from the Butterfly Butcher's history and the unsolved murders that still lingered at the manor.

Brutal strangulation.

Dead butterflies.

Marian Arnold lying in a pool of blood in the room just off Remy's bedroom.

She shivered, clicking her phone screen off. Darn it. She wanted to make sense of the entire sordid saga. What had encouraged Elton Floyd to purchase and then move into the very place where the Butterfly Butcher had apparently run rampant? Was it to get the full effect of what happened here while he wrote?

Remy was struck by how little she knew of Elton Floyd, the biographer. She knew of his books; they had always been popular. His bio printed on the dust jackets stated he lived in Upstate New York. So why the move to Wisconsin last year? A person could simply visit the location of their subject—they didn't have to *buy* it.

A clatter behind her sent Remy springing to her feet. She spun around from the table, scanning the room. It sounded like a stainless-steel pan falling into the sink. She eyed the sink and saw it was empty.

"Hello?" Her voice sounded loud in the lonely kitchen. Who was she greeting anyway?

Remy investigated the corner by the pantry, the only place in the kitchen that wasn't well lit. She didn't see anything, though she was sure her imagination could conjure a figure hunched in the corner, staring back at her.

The Butterfly Butcher's ghost?

Okay. Nacho cheese and chips were *so* not worth this.

With no idea as to what had caused the clatter that sent her heart into her throat, Remy stuffed the jar of cheese back into the fridge and rolled up the bag of chips. She hurried to the kitchen sink, grabbing an empty glass from an open shelf on the wall, and flipped the faucet on. As she filled the glass with tap water, Remy peered out the window that overlooked the back lawn.

From here, and with it being the middle of the night, Remy couldn't make out the glass house. But she knew it was there. She studied the trees that were a bluish hue against the sky. Pinpricks of starlight peeked through their branches at her, a reminder that the heavens saw everything. The good and the bad. These same stars had hung in the night sky as witnesses to the Butterfly Butcher's evil deeds, who'd crept through the shadows of the manor looking for the next victim.

Movement snagged Remy's attention. She shut the water off, her awareness sharpened as she squinted to see through the window. Reaching over, Remy flicked off the light switch, plunging the kitchen into darkness. It made it easier for her to see outside, and made it more difficult for anything outside to see her.

There it was again. Remy set her glass down, water sloshing over its rim into the sink. She could barely make out the silhouette of a man. At least she assumed it was a man. Broad shoulders were usually a dead giveaway, though not always.

Remy debated whether to remain there watching the man as he moved across the yard in the direction of the butterfly house or retreat to her room and lock the door. She was about to opt for the latter when the figure outside stilled and turned in profile, making it slightly easier for her to see who it was.

Was that Tate Arnold?

Remy's caution waned a bit as she craned her neck to see better. Yes, it was him. Why was Mr. Arnold walking around outside at this ungodly hour? Remy rolled her eyes. She was never going to sleep now. Not with her curiosity piqued and her nerves on edge after reading about the Butcher.

She padded from the kitchen into the adjacent hall reserved for house staff to exit to the back property. Remy made her way out the door and into the yard, cautiously approaching the man. As she drew nearer, she saw it was most definitively Tate Arnold.

He stood still, his face turned up toward the sky, hands stuffed into the pockets of his joggers. He had on a hoodie sweatshirt to ward off the chill.

Remy meant to ask if he was okay, but it came out as, "What are you doing?"

Tate jumped, jerking his head in her direction. He must not have heard her approaching, for his expression said she'd startled him.

He stared at her—stared *through* her. It was absolutely eerie! He was there, and yet, Remy could see, his mind wasn't.

"Are you okay?" Remy asked.

Tate blinked a few times, then nodded. "Yeah. Yeah, I'm good." His tone made it sound as though he were trying to convince himself of it more than Remy.

She didn't believe him. "Are you looking for something?" Remy eyed him.

"No," Tate answered quickly, looking back to the sky. "I'm just out for a walk."

"All right then." A moment later, realizing he had no intention of conversing with her, Remy tried to fill the awkward silence. "Are you a stargazer?"

Tate didn't respond.

"When I was a kid," Remy offered, "one of my foster parents told me the stars were holes in the floor of heaven and that God would put His eye over the one directly above you so He could watch you. I think they meant it to be comforting, but I sort of felt creeped out by it. Like God was stalking me."

Tate glanced at her. "Was He?"

A strange response, but Remy allowed it. "No." She crossed her arms over her chest and followed his gaze toward the heavens. "No, I've come to believe that God isn't a stalker, or an angry old man waiting to pounce, but instead He has that watchful, protective eye. You know, the guardian type. What every little kid wishes they had at night when they go to bed after someone turns the lights out. That knight standing by the door, brandishing a sword and daring anyone to try to get past them to harm you."

"Or like a sniper waiting to take out the enemy," Tate added.

Okay. That was a bit violent. Again, Remy decided to give it to him anyway. "Sure. We all want to be protected, don't we? At least as kids."

Silence drifted between them. Remy watched one star in particular. She remembered being little, being small, being . . . terrified. Security wasn't something she'd ever really experienced growing up. It had taken her years to realize such a thing could exist. That God was there and was personal enough to invest in her life. Remy didn't have it all figured out—faith wasn't a one-and-done thing by any means—but she knew enough now to understand that she'd been created for a purpose. And regardless of her upbringing, she wasn't unimportant. She was worth protecting.

"'In peace I will lie down and sleep, for you alone, Lord, make me dwell in safety.'" The verse slipped off her tongue, smooth as melted chocolate.

"Where'd you hear that?" Tate looked down at her, and Remy could tell he saw her—really saw her. The dazed look on his face had dissipated, replaced by an unexpected form of vulnerability.

"The Bible?" Remy responded. She'd learned the verse somewhere in her journey through foster care. Maybe it was back in that one home where they'd made her join a Bible club for kids. She didn't remember. She also didn't remember where in the Bible the verse was located.

Tate grunted in acceptance of her pithy answer. "The Bible," he repeated.

"You should read it sometime." She meant it in jest, but Remy realized it came out a bit snooty.

Tate's response surprised her. He nodded. "Yeah. I probably should."

After a few long moments with nothing more said between them, Remy returned to the manor. She felt Tate's eyes drilling into her back, but when Remy turned to look, he was staring at the night sky again.

Remy returned to the kitchen to set the room to rights before heading back to her bedroom for the night. The conversation with Tate had been so odd. So random. Spiritual and . . . personal? Maybe too personal. Remy's insides felt stirred up in ways that had nothing to do with the Butterfly Butcher. Instead, memories were assaulting her. Memories of growing up. Memories that were just outside her vision. Shadows that should be clearer, more easily grasped, but still danced beyond her reach.

Whatever. It was the middle of the night. Remy ran her fingers through her hair and drew a cleansing breath, resolving to set aside her worries for the sake of sleep. She wound her way through the kitchen toward the door, then stilled as she cast a glance at the table where she'd sat only minutes before.

In her place was a newspaper clipping. It had been torn from the paper, but the edges were so carefully ripped, it was evident it had been extracted with care. Remy looked around the kitchen. Empty, no one there. Yet she knew the clipping hadn't been on the table when she'd gone outside to talk to Tate. Someone else had been here. Had left it on the table.

Reaching for the clipping, Remy lifted it.

Her hand froze with the paper clasped between her thumb and fingers. Numbness crept up her feet and legs and into her arms until she collapsed onto a chair at the table. She couldn't unlock her stare at the clipping. So familiar, but so long ago.

This had to be a cruel prank.

Who would have come into the kitchen when she'd been outside with Tate and left this there for her to find? *Was* it meant for Remy to find, or had it been placed here for anyone, even the cook, to discover?

Remy's hand shook as she laid the clipping back on the table. She stared down at it. At the large brown eyes of the girl looking back at her. At the lopsided pigtails and the worn My Little Pony T-shirt. The girl, no more than four years old, hugged a teddy bear. The caption screamed at Remy, even though the words were printed in a tiny font.

> *Four-year-old girl survives Dowell Street apartment fire. Two other family members, including the girl's mother, were found deceased. The cause of the fire is yet unknown.*

Remy shoved away from the table, her chair toppling backward onto the floor. She snatched up the clipping, crumpling it in her fist, and charged from the room. She hadn't remembered for a reason. She had specifically made it a point to forget. And while Remy knew it was never far beneath the surface, at no time had it been so poignantly shoved in her face.

As she sprinted up the staircase toward the debatable retreat of her room, Remy clenched her fist tighter around the clipping. Distant screams flooded her memory—and the flash of a smile. Someone she didn't know, or couldn't remember, or refused to recognize. But it was there in the recesses of her mind. Someone's mouth stretched into a satisfied grin as the searing heat from the blaze licked at her bare feet.

Remy flung the newspaper clipping away from her. It bounced against the wall and landed on the hallway floor. She saw the door to her room and made for it, breaths coming raggedly, the sensation that whoever had smiled that toothy grin was chasing after her. Her bedroom before her, Remy reached for the doorknob and shoved the door open.

She stumbled, grabbing on to the corner post at the foot of her bed. Her chest heaved, her face hot from the memory of the fire. All Remy wanted was to fling herself onto the bed. Bury herself beneath the blankets. Hide her face under the pillow.

But she couldn't. She couldn't throw herself onto her bed because it was covered in butterfly wings. Like a blanket of confetti or rose petals thrown by a flower girl, orange-and-yellow wings torn from butterflies scattered about the white comforter.

There were no bodies. Nothing but broken wings and the memory of someone who smiled when death came to call.

11

"...left butterfly wings on the eyes of his victims."

Elton's gravelly voice finished the sentence as Remy burst into his study. It was the morning after she saw Tate staring aimlessly at the night sky. The morning after she discovered the newspaper clipping of her as a little girl. The morning after she'd found butterfly wings spread over her bed and had finally fallen asleep in a huddled ball in the corner of the bedroom.

Both Elton and Tate looked up at her in surprise.

Remy tossed the balled-up newspaper clipping at Tate. She'd recovered it from where she threw it on the floor last night.

"What's this?" Tate was sharp today. Aware. He seemed completely different from the Tate of last night. His eyes weren't distant but instead were focused. Maybe a nighttime walk did some people good, but then Tate Arnold hadn't had a demon from the past visit him.

"You tell me," Remy answered accusingly. She darted an offended look at Elton. "Do you know who would do this?"

"What are you jabbering on about?" Elton reached for the clipping, snapping his fingers for Tate to hand it over. He smoothed the paper between his hands, his brow creasing as he read. Looking up at Remy, he asked, "Was this you?"

"Yep," she snapped. The lack of sleep, the disturbing events of last night, and now this? It had her on edge. She wanted to accuse Tate, but that didn't make sense in retrospect. She'd been with him outside and returned to the kitchen to find the clipping that hadn't been there prior to her going to meet him. He was innocent. Elton? Elton couldn't get down the stairs by himself. He was in no way responsible. Which left the question open as to who had put the clipping—the awful memory—on the table for her to find?

"You were a pretty little thing," Elton observed, ignoring Remy's frustration. He studied the black-and-white print.

"And the butterfly wings? What about them?" Remy choked out as tears threatened to surface and spill over.

Worry flashed across Elton's face. "Butterfly wings?"

Tate leaned forward in his chair—actually *her* chair—concern on his face as well.

Remy swallowed hard, willing the tears to go back to their rightful place. She robotically recounted the events from the night before, stifling the awakened emotions she'd long since avoided. She did not regale them with the leering smile of her memories. That was hers to deal with, and to fear. She also didn't need Tate Arnold seeing her all emotional. She tucked her pink strands of hair behind her ear to partner with the rest of her naturally colored hair and attempted to compose herself.

Elton laid the uncrumpled article on his writing desk. His face had taken on a stern expression, and Remy appreciated that he saw fit to take this seriously. "I was afraid of this." His words confused Remy. Elton met her eyes. "The Butterfly Butcher. This is his *modus operandi*. Taunt, terrify, torture psychologically. He thrived on toying with his victims before finally squeezing the very life from their throats."

Remy stared at Elton. The writer's white wispy hair was neatly combed from his forehead, his face cleanly shaved by Nurse Aimee, his cardigan buttoned and tidy. For all sakes and purposes, he was practically Captain von Trapp from *The Sound of Music*, only he was decades older and significantly more bald. But his explanation contradicted that austere image he projected. He had lost his mind! The Butterfly Butcher?

Tate found his voice before she did. "You're saying the Butterfly Butcher did this?" He pointed to the newspaper clipping. "A killer from over a century ago?" The doubt lacing his words deemed it unnecessary for Remy to voice her own.

Elton shifted his attention to Tate. "Well, not him *per se*, but it's certainly in line with everything I've read and have been writing about him. Butterfly wings? We were just saying before Remy arrived that the Butcher would leave butterfly wings on the closed eyelids of his victims. Like the old-fashioned tradition of coins, only the gossamer wings are of a much more delicate nature."

Remy crossed her arms, thankful she had an oversized sweater on as it felt like a shroud of protection. Protection from what? A serial killer's ghost? "That doesn't explain the clipping. Or the butterfly wings on my bed. Are you saying the manor is haunted by the Butterfly Butcher now too?" If he was, then she needed to rethink the concept of working for a delusional writer—not to mention the credibility it gave to Tate's demand to verify that the biography was factual.

"Well, that all depends on how you feel about ghosts," Elton answered, albeit cryptically. "But you're right. My observations don't account for the newspaper clipping or the butterfly wings. That is a *humanly* influenced action. Ghosts aren't adept at making organized messes."

His wink and attempt to insert humor did little to calm Remy's nerves. She exchanged a look with Tate as Elton continued.

"My observations about the historical methods of the Butcher merely tell us that *this*"—he tapped the clipping—"is not a fluke. Whoever sprinkled butterfly wings on your bed is aware of the Butterfly Butcher and what we're doing here. And they somehow resourced those deceased insects because they certainly did not find them in Wisconsin in the middle of October." Elton stared directly at Tate, taking a breath and clearing the old-age rasp from his throat. "I would be concerned it was you, but from the way Remy seems not to accuse you, I gather she's eliminated you from her list of suspects."

"Me?" Tate drew back.

"Yes." Elton reached inside his sweater to his inner shirt's chest pocket. He withdrew a pipe and closed his mouth around it without lighting it. "You arrived here with the intent to stop me from writing about your great-grandmother. When that was unsuccessful, you agreed instead to stay on and offer your critique so as to have a say in what was published. One could assume you were resorting to rather devious measures to frighten us away from the project altogether."

"I had nothing to do with this," Tate insisted firmly.

"He didn't. I was with him," Remy inserted. She caught Elton's quick raise of his brows. "Outside. Looking at the stars," she explained, although somehow that didn't seem to help.

"Stargazing," Elton corrected.

"Yes, stargazing," Tate confirmed.

"Well then," Elton concluded, the pipe flopping at the corner of his mouth precariously, "we've established your innocence, Mr. Arnold."

"What do I do then?" Remy asked. She hated the feeling of being at a loss, but this was new and wicked territory. Her upbringing in the foster system had done an adequate job training her to guard her heart, to build walls before allowing people access to her inner person, and to process the various forms of emotional and verbal abuse. Yet it had not prepared her for the psychological act of someone toying with long-buried, personal memories and making threats through symbolic measures.

"I'm afraid there's nothing we *can* do," Elton said. "There's no crime to report."

Tate frowned. "Even so, we can't just ignore this. It's an act of aggression."

"Thank you." Remy shot him an appreciative look. Doing nothing wouldn't help her to sleep at night.

Elton removed the pipe from his mouth and eyed her. "Three victims point to the Butterfly Butcher being responsible for their deaths, but the first may not have been his. Percy Hahn. The second—more than likely his first, Loretta Habington—and the third, Marian Arnold herself, or so goes the story."

"Your point?" Remy folded her arms across her chest again.

"My point is, who in today's world would want to replicate that?" Elton raised his brows. "And I do not mean that as a rhetorical question. Once we uncover the answer to this question, we'll uncover who put those butterfly wings on your bed and dredged up your past."

"But why me?" Remy felt herself sinking into the mire of confusion and fear.

Tate met her eyes with a disturbed flicker as Elton concluded, "Why you indeed."

Was it wrong to be in her car again to go get coffee? Mrs. Flemming had given her the stink eye when she left the manor, and Aimee had stared out the third-floor window, waving wildly either in farewell or a desperate attempt to have Remy pause so she could place her own coffee order. Remy didn't wait to find out. Aimee got on her nerves, and while she knew that wasn't kind, the truth was the truth. She couldn't take Aimee's incessant one-upping of information and gossip today. At least she knew it couldn't have been Aimee who'd left that newspaper clipping. Aimee was too needy for the limelight. If it had been her, she'd have framed the clipping and bestowed it on Remy in some sort of ceremony designed to laud Aimee with praise for finding the souvenir.

Unfortunately, Remy still hadn't moved fast enough because somehow Tate ended up sitting in her passenger seat, filling up her small car and smelling like a deodorant stick from heaven. He'd asked if he could come as she was hurrying out the door. She'd nodded without thinking. There was no good excuse to tell him no except that she wanted to be alone. Maybe even that she wanted to get in her car and keep driving straight through town and away from *el creepo* fest that Müllerian Manor was fast becoming.

"Overall, I'm normally a happy person." Oops. She hadn't meant to state that out loud, but she had and she could see Tate smile a bit from the corner of her eye as she drove. Fine. Now she had to finish her thoughts out loud too. "But this newspaper article thing and the butterfly wings? I don't have anything to hide, so I don't get why I'd be a target for someone's mocking."

"But maybe you have stuff to hide *from*?" Tate offered.

His question didn't even bother her, which solidified all the more how random it was that this had happened. Remy adjusted her grip on the steering wheel. She craned her neck to look both ways at the railroad tracks she needed to cross. "The only things I run from are memories. Don't we all?"

"You were supposed to yield," Tate instructed absently as she drove over the tracks without pausing.

Remy ignored him. "God knows I've worked really hard to nurture peace in my life. I thought this job would continue that. Research assistant? History is just that. *History*. It's not supposed to come *alive!*" She turned her blinker on and slowed to a stop. "And Aimee says the manor is haunted by Marian Arnold. I didn't believe that, but your ancestors' house is really odd."

Tate chuckled but kept his attention averted out the window. "Or creatively constructed."

"Okay, we'll go with that if it makes you feel better." Remy was trying to be funny, but she noticed Tate had grown quiet.

He came off as a moody guy, and she wasn't totally comfortable with him yet. "Where'd you grow up?" Small talk was safer. For both of them.

Tate shifted, the seat belt rubbing against his waffle-knit Henley. Dusty blue, her favorite color. He reminded her a bit of a Hallmark Christmas movie hero. She wasn't sure she was keen on that—her with the nose ring and pink hair. They weren't exactly a perfect pair.

She shut down her thoughts as Tate responded to her question.

"I grew up near Madison. About a two hours' drive from here."

"Yeah? I didn't realize you were from Wisconsin." Remy wasn't sure why it surprised her. Maybe because his appearance screamed wintery Vermont. Scruffy goatee, unruly curls, outdoorsy.

"My hometown is small. Lots of tourists in the summer, empty in the winter." He supplied the brief description with zero personal information.

Remy felt it was only fair she knew something about him. "Do you have family there?" She also asked because she was curious to see if his response went along with Aimee's claim that he was the "last of the Arnolds."

Tate shifted again in his seat and cleared his throat. Nervous? Or just uncomfortable, squeezed as he was into her little car? "No family."

So that part was true. Score one for nosy Nurse Aimee.

Remy spotted the coffee shack ahead, which was in the corner of the hardware store parking lot. She turned and drove toward it but was unwilling to let Tate off the hook just yet.

Elton was right. If she hadn't been with Tate last night, she would have pegged him for the person who'd left that old article of her on the table, plus the butterfly wings on her bed. How had anyone even *found* that article? She'd never seen it before in her life. But she certainly recalled the fire.

"*Did* you have family?" Remy asked as she came to a stop behind another car that had pulled up to the shack's drive-through window before her.

Tate drummed his fingers silently on his leg. "That's an odd question. Everyone has family in their history."

"Depends on how you look at it. I didn't. I grew up in foster homes."

"Oh. Sorry." Tate cleared his throat again.

Remy gave him a sideways glance. "Don't be. I'm not the stereotype people slap on foster kids. I am a stable human being with a lot to offer the world, and I have committed no crimes. But still, I meant did you grow up with family?" How hard did she have to push this guy to get him to give her something beyond vague answers?

Tate shook his head. "I don't know if I should say 'good for you' or 'I'm sorry you grew up without your family.'"

At least he was honest, she'd give him that. "I don't talk about it a lot," Remy said. But she didn't bother to keep it a secret either. "That article from last night, the newspaper clipping? That was the catapulting event into my future without family." She'd always been envious of kids in school who had families to go home to. Families that shared a last name and at least a modicum of love. Even divorced homes weren't "broken" to Remy—not like the people in the churches she'd attended at various points in her childhood had called them. Divorced homes were still homes, and the kids were lucky enough to have two homes. She didn't even have one.

"That's rough," said Tate. "The fire, I mean, and getting thrown into the system."

"It's okay. I aged out. I worked my butt off through high school. I came out all right." Traumatized in ways she didn't care to explore, but all right overall.

Tate gave her a direct look. "Yeah, I had a family. My mom

and dad were killed in a car accident a couple of years ago. I was an only child."

There. Something personal. That was nice. He seemed more human now, though still withdrawn. Still guarded.

"Did you have a dog growing up?" Remy teased with a grin, attempting to coax one out of Tate.

"No." His eyes grew distant, and he stared beyond her as though transported to some faraway place.

Remy wanted to push with another question, but she stopped herself. Tate was wounded. She could see that he had gone somewhere deep in his soul. Somewhere she couldn't follow. Somewhere no one was invited.

She pulled ahead to the coffee shack window. Sometimes coffee really was all a person had to make the bad feel a little bit better.

12

MARIAN

IVO'S WORDS SUNK into the pit of Marian's stomach. She tried not to stare at him with utter horror, but she couldn't help it. This was a different type of anxiety altogether.

"A dinner party?" Her voice squeaked as she tried to temper her shock.

Ivo's grin stretched into dimples in his chiseled face. "You won't have to worry about a thing. I'll finance the entire dinner. In fact, I'll hire some outside staff so that your Mrs. Dale doesn't have to manage it all herself. See? And then you can just dress up like the doll you are. Let me spoil you."

"I don't think I need that kind of spoiling." Marian attempted a small laugh in hopes of lightening her mood.

"Nonsense!" Ivo strode across the library and gripped her upper arms lightly, leaning in toward her, his eyes sparking with energy and life. "Marian, you need to live a little. Experience *life*! Aunt Verdine never wanted you to be so serious, yet here you are, as stoic as your father."

Marian was certain she didn't like being compared to her daunting father, a man she couldn't remember ever laughing.

He's trying to trick you. He wants to hurt you.

Marian shot a glance to her side as she heard the whisper in her ear. No one was there. Ivo still held on to her arms. She wriggled free, and he released her. A cursory scan of the room told Marian she was still alone with Ivo.

"I can trust you?" she asked, knowing of course that Ivo would say yes. Why wouldn't he? He wasn't going to hurt her. He was family. She *needed* family.

"Marian." Ivo shook his head, his expression gentling. "Darling, you know I'm here for *you*. I wouldn't do anything to harm you—who do you think I am?"

"I know." Marian offered Ivo a reassuring nod. "I know. I just get worried. Mother wasn't fond of too many people here, and I'm not sure we've ever had a dinner party at Müllerian Manor."

"And it's time that changed!" Ivo grinned and snapped his fingers. "Loretta is resting for the afternoon. You should go for a walk. Let me worry about the party. I'm only thinking six or eight couples anyway. Nothing too grandiose."

With a flourish, he kissed her cheek and strode from the room, leaving Marian bewildered and feeling topsy-turvy from his announcement. But it would be rude to argue, rude to tell him no.

She heard movement beside her and jumped, startled by her sensing another's presence. This time, though, it was Frederick. The butler had entered from the opposite doorway from which Ivo had left. His brows were pulled into a grandfatherly look of concern, yet he maintained the appropriate distance due to her being his employer.

"Did I hear correctly? There's to be a dinner party here at Müllerian Manor?"

"Yes." Marian spun to face the dear man. "But you won't have to worry. Ivo will hire additional help. Mrs. Dale needn't be overwhelmed."

Frederick's trimmed yet bushy white brows drew together. "But with the recent events, do you think it wise?"

He was overstepping now, but Marian didn't mind. She relied on Frederick more than she should probably admit, but then who was left to shame in the family anymore? No one. The only shame of confiding in her employee would be from people whose opinions didn't matter, and Ivo certainly wouldn't judge her.

"I don't know." Marian nibbled at her fingernail. She winced. "What do you think?"

Frederick appeared taken aback that she would ask his opinion. He cleared his throat and dipped his head. "I think we proceed with caution, miss. We cannot be cavalier about Mr. Hahn's passing and what—*who*—may have had a hand in it. Will the police have any issue with outsiders descending on the manor while they're still investigating the death?"

"I-I don't know." She felt altogether helpless, and she couldn't very well call the police to ask permission to throw a dinner party! "The authorities gave me no further instructions. Perhaps it was of Mr. Hahn's own hand as has been suggested? Not a killing at all. You don't believe I'm being as concerned as I should be? Perhaps I should inquire with the authorities, or—"

Frederick held up a hand with a grim smile to pause Marian in her jumbled thoughts. "If there was nefarious intent behind Mr. Hahn's death, then we should be cautious. Why the milkman? Why here at the manor? These questions worry me."

"The police have suggested he may have died by his own hand." Even as Marian stated it aloud, she wasn't convinced she believed it to be true. Why would the milkman pile dead butterflies beneath his feet before he hanged himself?

"Perhaps." Frederick nodded slowly. "Be that as it may, I will follow your wishes, miss, even while keeping an eye on you as if you were my own ward."

A warmth spread through Marian—perhaps the first since her father's passing. Knowing that Frederick's affection was so loyal made her feel just a bit more invincible and much more comforted. More so than what she had received from Ivo. His obliviousness to her situation stung. She had hoped that he would sweep into the manor and take charge in a way that allowed her to rest and regain her stability. Instead, he had brought Loretta, and while lovely and kind, Loretta was the surety that Ivo was only here for a moment in time. And when that time was over, Marian would be, once again, very alone.

"Frederick?" Marian captured the butler's attention as he moved to take his leave.

"Yes, Miss Arnold?"

"Was my mother happy here? Alone, I mean?"

Frederick frowned. "Miss?"

"When Father and I weren't here, was she . . . sad? Lonesome? Was she heartbroken we didn't stay longer?" Marian had always wondered, yet Father seemed to have no patience for Mother's fancies, and Mother had been so distant from Marian that the idea of not being near her felt as if it wouldn't matter. But now, as Marian experienced her own aloneness, she worried it had all been a facade. That deep down, Mother had cried when they'd left her behind at Müllerian Manor, that she had been forsaken by them merely because she viewed life through a unique lens.

Frederick folded his hands in front of him, his expression proving he chose his words with thought and with care. "Your mother was never truly alone." He opened his mouth to continue, thought better of it, and closed it.

"What do you mean?" Marian tilted her head, studying Frederick's face.

The older man drew in a deep sigh and closed his eyes for a moment, then opened them. "Your mother found company with her butterflies, Miss Arnold. She spoke to them, and they . . . they spoke to her."

An earsplitting scream pierced the air.

Marian bolted upright in bed, simultaneously throwing the covers from her. She heard the pounding of footsteps in the hallway and hated the sound of them and the emotions that emerged.

Tonight had been misery. Absolute and sheer misery. Ivo had not told her that his guests for Friday evening's dinner party would arrive the evening prior. He had not explained that by ten at night, Müllerian Manor would be filled—every suite—with young men and women. That cigarette smoke would hover in the rooms, glasses would tinkle with the sound of ice against their sides just before brandy was poured. Brandy? From where? What if the police came to call? Which they certainly might considering the death of Percy Hahn.

Marian had retired early, not just annoyed but hurt by Ivo's lack of sensitivity. She should have listened to that voice that had almost audibly whispered in her ear earlier. He was hurting her—he just didn't mean to—and for that reason alone, Marian felt she should forgive him.

Pounding on her bedroom door caused Marian to tumble from her bed and hurry to answer it. She opened it a crack, peering through to see Ivo's eyes, wide with panic and bloodshot from too much enjoyment from the evening's entertainment.

"I need you," he urged. "Loretta has had a horrid fright."

Marian nodded, opening her door fully and snatching up her housecoat. She shoved her arms into it as they hurried down the twisty hall, down some stairs, through an oddly positioned doorway, up another set of three stairs to the open door of Loretta's suite.

Upon entering, Marian quickly took in her houseguest's

frazzled appearance. Loretta was perched on the edge of her bed, the bedclothes having been tossed to the floor. She wrapped her arms around herself, clad in a silky, flimsy nightgown. Her bobbed hair wasn't perfect any longer but was tousled and matted. Kohl liner was smeared beneath her eyes, and it was apparent Loretta had been crying.

"Oh, Marian!" Loretta swept from the bed and threw herself into Marian's arms. The unexpected embrace and the surprise that Loretta hadn't thrown herself at Ivo left Marian staggering to keep her footing.

"What happened?" she asked, looking sideways at Ivo as she held Loretta.

Loretta pulled away, sniffing. "I came to the bedroom. I had changed and I went to put my stockings in the drawer, and I saw . . . *that!*" She pointed to the bureau whose top drawer had been pulled open.

Marian exchanged looks with Ivo. She moved to the bureau to investigate further. The skeletal remains of a small animal lay in the open drawer, and atop the skeleton, a dried monarch butterfly with its wings outstretched as if it had been pinned to a board for display.

"What is this?" Marian turned to Ivo, her eyes startled.

He shrugged and threw his hands in the air. "Darned if I know, Marian!" Pointing at the drawer, he jabbed with his index finger. "Bones? A dead butterfly? What superstitious goon has the gall to leave such things in a lady's room? Or any room for that matter?" Ivo transitioned swiftly from being appalled to being furious.

"I think it's a cat." Loretta sucked in a shuddering sob.

"There's no skull." Marian looked again at the pile of bones in the drawer. "I doubt it's a cat. There aren't enough bones, nor are they large enough."

"Does it matter what it is?" Ivo protested. "This is reprehensible!"

Movement in the doorway alerted Marian to the presence

of three more people—all of whom she didn't know. Two were men, one a woman, all in their nightclothes and remarkably unconcerned about modesty.

Marian was relieved to see Frederick push his way in between them, his feet in house slippers, a housecoat wrapped properly around his waist, and spectacles perched on his nose.

"Miss Arnold, what is the commotion?" Worry etched the lines deeper between his brows.

Marian pointed along with Ivo to the open bureau drawer.

Frederick approached, looking down to see the macabre display. "Good heavens!" he muttered and then stiffened. He eyed Ivo, then looked to the guests in the doorway, then to Loretta, who was huddled back on her bed. He turned and pushed the drawer back into place to hide the gruesome sight. "I will summon the authorities immediately," he stated.

"No!" Ivo shouted, startling them all. He coughed. "I mean, I don't believe that would be necessary."

"Indeed." One of the houseguests in the doorway stepped into the room, extending his hand to Frederick in greeting—which was quite out of place for a guest to acknowledge house staff in such a way. "Cecil Adams."

Frederick ignored the man's hand. He turned instead to Marian, effectively transferring all authority to her as the mistress of the home. "Shall I call the authorities, miss?"

Marian looked desperately at Ivo, who gave her a quick shake of his head. She glanced at Loretta, whose eyes had widened again. Taking into inventory the guests, the bloodshot eyes, the faint scent of alcohol in the air, Marian knew precisely why they were not willing to risk the police being summoned over a dead animal's remains along with a butterfly in the bureau drawer.

"I-I . . ." She fumbled to decide. Frederick would be disappointed in her if she capitulated to Ivo and his friend's wishes. And Ivo would be in danger of being arrested. "No, Frederick," she answered. "You needn't call anyone. Let's just clean up this mess and . . ." Marian struggled to find words, to give instructions. The light from the wall sconces seemed to glow brighter. She saw a flicker from the corner of her eye, and for an instant she was sure a black shadow swept across Loretta's bed and shot toward Cecil Adams. "Just clean it up," she finished.

"Good plan." Ivo collected himself. He waved Cecil over. "Come. Take the drawer out of here and dump what's inside into a burn pile at the back of the property, then give the drawer a thorough scrubbing." He turned to Frederick. "You've that groundskeeper, yes? Felix? Summon him and have him take care of it for us."

Frederick's mouth was set in a grim line. "Very well." He did as he was bidden and exited the room as Cecil tugged the drawer from its place and hefted it over his shoulder so that no one had to see inside it. He appeared similar in age to Ivo but was balding and thin. He gave Marian an apologetic smile as he moved past her. "I'll take this downstairs for the groundskeeper."

The moment he had exited, the other woman flew into the room and pounced next to Loretta on the bed. "Oh, honey, that was just the worst!"

The remaining man was muttering in low tones with Ivo.

Marian watched them all as she stood alone by the bureau. The overwhelming nature of the event was beginning to sink in and take hold. A dead butterfly. Not unlike the dead butterflies lying beneath the milkman's body as the rope creaked from his weight.

Marian felt her knees give way, and she grappled for the bureau, holding on to it and regaining her footing. The others in the room hadn't noticed. They were huddled together, murmuring about brandy.

"Gonna need to put down another, I think," Marian heard Ivo state.

Within moments they had exited the room, the two women

clad immodestly in their slinky nightgowns, and the men apparently quite used to that state of undress.

Marian tugged her housecoat tighter over her old-fashioned cotton nightgown.

They won't care about you. You'd be better off dead.

Marian spun toward the whispered voice. But there was no one there. She darted a frantic look to the far corner just as the black shadow swept beneath the bed.

Better off dead, the voice whispered again.

Marian was frozen in place, her breath lodged in her throat. Motion in the doorway turned her attention toward it.

Violet stood there, just off a bit and in the shadows. She shook her head, and this time she looked . . . disapproving? It was difficult to tell, for as soon as Marian noted the woman from the butterfly house, Violet turned and slipped from view.

Marian sank to the floor, too frightened to follow.

Müllerian Manor was no longer a home. It was fast becoming a place of horrors. For the first time, Marian wondered if her mother had died for reasons other than natural causes.

Something evil lurked inside the manor. Something dark wove its way through the walls, whispering horrible things and demanding she follow them.

13

REMY

"THEY FOUND A DEAD ANIMAL in their houseguest's dresser drawer." Remy looked up from the notes she had taken from her morning jaunt to the local library to use their Wi-Fi. She tapped her handwriting with a pen.

Elton frowned, evidently piecing together elements from her research. "Well, that is intriguing information."

Remy leaned back in her chair and swung her right leg over her left knee, bouncing her foot. This was the part of research she enjoyed, but she really hoped Elton wouldn't be upset with her when she spilled the beans about something else. "Soooo, when I was at the library, I did some searching into Tate's background."

Elton's eyes narrowed.

Remy hurried to explain. "I just didn't want you taken advantage of by someone who wasn't who they said they were." Not to mention, Tate was a bit of an enigma to her, and her curiosity was becoming unquenchable. "Not to worry. His claims are accurate. He's from the Arnold family line—although, I'm not going to lie, the family tree is very sketchy and incomplete."

The old man's pipe shifted just slightly at the corner of his mouth. A spiral of smoke drifted toward the ceiling. Remy took his silence as a sign to continue.

"There is Marian Arnold, then what appears to be a brother, but unnamed and no dates of birth and death, just the indication of 'sibling-male.' There's no evidence that Marian ever married. The family tree extends from both Marian and her unnamed sibling, meaning the line from which Tate is a direct descendant is unclear."

"But he is a descendant," Elton confirmed as if he'd had no doubt.

Remy was just thankful he wasn't upset. "Short of a DNA test to prove—"

"I'm not requiring a DNA test." Elton's mouth thinned around his pipe.

"I know, I know." Remy laughed nervously. "I wasn't suggesting it either. But I did look into the Arnold trust and the estate. The manor was managed for some time after Marian passed—by a cousin of hers. After the cousin disappears from records, the manor remained in the Arnold trust, though there were occupants throughout the years. I found records that start up again in the sixties, with the residents being renters mostly. No one stayed for long, though."

"Because of Marian's ghost, I suppose." Elton drew his pipe from his mouth. "Nobody cares to argue with an angry ghost."

Angry ghost? Remy hadn't heard of Marian being angry before.

Elton must have read her mind. His eyes brightened. "When the estate put the manor up for sale, I was intrigued. What research I'd already done was to read accounts of various occupants through the years. It seems they all believed the place to be haunted by Marian Arnold, and she was blamed for being unwelcoming. It was a must-buy opportunity for me. To live with the spirit of the woman whose biography I was going to write?" Elton's eyes carried an element of confession. "Yes, I knew Tate was legitimate, Remy. When I purchased the manor, he was involved in the sale via the attorneys and real-estate agent. I figured it was only a matter of time before he pieced together who I was."

It made sense, and thankfully Elton didn't think she'd over-stepped. Remy thumbed through her notes. "Okay, back to the animal bones and the dead butterfly. I found the newspaper archives dating back to the time of Loretta's murder. One of them referenced the testimony of a houseguest."

Elton nodded casually, and Remy could tell he was tallying up the information in light of what they already knew. "That was more than likely the first sign the Butterfly Butcher was going to strike again. They should have taken it more seriously when the bones and dead butterfly showed up in Loretta's room."

Remy's skin crawled. "Why the animal bones?"

"Because, my dear girl—" Elton paused to take a puff from his pipe—"killers are sadistic. Plain and simple. Those items were symbolic to the Butcher and are therefore another clue as to the identity of the killer. You must delve deeper in our research—starting with Loretta Habington. Have you even looked at her as I'd asked? Who was she *really*? Why was she staying at Müllerian Manor? I've a feeling much more was at play than just a lovely visit. Think of it. Prohibition. Bankruptcy of the Arnold Brewery. Marian's father dead, her mother dead . . . what was happening in this house? The era itself screams of mayhem."

Remy nodded and closed the notebook, settling back in her chair to eye the writer across from her. "Loretta Habington. I'll check the newspaper archives and ancestral records—that's probably where our answers are hiding out." She squelched a sigh. "Elton, you're slicing my Achilles' heel making me drive to the library for Wi-Fi."

Elton puffed on his pipe, the smell of tobacco permeating the air. "That's a bit dramatic." He blinked lazily at Remy. "Contrary to what you urbanites might think"—he removed the pipe and gestured with it in her direction—"it's not as simple as phoning some company to come and hook up a high-speed connection, not this far out in the country."

Remy tried again. "I'm just saying, it'd be easier to do proper research right here. I just don't want to miss something and give Tate a reason not to like the manuscript once it's done. He'll claim it's unsubstantiated. Can I at least *call* to see what options there are for internet service?"

"Don't insult me. I've already checked my options. I'm not an idiot." Elton glowered. "Contrary to popular perception, rural areas can't just snap their fingers and achieve the internet."

"Oh." Remy gave the elderly man a sheepish look. "Regardless, with Tate here, and you writing the biography, I need to do my job. Do proper research. Online. With a computer." She smiled. "Those boxlike things that plug into the wall and have screens and, you know, internet?"

"You're a pistol, Remy Crenshaw." A crooked grin reached his eyes. "And I like that." He sighed, followed by more pipe smoking. "Yes, yes, I know about computers and the internet. If I appear old-fashioned, it's because I'm *old*. It would cost thousands to get decent internet out here in the boonies, and with all the trees, I've been told satellites won't help much. So there." A petulant pout settled on his face.

"We can't get it through cellular?" Remy asked.

"Does your phone work here?" Elton countered. "Again, I may be old, but I'm not stupid."

It was said with annoyance and affection simultaneously. As she got to her feet, Remy had the sudden impulse to bend down and drop a peck on the old man's cheek. So she did. Their eyes met, and she gave him a straight look. "Not stupid, no. Stubborn, yes. I know you have more than enough money to run fiber-optic cable out here. You're just *old-fashioned* and don't want the internet anywhere near the manor."

Elton smirked. "And you rather like me anyway."

Remy couldn't help but smile. "Keep hoping," she tossed over her shoulder as she exited the room to return to the library.

Remy took off her reading glasses and laid them on the desk beside the library computer. Her notebook was filled with pages of random dates and information. She'd found newspaper articles from 1921 on the Butterfly Butcher but was surprised by how sketchy they were. If the Arnolds had been trying to keep things under wraps for whatever reason, they'd done a fairly good job. Elton's connection with the local police had informed them that any cold-case records dating back that far would have been destroyed in a flood back in the 1940s that had ruined most of the older files. That no one had ever solved the murders, identified the killer, or even honored the victims was a conundrum that Remy was pretty sure Elton wasn't going to solve in the biography. Except for honoring the victims; that part he had an opportunity to achieve.

Remy drummed her fingers on the desk, staring blankly at the screen. She'd been distracted while researching. Images of a fire, the reminder of the newspaper clipping . . . it all bothered her more than she cared to admit. In truth, she was at war with herself. She'd never allowed herself to reflect deeply on her early years. Especially those memories tucked away in the long-forgotten filing cabinets in her mind.

She had made it through the system. That was what mattered most. What didn't matter were all the things she couldn't change that were in the past. Her mother's death, her absentee father, grandparents who couldn't care for her. All of it had resulted in the state taking over. Remy had been in fourteen different foster homes since the age of four. She recalled the day at home number nine when she realized she wasn't ever going to be adopted. Not at thirteen. Teenage kids in the system came with too much baggage. They weren't cute anymore.

She'd been lucky in some ways. The last three foster homes were decent, the last being for the remaining two years of her high school career. The couple had been kind. Reserved but good at caregiving. Yet they'd never really invited Remy into their hearts and lives, and once she aged out, she also moved out.

She was ambitious, though, and highly motivated. She had enough initiative and drive not to become a foster-care statistic. It was why she was here now, working with Elton.

Remy continued to stare at the blank computer screen. She barely remembered her mother—just little memories. Her father had no face; she didn't even know his name. There were ways she could find out, but she never had. Uncovering potential ties to a living family would be akin to opening Pandora's box. Could be good, or it could be very bad.

Then there was the fire. Always the fire. She could still recall the crackling of the flames, the echo of someone's laughter, the smoke that had choked her. Her only other memory was the firefighter who'd scooped her up into his arms and carried her to safety. She remembered his blue eyes, bright with concern but steady, comforting. *"It'll be okay, kiddo."* His words, so simple, had brought such promise.

But had it been okay? In terms of the fire hurting her physically, he was right. But in terms of the rest of her life?

Remy blinked, breaking her empty stare.

Why dredge up the buried memories? It would be exhuming remains better off left in the grave. She felt anger rising toward whoever had found that newspaper clipping and left it for her to find. They had taken shovelfuls of earth from the burial plot of her childhood memories and exposed what shouldn't be unearthed. What was their motive anyway? To unsettle her? Entice her to leave the manor to go off chasing her past? Who would want her to leave the manor, and who in this area even knew about the fire?

What was worse, her memories were incomplete, and that was almost as unsettling as remembering in the first place. At least a complete memory could potentially be reburied, but the snippets? They were like slow poison that was difficult, if not impossible, to get out of one's system because they left questions in their path.

Remy's job was to answer questions—but not hers, other people's. The questions surrounding Marian Arnold. Had the Butterfly Butcher truly murdered her? Were the tales accurate, or had something else occurred to make Marian Arnold disappear from history? Why did the Butterfly Butcher kill to begin with? What was the motivation? Why, if such an intriguing case, was there so little recorded about it, the facts so hard to come by?

These were questions Remy was anticipating digging into more deeply. But her own life? Her missing memories? They'd never haunted her because Remy hadn't allowed them to. She didn't want to become the troubled heroine of her own story. She had always wanted to rise above her circumstances, to be strong in her own right.

But Müllerian Manor wasn't allowing her to.

Remy released a low growl and slid her glasses back on her face. She clicked the computer screen on and typed into the search bar the information from the newspaper clipping. Several links appeared. She clicked on the top one. It was the same clipping that had been left in the manor's kitchen—and apparently inspired whatever sadistic mind had put it there to also sprinkle butterfly wings on her bed. Butterflies had *nothing* to do with Remy's past but everything to do with the manor's.

Remy exited that web page and selected the next. It was impossible to drag her stare away from the article. Numbness entered her body, along with a strange familiarity with the words on the screen. Though she'd never read them before, she had been there. Snatches of images shot to the surface in Remy's mind as she read:

> *An apartment fire ripped through the Dowell Street apartment complex at 2:47 a.m. yesterday morning. Residents who had not already escaped the blaze were evacuated after the 911 call came in and the fire department arrived on the scene. Two individuals were unable to be revived and died from smoke inhalation at the scene. Their names will be withheld until the families are notified.*

Remy knew the names. It was her mother—who had probably been strung out and unaware of the fire—and her mother's boyfriend. Remy didn't remember much about the boyfriend. Just a vague outline of a thin man with pockmarked cheeks, but she wasn't even sure if that was him.

She squeezed her eyes shut, but the images remained. She could see her mother in a chair, sprawled out and sleeping. She saw a smoky haze. Remy's eyes flew open as the next image flooded her brain.

That smile. That satisfied grin from someone else. Yes, someone else had been there that night, and Remy knew in her soul it wasn't her mother's boyfriend. That smile was awful. It was what she'd seen on the faces of villains in thrillers and horror movies right before they tortured, dismembered, or murdered their victims. That grin that said "I've got you!" which made her skin crawl.

Remy pushed away from the library desk and pounded her finger against the mouse, shutting down the apps and the reminders her toddler brain had shut down long ago. She jammed her notebook into her bag, threw in her pen and Post-its, and snagged her glasses off her face, stuffing them in their case.

She needed to breathe.

Her fingers trembled as she tried to zip her bag shut.

She needed fresh air. Remy could smell smoke—the memory of it so strong it was still in her senses from more than twenty years before.

Giving up on the zipper, Remy hugged her bag and hurried through the library, slipping between desks and muttering apologies as she accidentally kicked over a metal mesh wastebasket by another station.

She pushed through the main entrance door and burst into the fresh air. Sucking in deep gulps, Remy sagged onto a nearby bench, still hugging her bag. Two sparrows pecked at the lawn beside her. The oak tree overhead swayed gently in the autumn breeze, its golden leaves rustling like a calming lullaby.

Remy sucked in a shuddering breath, willing away this surge of unfamiliar and unwanted emotion. She had to control it. She had to bring herself back to the present. To the place she was now, not the place she had been. There was a reason her four-year-old mind had buried away the memories, and this was the reason. They were disabling.

Minutes ticked by until finally Remy found herself able to breathe more consistently. Her grip on her bag had loosened and she was able to zip it shut and sling it over her shoulder.

God had a funny sense of humor, creating the human brain the way He did. He allowed it to block harmful memories to protect one's psyche, but then He didn't stop them when they tried to revive their ugly selves. Remy struggled to believe in the small vestiges of faith instilled in her through hodgepodge resources throughout her growing up. The Bible club, the elderly neighbor with the cookies and Scripture verses when Remy lived in foster home three, a friend from high school. They reinforced the belief that God protected, that He provided a place of safety.

Remy had clung to those promises as a child. As an adult, she didn't want to be convinced they were merely a fairy tale. But sometimes it seemed that way. That God wasn't protecting, and maybe He didn't even exist. And yet, in spite of all the arguments for or against, Remy couldn't shake it. Couldn't shake Him. She knew in her soul God existed. It was just difficult to understand Him. Why it was He protected sometimes, while other times He let the fires rage.

Her car was parked close by, and Remy hit the key fob in her hand, unlocking it. She went and opened the back door and tossed her bag onto the seat.

She would head back to Müllerian Manor, collect her notes, outline them, and start to compare what she had learned to what was already known about the Butterfly Butcher story. The little info she had on the victim Loretta Habington had given Remy a few more ideas to research, but her energy was sapped for now.

Remy shut the back car door and opened the driver's door. She moved to get in, then froze when she noticed something on the seat. Her shoulders tightened as the rest of her body was paralyzed from further movement. She couldn't react. The power to scream or flee had been stolen from her by the inanimate objects on the seat.

A pile of small animal bones had been placed there. On top of them, a dead monarch butterfly. Beside them, another newspaper clipping. This one showed a picture of Remy from high school, running in a cross-country race in which she'd placed second. Taped to the clipping was a scribbled word in blue ink.

Hi.

A hello had never been so terrifying.

14

R EMY HAD DECIDED to call the police. It was the only
thing she could think to do. But other than filing a report, there wasn't much the police could do either. A
few photos were taken, the items confiscated, a "We'll look into
this," and then it was over. She was now alone in her car, driving
back to the manor, and experiencing the worst case of emotional
whiplash.

Arriving at the manor, she parked the car, exited, and grabbed
her bag from the back seat. At this point she was anxious to
dig back into the research on Marian Arnold and the Butterfly
Butcher. It would be a great diversion. And Remy needed a diversion right now, even if it was in researching a dead serial killer.

"Hey."

A scream ripped from Remy's throat. She spun, swinging her
bag like a weapon. Tate's hands shot up to block it, and the bag
flung back and hit Remy in her jean-clad legs.

Tate winced. "I didn't mean to scare you."

Remy caught her breath and waved her hand at him. "No, no,
that's okay. It's been that kinda day."

At Tate's questioning look, she filled him in on the situation, leaving out her personal perusal of articles regarding the apartment fire.

"What'd the police say?" Tate walked beside Remy as they headed toward the manor from the more modern garage area.

Remy's shoes crunched on the gravel drive. "Not much. Classic case of stalker but no suspect, messages but no crime."

"He broke into your car. That's a crime," Tate said.

Remy gave him a tight smile. "It's under debate whether I'd locked my doors. I thought I had, but I honestly can't remember."

Tate adjusted the brim of his baseball cap. "Do you have a second?"

Remy paused on the front step of the manor.

Tate continued, "I found something, and I think it might . . . well, it's easier just to show you."

"Let me put my bag inside." Remy's discomfort from the day was ebbing, but now Tate's cryptic announcement revived some of it. She dropped her bag in the manor's entryway, knowing Mrs. Flemming would be irritated at the sloppy discard of personal belongings. Joining Tate once again, he nodded toward the back lawn.

"It's in the glass house," he said.

Remy followed Tate across the yard, stealing a few sideways glances at him. He appeared relaxed today. Blue jeans, flannel shirt, baseball cap—it all lent itself toward a casual, very Wisconsin air. Yet there was something else about him Remy couldn't place, and it bothered her that she couldn't identify it. Most of the men she knew were self-confident, snarky like Elton, or dismissive. She'd met a few timid men too, but Tate's issue wasn't timidity. It was something altogether different. Secretive? Maybe. Things he didn't want to share, or maybe things he *did* want to share but didn't know how to.

"In here." Tate motioned to the glass house, and because the structure was missing its doors, they both entered side by side.

"This place is a mess," Remy muttered.

"I'm going to work with Boggart to get it cleaned up," Tate said. "Part of my working for Elton is to help out around the manor—cleaning, making repairs and such."

"I thought you were going to help with the biography of Marian Arnold?" Remy countered.

"Yeah. I will. But there's not always stuff for me to do." With that, Tate closed his mouth in a grim line and moved ahead of her. "It's back here. What I want to show you."

Remy followed until they'd woven their way around piles of cardboard and bins of glass to the stone grave at the far end, where Tate looked at her with an expectant expression.

She nodded. "Yeah, I saw that already. It's Marian's mother's grave."

"Right, but did you see this?" He squatted next to the stone sarcophagus and ran a hand along it, pushing aside dead vines and branches that crumbled under his touch.

Remy frowned, bending to see better. She felt the warmth of Tate's body, and being so near him flustered her. "What is it?"

"There." He touched the side of the granite coffin, his hand sliding to the bottom where it met with the floor.

"Is that writing?" Remy leaned in closer. "I can't make out what it says."

The message was small, written with brushstrokes of black paint that had since chipped and faded.

"I think it says 'He will haunt the future.'" Tate crouched low, squinting to read the words. "Yeah. That's gotta be it."

Remy nudged him. "Let me see."

Tate shifted to the side on his knees, giving her space.

Remy kneeled and peered at the words of the message. It certainly looked like what Tate had interpreted. "What does it mean?" She looked at Tate, who met her eyes with a perplexed expression.

"I don't know. But there are initials with it. Did you see them?"

Remy leaned back in and looked, then sat back on her heels in surprise. "M. A.?"

"Marian Arnold," Tate said.

"Possibly," Remy agreed.

"Who else would it be?" Tate tipped his cap back on his head, dark curls sticking out from beneath it. His look was almost boyish, and if Remy wasn't trying to process everything from today, she knew she'd be in danger of being a bit enamored with the guy.

"You're probably right, but I don't want to assume." Remy let out a sigh and looked around them at the butterfly house ruins, the garbage, the remnants of the past, so hallowed here and yet buried by time. "Marian Arnold would have come here regularly, I mean with this being her mother's grave. But why would she write 'He will haunt the future'?" Remy didn't try to hide her apprehension as she met Tate's eyes. "Did she mean the Butterfly Butcher? How would she have known—?" Remy bit off her words because the idea was ludicrous.

"How would she have known that someone in our time would start leaving the Butcher's marks? Dead butterflies?"

"And a pile of bones," Remy mumbled. "Like in Loretta Habington's dresser."

"You know what concerns me the most?" Tate ventured.

"What?" Remy waited, studying his face.

"What happened with the milkman, Percy Hahn, and then Loretta Habington, the dead butterflies were . . ." He broke off as if he were hesitant to say it for fear of frightening Remy.

But she'd already put the pieces together. "The butterflies were omens of their murders," Remy finished. She glanced back at the obscure message from the past. "If he *will* haunt the future, then . . ."

Her words hung between them.

She'd been visited with dead butterflies twice already, and now it seemed Marian Arnold was speaking from beyond the grave to warn her. Warn her of something—*someone*—dark and threatening.

"Don't be irritated if you have me hanging around you a lot more." Tate's words coursed through Remy with a sense of gratitude but also trepidation. He didn't mean it flirtatiously, that was evident by the scowl on his face. "I'm not convinced you're safe here."

Remy wanted to argue, tell him she could take care of herself. She wanted to say this entire thing was ridiculous. Dead butterflies? Animal bones? Messages from ghosts? But everything inside of Remy was a red alert going off. She was afraid that Tate Arnold was right.

Remy wrapped a sherpa blanket around her shoulders and made her way to the veranda at the back of the manor. It was after seven in the evening, and Mrs. Flemming had left for the night. Aimee was helping Elton prepare for bed and chattering like a magpie. Remy, her nerves taut after today, curled up in a papasan chair on the veranda. It was roofed with large potted ferns adorning the corners, carved lions sitting regally at the top of the stone steps that descended to the lawn and joined the path leading to the butterfly house.

With dusk settling in, Remy wondered if it was wise for her to sit out here alone. She'd never had to think about her safety in such a way, but now she was comparing herself to the victims at Müllerian Manor who'd lost their lives over a century ago. What had they sensed before they died? Someone lurking in the shadows? Had they all received threats like Loretta Habington had with the bones and butterflies? What was the significance of the animal bones anyway?

That last question made Remy pull out her phone. She checked its signal bars and was pleasantly surprised to see the LTE network flickering. Maybe she could get a strong enough signal here on the porch to do some quick research. She was waiting for pages to load when the door opened to the right of her.

Tate stepped out and scanned the lawn, the woods, and then settled into a lounge chair not far from Remy's. "Didn't want you to be alone out here," he said, clasping his hands behind his head, elbows sticking out. He focused on the property and not on Remy, which gave her a few seconds to study him.

His curly hair was damp from a shower. He was sans his baseball cap, and truth be told, Remy rather liked that. She could smell his deodorant from where she sat, a mixture of pine, peppermint, and something else.

She had to break her attention from admiring him. Remy adjusted her position in the round and comfy papasan, bringing attention instead to her phone. "Did you know that cats and their skeletons have been used for centuries in superstitious rituals?"

Tate's questioning grin was a bit too toe-curling when he looked at her sideways like that. She had to get ahold of herself. Remy nodded as though Tate had asked her a question, only he hadn't.

"In New England," she went on, "the Puritans used to say that if you saw a cat sitting with its tail toward the fire, expect bad luck."

Tate chuckled. "Sure. A cat's tail probably started on fire once. That's bad luck."

Remy laughed along with him. It felt good to laugh for a moment.

Tate grew serious. "I thought animal bones and the like were used mostly in voodoo."

Remy glanced at her phone. "From what I'm finding, they've been used going back to ancient Egypt. Archaeologists have found cat skulls in various sites around the world. Other occult practices have used them too. I came across a site with instructions and a warning not to *kill* the cat but find its bones in the woods to be more humane."

"Not gonna lie," Tate said and shifted in his chair, "that stuff makes me uncomfortable. Why the fascination with dead cats?"

"I wonder if that's what the bones were. Imagine finding a cat skeleton in the front seat of your car or in your dresser drawer." Remy shook her head. "Do you think there's witchcraft involved here? Do you know your family's history well enough to know—"

"No," Tate interrupted. "The Arnold family has always been one of Christian faith."

"That doesn't mean that the Butcher—"

"No," Tate snapped again. "I don't want to mess with that."

"But there were bones in my car today, Tate, and bones found back in 1921 here at the manor. We can't just ignore that."

Clearly frustrated, Tate blew out a breath and leaned forward in his chair. He stared out at the back lawn. "There used to be a tradition around this area of using small animal bones to ward off negative energy—a superstition. I don't know where it started, but it wasn't tribal. It came from Europe. They'd place the bones under porches and other such places."

"Dead things ward off dead things. Got it." Remy didn't mean to sound so sarcastic.

Tate shot her a look. "Do you believe in superstitions?"

Remy was taken aback by his question. She contemplated for a moment, then shook her head. "No. I don't think so. I've walked under ladders without anything bad happening to me. But just because I'm not superstitious doesn't mean I'm not creeped out by finding a bunch of bones and butterfly wings on the seat of my car . . . not when they're the supposed calling cards of a killer."

Tate twisted in his chair to face Remy directly. It was harder to make out his features now that it was getting dark.

"I was a sniper in the Marine Corps," he began.

Remy stilled, waiting.

Tate picked at a fingernail. "They say every sniper has a bullet with their name on it. That's the one that's going to end you." He sniffed. "But if you can get ahold of that bullet with your name on it, you become invulnerable."

"Did you get your bullet?" Remy asked cautiously. The conversation was taking an oddly personal turn. Moments before he'd just been Tate Arnold, the concerned descendant of a legendary woman. Now he was an ex-Marine with a story to tell.

"No," he answered. "I wasn't about to break cover to try to take one from my dead enemy's chamber. No, I served my time and then got out. Guess that's how I avoided the worst."

"Why did you leave the Marines?"

Tate ignored her question. "Point is, everyone—every culture, organization, et cetera—has their superstitions. But in the end, that's all they are. Superstitions. If I'd hung my enemy's bullet around my neck, I could just as easily have died from a fatal shot the next day. And putting animal bones under your porch won't keep evil from entering the house. If Marian was superstitious, maybe that's why she left the warning on her mother's grave. But that doesn't mean superstitions supersede real faith. There has to be a God who is bigger than all of that. Bigger than a killer's calling card—if that's what the bones really are about." Tate sounded as though he were trying to convince himself and not just her.

"What then does a person do to ward off the bad?" She was surprised when she realized how much she wanted an answer to her question. Current events aside, life itself seemed to be a consistent string of bad.

Tate breathed in deeply, then let it out and turned his attention back to the lawn, shrouded now in the darkness of night. "Pray? Maybe? Or like my grandma used to say, 'Wash yourself in the holy blood of Christ.'"

"That's just weird," Remy stated without thinking. "Kind of gory, if you ask me." Even though she knew the story of the crucifixion, she'd never quite understood the religious terms Christians used to describe it, throwing them out like candy at a birthday party.

Tate's chuckle surprised her. "I think it's in reference to the willing sacrifice of His life to save ours, that there's nothing greater than someone giving their life for you. I saw it in the military. I've seen it in my family. It's a legacy. Sacrifice is far more powerful than any superstition."

"Who taught your grandma that?" Remy asked, unsure whether she understood Tate's theories any more than she understood the omens of the bones and dead butterflies.

"*Her* mother," Tate answered.

Remy nodded. That would mean Tate's grandmother's statement of belief had come from . . . "Marian," she whispered.

But Marian had supposedly been murdered by the Butterfly Butcher. According to Aimee, she'd been found in a pool of blood in the room just off Remy's bedroom. No one knew what had happened. Some debated whether Marian *hadn't* been a victim, as the story was told. That maybe she had disappeared, and no one knew where she'd gone. There were no records of Marian Arnold after the year 1921.

"How could Marian have told your grandmother that if Marian was murdered by the Butterfly Butcher?" Remy posed the question with hesitation. Another thought popped into her mind. "Unless Marian *did* have a brother, like Nurse Aimee claims, and *his* wife was your however many greats-grandmother, not Marian."

Tate's low laugh rippled through Remy and left her feeling adrift at the lack of clarity being offered. He shoved off the chair and stood over her. Remy could feel his eyes on her. "It's been a long day. You'd best come in for the night, get some sleep."

"You're not going to answer me?" Remy frowned.

"It's why I'm here, Remy," Tate stated, "the real reason." The set of his mouth was grim. "I protect my family because they protected me. So no. Some stories were never meant to be told. Especially by Elton Floyd—or you for that matter."

15

MARIAN

THE MANOR WAS ABUZZ this afternoon with the guests tantalizing each other with lurid retellings from the night before. It was almost as if they'd simply shared a nightmare, and it hadn't actually happened.

Marian herself had not slept. Her body was exhausted, and she could feel the strain in her muscles. Her eyes hurt, the world around her a bit fuzzy, yet she found her feet taking her hurriedly toward the butterfly house. She knew who it was she'd seen outside Loretta's room last night. Violet. As to why Violet had given Marian a disapproving shake of her head as though she was to blame for the events . . . well, Marian was determined to find that out.

She unlatched the door to the house and stepped inside. Again the misty warmth assaulted her senses, this after being outside in the crisp autumn air. Butterflies fluttered around her, then continued their trajectory toward the domed glass roof. They darted in and out among the vines and leaves.

"Violet?" Marian called softly, unsure whether the woman would be here. She paused to listen for a response. There was none. "Violet?" she tried again.

She doesn't want to see you. The whisper in Marian's ear caused her to jump, swiping at her hair as if a butterfly had taunted her. When a monarch winged its way in front of her face, a blurry form that dipped and rose, Marian blinked rapidly to clear her vision. Butterflies didn't whisper. Butterflies didn't speak.

"Ignore them." Violet stepped out from behind a large-leafed plant. As before, she remained just out of clear view.

Marian took a tentative step toward her, but something about Violet's presence made her stop.

"You're going to hurt yourself." Violet's voice held judgment. She laughed quietly, then added in a more serious tone, "You need to be careful."

"What's happened here? At the manor?" Marian took a half step forward. As she moved toward Violet, inch by inch, she realized that perhaps she was invading the woman's privacy.

Violet retreated behind the plant. "I tend the garden," she said.

"You do?" A smile teased Marian's lips. "I didn't know you were caring for my mother's butterflies."

"If I don't, they'll die." The bluntness of the words startled Marian. "You will die," Violet stated. Her fingers plucked at something on one of the plant's leaves. "We all will. Why not enjoy beauty before we breathe our last?"

Marian swallowed hard. "Did you know my m-mother?"

"Did *you*?" Violet retorted. She laughed again as if it somehow made everything better. Kinder. More palatable. "Do we ever really know anyone? Or are they all just strangers to us?"

"I feel like I know people." Marian toyed with the brooch on her collar and wrapped her other arm around her waist. "I know Frederick well. I know Mrs. Dale and Felix."

"You do?" Violet challenged. She disappeared farther behind the plants, but her voice still carried in the enclosed space. "What is Felix most afraid of?"

Marian struggled to answer the question. "I-I . . ."

"What does Frederick most despise?"

Again Marian fumbled for an answer. She heard Violet moving in the garden and strained to see the woman, but Violet had hidden herself well.

"You see, you don't know. You think you do. You want to believe you do. But in truth, you are all alone, and no one knows you. You don't know anyone else. This is why a man hangs himself. See? There. Where the milkman hung. It's empty now, but it wasn't. He swayed and danced, and his feet tapped the air until finally he was still. Why did he die? Did *you* kill him?" Violet's voice turned wistful, her words floating in the air without accusation so much as curiosity.

"No!" Marian pulled back. She was growing apprehensive of Violet. The woman who had seemed to be a friend, or perhaps someone in whom Marian could find kindness, now became unpredictable, even disturbing. "I didn't kill anyone."

"You will."

"No!" Marian scowled in the direction of Violet's voice.

"You should kill yourself, you know, like the milkman did."

Marian backed away from Violet, from the butterflies. She felt behind her for the doorframe so she could flee, and yet she didn't want to turn her back on Violet. She didn't trust her. Especially when she couldn't see her anymore.

"Run away." Violet's voice came from Marian's left. Marian spun toward the sound and saw Violet's form among the ferns—saw the beauty of her face, though not her expression. "Run away, Marian, before you're hurt. I don't want you to be hurt."

Confused, Marian stilled.

"This place is bad. The only beauty left is here, and the bad will come here too and will destroy the life in this place. It will destroy you. It will haunt you forever."

Tears burned in Marian's eyes. This place that had once been her mother's respite . . . had Mother met Violet here as well? Father spoke of Mother so rarely. She had never asked. She had obeyed her father, not inquiring into things she shouldn't bother herself with. But now the questions assaulted her. Had Violet persuaded Mother to . . .

Marian whirled around and fled the butterfly house. She pulled the door shut, locking it from the outside. A butterfly kissed her face as it fluttered and made its escape. The orange-and-black monarch hovered before Marian for a moment before flying off, disappearing among the matching orange hues of the trees.

It's going to die.

This time it wasn't a whisper Marian heard. It was her own spirit speaking. The butterfly would never survive October's chilly bite.

She faced Müllerian Manor and its looming, angled architecture with the stone lions guarding the steps of the back veranda. Scintillating laughter floated out, along with the sound of glassware and ice clinking. The brandy was being poured. The naive were beginning their dinner party, ignoring the pallor of death that hung over the place. A pallor only Marian could see. She could more than see it, though. She could *feel* it. And that made it all so much worse.

In her haste to return to the manor, Marian almost missed Felix Dale as he balanced precariously on one leg with his crutch while he reached up to pull a dead branch from an oak tree.

Thankful for the distraction, Marian hurried forward. "I'll help you," she offered.

Felix shook his head. "I've got it." And he did.

154

"I'm sorry." Marian blushed, ashamed for having assumed he wasn't capable.

Felix tossed the branch onto a pile of brush. Facing her, his eyes were cloaked with a gentle reprimand. "In my humble opinion, you're too hard on yourself. You didn't offend me. There's no need to apologize. Just be assured, I'm capable."

"I'm sorry," Marian responded instinctively, then blushed again. "I mean, I . . ."

Felix only smiled. He seemed at peace today and took on an air of safety. Or perhaps it was because Marian was so rattled and unnerved that he offered a familiarity she could trust. Childhood memories overwhelmed her.

They hadn't played much together; differences in life's positions had influenced that. But she recalled moments when they were young and would play hide-and-seek on days Marian's parents were oblivious to her whereabouts. Occasionally, Felix would bring her something he'd found on his jaunts through the woods. An interesting rock, a bouquet of colorful leaves, a flower . . .

"You're not all right." Felix was assessing her, and Marian wrapped her arms around herself, hugging her body as if to keep her fears close to her. But he didn't allow that to stop him. "Is it last night that has you disturbed?"

Marian nodded. He was aware of what had happened. He had been the one to dispose of the bones.

Felix's eyes softened. "If it makes you feel any better, the bones weren't those of a cat or house pet." His crooked grin did something funny to her insides. "They were squirrel bones. I find them all the time in the woods. Nothing nefarious or superstitious about a squirrel—unless a person just wants to frighten someone with them."

"They frightened me," Marian admitted and released a breath she didn't realize she'd been holding. She looked over her shoulder toward the butterfly house and almost asked Felix how long

Violet had been tending it. But she bit her tongue. She didn't want to talk about Violet. She didn't want to think about the happenings here at the manor. She wanted . . .

"My mother made pumpkin muffins this morning." Felix tipped his head in the direction of the groundskeeper's cottage at the far end of the property. "I'm sure she'd be all right if I shared one."

Marian hesitated. "Don't you have work to do?"

"I don't know, do I?" he joked, and Marian gave a small laugh. She was the owner after all, and he her employee.

"Very well," Marian said.

Felix nodded. For a moment, neither of them said anything, and Marian wondered if he felt peaceful and serene. Could he be more to her than a childhood memory? Could he be the child-hood friend who called her "girl" and winked at her and made her feel valued?

As Marian walked beside him toward the cottage, she admired how unhindered he was by his war injury. She was tempted to ask him what had happened but didn't want to revive painful memories and strip him of the peace he had found today.

The small cottage was built of brick and stone, with four-paned windows and red shutters. Pots of chrysanthemums set here and there added splashes of yellow and purple.

"Ma is at the manor helping the hired staff prepare for the dinner party tonight," Felix explained. "I'll, uh . . ." His hesita-tion had nothing to do with his crutch, and everything to do with being unsure how to properly host a pumpkin-muffin respite for a lady.

"May I?" Marian offered.

His relief was evident. "Thank you. I'll just wait here."

Marian admired Felix's gentlemanly efforts. He was old-fashioned. She appreciated that. Ivo would have just followed her into the cottage and kept her company, which on one hand would have been nice, but on the other inappropriate according to tradition and propriety—in spite of their familial relation. Times were definitely changing, but Marian had experienced enough change, so she took comfort in Felix's sensitivity.

Inside the cottage, she was struck by the comforting aroma of baked goods with spices that permeated the air. A bouquet of fall leaves in a pottery jar occupied the center of the table. A half-full coffee mug, probably from breakfast, sat beside the autumn bouquet. The mantel over the fireplace held a framed photograph of a man Marian assumed was Felix's father—he'd died when Felix was a baby. A matching pair of small bookcases took up the corner, along with a reading chair. Suddenly, Marian never wanted to leave Dale Cottage. The difference between it and Müllerian Manor was stark. This was a home. A true home. Warm, inviting, *safe*.

Marian walked into the kitchen and spotted the basket of muffins on the counter wrapped in a cloth. Finding a plate in the cupboard, she placed two muffins on it and then glanced around for a pitcher to fill with water. A few moments later, she lifted a tray with the plate of muffins, glasses, and pitcher of water, then headed back outside.

Felix had arranged two wooden chairs by the front door. A little table made of rustic wood was between them, and he motioned for Marian to set the tray on it.

"Please, sit down," she said. "I'll serve you." Marian wondered at the look that flickered across Felix's face. Handing him a muffin on a cloth napkin, she poured him a glass of water and left it on the tray. She took her own muffin and seated herself, and for several minutes they were both silent.

Marian's world was beginning to slow its wild spin. The trees were coming into focus. The fear and anxiety of the unknown were being quashed by the peace at Dale Cottage and by the security she felt in Felix's presence.

The realization dawned then that if anything threatened her in this moment, Felix would be there. He had faced war. The battlefields. He had sacrificed for his nation. He would sacrifice for her too.

Warmth crept up Marian's neck as she tried to collect her thoughts. They were wayward, going in directions she'd never considered. All because of fall foliage, pumpkin muffins, and solitude with an old friend.

"Are you happy here?" Marian ventured to ask.

Felix nodded as he finished chewing and swallowing a bite of muffin. "Yes. It is home."

The word opened a chasm in Marian's soul. *Home.* What was home? Had she ever known one? The expansive and showy estate in Milwaukee? Here at her mother's eccentric summer home?

"Are *you* happy here?" Felix asked.

His reversal of her question surprised Marian, yet she didn't have the heart to lie to him. "No," she replied.

His silence invited more, and suddenly Marian needed to tell him. Needed to unburden her spirit.

"It's frightening here, Felix. And the guests, Ivo and Loretta, their friends . . . they are—"

"I saw the liquor."

"It's nothing I'm not used to." Marian laughed a little. "My family was built around the brewing industry, but Father never *abused* liquor. Besides, liquor is—"

"No longer legal," Felix finished.

Marian gave him a concerned look. "Am I too uptight? Perhaps if Father were here, he'd be pouring it himself."

Felix pursed his lips, eyes narrowing as he considered his response. "I would say that you have scruples. You desire to be obedient to the law."

Marian released a sigh of relief. He understood. How many times would Felix have understood her if she'd given him more of her childhood time and attention?

"But it's more than that." Marian didn't want to discount the partygoers' illegal imbibing, but in light of recent events, it was less of a concern. "The milkman's death in the butterfly house, and then last night . . ." She stopped. She couldn't tell Felix about her visions. He would think her ridiculous, not in her right mind, which was an entirely different subject altogether. There were places for people who saw things, who spoke to the dead. They were either around séance tables as spiritualists making a living, or they were in institutions where people were sent and never seen again.

Felix leaned forward, propping his forearms on his knees. His crutch leaned against his chair, but he ignored it and instead rubbed the end where his leg should have been but wasn't. "Fear isn't always something we can control, Miss Arnold."

"Marian," she invited gently.

Felix's attention flew to her face for a second and then dropped back to his lap. "Girl," he said, smiling as he looked up at her.

Marian matched his soft grin, and their eyes locked.

Felix cleared his throat. "Fear attacks like an enemy in hiding, and it can paralyze." His voice grew distant, and Marian could tell he was revisiting unshared memories. "I saw men in trenches weep like babies because of fear. And I learned something profound."

Marian waited, wrapping her hands around her water glass now that her muffin was consumed.

Felix stopped rubbing his leg. "It is all right to be afraid."

Marian's breath caught. She'd not expected that.

Felix looked at her, poignantly, without disguising the depths of his internal struggles. "It's what we do with that fear that's important. What we allow it to shape us into. Someday, Lord willing, I will have my own children. I don't want them to have a father paralyzed by such a feeling."

Marian let his words sink in. "How do you not allow fear to paralyze you?"

Felix's expression was distant as he searched for words and then found them. "You have to choose to believe that when your world is shuttered and dark with unknown dangers, life is still worth fighting through. That God sees into it even when you don't. That you'll come out the other side with purpose."

"But not unscathed," Marian concluded.

Felix gave a short laugh and tapped his leg. "No. Not unscathed. But hopefully stronger—and with something to offer others that you couldn't before. You're richer for the pain, for the fear. In its twisted agony, God makes it so that life becomes deeper, more meaningful, and you can look into your future and hear the voices of the generations to come and ask yourself, What will I leave behind for them? Fear?" Felix met her eyes with a dark but naked starkness that made it impossible for Marian to inhibit the tears from slipping down her face. "Or faith?" Felix took a sip of his water, then breathed deeply. "I chose faith—even though I'm still very much afraid most days."

16

AND THEN PEACE was shattered.

The cries from the manor came in waves, growing in volume until both Marian and Felix were hurrying back into the very place Marian had just been grateful to leave behind.

"Someone telephone the police!"

That wasn't a good omen at all. Hearing that shout, Marian knew something dreadful had happened. Ivo and his friends wouldn't have wanted the police called otherwise.

Frederick met Marian at the manor's front entrance. His face was gray, his mouth a grim line. "I've already summoned the authorities, miss."

"What happened?" Marian looked over Frederick's shoulder.

Cecil Adams, Ivo's friend, charged down the staircase, luggage in both hands, his slicked-back hair flopping against his forehead. His lady friend was fast on his heels. He approached Marian and, with panic-stricken eyes, said, "This place is one wild joint!" He dropped the suitcases to the floor and rummaged through the umbrellas in the stand to retrieve his. "People gettin' knocked off now? No dinner party is worth this!" Cecil grabbed his umbrella and handed it to his lady friend, then picked up the luggage. "We're leaving at once. We'll wait at the end of the drive for our ride—I already called 'em. I'm not staying in this house one minute longer than I have to!"

Frederick held out his hand, palm out toward Cecil's chest. "You shouldn't leave. The police will want to speak with you."

Cecil snorted. "Let 'em think I did it and I'm on the run. That's better than staying in this horrid place!" With that, he pushed past Felix and Marian, ignored Frederick, and marched toward the front entrance. The woman hurried after him, holding on to her hat and the umbrella as her heels clicked on the hardwood floor.

Felix maneuvered his way to the entrance, watching the couple descend in haste down the stone steps toward the drive. He spun around. "What happened?"

"She's dead!" Ivo pushed into the foyer, his eyes bulging. "Oh, God in heaven, Loretta's dead!"

Marian grappled for something to hold on to as her knees buckled. Felix's arm, still holding his crutch, shot around her, pulling her to his side and using the crutch to hold them both upright.

Ivo's face grew paler if that was possible. "She went upstairs!" His voice broke. "When she didn't come down, I went and checked on her." He moaned and dropped onto a lounge along the wall meant for those who needed a temporary respite in the foyer.

Marian couldn't help herself. She clung to Felix as her only source of strength at that moment.

Frederick took a step toward them, lowering his voice. "Miss Habington was found in her bedroom."

Marian pushed against Felix, a surge of hope rushing through her. "Maybe she can be saved still!" She raced for the stairway.

"Marian!" Felix's shout followed her up the stairs. She heard his crutch thudding behind her, heard Frederick announce, "I'll stay for the police." Ivo's sobs echoed and prompted Marian to move faster.

She ran through the manor, opening doors to pass through, avoiding dead ends and corners that made no sense. At the door of Loretta's room, she burst inside.

Just as Frederick had said, Loretta was lying on her bed, silent. Still. Marian flew to the bedside, pulling up short at the sight. She clapped her hands over her mouth, stifling her cry.

Loretta lay there, her gauzy green dress positioned neatly with its hem in the middle of her calves as it should be. Her stockings were still on her legs, her shoes still on her feet. With elbows bent, Loretta's arms crossed over her chest, her palms flat at each shoulder. Her face was turned upward, but it was the butterflies. The butterflies! A butterfly spread its wings over each of Loretta's eyes.

She was dead.

There was nothing Marian could do to save her.

Marian noticed red lines around Loretta's neck, scratches, as though Loretta had struggled to free herself from whoever choked her and strangled the life out of her.

Felix's soft exclamation as he arrived in the room brought Marian's head around. In shock, she stared at him, not bothering to mask her tears. "Who did this?" she demanded, and yet she knew Felix had nothing to offer. He had been with her. Thank God, he had been with her! At least she could trust Felix in this deathtrap of a house.

"I want to move," she declared. "Sell it. I don't want this house anymore." Marian shook her head vehemently, her hair bobbing around her face.

Slowly, Felix stepped toward her. "Marian, shhh." He tried to soothe her oncoming panic.

"It's going to kill us. Everyone. We'll be butchered in broad daylight." Marian's feeling of terror clawed at her throat, mimicking the strangulation that Loretta had suffered.

Felix attempted to reach for her. "Marian . . ."

She stepped back, her legs hitting the bed frame. "It's not safe here. It's not safe!" Violet in the butterfly house had said as much. Maybe that was what she'd meant when she told Marian to kill herself. Sparing her the trauma of someone else doing it for her.

"Marian," Felix tried again.

She heard his voice like a distant echo.

It's all going to end.

The whisper. Violet. She glimpsed a brush of black shadow at the doorway.

You'll be next.

Marian heard Felix shout as if in the distance. A dizzying wave rolled over her, nausea rising in her throat, and then blackness shuttered her eyes as she fell backward onto the bed—onto Loretta's butterfly-adorned corpse.

17

Remy

OCTOBER, PRESENT DAY

DO WE HAVE the family tree right?" Remy spread out her notebook and showed Elton. The wizened writer leaned forward to peer at her notes.

"You have dreadful handwriting," he observed.

Remy tapped the paper. "Pay attention, Elton."

He chuckled. "Very well."

Remy gave him a reprimanding look, then tapped her pen over the haphazard family tree she'd composed. "I'm not convinced we have the Arnold family tree right, and I'm pretty sure Tate knows more than he's saying."

"Of course he does," Elton said. "Why do you think I wanted to hire him as a consultant?"

Ah, that made sense. Remy nodded. "So Tate knows something we don't know. Why not just ask him? 'Hey, Tate, mind helping us with this biography by telling us *everything* you know.'" Remy sat back on the footstool she was perched on next to Elton's chair, placing her notebook on his writing desk.

"And you believe that would work?" Elton's smile was patronizing.

"Okay, fine." Remy scratched her head. "But just look at the family tree. There's Marian's parents, then Marian, then a reference to a nameless male sibling."

"Exactly." Elton didn't seem surprised, for the gaps and lack of clarity concerning the Arnold family history were many.

"It's obvious that Tate is an Arnold, but whether from Marian or this unknown brother? Tate claims Marian, but I'm not so sure," Remy challenged. "Your nurse, Aimee, seems to think Marian wasn't Tate's matriarchal grandmother, but instead he comes from the brother's line."

"She also believes in aliens. Did you know she was abducted as a child and experimented on?" Elton adjusted his glasses. "I believe that explains quite a bit."

"Elton." Remy glared at him.

"I'm just saying I've never found a credible resource about Marian having had any secret siblings that history simply forgot to mention."

"They didn't forget. He's listed right here." She slammed her index finger on the reference. "But he's unnamed. Which makes him virtually a ghost."

Elton smiled, enjoying this far more than she was. "Ahh, so he joins the family tradition of haunting the manor?"

Remy blew a frustrated breath, ignoring the quip. "I searched graves through the United States. Plenty of Arnolds. Nothing linked to this family or the Arnold Brewery. There are no historical business records with any names of offspring or relatives associated with running the brewery before it went bankrupt during Prohibition. In fact"—Remy leaned forward and flipped a page in her notebook—"the only family I *have* discovered proof of is an Ivo Lott. A second or third cousin on Marian's mother's side. He'd potentially be the closest to a sibling I can find. He also appears to be the one who originally sold the manor after Marian's death."

Elton snapped his fingers. "That's probably who Aimee is associating as Marian's brother. She's a conspiracy theorist, Remy, and if you take her word as part of your research, then I'd rather have you ask a medium."

"No." Remy rolled her eyes. Elton was probably right about Aimee. But Tate *had* blatantly skirted her inquiry about his family line. "It still doesn't answer *how* Tate is an Arnold. He's male so he would have taken his father's surname, which wouldn't be Arnold. If Marian had married and had children, she would have taken her husband's surname. Meaning—"

"I know what it means," Elton interrupted. "The Arnold name should have ceased with Marian and not carried down generations to Tate."

"Which leads me to believe there was a brother, and Aimee is right—Tate doesn't descend from Marian but from this mystery sibling."

Elton flipped Remy's notebook page back to her sketch. "We don't really *have* a family tree, do we? Not with three people, Remy. Marian's father, his wife, Verdine Arnold, and Marian? Then the trail leading to Tate. That's barely a family stick."

Remy reached into her bag at her feet and pulled out a manila folder. She slapped it on the desk and opened it. A copy of a photograph and an obituary stared up at them. "Meet Loretta Habington."

"Ah!" Elton's eyes brightened. "So you *did* find something else!"

"I did, and here's where it all gets murkier and weirder. Loretta Habington was *engaged* to Ivo Lott, Marian's cousin. When I traced Loretta's family tree back, I found that she was the daughter to Arnold Brewery's stiffest competitor."

Elton raised a brow. "Pabst or Miller?"

"Neither." Remy grinned, pleased she knew something Elton didn't. "No, we're talking about the Habington Brewery of Milwaukee, which went under right around Prohibition—they went bankrupt when Habington made deals under the table that stripped the Habingtons of their investors. There are newspaper articles to cover *that* story, even if they all but seemed to ignore a serial killer."

"This is getting interesting!" Elton jotted in his own notebook. "Keep talking."

Remy cleared her throat. "I don't have much more than that. I did find it more than coincidental that the Habingtons were infiltrating the Arnold family line—even if it was through Verdine Arnold's side, Marian's mother."

"That doesn't account for why Tate is an Arnold and not a different surname," Elton pointed out.

Remy hefted a sigh. "No. It only adds another loose end to an already knotted pile of threads."

"So was the Butterfly Butcher," Elton mused aloud, "killing with his own personal motives, or were the murders somehow tied to the breweries and Prohibition?" He tapped his pencil on his desk. "And if it wasn't connected to Prohibition, then what exactly was his motive?"

"What about the milkman?" Remy studied the copies of Loretta's and Percy Hahn's obituaries. "The police seem to have concluded he'd hanged himself. In the butterfly house. A suicide."

"See?" Elton nodded. "I told you it didn't fit the M.O. of the Butcher."

"No, but there's still the pile of butterflies the newspaper article referred to," Remy stated. "What if the Butcher came upon the dead milkman and decided to claim the man's demise as his work, another victim, placing the signature butterflies and getting the credit for it?"

Elton squinted in thought. "In other words, we have an attention-seeking killer in the Butcher?"

Remy nodded. "He liked the limelight? Or maybe the killer was trying to make a point, and Percy Hahn's suicide muddied the waters."

"Why would the milkman choose to kill himself on the property of one of his customers?" Elton challenged. "In the butterfly house no less?"

Remy flipped to the next page she'd printed at the library from her research. "Percy Hahn once worked at Müllerian Manor. After the Arnolds went bankrupt, most of the staff was let go. Percy was forced to leave his position as a footman and become a milkman. Depressed, maybe he returned to end it all where he'd felt he had a future. A last slap in the face for the family who'd released him to the menial future of delivering milk."

Elton clapped his hands together. "Brilliant!"

"It's just a theory," Remy reminded him.

Elton's eyes sparked. "Yes, but it makes perfect sense. And you have the evidence to support it. The police determined it was suicide. The milkman used to be employed at the manor. It all fits."

"But this doesn't really help solve anything, does it?" Remy ventured. "I mean, if Percy Hahn's death really was a suicide, it only takes one body from the Butcher's body count. It doesn't exactly solve any mysteries."

"Well, the more revealing information would be that Hahn was employed by Müllerian Manor. In my reading about the Butcher, I've not run across the link tying Hahn to the manor via employment records." Elton paused, then added, "Odds are Marian didn't even know Percy Hahn's connection to the manor, considering she stopped visiting the manor after her mother passed away. So one could argue that both Hahn and Loretta Habington were inadvertently tied to the Arnold family. One through employment, and one through engagement."

"Okay, but that still doesn't answer motive, or why the Butcher killed Loretta and supposedly Marian. Not to mention it still bugs me: *How* is Tate an Arnold?" Remy moaned, tipping her head back in frustration.

Elton chuckled. "Well, I'd recommend asking him again, but he's as guarded as they come."

"Can we even trust him?" Remy asked. Although, after her chat with Tate a few nights ago, she'd felt better knowing there was a military sniper in the manor. Knowing that he had appointed himself as her guardian. She could sort of pretend the butterflies and newspaper clippings and bones weren't threats that someone would actually dare to carry out.

She waited, watching Elton as a shadow flickered across his face. "I don't know," he finally said, bending over his journal and scrawling something with a pencil. "Can we trust anyone?"

"Whether I be false or true,
Death comes in a day or two."

Remy sprang up in bed, the audible words startling her awake. She was so tired, and the last few nights—since Tate had come—she hadn't heard the whispered words. She hadn't heard the creaks of the floor in the room next door. Nor had she wondered if she was losing her mind, or if Aimee was right and the ghost of Marian Arnold truly did wander the room in which she'd been killed.

Boggart the groundskeeper believed as Aimee did that Marian Arnold was still influential on the manor, that her spirit lingered and had yet to "pass over." Even Elton seemed convinced of it, or else he just reveled in being mysterious. Remy wasn't so sure. Hearing noises and whispers was one thing. Being convinced it was evidence of a dead woman was an entirely different thing.

Slipping from the bed, Remy moved to the door. Scared, sure. Willing to start losing sleep again? No.

"Butterflies are white and blue
In this field we wander through."

As the words filtered through the crack between the floor and the door, Remy grabbed the doorknob and twisted. It caught her by surprise when it resisted.

Locked? When had anyone locked the door?

Remy flicked on the lights in her room and eyed the mechanism. There was no lock to unlock. That meant it'd been locked from the inside. Which also made no sense because there was no other way out. That realization brought a chill to Remy. That also meant there was no way in but to creep past her in her bed and use the door.

Remy's skin crawled. She knew no one had been in her room, nor had they snuck past her as she tried to sleep. They would have had to have been a ninja. The image of a man in all black maneuvering silently through her room unnerved her.

She tugged on the door again.

The whispers stopped as quickly as they had begun. Silence enveloped Remy. No footsteps. No creaking floor. Yet she sensed someone there, just on the other side. She could picture a wraith with hollow black eyes, leaning their pale-skinned forehead against the door, straining to see through to Remy.

"Hello?" Remy said cautiously. Silly. Ghosts weren't known for responding politely. And did she believe it was a ghost? No. No she didn't.

"Whoever is out there, this isn't funny." Remy opted for the human-to-human straightforward approach. There was still no answer, not that it surprised her. She rattled the doorknob, growing in irritation as it refused to budge. Whoever had locked it refused to cooperate.

"Enough with the whispers!" Remy opted for a firm approach. Silence greeted her.

She sagged against the door until she slid down with her back against it. Seated on the floor, Remy was now so wide awake, she knew she wasn't going to sleep.

The whispered words . . . they were poetic. Remy couldn't

help but wonder if they were a recitation of something versus the chortled words of an anxious but very dead Marian Arnold.

Recalling that she'd gotten a signal, albeit a weak one, on her phone on the back veranda the other night, Remy pushed to her feet. It wasn't ideal. She'd rather not traipse through the manor past midnight, and she'd rather not go outside with some weirdo leaving dead butterflies and bones around, but she couldn't say that she felt any safer in her own room.

After pulling on a sweatshirt and a pair of fluffy socks, Remy slipped her feet into her moccasins, unplugged her phone from its charger, and turned on its flashlight app. She checked to see if there were any signal bars. No Service.

Minutes later, and out of breath from avoiding imaginary threats, Remy made it to the back of the manor. The rear door was different from the servants' exit to the back lawn. This one was a heavy wood door with stained-glass windows of red and green in the design of a lion's head. She unlocked the door and pulled it open, the door straining against its brass hinges with the classic groan of a haunted house.

Remy winced as cold night air hit her. She probably should have put on joggers over her sleep shorts. Oh well. There was no way she was running back through the maze of the manor to get pants. She hurriedly found her place in a chair, thankful the sky was clear and the moon casting its light over the lawn. Remy scanned the yard and shrubbery. No lurking figures. No imminent threats. And no choir of wraiths floating above the lawn, weaving back and forth, wailing.

A major plus.

She turned off the flashlight and clicked open a browser. It struggled to load, instead sticking on its white, wordless screen with a stubbornness that irked her.

"C'mon," Remy muttered. She held the phone in the air in the hope it would summon the signal gods and . . . Yep, she was losing it. Remy rolled her eyes at her own silly thoughts. Ancient signal gods?

"Are you okay?"

She screamed. A bloodcurdling, throat-ripping scream that left her with no voice and anyone in proximity with ringing ears. Remy spun around and attacked. She swung with her right hand, phone flying from it, and the phone smacked against flesh. The hard flesh of a larger hand that curled around her fist and shoved her arm away.

"Hold on!" Tate's command was as effective as a slap across the face.

Remy staggered back, right hand over her heart, glaring at him with invisible but very real daggers. "Why'd you sneak up on me!"

Tate eyed her. "You were jogging through the manor like a ghost was chasing you, and then you came outside. I told you I'd be keeping an eye on you for your own safety."

Remy hugged herself and wished for the second time she had on pants versus sleep shorts. She had to look a mess in her oversized sweatshirt, neon-pink cotton shorts, and yellow fluffy sock-covered feet jammed into moccasins. "And your keeping an eye on me involves twenty-four-hour surveillance?"

A small smile tweaked the corner of Tate's mouth. "No. Actually, I was up anyway."

Remy stared at him with skepticism, then gave up trying to understand the man and instead bent to retrieve her phone she'd flung in the chaos. She didn't owe Tate any explanations, but she rambled anyway as she scooped up her device. "I came out here looking for a stronger signal. I'm tired of whispering ghouls at midnight. I thought they'd quit, but nope!" Remy gripped her phone and straightened, looking Tate directly in the eyes. "I need Wi-Fi."

He grimaced. "Whispering ghouls?" His eyebrow rose up.

She'd always admired people who could quirk one eyebrow. It

also made his rugged features a bit cuter and less solemn. Remy pushed that thought away. Midnight thoughts were dangerous.

She chose to answer him and divert her attention back to her phone as she tried once again to load a browser. "They stopped for a few days," Remy went on, "but now they're back. And they locked the door. Which doesn't make sense because how do they expect to get out. There's no other entrance. But seriously, the whole 'death comes in a day or two' is getting old and fast."

Tate's hand wrapped around her wrist, his skin hot against her flesh. Remy jerked her head up from the perusal of her phone screen. His touch wasn't invasive. It was calming—meant to cease her talking—yet the concern on Tate's face was intense.

"Death comes in a day or two?"

Remy sucked in a breath. "Yeah. Nice to wake up to, isn't it? And someone shuffling around in the room? Aimee swears it's your dead great-grandmother. I guess it's the room they say she was found dead in? Assuming that part of the story is factual."

"Hold up." Tate released her wrist. "Fill me in," Tate said, and Remy found herself doing so—explaining Aimee's tale of murder, the pool of blood that supposedly Marian Arnold had been found in, the Butterfly Butcher's last kill, and the whispers and shadowy movements.

Crickets filled the air with their night song. A cool wind sent a shiver through Remy, and she pulled her sweatshirt as far as it would go over her hips. "I have this feeling the message 'death comes in a day or two' is from something. It's too lyrical. That's why I need access to a web browser."

Tate pulled his own phone from his pocket and checked. "I have a little signal strength. Might be enough." Within seconds, he had miraculously produced a list of possibilities on a browser.

"I need to switch carriers," Remy muttered as she sidled Tate to see his phone screen better.

"That one." Remy pointed to a link, and Tate clicked on it.

Soon a new page loaded. Remy skimmed it. "Wow," she whispered.

"Yeah." Tate scrolled the page so they could read the entire poem.

> *Butterflies are white and blue*
> *In this field we wander through.*
> *Suffer me to take your hand.*
> *Death comes in a day or two.*
>
> *All the things we ever knew*
> *Will be ashes in that hour,*
> *Mark the transient butterfly,*
> *How he hangs upon the flower.*
>
> *Suffer me to take your hand.*
> *Suffer me to cherish you*
> *Till the dawn is in the sky.*
> *Whether I be false or true,*
> *Death comes in a day or two.*

"I've never heard that poem before," Remy said, the poignancy of its meaning barely sinking in.

"Edna St. Vincent Millay. An American poet." Tate clicked on another link, but this time his phone's service resisted opening the page.

"Butterflies? Again?" Remy was tempted to lean her head against Tate's shoulder, but then he turned to face her, stuffing his phone back in his pocket.

"This is a death threat." His statement made Remy scoff. "I'm serious. A veiled threat maybe, but still."

"Isn't that a bit extreme?"

"Bones and butterflies left in your car? And using this poem to taunt you from the next room? No. Not extreme." Tate's chest lifted in a silent sigh. "I need you to show me the room."

"The room." Remy knew what he meant, but she was devoid of clear thought at the moment. Death threat?

"Yes, the room next to yours where you're hearing these things. I need to see if there's evidence someone was there."

Elton's words from earlier in the day fluttered through Remy's mind. "Can we trust anyone?"

Remy knew the answer was generally no, but she also knew she was being tugged toward trusting Tate more and more. Maybe it was his strength, his self-confidence? Maybe it was the mystery of his silence, the pieces of him that he kept hidden that somehow played on her sympathies? All Remy knew for certain was that she didn't want to stay on the back porch alone, and she didn't want to go back to Marian Arnold's old bedroom alone either.

"This isn't exactly what I imagined when inviting a guy back to my bedroom." Remy's quip was ill-timed and out of place. She followed Tate back into the manor, noticing how he didn't respond. Instead, he seemed alert, focused.

Good. Maybe he would go all fight-to-kill on whatever was in the manor haunting them. Spirit or human, Remy decided that, come morning, she'd be moving to a different bedroom—and maybe moving from this place altogether.

18

TATE TRIED THE DOORKNOB and then, before Remy
could prepare herself, he kicked the door open with all
the finesse of a professional kickboxer. It flew open,
banging against the wall.

"Holy buckets!" Remy cried. "You're going to wake up the
rest of the house!"

Tate's hand swept along the wall just inside the door and
found the old-fashioned, push-button light switch. Yellow light
spread over the empty room, its reach minimal from the vintage
fixture mounted on the ceiling.

He hesitated for a brief second, holding a hand out behind
him to stop Remy. "Stay there."

"Why?" No way was he going to explore her personal nightmare without her. Remy followed, but her body froze when she
saw the crumpled form, curled up on the floor near the table in
the center of the room.

"Tate!" Her voice shook.

"Stay back." Tate's command met with no argument from her
this time around. He approached the form and knelt, his body hiding much of the one on the floor. Two legs stretched beyond him—
the backs of legs, with bare feet, pulled up into a fetal position.

"Tate, who is it?" Remy ventured a step. "Is the person okay?"

He waved her back with his left hand, his right reaching forward to check for a pulse. "Call 911." Tate's statement was direct, emotionless. "Tell them we have a DOA but need assistance immediately."

"DOA?"

"Aimee's dead, Remy. Call 911 now."

Nausea slammed into Remy's gut without warning. She whirled around and raced into her bedroom, grappling for the landline phone on the dresser. Dialing the number, she waited.

The 911 dispatcher answered quickly, and Remy stammered out the request.

Dead body.

Her employer's nurse.

Aimee Prentiss.

Yes, they knew she was dead.

The dispatcher offered to stay on the line until help arrived at the house, but Remy refused. She needed to summon Mrs. Flemming, have the housekeeper come to the manor immediately. Mrs. Flemming should be present in case the police and EMTs had questions or needed assistance.

"Oh my gosh! Elton!" Remy sprinted for the door. Tate's shout behind her didn't stop her. If Aimee lay dead in the room beyond, then where was Elton? Was he dead too?

"Remy! Don't go—"

Tate's voice was cut off as she bounded up steps, around corners, and made her way to Elton's quarters. Without bothering to knock, Remy burst into Elton's bedroom. She'd not been in it before, and another time she would have smiled at the tobacco-scented room with its dark, masculine furniture.

Remy raced to Elton's bedside.

The writer's eyes shot open in bewilderment. "Remy? W-what is it?" His voice was wobbly from sleep.

Remy sagged against the bed. "Oh, thank God," she breathed.

"Thank God? For what?" Elton pushed himself up on his pillow, his nightshirt open at the chest, his old-man skin parchment thin and spotted with age. "What's going on? Why are you in my bedroom?"

Remy hadn't thought far enough ahead. The image of Aimee's crumpled body washed over her. How would she tell Elton—?

"What is it?" he repeated, sensing the seriousness of the moment. "Spit it out."

"Aimee . . . she's dead."

"Dead!" Elton grappled with the covers, his eyes filled with dread. "No. This is not good. Not good at all."

Remy reached for him. "Elton, there's nothing you can do. I just needed to make sure you were all right."

"I need to see her at once."

She had underestimated his affection for the nurse and conspiracy theorist.

"But there's nothing you can do," Remy said, urging him to stay where he was. "Tate is with her. The authorities are on their way. I need to call Mrs. Flemming."

"There. Use my phone." Elton wagged his finger at a rotary phone by his bed.

Remy nodded.

"Just pick the number you want and spin the thing with your finger!" Elton swore under his breath as Remy hesitated.

She dialed the first number, rotating the dial and watching it spin backward. At Elton's grunt of frustration, Remy glanced at him.

"You have to lift the receiver!" he barked.

"Oh." Remy knew that. At least she thought she did.

"Blasted cellphones." Elton shifted in the bed while Remy finished the rotation of numbers, grateful he had Mrs. Flemming's number printed on a list next to the phone.

At the housekeeper's irritated "Hello," Remy made quick work of explaining what had happened. To the crotchety older woman's credit, she turned professional and stated, "I'll be there as soon as I can."

Satisfied she'd have the support of Mrs. Flemming for anything the authorities needed, Remy sank onto the edge of Elton's bed.

"Don't sit here with me!" he said. "Go unlock the doors for the police. And where's Tate?"

"He's with Aimee." Remy had already told Elton this but didn't blame him for not remembering.

"Leave me be and get back to Tate. I don't want him handling everything like he owns the place—he already thinks he does!"

Remy was caught off guard by Elton's sudden criticism of Tate.

"I don't want to leave you alone," Remy argued.

"Get me my gun and I'll be just fine," Elton groused.

"Your *gun*?"

Elton rolled onto his side and tugged open the drawer of his nightstand. He reached in and gripped a revolver.

Remy ducked as he swung it around. She held up a hand. "Whoa! Careful with that thing!" she cried.

Elton checked the cylinder, revealing six chambers, all of them loaded. He gave a satisfied nod. "I'll be fine."

Remy eyed the revolver as Elton pushed the cylinder back into place. "Don't go Jesse James on us, Elton," she admonished.

He waved his free hand and fixed his eyes on the door beyond. "Anyone tries anything, they'll know what it's like to be bested by an old codger. Now go. Get back to Tate."

Remy started heading for the door, then spun around to give Elton a stern look. "Don't shoot the cops."

Elton waved the revolver in the air. "What do you think I am? Nuts?"

Remy didn't answer that.

Elton with a gun. Tate with a dead body. And she? She was running through the maze of the manor to get to the front entrance as sirens sounded in the distance.

The hard truth was, Aimee the nurse was dead.

Death had come. Just as the poem said it would.

It had been chaos for hours.

Mrs. Flemming, in her brisk, no-nonsense way, had been a godsend. She'd managed the ins and outs of all the various areas of emergency response with ease, taking them where they needed to go and answering manor-related questions.

Remy had alerted the police as to Elton's presence in his bedroom upstairs. She'd told them he was armed, which set off a rather hurried and organized approach by the police to disarm—literally—the situation before events grew worse.

Now Remy slouched in a chair in the library downstairs, still wearing her ridiculous pink shorts and fluffy socks. Tate stood off to the side in conversation with a detective, who was busy taking notes. Remy had already done her part answering the detective's questions.

She heard the words "crime scene," and then Tate muttering "elderly" and "partially disabled." She could tell he was lobbying for them to be able to remain at the manor. Remy, however, wished the police would kick them all out.

The detective, who'd introduced herself as Detective Ambrose, cleared her throat, a cue that she wanted Remy's attention also. Remy slipped from her chair to stand beside Tate. She glanced at the clock and saw it was already nine in the morning.

"So," Ambrose began as if preparing to summarize, "we won't know for certain until an autopsy is performed, but it appears Nurse Prentiss died of strangulation. Since all of you are each other's alibis, I'm asking that none of you leave town."

There went Remy's plan to quit her research job with Elton and flee back to the Twin Cities.

Ambrose shifted her gaze between them. "Neither of you saw anyone else?"

"Like she stated earlier"—Tate spoke for them both—"Remy heard a voice in the adjoining room."

"And the door was locked when you went to investigate," Ambrose concluded.

"Yes," Tate answered.

Ambrose's brow furrowed. She was rather pretty. Remy looked at Tate, then at the detective. There seemed to be a vibe of mutual respect between them. Or was Ambrose considering Tate as a potential suspect?

Ambrose continued, "How do you propose the killer exited the room if the locked door was the only way out?"

It was like a flipping game of Clue, and Remy was not amused. "So the rope, in the empty room, and who? Professor Plum?"

Tate and Ambrose both frowned at her.

Remy shifted uncomfortably and bit at her thumbnail. "Sorry," she muttered. "I get quippy when I'm stressed."

Ambrose ignored her excuse. "The voice you heard, was it male or female?"

"I don't know." Remy shrugged. "It was more of a whisper." She'd already told Ambrose this earlier.

"All right." The detective was all business, and she spoke to Tate as if he were the one in charge at the manor. "We'll need to keep that wing of the manor blocked off until forensics is finished. For now, it's a crime scene. No one but the forensics team goes in or out."

"Can I get a change of clothes?" Remy asked. She really didn't want to be wearing neon-pink shorts and yellow fluffy socks all day.

Ambrose gave her a once-over, and her pretty mouth quirked. "Sorry, but no. Everything in that area could be potential evidence. You'll have to wait until it's been cleared. That includes, of course, Nurse Prentiss's room."

As if Remy had intentions of stealing clothes from a dead woman. She glowered at the detective.

Tate cleared his throat. "I've got stuff she can wear. I don't sleep in that wing."

"Thank you." Ambrose smiled at him. Too warmly? Remy grimaced but tried to hide it. Aimee had been murdered, and now the detective on the case was crushing on Tate?

She edged between Tate and Ambrose. "You're going to cross-check this with the report I filed a few days ago, right?"

The detective shifted her attention to Remy. "Of course. We don't take any of that lightly."

"Detective?" An officer summoned her. Ambrose nodded politely at Remy and then smiled warmly at Tate.

"Don't go far," she admonished them. The officer approached her and murmured something in her ear. Ambrose's eyebrows shot up, and she motioned to Tate and Remy. "Actually, can you both come with me?"

They exchanged glances and followed. As they went upstairs and returned to the wing where Aimee had been found, Remy felt her gut gnawing at her. She hadn't eaten, and she was exhausted and unnerved. She wanted to go check on Elton, although they'd been assured there was an EMT with him. But going back to the scene of the crime wasn't on her top list of things to do.

Detective Ambrose stopped them just outside the bedroom door. A couple of investigators were canvassing the room. The flash of a camera went off in the side room, where Aimee's body still lay.

Ambrose turned to Remy. "Do you see anything out of place?"

Remy scanned her bedroom. Her flannel shirt was still draped over a chair. Her bag lay on the floor, and other belongings were scattered about. She shook her head. "Everything looks normal."

"What about your bed?" Ambrose tilted her head in the direction of the bed.

Remy peered into the room from the doorway. The blankets and sheets were twisted where she'd left them, but there was a lump in the middle of the bed where she'd been lying last night. She frowned. "What is that?"

Ambrose snapped her fingers at one of the investigators, who brought over his digital camera and turned it so Remy could see the photo.

A doll lay faceup on the bed. Over its eyes . . .

"Butterflies." Tate's voice rumbled in Remy's ear as he looked over her shoulder.

Remy didn't even bother to try to stand on her own. She sagged back against Tate and felt his arm slip around her for support. "What is that thing?" she hissed, unable to peel her eyes away from the camera.

Ambrose nodded to the investigator, who took the camera and went back to his job. "We saw the doll lying there when we arrived. I'm guessing with your focus on getting into the room where the victim was found, you didn't notice it."

"A doll. Butterflies." Remy turned, splaying her hands across Tate's chest, staring up at him with frank insistence. "We need to get Elton out of Müllerian Manor."

Remy hoped to find security in his eyes, but instead Tate eased away from her. His eyes darted to Ambrose. "Is it possible for us to move Elton and Remy away from the house? For their safety."

Ambrose nodded. "Of course." She waved toward the doll. "That is definitely something we need to look into, especially in light of what happened with your vehicle the other day, Miss Crenshaw."

Remy, embarrassed by the physical contact she'd initiated with Tate, and his subtle snub as he'd extricated himself from her, shook her head. "I don't want to be here any longer. This place is a deathtrap."

Ambrose nodded, her voice grave. "I'm not going to disagree with you."

19

MARIAN

OCTOBER 1921

MARIAN HELPED Mrs. Dale strip the bed that Loretta's body had been laid out on. Her mind was still so fuzzy, and she knew she was pale from the fright of it all, but after sipping cold water and being revived by Felix and his mother, Marian couldn't leave it all to Mrs. Dale.

This was her responsibility.

Her guests were her responsibility.

She had failed them miserably.

"You don't need to help me, Miss Arnold." Mrs. Dale's eyes were soft like her son's, and concern emanated from her.

"I need to." Marian's response was brisk, and she hoped Mrs. Dale didn't take it personally. "I mean . . ." Marian stumbled over her words. "It's my responsibility."

Officer Petey, who'd been there when the milkman had been discovered, circled the room, lifting her hairbrush and setting it back down, running his fingers along the windowsill, bending to look at the floor.

Marian could hear two men hefting Loretta's body down the hall.

Detective Fletcher stood in the doorway of the room, his arms crossed over his bulky chest as he watched them.

Officer Petey stood, and Marian edged around him, focused on pulling off the bedsheet.

"Don't look like anyone came through the window," the officer announced.

Detective Fletcher huffed. "Nothing else here then to help. You said two of your houseguests took their leave already?"

Marian hesitated, thinking of Cecil Adams and his girlfriend as they'd catapulted through the front door, luggage in hand, after the grisly discovery of poor Loretta. She nodded.

Mrs. Dale remained quiet, balling up the bedsheets in her arms and putting them in a basket.

Detective Fletcher eyed Marian. "Do you know them well?"

Marian reached for the footboard to steady herself. "No. They're my cousin Ivo's guests."

"Mm." Detective Fletcher nodded. "Your cousin Ivo who carried a torch for Miss Habington?"

Marian nodded, thankful Mrs. Dale was making a pretense of puffing the already puffy pillows that Marian knew they'd burn later. No one wanted to rest their head where a dead woman had lain. "Loretta was Ivo's fiancée."

"Yes." Detective Fletcher pursed his lips, eyeing her. "You think I'm a chump, Miss Arnold?"

Marian sensed Officer Petey standing behind her. "Excuse me?"

"You think you can con me?" the detective asked again.

Marian shot a nervous look to Mrs. Dale, who had frozen in place, bent over a pillow. She raised her brows in concern.

"Your cousin Ivo Lott. He's in trouble back in Milwaukee, and you didn't think I would find out?"

"I don't know what you mean." Panic started clawing at her throat. Ivo wasn't behind this. He was downstairs and distraught. "Ivo would never hurt Loretta."

"Detective Fletcher didn't say that he had," Petey drawled lazily behind her.

Fletcher shoved off the doorframe with his shoulder and took a step into the room, his chest sticking out in a way that communicated he knew more than Marian. "Ivo Lott. He gets around the speakeasy rotation."

"Loves his giggle juice," Petey goaded.

Detective Fletcher shot Petey a look that shut him up. He then returned his attention to Marian. "Your cousin is connected with people running hooch through the city. Funny, he came here right when things were getting hot."

Feeling helpless, Marian tightened her grip on the footboard, unable to respond. She noticed Mrs. Dale from the corner of her eye straighten and drop the pillow onto the bed. Mrs. Dale addressed the detective, "Sir, Miss Arnold is not feeling well. Can this wait?"

God bless Mrs. Dale.

Fletcher looked between them. "I'll be taking your cousin in for questioning, the others too. Most of them are tied up in illegal activity, and you, Miss Arnold, were at the center of their little fun this weekend." He pointed to the bed, now vacant of Loretta's corpse. "And they left you a stiff to remember them by."

Marian let the words sink in and then realized what the detective was insinuating. She shook her head emphatically. "Ivo didn't do this! He didn't!"

"One of you did. Maybe that fella who already skedaddled out of here? Or are you going to claim the prize?"

Marian winced. "No, but . . . the dresser drawer!" Her eyes flew to Mrs. Dale's. "We can show Detective Fletcher the drawer with the butterflies and bones!"

"Butterflies and bones?" Petey repeated as if he hadn't heard her right.

Detective Fletcher's eyebrows shot up.

Mrs. Dale grimaced and reached across the bed toward Marian, but her arm was too short so she dropped the comforting hand to her side. "Felix destroyed it. Remember? On Mr. Lott's instruction."

"What are you going on about?" Detective Fletcher demanded.

Marian hurriedly filled him in on the night Loretta discovered the macabre pile in her dresser drawer. She reminded the detective of the similarity to the dead butterflies beneath the milkman.

Fletcher's eyes narrowed. "Miss Arnold," he began, and Marian knew instantly she had done nothing but convince him she was creating answers where there were none, "I'm afraid if you don't have evidence of this, there's nothing I can do."

"But—"

"Best you just take it easy now. We'll be gone soon, and your cousin too. This place should—" he gestured toward the room, and then his eyes came to rest on Marian—"well, this place should quiet down now."

"Yes, but—"

Petey moved from behind Marian, and she shrank away from him as he moved to join the detective. "Fact is," Petey added, "once your cousin sings, you'll need to be rested so you can testify in court."

"Petey." Detective Fletcher glowered at the officer, who ducked his way from the room. "Sorry about that," he said before taking his leave as well.

Marian collapsed onto the stripped bed, all strength sapped from her body. She stared emptily at the wall.

"Oh, Miss Arnold!" Mrs. Dale swept around the bed and took the liberty of sitting beside Marian and putting a motherly arm around her. "I'm so sorry this has happened!"

"Ivo didn't do this," Marian insisted, still staring at the wall. "Oh, the alcohol, the drinking, I suppose he could be in that sort of trouble." Marian didn't want to believe it, though, not about Ivo. His twinkling eyes, his handsome face. But more than that, he was . . . well, he was family.

"I know it's in you to be loyal." Mrs. Dale's tone was comforting. "But maybe—"

Marian jerked her head up to look Felix's mother in the eyes. "No. And I'm not being naive either. Ivo did *not* kill Loretta. He didn't leave bones in her dresser. He wasn't even *here* when I found Percy Hahn in the butterfly house. Ivo didn't have anything to do with this."

At the mention of his name, Marian heard Ivo's shout in the distance, coming from the floor below. She leapt to her feet. The cops were going to take Ivo in for Loretta's murder with nothing to go on but rumors of his exploits back in Milwaukee? What about Cecil, who had already fled the manor? Or any of the other guests?

The detective wanted an easy-to-close case.

But nothing—*nothing*—about this *butcher* had been easy.

"Don't let them do this, Marian!" Ivo's plea made her insides wrestle between pain and the need to insert herself between Ivo and Officer Petey, who had put him in cuffs. The other guests had been escorted out, people Marian hadn't spent much time with, let alone remembered their names.

Had she been foolish to trust Ivo? To allow him to invade the manor with his cavalier persona? Maybe he *was* a darker version of his old self. Maybe Detective Fletcher was right and—

"Marian, are you listening to me?" Ivo's expression was desperate as Officer Petey grumbled something to the detective. "I didn't have anything to do with this!"

Marian hurried toward him, but Detective Fletcher stepped

between the cousins. "Now, now, Miss Arnold. I'm afraid I can't have you interfering."

Officer Petey began to drag Ivo away toward the entrance. Ivo looked wildly over his shoulder at Marian. "Give my lawyer a ring for me, okay, Marian? Raymond Paske. Ring him up. His card is in my luggage."

"Paske, huh?" Fletcher's expression was not one of surprise. "You do like to dance with the devil, don't you?"

The lawmen led Ivo from the manor. Marian hurried after, helpless to do anything and terrified there was more to Ivo than she knew. Still, murder? Loretta?

None of it added up to Marian, not that she was smart in any way that mattered. Her self-deprecation ended with the slam of the police car's door, Ivo pleading desperately with her through the window glass.

"Call my lawyer," he mouthed.

Marian nodded. It was the least she could do.

"Miss Arnold." Frederick's calming voice sounded by her ear.

Marian whirled to face him. "Frederick, what do I do?" She studied the butler's face, anxious to hear words of wisdom that would give her direction.

Frederick's grim face didn't provide much hope. "You pray, Miss Arnold. I'm afraid that is all we can do now. Prayers for Mr. Lott and his friends. For the family of Percy Hahn and now Loretta Habington."

"But I need to do something. I—" Marian bit her lip. She what? Had a premonition something terrible would happen? She'd had a feeling Ivo hadn't kept to the straight and narrow, and neither had Loretta. But such extremes hadn't been on her mind as real possibilities.

The pity in Frederick's eyes hurt Marian's insides. She didn't want to be pitied as a helpless victim of her father's stubbornness against Prohibition that made them lose everything. She didn't want to be felt sorry for because a cousin whom she'd long admired now had a shadow cast over his reputation.

"I'll be fine," she concluded aloud. She met Frederick's eyes with determination. "I think I will go for a walk. To clear my mind."

Frederick's brow creased.

Marian reached out and squeezed his hand. "Truly. I'll be all right. A walk will do me good."

She knew Frederick didn't believe her. How could he when she didn't believe herself?

20

S HE MEANT TO GO to the butterfly house, so now Marian couldn't explain how she'd ended up in her mother's secret art room. She hadn't wandered back here since the day she arrived at the manor. Now she stood in the inner sanctum of Verdine Arnold's private room. The paintings were undisturbed since Marian's last visit. Paints, brushes, canvases—they were all there as if waiting for the artist to return.

She never would.

Her mother was dead. She lay in the butterfly house, surrounded by her precious winged creatures, in a state of repose. Death could be elegant. Then again—Marian recollected Loretta's body on the bed, neck raw from strangulation—death could be grisly.

Marian ran her fingers over the tubes of paint, still in a tidy row. It felt like ages since Mother had died, and yet Marian recalled her father when he'd broken the news to her.

"Your mother is dead."

The four words not cloaked in gentility or grace. That was

Father. His manner was matter-of-fact, unemotional. Marian was almost convinced she'd heard relief in his voice.

"What happened?" she'd asked as carefully as possible. Any show of emotion and Father would accuse her of being irrational. Dramatic. Overly sensitive.

Father had sat behind his desk, his handlebar mustache a carry-over from the style of his younger days. His muttonchop sideburns almost touched his shaven chin. He'd lifted his eyes, and his look was impatient. Offering an explanation was a chore, Marian could tell.

"It was probably her heart. At least that's what the doctor said. We all know your mother was not in the best of health."

Mother was eccentric, a free spirit. She suffered from melancholy. She was closer in fondness with her butterflies than her own daughter. But she hadn't been sickly.

"Her heart?" Marian's questioning tone wasn't meant to challenge.

Her father had glared at her. "Yes. Her heart." It was stated in such a way that Marian knew no more questions would be welcome, and no more answers were forthcoming.

Marian eyed the canvases. Several were piled together and leaning against the wall. She went to the canvases and flipped through them.

Purple butterflies. A beautiful painting of a tiger butterfly, its yellow more vibrant than an actual one. A canvas toward the back caught Marian's attention, and she pulled it from behind. This one unsettled her. She studied the butterfly—a figment of her mother's imagination, for she'd never seen a butterfly like this. Almost all black with violet centers in the wings that gave it the appearance of two eyes staring back at Marian. The bottom part of the right wing was painted in such a way that it looked broken, barely hanging on to the thorax. Her mother had painted a thin red line at the edge. Butterflies didn't bleed, but in Verdine Arnold's mind, they must have. It looked like blood.

Broken wings. Marian narrowed her eyes as she noticed something tiny and curved along the edge of the broken wing. She lifted the canvas and bent to look closer.

He will haunt the future.

Marian dropped the canvas, and it banged against the others, then fell flat onto the floor. She stepped back.

Who will haunt the future? What did the cryptic message mean? Were her nightmares at the manor older than originally thought? Had her mother come into contact with the one who left dead butterflies and bones as omens? The being that had haunted her mother, was it the same one that haunted Marian now?

You're going to die.

The whisper was back.

Marian spun, but no one was behind her. "Go away!" she commanded the empty room.

They're going to find you.

"Stop!" Marian whirled back toward the canvases. She was still alone.

Warn them, Marian.

Her mother's voice—clear as a tune on the piano—rang in Marian's ears. Warn them. Yes. Warn them. Impulsively, she reached for a jar of black paint and grabbed a paintbrush from its container. Slipping them into the pocket of her sweater, Marian backed away from the offensive painting and its message.

This darkness, this *evil* in Müllerian Manor, was more far-reaching than Marian had expected. It could reach from the past into the present, and Marian was convinced that it could also reach its clawlike fingers into the future, ruining those lives as well.

Marian fell to the floor of the butterfly house at the edge of her mother's grave. Violet was nowhere to be seen. Her mystical existence was a frustration as Marian searched for her and came up empty. The feeling of urgency hadn't left Marian. Maybe it was strange that she was worried about the future, worried about generations to come in the Arnold family—or anyone who came to live in the manor someday. This evil that lurked here had soaked into the framework of the house. What if it had nothing to do with flesh and blood, but truly was the owner of the whispers, the master of the mysterious Violet, the taker of life?

She dipped her mother's paintbrush into the paint. Maybe the paint wouldn't take to the stone. Perhaps it would fade or chip away after a time, but Marian knew she needed to leave the message. She needed to let them know—her future descendants—that the manor wasn't safe. That . . .

He will haunt the future.

Marian painstakingly crafted the words at the bottom edge of her mother's grave. She painted over them, making them blacker and more apparent. Yet if someone wasn't looking, they probably wouldn't see the words, and that concerned Marian. She couldn't make them too obvious, however, or someone would scrape them away. She eyed the finished words and decided it best to add her initials. If she had grandchildren or great-grandchildren, they should know it was she who was warning them. She who was urging them to look over their shoulder, to not be lazy in their vigil.

He will haunt the future.

"Marian?" Felix's voice broke into Marian's worrisome thoughts. She shoved the paint and the brush deep into the foliage and stood quickly, rustling her dress so it fell neatly to her calves.

Felix rounded the corner, arm clutching his crutch as usual. He seemed relieved to see her. "My mother was worried about you. Frederick didn't know where'd you gone."

"I'm fine." Marian heard herself and realized her voice was far too bright for the current circumstances. She did not want

Felix to see her message to the future. He would think she was on the brink of exhaustion, or worse, losing her mind. She stepped toward him, hoping to jar his attention away from where she'd been sitting. "I suppose it will get dark soon. I shouldn't be outside alone."

"No." Felix frowned, looking past Marian.

She stepped to the side to block his view. "I'll come inside now."

Felix issued her a questioning, thin smile. Marian sensed his eyes on her back as she hurried through the butterfly house.

"Aren't they beautiful?" she asked over her shoulder in an effort to avoid giving Felix the opportunity to ask questions about what she'd been doing. "The monarchs were my mother's favorites. Mine too!"

A quick glance at Felix and she didn't relax. He was still frowning and had increased his pace to keep up with her. Marian slowed as she reached the door of the butterfly house. At Felix's approach, she explained, "I'm waiting for you, but there's no hurry. I just don't want to let the butterflies out. They'll never survive if it frosts tonight."

Felix gave her a nod and didn't respond. Together, they exited the butterfly house, Marian careful to latch the door behind them.

"Marian?" Felix's voice traveled down her spine.

"Yes?" She looked up at him, mustering a smile she knew could not have met her eyes.

"I don't mean to overstep . . ." He stopped, leaning on his crutch, forcing her to pause along with him. "But I think you need to rest, really rest tonight."

"Oh, I will!" Curse the way her voice sounded. Watery and cheery simultaneously. The perfect giveaway that she was on the verge of bursting into tears.

Felix seemed to gather some sort of courage for something, and then he continued. "I think you should come to Dale Cottage.

At least for the night. We have a spare room. Mother agrees. You shouldn't be alone in the manor tonight. Not after what has happened."

The very idea, the very solace of that beloved idea, sent relief coursing through Marian that she hadn't realized she needed. Tears made her gasp, and she covered her mouth with her hand. "Really?"

Felix shifted his weight, and he didn't seem particularly over-joyed himself, but Marian assumed it was because of the unconventional idea that the employee was asking the mistress to stay in the servants' cottage. "Mother would have asked you, but . . ."

"But she couldn't find me," Marian finished for him.

Felix nodded, a redness creeping up his neck into his beard. "And if you're uncomfortable, I will sleep in the shed."

"The garden shed?" Marian swiped at an errant tear of relief. "No, no. I'm quite unconcerned, Felix."

When she said his name, it came out more like a whisper. It was honey and sweet on her tongue, and she wondered how she could have ever forgotten him after they'd grown. Felix with his quiet, unassuming way, his dark curls and even darker eyes that were so expressive, so . . .

His fingertips grazed her cheek, and then awareness flooded his face. Felix dropped his hand, righting himself. "I'm sorry," he mumbled, taking off for the manor. "Check in with my mother. She'll get you settled for the night."

"Felix!" Marian called after him, but he moved efficiently, and his broad shoulders slumped from embarrassment. "Felix!" she tried again, but to no avail. The man refused to turn around and instead disappeared behind a row of bushes, striding away from her.

Marian was left disappointed. She'd barely had time to register Felix's fingertips on her skin and then they were absent. She could not relish the sensation, but she understood the emotion he left behind him.

Security.

The world around the manor suddenly seemed less chaotic. The voices had ceased. The panic had been assuaged and shifted into wary concern. Even her worry for the future seemed a tad melodramatic now, and Marian wished she hadn't defaced her mother's grave with the ominous message.

She drew in a deep breath, the fall air crisp and brittle in her lungs, awakening her to a deeper reality. One she'd never taken note of before. In the shadows of the manor were good people. People the world outside questioned because of the war. German people whose hearts were caring and faithful. Inside the manor, the legacy left by her father and her mother remained. Separate entities with obsessive dreams and realities that created barriers between them, cloaked their relationships in a cool distance, and produced a daughter who had never known what it felt like to be home.

Simply that. Home.

Home should be a safe place, shouldn't it? Marian mused to herself as she made her way back to the manor that was draped in the shroud of death itself.

A legacy should be like the warmth of the hearthstone, the inviting scent of baked bread, the safety of undying loyalty. Instead, the Arnold legacy was one of cold wealth, wooden walls that hid secrets not even Marian understood, and the constant wondering of her place both within and without its walls.

As Marian's foot found the bottom step of the manor's back veranda, it dawned on her. *She* was the last of the Arnold line. She had no siblings. No direct cousins—Ivo being distant—and no aunts or uncles. It was up to Marian to build a legacy worth securing for the future ones who stepped on the manor's soil. It was up to her to make sure the manor was safe and that the evil within it was banished. It was up to her to uncover what made Müllerian Manor the house of horror that it was.

But tonight? Tonight she would take a respite in Dale Cottage. She would watch Felix and Mrs. Dale interact as mother and son. She would allow herself to wish, just once, that their life could be hers and she could leave Müllerian Manor far behind. Forever.

21

REMY

R EMY SLUMPED onto the hotel room bed. There were a gazillion words rushing through her head, and not one of them was appropriate to express out loud. Elton had thrown the biggest tantrum she'd ever witnessed in an elderly man. Refusing to leave the manor had only been the beginning, for when the aides from a local assisted-living home came, Elton had blown a gasket.

"I'm not *dying*! I didn't break a blasted hip!" he'd protested. "There's *no* reason to stuff me into an old folks' home." He batted away all of Remy's attempts at being helpful. It'd taken her a full hour to convince him that no one thought he was dying or incapable of living on his own. That the manor was currently a crime scene, and until the police cleared it, no one was allowed to stay there.

"Take me to your hotel then," Elton had insisted as a compromise.

Remy explained that she wasn't knowledgeable enough about his medications and how to administer them. There were also his bathroom needs and protective undergarments, checking his vitals periodically—the kind of care Remy wouldn't be able to help him with. That he had the finances for private nursing was wonderful, but unfortunately his nurse was dead, and until another one could be hired, a retirement facility was the best they could do.

Elton had finally acquiesced—after extricating a promise from her that the moment they could return to the manor, Remy would summon him immediately. She promised and then wished she hadn't when Tate reminded her that they'd still need to hire a nurse before Elton could return to the house.

Remy fell back onto the hotel mattress. Her body ached. She'd been awake since she heard the whispering from the other room, and now Aimee was dead. Strangled, Detective Ambrose had said. Which meant somehow not only Aimee but the killer had gotten past Remy's bed and into the room next door. The very idea made her grateful to be in the hotel tonight. She weighed whether to quit her position with Elton and drive back to the Twin Cities, regardless of the police requirement that she stay close by. But she couldn't just up and leave him. Not only had the writer weaseled his way into her affections, but he'd managed to get her to promise she wouldn't quit. Another promise Remy now second-guessed.

She'd arrived at the hotel with Tate, and they'd both booked rooms. It was a little awkward when the hotel reception booked them adjoining rooms.

"We don't need adjoining," Tate stated.

The guy behind the desk had simply shrugged. "Don't use the door then. It has a lock."

So here she was in adjoining rooms with Tate Arnold. And she *had* locked the door. Granted, she didn't suspect Tate of being responsible for Aimee's death, but she still felt better locked away in her own room.

Remy pushed herself off the bed. She had squeezed into a pair of Tate's fleece pants that he'd loaned her since she couldn't access her room in the manor. Just because a guy was taller and his shoulders broader didn't mean his hips were wider. His pants barely fit over her backside. She was grateful his T-shirt and sweatshirt were overlarge, as they covered the tightness, but she wanted out of the pants. She slipped them off and grabbed the pink sleep shorts from her bag. The bonus of wearing Tate's shirt was that it smelled like him. And Tate Arnold smelled amazing. She chose to leave his shirt on.

She glanced at the clock on the nightstand. Midnight already. With exhaustion overwhelming her, Remy opted against her nighttime bathroom routine and slipped between the sheets.

Heaven.

She was safe tonight. That too was a bonus . . .

Remy's eyes shot open.

How long had she slept?

She'd forgotten to turn off the hotel room light.

Another thump on the wall alerted Remy as to why she'd awakened so abruptly. She sat up, frowning. Low murmuring coming from Tate's room met her ears. Remy leaned closer to the wall, unashamed that she was trying to eavesdrop. She could hear him intermittently.

"Stop."

His voice held a questionable element of anxiety that she'd not heard from him before.

"Knock it off!"

Concerned, Remy eased from the bed and tiptoed to the door that led to his room. She hesitated. He probably had locked his side as well.

"Tate?" Remy called softly, hoping to get his attention. Maybe he was dreaming. They'd been under enough stress to induce bad dreams, that was for sure.

"No." His response was muffled, and the tone gave Remy the impression he wasn't responding to her.

She quietly unlocked the door . . . and was surprised when it opened effortlessly. Tate hadn't locked his side.

His room was dark. Only the light over the desk was on. Remy saw Tate sitting on the edge of the bed, the hood of his sweatshirt pulled over his head, his hands stuffed in its front pocket. She was reminded of the night she'd watched him in the backyard at the manor as he stared at the sky. He seemed to be somewhere else entirely.

"Tate?"

He didn't answer, his eyes fixed on the wall.

"Tate?" Remy tiptoed farther into the room.

He jerked, his body twitching, and shot her an anxious look. "Go away."

Remy knew immediately something was terribly wrong. She approached him with caution. A glance around the room told her he'd not unpacked his things. His bag sat on the floor in the corner. The bed was made, the curtains pulled.

She kneeled on the floor before him, reaching out to touch his knee. He jerked it away.

"Tate?"

He moved away from her, and his expression didn't resemble the capable and strong Tate she was coming to know.

"It's me. Remy."

He hunched his shoulders. "Go away."

She had seen this before. Years ago. The memories came back from one of her foster-care homes. A foster brother. Remy recalled her foster mother—one of the good ones—and how she'd come alongside him. Did Tate have PTSD from serving in the military? It didn't matter. He was obviously not himself.

Remy softened her voice. "Tate, it's me, Remy. We're in the hotel tonight, but I get it can be overwhelming."

He glanced at her.

She tried again, adjusting her position on the floor, being careful not to touch him. "You can tell me how you're feeling if you need to."

Tate stayed silent but didn't move farther away from her. Remy decided to sit with him, and then after a moment, she tried something different.

"This room is nice. It's safe."

He glanced at her again.

Remy smiled reassuringly. "I always like to check my surroundings when things feel out of control. I know you do too."

Tate bent his head to look down at his hands hidden in his hoodie's pocket.

"You're a natural protector," Remy went on. "I get that too."

"Is the door locked?" Tate ventured, his voice gravelly and uncertain.

"I'll double-check," Remy said. She got to her feet and checked the locks on the door. "Locked and bolted." She saw his shoulders lower a bit. She moved past the bed to the window and checked it. "Window is locked too." She moved to the door that joined their rooms, shut it, and locked it. "All good."

Tate twisted in his spot on the bed. "There's access on the roof—across the street."

Access? Remy tried to comprehend what he meant and then it dawned on her. His sniper training had him processing their surroundings. "The drapes are closed," she said. "No one on the outside can see into your room."

He nodded in agreement.

"Let's just hang out here for a bit." Remy didn't ask, but instead crawled onto the bed.

Tate eyed her for a second and then joined her, leaning back against the headboard, his hands still in his sweatshirt.

Remy smiled. "How about I tell you my life story?"

He gave a small chuckle.

"It's long, and it's boring," Remy warned. "It'll probably put you to sleep. But at least you won't be alone."

Tate nodded, wordless.

"So I was born at a very young age . . ." Her joke fell flat as he stared unblinking at the wall. She continued anyway. "I never knew my dad. My mom died in . . ." She hesitated. Maybe talking of trauma wasn't such a wise idea. Remy shifted her story. "I've never tried to find my blood relatives. I've just worked hard and made a life for myself. I like to knit." She laughed lightly and noticed Tate's mouth tip up in a weak smile.

Taking encouragement, Remy reached over and attempted physical contact with him. To help ground him. To help Tate know he wasn't alone. She slipped her hand slowly into the pocket of his hoodie where his hands were. He stiffened at first, but as her fingers found his, Tate's hand turned and grasped hers. Remy drew in a careful breath.

"The only time I wish I had family is at Christmas. I love all the twinkling lights and the trees decked out and Bing Crosby crooning and all the snow. But I don't really have anyone to celebrate with. What's the best Christmas you can remember?"

She waited.

Tate didn't answer.

"It's okay," Remy said. "I have one. I was fifteen, and my foster family had bought gifts for me and another kid. We were allowed to open them Christmas morning. They'd gotten me a stuffed dog. So there I was, fifteen years old, holding a stuffed animal. But the funny thing? I loved that dumb dog because it was mine. Like God had looked down and nudged my foster parents to give me something I could hold."

Tate blinked.

His fingers curled tighter around hers.

"Sometimes we just need something—someone—to hold

on to. Someone who doesn't ask questions. Someone who's just there."

Silence.

Remy dared to lean her head against Tate's shoulder. He didn't move.

"I'm here, Tate," she whispered. She was coming to understand that Tate struggled with something much deeper than she'd originally imagined. Monsters other than the ones at Müllerian Manor. But whether the monsters were tangible or intangible, they were still real.

Sometimes it was better not to be alone.

The sound of Remy's pealing phone awoke her. She reached for it, her hand slapping the nightstand.

"Hello?" She could hear the grogginess in her voice.

"Miss Crenshaw?"

"Yes?"

The caller on the other end sounded familiar.

"It's Detective Ambrose. I wanted to let you know we'll be out of the manor by end of the day. If you need to make arrangements for Mr. Floyd's care and return, I just wanted to give you a heads-up."

"Thanks." Remy appreciated the thoughtfulness, although she couldn't say she was happy at the thought of returning. She ended the call and, with eyes half closed, put the phone back on the nightstand before rolling over toward the middle of the bed to return to sleep.

Her eyes flew open.

Tate Arnold faced her, his eyes shut in slumber, his hoodie still pulled up over his head. He was on top of the blankets, she beneath them. Awareness flooded Remy as she remembered the night before. They had sat on the bed for what seemed like hours, until finally Tate had relaxed enough to fall asleep. Worried about him, she hadn't thought it a good idea to leave him alone. Instead, she slid fully dressed beneath the covers and allowed herself to drift off into her own much-needed slumber.

Now she studied Tate's face. The angles were softer when he slept. His face was covered in dark, overnight stubble. His breathing was silent, his chest moving up and down rhythmically. He didn't even snore! If a man could be perfect, Remy was close to thinking this might be the one.

She rolled onto her back and stared at the ceiling. Last night had been enlightening, but it had also dredged up long-forgotten memories of her foster brother Lucas. She had never gotten to know him well. She'd been in that foster home for only eight months. Remy remembered Lucas lived with a mental illness, and though she had never been given a name or explanation for it, it had manifested not unlike Tate's experience last night. There were medications for Lucas, and Remy didn't think she'd have known about his illness had she not lived in the same house. Their foster mother had been validating toward him, calmly diverting his attention while also acknowledging what he was feeling. That had always stuck with Remy. Not so much witnessing the shift from his usual behavior, but the fact that both he and their foster mom had been unified during it.

Remy turned her head to look at Tate.

His eyes were open and clear.

"Hey," Remy said softly.

"Hey," he acknowledged, his voice husky. There was a flicker in his eyes. Shame, question, apology? She wasn't sure what exactly it was that she saw there.

"Are you okay?" She had no intention of revisiting last night unless Tate initiated it.

"Been better." That was all he was going to give her, and Remy respected that. She was determined not to pry or inquire further. It was Tate's story to share, whatever it was, and in his own time.

Yet she found she couldn't move from her place on the bed. He was looking at her, wordless, studying her face, his dark lashes framing expressive eyes that harbored his story. His untold story.

His hand came up, and he traced her cheek with the backs of his fingers. "You stayed."

Remy swallowed. Okay. She wasn't expecting the flood of emotion. Tears sprang to her eyes. "Of course," she murmured.

"I'm sorry."

"Don't be." She managed a wobbly smile as she felt his fingers graze the skin along her neck before he withdrew his hand.

"I don't like people to have to deal with me when I'm like that," he admitted with no further explanation.

Remy weighed her response. "I didn't *deal* with you, Tate. I was just there."

With a tight smile, he said, "Yeah, well, you didn't have to be."

Remy didn't know if it was a rebuttal or a way to excuse her from something he was afraid she'd find burdensome. "I know I didn't," she responded. "I wanted to be."

Tate moved toward her. She could feel his breath on her skin. The covers over her tightened as his body slid nearer. Remy couldn't gather her thoughts, let alone her wits. Tate's lips settled gently on her forehead.

Remy closed her eyes. This was unexpected. But there was an unspoken thread between them now. Hurting pasts. Unspoken memories. Secrets that hovered so close to the surface they could almost guess the other's worst fear.

Tate lifted himself onto his elbow so he could trail a kiss down to her cheek. Her neck. Then hovered over her mouth.

Remy opened her eyes. His were pools of uninterpretable emotion.

His mouth covered hers. Soft at first, then needy, pressing against hers with a barely suppressed desire to become a part of her. To know her not physically so much as emotionally. She could feel it in his kiss, in the way his lips searched hers. They both felt it. Two lost souls in a world that spiraled around them with no explanation.

Remy's arm stole up around Tate's neck, drawing him closer. He lifted his face and claimed her mouth again, this time more urgently, more—

Tate rolled away and swung his legs over the edge of the bed, his back to her.

The room fell silent.

Remy's lips thrummed with the absence of his, but with the memory—the taste—of him.

This was nuts. Not what she'd signed up for. This was no longer just coming alongside Tate Arnold, it was being invited *into* Tate Arnold. Into his world, his feelings, and next would be his thoughts and his story and . . . Well, it frightened her as much as it made her wish his back wasn't to her.

Remy managed to sit up. "I should get back to my room."

Tate didn't say anything as she eased from the bed, adjusting her shorts and shirt. She was sure her hair was a mess, but it didn't matter. Her bare feet felt the coarse carpet of the hotel room. She gave Tate a questioning look over her shoulder.

"Did you want me to open the drapes?" she asked.

He shook his head.

"Okay then." Remy approached the door to their adjoining rooms and unlocked it.

"Remy?" Tate stopped her.

"Yes?" She turned.

"Thanks."

She smiled. "No problem."

But their words said so much more. Only Remy wasn't certain how to interpret them. She just knew that Tate Arnold was no longer a stranger. He was someone who in one night her soul had connected with in the darkness that was his world, and in the questions that were her world. Places both of them avoided.

Places one of them feared, and the other didn't want to acknowledge. She was the latter.

Acknowledging questions meant they would need to be answered someday. Life was fine the way it was, Remy determined. She didn't need to unearth the past. There was too much trauma in the here and now. Too much pain swirling around Tate Arnold. Dredging up her own pain? She'd save that for another day—or never.

22

WAS IT SAFE TO RETURN to the manor? Remy didn't feel safe. The place screamed *I'm haunted* the moment she stepped back into it. The air in the manor was stagnant. Mrs. Flemming met them at the door, ushering them back as though they were new guests and not returning occupants.

"I've set you up in a different room." Her heels clicked on the hardwood floor as she led Remy back up the winding stairs. "Unfortunately, you're merely exchanging one ghostly room for another." The housekeeper didn't mince words. "Since Marian Arnold's rooms are now . . . well, I suppose no one will ever want to sleep in them again now that *another* death has occurred there. Anyway, I've put you in Verdine Arnold's rooms."

Marian's mother's rooms. Wonderful. Remy eyed Mrs. Flemming's ramrod-straight back as she led the way. "Isn't there another room? I'm sure there are guest bedrooms."

"Yes, of course," Mrs. Flemming snapped. "But they're farther away from Mr. Floyd."

"I'm not his caregiver." Remy didn't think it mattered that she be close to Elton after they'd all retired at night.

"Nevertheless." Mrs. Flemming's conclusion was not even close to satisfactory. They turned down a corridor and passed a door before reaching the already open bedroom door.

"Where does that go?" Remy inquired of the one they'd just passed.

"To a set of rooms that make no sense." Mrs. Flemming pursed her lips. "They're supposedly rooms Mrs. Arnold used to paint in before her death."

"How did Verdine Arnold die?" Remy ventured.

Mrs. Flemming's eyes widened. "How am I to know? You're the research assistant."

Her barbed response convinced Remy not to ask more questions. She'd merely inquired to see if the aged employee had more to add to the story. The woman was as approachable as an invasive thistle in a flower garden.

Once Mrs. Flemming departed, Remy quickly assessed the bedroom and its attached bath. It was smaller than Marian's, but more inviting. Probably because there was no odd, attached room with a butterfly in a globe set in its middle.

At that, Remy froze.

The butterfly. There had been a butterfly in a globe on the table in the middle of the room, but in retrospect, Remy didn't recall it sitting there when they'd discovered Aimee's body.

She knew she'd have to go back and check. If it was missing, that would be important information for Detective Ambrose. What significance it had on Aimee's death, Remy had no idea.

Resigned to the fact she now occupied the room of Verdine Arnold—currently lying at rest in a stone grave in the glass house—Remy took note that her belongings had been moved into the room. Mrs. Flemming had outdone herself, and Remy wasn't sure how she felt about the housekeeper handling her things. She could have relocated herself. Thankfully she wasn't the type to have a diary hidden in her underwear drawer. There wasn't anything Mrs. Flemming would have seen that would create an issue, but it just seemed violating to Remy's privacy.

She exited the room and made her way back to the main part of the manor, hesitating outside the closed door to Verdine Arnold's painting rooms. She hadn't known Marian's mother had been a painter. Remy pushed on the door and peered inside. The room was windowless, devoid of furniture, and cold. She dared to enter, her footsteps echoing off the walls.

Verdine Arnold.

Remy surveyed the ceiling and the walls as if to find clues there that would somehow clarify all the rumors. But there were no clues. Just a small door on the far wall that stood open by a few inches. If closed, Remy realized, it would mesh into the wall seamlessly. It tempted Remy to look deeper. She opened it further, her hand brushing a latch on the outside of the wall that at one time must have been hidden to keep the room secretive. A painting hung over it would have done the job. Remy's gaze swept the room. An empty easel, a vacant table, and, in the corner, a sheet shrouding a pile of something.

Intrigued, Remy went to the corner, reached for the covering, and carefully lifted it. Beneath the sheet was a stack of painted canvases, leaning against the wall. She dropped the sheet on the floor, then squatted in front of the paintings. The first one was of a butterfly with a broken wing that appeared to be bleeding, which made little sense to Remy. The canvas was yellowed and frayed at one of the bottom corners. Pulling the canvases toward her, she glanced at each one. A group of five paintings, all of them of butterflies. Species that, to Remy's knowledge, didn't exist. They were beautiful figments of Verdine Arnold's imagination, made evident by her looping signature at the top left of each canvas.

"Who were you, Mrs. Arnold?" Remy asked the empty room as she repositioned the paintings against the wall. Her research revealed that Verdine Arnold had lived here alone, had been responsible for the unusual architecture of the manor, and had suffered a heart attack and died prior to Marian Arnold moving into the manor.

"You were a creative, weren't you?" Remy's voice bounced off the walls, but she didn't mind. She was speaking to a dead woman who couldn't answer, and there was no one to witness it. "I wonder if you were lost in time to the memory of Marian and the Butterfly Butcher. What could you tell me that no one else would be able to?"

And yet Verdine Arnold remained silent in her grave. The paintings were the only remaining evidence in the manor that she had even existed, outside of her sarcophagus in the glass house. Still, she'd left behind a legacy, hadn't she?

In some ways, Remy could relate to the woman. The whole not-knowing-who-you-were concept. Who was Verdine Arnold in the story of Müllerian Manor? Who was Remy Crenshaw in the story of her life?

Remy was beginning to feel as though the manor were drawing her into itself. Pulling her in like an invisible specter. Taking hold of her soul and desperately wanting to tell her something. The secrets of the butterflies in the glass house.

Remy stiffened. Butterflies. Verdine Arnold's obsession with them was clear. It was known. But so was the Butterfly Butcher. There had to be a tie that bound the two together. Somehow the butterflies connected Mrs. Arnold to the Butcher, not Marian. Marian Arnold had no compulsion toward butterflies that Remy had uncovered. None outside of what her mother had begun.

"Thank you, Verdine Arnold." Remy moved to replace the sheet over the paintings and return them to the darkness of their shroud. Verdine Arnold had spoken.

The key to the Butcher couldn't be Marian.

It had to be Verdine.

She'd have to think more about that, but right now Remy increased her pace. It was already two in the afternoon. Tate had retreated to his room—or wherever he'd decided to go. He'd been quiet most of the day, but there was a steadying confidence in him again that was familiar, and Remy was relieved to see it return despite the fact that she had to keep herself from touching her lips and remembering his caress like a crushing teenager. She'd received a call that Elton would be moved back to the manor by seven, and the agency was sending Aimee's replacement.

As Remy descended the stairs to the main entrance, she heard Mrs. Flemming's voice greeting a newcomer. That had to the new nurse.

"Ah, you're here." Mrs. Flemming noticed Remy. She addressed the man before her. "This is Miss Crenshaw, Mr. Floyd's assistant. She will show you to his rooms."

She would? Remy hadn't expected Mrs. Flemming to dump the new employee on her, but then it was probably for the best. The last thing they needed was for the nurse to take off after being soured by Mrs. Flemming's manner.

"Remy." She extended her hand.

The man facing her looked to be in his late thirties. He was lean and a bit angular, a full beard covering his face, and his smile was friendly. "Dean." He gave her a firm handshake.

"I take it you're the nurse?" Remy asked.

"That's what I hear." His jovial manner belied the recent events in the manor. Remy wasn't sure if Dean knew of those recent events, but she didn't feel like revisiting them with him and risk sending the poor guy running.

"Let me show you to your room, and I'll give you the quick tour of Mr. Floyd's quarters. He likes to hide out on the third floor in the attic space."

"And how does he get down to take walks every day? I know he's not very mobile—according to his charts." Dean followed Remy as she made for the stairs.

She stopped, pondering Dean's question. "You know, now that I think of it, Elton doesn't go outside ever. He stays put either in his study or his bedroom."

Dean gave an understanding nod. "Well, now, that isn't healthy, is it? We'll have to inspire him to get some fresh air."

"He'll just tell you to open a window," Remy laughed. At Dean's taken-aback expression, she reassured him, "He's feisty, but he doesn't bite."

"Just open a blasted window!"

Elton was cranky. More so than Remy had seen before. But could she blame him? No.

"He's just trying to do his job." Remy positioned herself in her customary chair. Elton said he wanted to get some work done, no matter that it was nine at night. He was still irritated that he'd been kicked out of his home, even if it was for just a night and a day. Remy wanted to tell him how lucky he was. The police had told her a lot of places where murders occurred weren't available to be inhabited again until weeks afterward.

"Aimee didn't make me go outside," Elton groused. He yanked his writing desk, which was on wheels, closer to him. "She didn't make me take vitamin D either."

"Wow," Remy teased. "Vitamin D, huh? Dean is bringing out the big guns to take care of you."

"Shush." Elton waved her off and fumbled for his pipe. "He'll probably make me quit smoking too."

"Probably." Remy bit the inside of her lip to keep from smiling. With all that had transpired, and as awful as it had been, it felt like it'd been days since she worked with Elton on the biography.

"I don't like him," Elton said. "Asinine they sent me a man. What kind of man is a nurse?"

"Lots of men are nurses, and you're buying into stereotypes," Remy pointed out.

"Pfft." Elton opened his tobacco pouch. "When I was a lad, nurses were women, doctors were men."

"And the world was dark and oppressive," Remy finished for him.

"You have a mouth, Remy." Elton glowered.

"So do you." Remy's quick comeback silenced the old man, and he finished preparing his pipe before lighting and puffing on it. Remy was certain she would forever associate the smell of pipe tobacco with Elton Floyd.

"Well, I miss Aimee." Elton's admission was a bit less emphatic and wobblier.

Remy offered him a sympathetic look. Aimee might have been a bit pesty and a know-it-all about the Arnolds and their history, but it was apparent now that she had been a huge part of Elton's life. As Remy considered the loss of Aimee, guilt sliced through her as she realized she hadn't actually thought much about her, about her grieving family, and the fact that she was gone. She'd been a critical part of Elton's life. Remy reminded herself to be more sensitive to Elton. He might be the only one in the manor who was grieving and not just processing the ramifications of the traumatic event.

"You had a good rapport with Aimee," Remy acknowledged.

Elton's eyes shot up to meet hers. He puffed on his pipe. "I don't want to talk about it."

Man, he was cross! Grief did that to a person, though. "No. Of course not." Remy nodded. She sought a distraction and quickly found one. "What do we know about Verdine Arnold?"

"Marian's mother?" Elton's bushy brows knit together. "Hmm . . . well, she passed away about a year before Marian took over the manor, and before the Butterfly Butcher killings began."

"She was a painter, wasn't she?" Remy asked.

"A painter? Yes, but she wasn't known for her paintings. Verdine was known for the butterfly house. She was obsessed with butterflies and spent most of her waking moments there." He took a puff on his pipe. "It's why she's buried there in the glass house."

Remy opened her notebook. "How did she die?"

"Heart attack," Elton answered. "You knew that already."

"But do we know it for sure?" Remy challenged.

"It's not like there are autopsy reports from back then you can look up online. What did her death certificate say?"

"Heart," Remy replied.

Elton shook his head. "It doesn't make any difference how Verdine Arnold died. She has nothing to do with the Butterfly Butcher's case."

"Yes, but she *was* Marian Arnold's mother. Sometimes working backward can bring clarity on what's in front of us. Any researcher worth their salt knows that." Remy tapped her pen on her notebook. "She died here, yes? At the manor?"

Elton eyed her like she was daft. Sure, she knew the answer, but she was hoping to distract Elton from his grief. He seemed to gather that this was her ulterior motive. His lips thinned. "You know what I know, missy. I will say this, however. From what I've read about Verdine Arnold, I get the feeling this place was where she was tucked away."

"Tucked away?"

Elton tossed Remy a wan smile. "Tucked away as in *hidden* here. Ostracized. Kept. It was better than an institution."

"I haven't found any records that Verdine Arnold experienced mental illness, just that she was eccentric."

Elton stifled a yawn. "Anyone who behaved outside the box in those days was threatened with being institutionalized. The 'crazy farm' they used to call it."

"That's awful." Remy was repulsed by the term. An image of Tate from last night raced through her mind, making it more personal.

"It was harsh, yes." Elton frowned. "My own mother spent two years in a mental ward after she had my sister."

"She was hospitalized?" Remy drew back in surprise.

Elton nodded. "Back in those days, when women had babies

and then spent hours crying and ignoring them, well, that wasn't right. They needed help."

"It's called post-partum depression, Elton." Remy would never stop being surprised at how what was misunderstood in one generation was sometimes so much more carefully approached in another.

"Is that so?" Elton replied. "Well, my mother got better. She came home when my sister was two. She never had any more issues. But she didn't talk about the hospital much either."

"Probably because of how she was treated there," Remy said with a shiver.

"Perhaps," returned Elton. "Anyway, my theory is that this manor was how the brewery baron Mr. Arnold kept his wife, Verdine, away from the public eye."

Remy nodded. "I wonder if—"

A knock on the door startled them both. Dean, the new nurse, poked his head into the room. His smile was genuine, and his apologetic expression offered out of politeness because his next words were firm. "It's well past time for you to prepare for bed, Mr. Floyd. We have medicines for you to take and other things to tend to."

Elton's eyes narrowed. He eyed the nurse and waved his pipe in the air dismissively.

Dean tilted his head and gave Elton a smile that was kind but communicated that he wouldn't be talked out of the care that was necessary for the man's well-being.

Remy knew Dean was correct. She closed her notebook and leaned over to drop a peck on each of Elton's cheeks.

He blustered, his blue eyes filled with question.

"You have a good heart, Elton Floyd." Remy wasn't sure why she needed to say it, but she did. It was a reminder that someone in Müllerian Manor was worth staying for. Otherwise, this place was just a tomb that held the pain of the past between its walls and only continued to compound it.

23

MARIAN

OCTOBER 1921

MARIAN SIPPED TEA—*tea!*—just as she'd always imagined herself doing on an autumn evening, with leaves falling intermittently from the trees, the sun descending beyond the woods, and a blanket of peace enveloping the cottage in which she sat. It seemed rather awful that she was enjoying it so immensely in the wake of Loretta's death. But Marian could feel the stress seeping from her muscles, and for the first time in a long time, she had a clarity, a hopefulness, which was something she'd not experienced until now.

Mrs. Dale rocked in the corner, her knitting needles flying with such adept speed that they mesmerized Marian for a long moment. There was a companionable silence here at Dale Cottage. Felix was reading a book while Marian was content sipping her tea. Here they sat, in the shadow of Müllerian Manor.

Felix sniffed and set his book on the hearth. He had been standoffish since he'd brushed her cheek. He kept his eyes averted from her most of the time, although he'd never once wavered from being gentlemanly and polite. If Mrs. Dale noticed her son's discomfort, she didn't draw attention to it.

He reached down to where his trousers were pinned at his knee, and Marian observed as he massaged the area with his fingers. Was it paining him? She'd heard of phantom pain, but she didn't want to ask. She didn't want to be rude. Marian shifted her eyes away. Staring was rude as well.

"Sometimes it hurts." Felix had noticed her attention and answered her unspoken question anyway.

Mrs. Dale's needles didn't stop clicking. "Do you need some powders?"

"No, Ma, I'm fine."

Marian assumed the powders were for the pain. How did one treat the pain from something that wasn't even there?

"Did you tell Miss Arnold how you lost it?" Mrs. Dale's pointed question stunned Marian. She turned a shocked gaze at Felix, who didn't seem taken aback in the slightest. He merely continued to rub his leg.

"Nope."

"I'm sure she'd like to know," Mrs. Dale said.

Felix snuck a look at Marian, then shifted his attention back to his leg. "I lost it in the war."

His answer was not at all what Mrs. Dale had intended, but Marian could tell that Felix had no desire to revisit it.

"He has a prosthetic." Mrs. Dale rocked and knitted, and if Marian hadn't already known how close the bond was between mother and son, she might have thought Mrs. Dale inconsiderate. Felix's mother added, "They fitted him with it before he came home from the war, but he refuses to wear the thing."

"Ma." Felix eyed his mother and shook his head.

Mrs. Dale flushed. The needles stopped moving. "I'm sorry, dear. I . . . I'm sorry." She then returned to her knitting, and that was that.

Marian took another sip of tea.

Felix pushed himself up from his chair and grabbed his crutches. "I'm going to get some fresh air." He exited the cottage, leaving behind a gust of cool air in his wake.

Mrs. Dale continued to rock, Marian sipping her tea.

"He suffers from nightmares," Mrs. Dale stated.

Marian met her eyes.

"He wouldn't want me telling you this, but if you hear him at night in distress, I don't want you to be alarmed or afraid."

"Of course." Marian nodded slowly.

Mrs. Dale gave her a sad smile. "Mind you, Felix has done well for himself. He's strong like his father. I just wish . . ."

Marian waited.

"I always felt he was meant for more, our Felix." Mrs. Dale waved her off with a knitting needle. "That's no offense to you, Miss Arnold. Your family has been generous in letting Felix continue in his father's position."

"I would have nothing less." Marian's response sounded dry even to her. She looked out the window beside the door. Felix was leaning against an oak tree, staring off into the woods.

What did a man, one who'd seen so much death on the battlefield, ponder when alone?

Marian moved to stand, and Mrs. Dale caught her eye. "If you're going to go be with him, Miss Arnold, go gentle on my boy."

Marian wasn't sure what Mrs. Dale meant.

The mother's expression softened, almost wistful. "He's admired you, Miss Arnold, for years. You must understand that beyond the fact you're far above him, he feels even less worthy now than ever before."

It was the concern and worry of a mother who shared her son's affections to the one he'd always wished for. Marian realized this even as she met the poignant expression of his mother, Mrs. Dale.

Go gentle on my boy. Her eyes seemed to say what her mouth could not. *He doesn't believe he'll be loved after I'm gone.*

The crunch of leaves beneath her feet gave away Marian's presence. Felix turned toward her, offered a shy smile, and then looked away. Now that she had gone outside to be with her childhood friend, after Mrs. Dale's words, Marian didn't know how she should process what she'd been told.

Honored? Flattered? Or perhaps in some curious way, unworthy herself. Not to mention they were from two separate worlds in so many ways.

"I hope you don't feel as though you owe me any explanation as to your experience in the war," Marian began.

Felix gave a short laugh and looked down at his foot. "My mother has a way about her."

"Yes." Marian recalled Mrs. Dale's words from only minutes before. "Yes, she does."

Felix was silent.

Marian drew in a deep breath of crisp autumn air, taking in the scent of wet leaves. She looked down and noticed how moisture had collected among the fallen leaves, which reminded her of the impending winter season. "You know, your mother loves you very much." Her words sounded inane to her own ears. Of course Felix would know of his mother's love! What he didn't know was that his mother had revealed to Marian his admiration for her.

Felix watched a hawk as it flew overhead. "She means well. It's been just us for years now."

"And just her while you were away." Marian winced, for without thinking, she had reintroduced the topic of war.

"Yeah." Felix adjusted his crutch, gripping it as he faced her. "I'm not quite what she expected to have come home."

Marian furrowed her brow. "But you came *home.* That's a mother's deepest wish."

Was it? Had her mother ever wished for Marian to come home to the manor? To leave Father in Milwaukee and return home to her? It was easier to bestow comfort on someone than it was to try to accept that same comfort as truth for oneself. Somehow Marian couldn't imagine her mother praying for Marian to come home.

"Your mother was good to mine," Felix offered.

Marian lifted her eyes.

"Not many people understood your mother, but she was a good person." Felix's assurance warmed Marian, as did his dark eyes. "I remember once I was trying to paint some rocks. I was about ten or so at the time. Your mother saw me and brought out her own paints—many more colors than I had. We painted butterflies on the rocks and then hid them in the woods. 'For the fairies,' she had said."

"You did?" Marian instantly wished that Felix's memory was hers.

"Lots of folks—even your father—didn't understand your mother. But she was worth being understood." His words pierced Marian. Was he speaking of her mother or himself or perhaps both? Felix provided the answer. "People have this measuring stick they use and hold one another up to. If you're running a tad short, then something's wrong with you. There's a place to put people like your mother and me. Put the crazies in the hospital. Put the *jumpy stubs*—that's what they're calling boys like me these days—in jobs that pay a lesser wage just to make the *normal* folk feel better about themselves. Like we don't have anything left to offer folks." The words were flowing now, and Felix didn't seem prone to stopping them. "Throw in the fact you're German, and nowadays, since the war, that alone can get you in trouble. It'll take some time for folks to relax about us and not think we're out to wage war for the motherland."

Marian swallowed hard. She'd not expected Felix to share his thoughts on the prejudices and limitations imposed on him—imposed on her mother.

He cleared his throat and didn't disguise the hurt in his eyes. "Makes a man sore, you know? Am I less for having one leg instead of two? Considering I gave that leg up for the rest of you all?"

"No. You're not less," Marian whispered. She took a step toward him, anxious to communicate the opposite to Felix.

"Was your mother less because she painted butterflies that don't exist, danced with fairies in the woods, and had fears that kept her away from folks?"

"No." Marian took another step toward Felix.

His voice quieted with each question, became less accusatory and more a plea to be understood. "People think I need help and can't do things on my own, but I can do things. I'm no less a man now than I was when I went to France. I'm no less a man now than I was when you—" He bit off his words and lowered his chin.

"When I what?" Marian stood directly in front of him now. She tilted her head to catch his gaze, to bring it back up from staring at the earth.

It worked. When Felix's dark gaze slammed into hers, his eyes were filled with remembering.

"You were thirteen when . . ." He reached into his pocket and pulled out a small crocheted cross. It was a bookmark she had made, edged in green thread. Marian remembered it clearly. "You gave me this." Felix held it out for her to see.

"I remember," she breathed.

"You said you gave it to me because I was the nicest boy you'd ever met. But then your cousin—"

"Ivo," Marian stated, knowing.

Felix ducked his head. "Yeah. He came around the corner, and even though I was your nicest, he was your most important."

"Felix. Ivo was family." Marian dared to step closer to him.

So close that she placed her palms on his chest. He leaned back against the oak tree, stabilizing himself with the crutches. "You, on the other hand, are the strongest man I know."

His expression reflected disbelief.

Marian tried again, a tear escaping from the corner of her eye and coursing down her cheek. "I-I get so frightened sometimes. Like my mother, I suppose. And you're . . . you're *safe*. You're safe to me, Felix."

A look of doubt still lingered in his eyes.

"I've never felt that way before," Marian admitted. Then she lifted a hand and gently ran her fingertips along Felix's jaw. He closed his eyes at her touch.

When Felix opened his eyes again, an understanding seemed to pass unspoken between them. Marian dropped her hand from his face.

They needed each other. They probably always had. Only now they were beginning to understand why. Neither of them was broken, but instead they were frightened. Frightened by being unwanted, which was worse than anything in the universe.

24

MARIAN RETURNED to the manor in the morning. Frederick met her with a question in his eyes. But he didn't dare ask her why she'd stayed at Dale Cottage last night, and Marian had no compulsion to tell him. Something had shifted last evening. Shifted not only between Felix and her, but in her own mind. Today she walked the relatively short distance from Dale Cottage to Müllerian Manor with one person weighing heavily on her mind.

Verdine Arnold.

Mother.

Something in the way Felix spoke of her mother the night before had awakened in Marian an intense desire to reconnect with the woman she'd known and yet had never known, not really. Father had trained her—whether purposefully or not—to keep her mother at a distance. Because of that, Marian had grown to know her only as the woman who fancied pretty things, hired workers to add strange nooks and crannies to the manor, flew with the butterflies, and the woman whom Father kept hidden from society.

The manor was eerily still this morning. Marian made her way through it toward her mother's quarters. All signs of houseguests were gone. Ivo was also gone. Loretta . . . Loretta was dead. The lump in Marian's throat grew thick. She'd rather liked Loretta with her caring and her flamboyant beauty. Who would have done such a thing to her? Not just stolen the breath from her but displayed her like a doll on her bed, butterflies over her eyes. A princess with broken wings. It taunted and it nagged at Marian.

Because it was a message for you.

Marian saw the shadow whisk by her down the hallway, yet its words remained. The solace she found at Dale Cottage was already slipping away. Yes. The butterflies, Loretta positioned on the bed just so, the bones in the drawer—they all pointed to one person.

Verdine Arnold.

Marian opened the door to her mother's bedroom. The air inside was stuffy from being shut in for months. She walked to the window and wrestled it open. A gust of cold wind blew into the room, lifting the lace curtains high into the air like the arms of a specter, reaching to embrace someone or something but finding nothing there.

Marian moved to her mother's bureau. Butterflies. It was always the butterflies. Omens of death as much as they were omens of life. She recalled once her mother explaining their significance. It was when they were at her grandmother's funeral. Mother had leaned in, her sweet perfume subtle but intoxicating. Her breath had brushed Marian's little ear in a way she could still feel now as she remembered.

"Look, Marian. Do you see the butterfly? It's your grandmother. When you see a butterfly at a funeral, it is the spirit of the departed wishing you farewell. Only be warned, my love. Butterflies live short lives. They were not meant to live forever, and once in bloom, they are no longer symbols of life but symbols of death to come."

Marian touched her ear, certain she could feel the feather-light breath of her mother even now.

232

"Bid your grandmother farewell, Marian. She will fly for only a little longer."

Marian had done as she was instructed by her mother. She had whispered goodbye into the wind, and the butterfly had dipped over the casket suspended above the earthen hole that awaited it. Then it had winged its way around the ensemble of people gathered in shrouds of black.

What a different thing it would have been had her mother leaned over and breathed promises of heaven, the hope of faith, and the joy of knowing the Creator. But no. It had been butterflies as omens of death that had swooped and followed Marian all her life. That made believing in sunrises and life and hope very difficult. Strange almost. As if to hope for something meant to enter a world that didn't exist and delude oneself into believing nothing but silliness.

Now Marian ran her fingers along the bureau until her hand connected with a drawer pull. She tugged on it, knowing what she would find before she looked.

Inside the drawer was a box covered in printed paper, flowers of reds and pinks, tied with a lace ribbon. Marian withdrew the box and set it atop the bureau. She untied the ribbon, letting it fall to the side, leaving the box ready to be opened.

Marian drew in a deep breath. She remembered her mother bringing her here. Remembered her mother pulling out this very box and whispering *"Tell no one, my love."*

Her fingers trembled as she lifted the lid of the box. She stared at the contents, sickened and repulsed and yet entranced by the sight. The box was filled with the dry, crumbling bodies of butterflies—hundreds of them, collected and stored away. Their wings had lost their colors, and their bodies had turned into such fragile remains a very breath would send them into dust. Mostly monarch butterflies. Marian touched the wing of one as lightly as she could. Even then it crumbled. Time and age were not friendly to dead things. In the end, decay was inevitable.

Marian replaced the lid and retied the lace ribbon. She finally understood her mother's fascination and obsession with the winged creatures. Her mother was collecting souls. The souls of the dead, or at least the memories of their reincarnated selves. A second chance to live in the life of a winged insect, only to die shortly after. This was her mother's homage to them. Every butterfly in her glass house that died, she had collected and treasured.

To Verdine Arnold, each butterfly was the spirit of someone who had gone on ahead. And Marian wondered if her mother heard the voices like she did when she opened the box.

You will join us.

You'll be here soon.

Death is coming.

You can hasten it.

Marian set the box back in the bureau drawer, using her hip to push it all the way closed and hide the box from sight.

Motion in the bedroom doorway caught her eye, and she glimpsed a woman, a frown on her face, before she slipped around the corner. Violet.

Violet had been watching her. Disapproving of Marian's rejection and fright of the butterflies.

You should embrace them, Marian heard Violet whisper as she vanished from view. *Soon one of them will be you.*

Marian stumbled into the butterfly house, this time uncaring as to the greenery, the butterflies, the beauty inside. In fact, she noticed the place felt darker somehow. The light had dimmed, as though the wickedness from Müllerian Manor had seeped through the earth and infected the last vestige of loveliness on the grounds.

Yet how could the butterfly house be a place of beauty when it was also a place of death?

Marian sagged onto her mother's grave, the stone cold on her skin. Her hand caressed the top, connecting with its roughness, her mind evoking the unbidden memory of Percy Hahn's dangling feet, the pile of dead butterflies beneath him.

"Why?" she whispered to her mother. But there was no answer. *Why did you believe what you did about butterflies? Was God not powerful enough to swallow death? Must our spirits morph into the limited beauty of an insect only to plummet back to earth in a second death?*

Then what? What good was there in such dark omens, what hope when the world of good and safety and warmth collided with that of the ugly and deadly and cold? They crashed into each other, a thunderstorm erupting, and now Marian was caught between them. What her mother had left for her was only questions and fear and the unknown. What her father had left for her was failure and greed and bitterness. In front of her, however, stood Felix, a man who *should* be all of that too, and yet he fought against it. He reached into the void, but instead of the momentary comfort of the soul taking wings in the delicate and fragile unknown of death, he somehow took comfort in the greater. The deeper. The truth that was sacrifice. That was family. That was greater than death and more palpable than fear itself.

Was Felix afraid? Oh yes. Yes! Marian had seen it in his eyes. She had seen the anxiousness that came with the questions of personal value. And yet he also stood there in peace, captivated by the unknown in a way that spoke truth into her soul. His unknown to her was not unknown to him. Felix had interlocked his grip with God's and refused to let go as the wildness of life and death brutalized him.

She knew that now.

Because of the cross.

That silly crocheted cross. It had meant nothing to her. Nothing really but an act of friendship. But to Felix it had meant everything. She knew without his telling her that it had remained in his pocket through battle. That the cross had become his symbol of willing sacrifice for those he'd left at home, a symbol of sacrifice greater than himself.

"No more butterflies!" Marian cried, the words reverberating in the glass house. "No more!" She dropped to her knees beside her mother's grave.

He will haunt the future.

Marian stared at the words she'd painted on the base of the stone grave. Words she'd intended to warn future generations of Müllerian Manor. The butterflies were not going away. They plagued her even now.

Marian swiped at a monarch that brushed against her cheek. It had become a pest. She reached into the greenery and retrieved the jar of paint and the paintbrush she'd hidden there the other day. Scrambling to her feet, Marian looked frantically around the butterfly house until she noticed the marble statue of a goddess, there among the beautiful ferns.

She pushed her way into the ferns toward the base of the statue. One day these plants would be dead, while the goddess would still be standing here with her stony smile. Dropping to her knees, Marian opened the jar of paint and used the brush to write a new message at its base. It was irrational to think someone of her line would one day discover it, but Marian wrote it anyway. She needed her descendants to know. Needed them to understand.

You are wanted.

M. A.

~~~~~

You're wanted?

Marian snapped from her intense focus on the words she'd painted on the base of the goddess statue. How long had she been sitting here, staring at the message as it dried? Praying that somehow God would preserve it so that the future of Müllerian Manor would not be so dark.

A pebble bounced on the walk beside her. Marian shifted, looking up. A shadow passed over her, and then she was there. Violet. Once again half hidden in the shadows and the plants, only this time the butterflies were absent. It was as if they had gone into hiding, afraid they too would soon join the box of butterfly corpses, preserved but no longer alive.

"You shouldn't have looked in the box." Violet moved among the plants, trimming dead leaves from the live vines.

"I had to," Marian responded, pressing her palm against the statue and pushing herself to her feet. "I need to know my mother. I need to know why the manor is so dark."

"It is dark because you make it dark." Violet's declaration brought Marian no comfort.

She stuttered, "I-I don't make it dark."

"You see the darkness that no one else sees. Because of that, it cannot stay contained, and it seeps out, touching the others who deserved to live."

Marian leaned against the statue for support. "It's not my fault Loretta was killed."

"What about Percy," Violet asked, "the poor milkman? Left destitute after you ended his employment."

"I didn't . . ." Marian's mind was reeling. Ended Percy Hahn's employment? "He w-was the milkman."

Violet yanked free a dead vine, her shoulder and back visible in her dark silk dress. "You know he was more than that. Remember? The footman your father employed when you were last here? That was Percy. And now he is dead because of you. Because he lost his position at the manor after your father went bankrupt and because you didn't do anything to help the employees. Instead, you let the lawyers speak for you. Percy lost his place here because of you."

Marian opened her mouth to protest, but no words were forthcoming. It was true. All of it. She remembered him now: Percy in his black suit, his back always straight, his formal approach with her father. He was a true footman in every sense of the English role, and Father had delighted in bringing the look of the old aristocracy to his estate in rural Wisconsin.

"We lost our brewery . . ." Marian began.

Though Violet's back was to her, she lifted a hand to silence Marian. "How many people have lost because of what you did?"

"What my father did," Marian corrected. "He was the one who wouldn't adapt. The government ruined the lives of my father and his associates. Because of the law, we were left with nothing—"

Violet's laughter was knowing, and it fluttered among the leaves like the flight pattern of the vanished butterflies. "There is always someone else to blame—until you hear the truth and embrace it. *You* are to blame. *You* are the last Arnold. There is no one else to bear the weight of Percy's suicide. No one else to bear the cost of Loretta's life."

"I don't know why someone killed Loretta!" Marian's protest was met with a long, silent pause. She took a few steps from the statue, having regained her balance, and started following Violet down the path in the butterfly house. Violet veered off until she was almost out of sight.

"You don't know why? Or you just don't want to admit the reason?" Violet's questions cut through the foliage, slicing Marian's conscience like a knife.

"What do you mean?" she asked, bewildered.

Violet stepped onto the path, her face turned so that Marian could make out the grim set to her mouth. "You know what I mean, Marian. Look around you. Really look. *You* can stop this. *You* can stop all of it." Violet's laugh was wicked this time and coiled around Marian like a vine that threatened to squeeze the life from her. "But you won't. And they will hate you for it."

25

REMY

REMY GAVE ABIGAIL a grin as the barista handed her an Americano through the window of the coffee shack. Abigail rested her arms on the ledge, her eyes filled with unconcealed curiosity.

"I know I shouldn't ask this, but—" Abigail bit her lip—"did they find whoever did that to Aimee?"

Remy sipped her coffee and then set it in her car's cup holder. "No. They're still investigating."

"Oh, that's creepy." Abigail shuddered. "To my knowledge, there hasn't been a murder in this town since way back when."

"The Butterfly Butcher?" Remy supplied.

Abigail nodded, her ponytail flipping to lay over her shoulder. "Yeah. And even then, he pales in comparison to other Wisconsin serial killers such as Ed Gein and Jeffrey Dahmer. I mean, the Butterfly Butcher got lost in time. Especially since no one figured out who it was."

Remy matched Abigail's regretful wince. "I know. So here I am, off to the library to dig some more."

Abigail offered a conspiratorial scrunch of her face. "Have fun?"

Remy shifted the car into drive. "If that's what you want to call it!"

Just minutes later she was at a computer station in the library. Prior to Aimee's death, Remy would have preferred to do her research at the manor. But now? Now she relished being away from the place. Although she felt bad leaving Elton behind. He'd been cranky since Aimee's death—not that Remy blamed him. While it'd only been a week, the more time went on, the less hopeful any of them were that Detective Ambrose would be able to identify who'd killed her. Meanwhile, Elton was trying to grow accustomed to Dean, whose caregiving turned out to be excellent. Still, he wasn't Aimee. Elton had lost his will to write, withdrawing further into himself. So Remy was anxious to uncover something that might rekindle his interest in the biography and bring some excitement back into the older man.

Remy slid the mouse to inspire the desktop computer to flare to life. She'd looked all over the manor for that globe with the dead butterfly, but to no avail. She thought back on the day Aimee had taken her to the room, showed her the lone table in its center, the odd heirloom with the butterfly, and explained how Marian Arnold had been found dead on the floor beside it, lying in a pool of her own blood.

Gory, yes, but was it even true? Or was that just Aimee's story? Remy had searched for death records and grave records, but again to no avail. There was no record of Marian Arnold's death. No record of anything that confirmed Aimee's tale of Marian's meeting a violent end at the manor. That was the question that aggravated Remy. Where had Aimee even heard that story, and why did Elton not challenge it? She knew it was a huge part of Elton's biography about Marian Arnold and the Butterfly Butcher.

But the more she researched and tried to find corroborating facts to make sure their story was as true to events as possible, the tale that Marian had been found murdered didn't line up. Even so, the fact that Marian disappeared from history after that, with no clear family records, made it appear as though the story was at least partially based in truth.

Another question nagging Remy was the missing glass globe and butterfly. It *had* been in the room—she'd seen it. She'd placed a call to Detective Ambrose to report it missing. Ambrose had been curious but vague in her response. Remy hadn't expected anything more, as the authorities weren't going to give them a play-by-play in the investigation.

Then there was Tate.

He'd been avoiding her, spending his time in the butterfly house, hauling out recyclables and garbage. She had attempted to talk to him at dinnertime, but often he'd come in, grab a plate of whatever had been prepared, and head off to who-knew-where. Remy wished he wasn't so standoffish. He had nothing to be ashamed of or embarrassed by. Though she wasn't sure what all Tate was dealing with in his life, it'd become obvious it was something he preferred to address alone.

She shifted her focus back to the computer screen and research at hand.

Verdine Arnold.

Remy scrolled through a newspaper article from the early 1900s. Interesting. It wasn't until after Marian was born that Verdine had taken her leave of Milwaukee society and moved to Müllerian Manor.

She slowed her reading. There it was. Evidence of the early days of Verdine's occupancy in the manor.

Curious happenings have occurred at Müllerian Manor. New construction has begun under the supervision of the mistress, Mrs. Verdine Arnold, originally from Milwaukee. Builders state she is

prone to changing her mind during the build and abandoning en-
tire portions of the construction plan, only to begin again elsewhere.
What is going on at Müllerian Manor? That is the question all of us
locals are asking.

A gossip rag to be sure, but it certainly helped her cause now. Remy wrote Verdine's name in her notebook and jotted down her observations. Verdine changed her mind frequently and with no apparent logic. She was known for her eccentricity.

Remy did more searching and came up with Verdine's obituary.

Mrs. Verdine Florence Arnold passed away at the age of forty-eight.
She was found by house servants. Dr. Timothy Parks stated she died
as a result of heart failure. However, rumors have been circulating
that Mrs. Arnold was in fact found in a secret room of the manor, and
murder is being considered as a possible cause.

Remy slouched back in her chair.
Murder?
This was the first she'd read about a potential killing prior to the supposed first victim of the Butterfly Butcher—Percy Hahn, the footman turned milkman.

Remy's fingers flew across the keyboard. She couldn't take an old gossip rag's story as fact, but it sure was raising questions. She ran more searches on the name Verdine Arnold and pulled up another article, noting its title was the *Coldwater Valley Scuttlebutt.* Heck, she'd pay for a subscription just to be entertained if it were still in print today. Remy scoured the article, pausing at another revealing sentence.

Whispered behind closed doors, word has it that Dr. Timothy Parks
admitted to being paid under the table to classify Mrs. Verdine Arnold's
death as the result of heart failure when instead it's been said Dr. Parks
was actually called to a grisly scene wherein he discovered Mrs. Arnold
lying dead in her own blood.

Remy reared back in the chair.

"What the what?" she exclaimed.

"Shhhh!" The librarian from across the room stern-eyed her.

Remy ignored the reprimand and leaned back in, closer to the screen. Was the rumor that Marian Arnold had died in a pool of her own blood actually more truthfully applied to her mother, Verdine?

God bless the internet—and vintage gossip magazines. Still, gossip was gossip in any era, and often untrue.

Remy ran a few more searches but came up short. This could change a lot in the perception surrounding what had happened to Marian Arnold! And it would definitely influence Elton's book.

She stuffed her notebook and belongings into her bag and logged out of the computer.

If Verdine Arnold was the one to have died in the same spot Aimee had been murdered, and if Verdine Arnold had been murdered beside the very butterfly globe she'd heralded in that strange, one-entrance-only room, that meant everything—*everything*—took on an entirely different light.

It meant the Butterfly Butcher had killed *before* Marian Arnold and the others. Maybe the Butcher hadn't killed Marian Arnold at all!

Remy quickly wove her way between desks and out the library doors.

~

Elton was napping. He always napped around one in the afternoon, after lunch and after taking his medications. Remy knew this, so it wasn't fair for her to skewer Dean with her annoyance. The new nurse was slipping into Aimee's role seamlessly, and it wouldn't be smart to insult him by being grumpy. He had enough of that to deal with from Elton.

But Remy wasn't one to process things on her own very well. She always did better if she could lay out her thoughts verbally, even if the person listening didn't offer any advice or input. Just hearing herself talk helped her make sense of things. Back in the Twin Cities, Remy would process life aloud to her therapist, but here? She needed an active listener.

Remy went hunting for Tate. She traipsed across the back lawn to the butterfly house and gave herself a brief tour. It was cleaner now, empty of trash. The structure was still abandoned and dilapidated, but she could tell Tate had been putting an effort into improving it.

When she exited, she almost ran into Boggart, who regarded her with narrowed eyes. Remy had a sudden desire to squint back at him so he'd know what it felt like to be ogled through little slits in another person's face. But again she refrained from acting on impulse.

"Boggart." Remy opted instead for a warm smile in an attempt to gain a friend and perhaps influence the groundskeeper. "Have you seen Tate?"

Boggart grunted. "Thankfully, no."

Remy cocked her head. "What do you mean 'thankfully'?"

"Man gets in my way." Boggart waved a bony arm in the direction of his cottage and shed. "Found him snooping in my tools. He took a rake and never returned it. Who does he think he is?"

"The last Arnold and heir to the manor?"

"Heir my backside!" Boggart spat. "This place belongs to Marian. Always has, always will." The groundskeeper stalked away.

Remy called after him, "Boggart!"

He turned, glowering at her.

"Why do you say that?" Remy took a step toward him. "Why are you so fiercely loyal to a woman you never met?"

Boggart's expression changed ever so slightly. He wrinkled his nose. "Never met? You make big assumptions for a little lady."

"So you *did* know Marian?" Remy heard the squeak of excitement in her voice.

Boggart eyed her and shook his head. "No. Never met her." He spun on his heel and marched in the direction of the grounds-keeper's cottage.

"I don't believe you!" Remy shouted after him.

The old man's hand came up in a dismissive wave.

Remy made a few quick calculations. If Boggart was in his early seventies, then it was possible for him to have known Marian Arnold. But only if she'd lived well into her middle-age years or beyond.

"Who are *you*, Boggart?" Remy mused aloud to the trees surrounding her as she watched his retreating form.

Her search to find Tate had only resulted in more questions. Remy hiked back to the manor, her mind whirling with the possibilities that *if* Boggart *had* known Marian Arnold, then the Butterfly Butcher could not have made her his victim.

But there were the butterflies left on her bed and in her car.

There was Aimee.

The Butterfly Butcher wasn't immortal—of that Remy was sure.

She walked through the manor, peeking behind some of the doors that led to nowhere and the hallways that were dead ends. Finally she decided she'd just suck it up and go straight to Tate's room. The man must have sequestered himself there for whatever reason.

Moments later, Remy approached his bedroom door in the wing opposite the one she'd used before being evicted from a crime scene. She rapped her knuckles against the dark wood of the door. "Tate?"

No answer.

She tried again. "Hello, Tate?"

Remy tried turning the doorknob. The door gave way easily, and she poked her head into the room.

"Tate?"

The room was dark, the curtains drawn. Remy pushed the door fully open, stepping inside. It was a spacious bedroom, probably one of the rooms originally reserved for guests. The bed was rumpled, pillows piled to one side. A sweatshirt was flung over the footboard. Tate's signature scent wafted in the air. Okay. This was going to be really embarrassing if he stepped out of the bathroom freshly showered, a towel around his waist.

Remy dared a glance toward the bathroom door. It was wide open and dark inside. Against all common sense, she made her way to the bath, then flicked on the light. The fixtures were vintage but updated for modern-day hygiene. The shower curtain was pulled back from its track that encircled the claw-foot tub. The showerhead looked dry. Remy glanced at the sink. Also dry. He hadn't been in here, at least in the last hour.

She noticed some prescription bottles sitting on the vanity top. Remy ignored the sting of guilt as she crouched to look at them closer. She was curious what medications he was taking—even though it was none of her business. Glancing at the labels, Remy didn't recognize any of the meds. If Tate was going to be all mysterious and aloof again, she wanted to make sure he was safe. He'd started out by being protective of her, but lately he'd been withdrawn. After Aimee's death, the veteran had pulled away rather than heightening his defense.

Feeling justified, Remy snapped photos of the prescriptions with her phone, carefully placing each bottle back in its original position. She made her way from Tate's bathroom back into the bedroom. His suitcase lay open on a trunk, clothes piled haphazardly inside it, a pair of shoes on the floor nearby.

Remy went to the wardrobe and opened it, peering inside. The shirts were askew, like they'd been hung hastily, and she noticed a bundle on the floor. She bent down to remove the sweater that lay on top of the bundle, so she could see what was beneath.

The butterfly globe.

Tate had taken the butterfly and its globe from the crime

scene. Or had he taken it *before* Aimee's death? Which meant he'd been in Remy's room . . . while she was asleep? Maybe. Maybe not. Maybe he'd just snooped around like she was snooping around in his things right now.

She dropped the sweater back over the globe. The questions kept piling up, one on top of the other. At some point she needed answers.

"What are you doing?"

Tate's voice startled Remy. She yelped and slammed the wardrobe door shut, spinning to face him, guilt saturating every pore in her body.

"I'm sorry, I . . ."

Tate stepped into the bedroom and closed the door. The sound of it latching was ominous. Remy backed up into the wardrobe.

His glare was chilling, not at all friendly. "You're going through my stuff?"

Remy thought of the photos she'd taken, now stored on her phone. "Tate, I—"

"Oh, you already *went* through my stuff." His conclusion was followed by an aggravated rake of his fingers through his hair. "What for?" His eyes speared her, demanding the truth.

"I-I . . ." Remy's stutter did nothing to assuage the growing tempest on Tate's face.

He launched at her before Remy could react. His hand came down over her mouth, pressing her head back against the wardrobe. Tate bent so his breath was hot against her face.

"I won't let you do it," he growled.

Remy tried to cry out. She wrestled against his hold, but Tate was unshakable. And in that moment, Remy realized so were his secrets.

26

MARIAN

HER SLEEP WAS RESTLESS. She tossed and turned until the majority of her bed covers lay on the floor, her nightgown tangled around her legs. She could sense it, feel it, but *it* was undefined. She didn't know what *it* was. A person? A being? A spirit?

Marian didn't want to open her eyes. She didn't want to look into the dark corners of her room. She could already picture Violet standing there, judging her in silence, expecting Marian to understand what she had no comprehension of.

She buried her face in her pillow, her breath stifled by its feather stuffing. God help her. Praying was not natural to her, but she believed in the Creator. And she desperately needed Him, here, with her.

Marian lifted her face from the pillow and rolled onto her back. She swiped at her cheek where something feathery tickled her skin. If she opened her eyes, would she see only the dark outlines of her quiet bedroom, or would she see something else? The presence that she felt, would it have a form? Would it be standing over her, there to strangle her, just as it had Loretta?

The tickle was back on her cheek. Distracted, Marian flicked at it with her fingers, this time feeling the object. It was pliable, soft. Instinctively, Marian grasped it and at the same time opened her eyes. No one loomed over her. She held the item close to her face so she could see it in the dark.

With a wild fling, Marian threw it away from her. Sitting up, she clawed at her bed. Butterflies. They were everywhere. Dead and sprinkled around her like a funeral shroud of flowers. They outlined her body where she'd lain, and there were more on the floor that had been cast aside in her tossing and turning. Marian scrambled away from them, pressing her body against the headboard and drawing her knees to her chest.

Butterflies.

Everywhere.

She had been coronated with them, like a princess in death with a crown of insects waiting to take her spirit into their bodies.

With a squeal of terror, Marian flung herself from her bed, kicking at the blankets tangled around her feet, hopping over the lifeless bodies of dried and crumbling butterflies. In her haste to get away, Marian's foot knocked into a box, and it went skidding across the hardwood floor.

Her mother's box! The butterfly box!

Marian clamped a hand over her mouth in horror. Someone—*something*—had poured her mother's collection of dead butterflies around her as she slept. Clutching the front of her nightgown, Marian stumbled toward the bedroom door. She had to get away from here. Away from Müllerian Manor. Away even from her mother's memory—her grave.

She tripped over the edge of a chair and fell headlong toward her bureau. Putting her hands out, she caught herself as she collided with the dresser, knocking off a porcelain figurine and sending her jewelry box flying. Necklaces and brooches scattered across the floor, adding sparkle to the dead butterflies. Marian steadied herself at the bureau, lifting her face to look into its mirror.

She froze.

It is time to end it.

The words were smeared across the mirror, reflecting back along with Marian's colorless face.

End it? End this? Yes, Marian agreed, but not violently as the message seemed to portend. She frantically swiped at the items on her bureau, finding the glass hatpin holder. Marian slipped a pin from it, wielding it like a weapon, though she knew it would do little against an assailant. Especially if that assailant wasn't alive but instead a spirit that permeated the walls of the manor and toyed with its occupants.

Marian pushed the hatpin holder away from the dresser's edge, and her fingers brushed the softness of yarn. Grabbing the item, she was almost afraid to see it for what it was, only she knew she had to. Whoever had left the message, the butterflies, had left this too.

It was a knitted scarf, one suitable for the winter season. Marian's fingers curled into it, recognizing it immediately. Mrs. Dale. The woman had been knitting this scarf the night Marian had taken refuge at Dale Cottage. Marian wondered if Mrs. Dale was behind it all—the butterflies, Loretta's murder, tonight . . . But what motive did she have? No! Marian refused to believe Mrs. Dale had anything to do with it. She was the epitome of a loving and faithful woman, an honored employee of the manor, a friend and the mother to Felix, who had been raised to be a person of integrity, to be *good*.

Marian dropped the scarf on the bureau, looking again to the words on the mirror.

It is time to end it.

She glanced down at the scarf, then at the butterflies strewn across her bed. As with Loretta and the butterflies and bones in her drawer, they had been an omen. An omen or warning before a death.

She jerked her gaze back to the scarf.

Mrs. Dale?

Was Mrs. Dale the next victim of the Butterfly Butcher?

~~~~~

Marian stumbled into the walls as she raced down the hallway. She'd give anything for the Dales to have a telephone in their cottage. She could get to hers at the bottom of the stairs and ring them. Warn them! Warn Felix!

Prayers slipped from Marian's lips—pleas on behalf of Mrs. Dale, on behalf of them all. Marian stepped on something soft and leapt back, staring at the floor of the corridor, the carpet runner a dark shadow in the night. She knew what the shape resembled as she drew her bare foot back. Another dead butterfly. She made her way to the light switch at the end of hall, jabbing it with her finger. The wall sconces lit the area, a golden hue mingling with the shadows. Marian surveyed the floor. Every few yards, another butterfly, like a trail beckoning her to follow.

"Oh no, no, no . . ." Marian whimpered, tears building in her eyes and quickly overflowing. Was Mrs. Dale already dead? The Butcher was taunting her. Taunting her with her mother's belief that butterflies would embody the spirits of the dead, enabling them to offer a second goodbye. Marian charged forward, a sob catching in her throat. She had to get to Mrs. Dale. Maybe there was a chance to save her! To spare her life! She would even offer hers up in return—

They're after you.

The whisper in Marian's ear caused her to trip. She landed hard on the floor, her knees burning along the carpet.

Get up. Run.

Marian obeyed the voices and whoever had whispered them. She struggled to her feet, then surged forward, noting the butterflies along the way, guiding her. She would follow them for Mrs. Dale.

Marian found her way downstairs and around corners until she reached the back veranda. The moon shone bright overhead, like a witness unable to do anything to stop what was coming. Another butterfly lay on the walkway, and as Marian reached it, the breeze lifted and detached one of its wings and blew it into the emptiness of the lawn.

The glass house.

Of course.

She was being led to the butterflies. Violet? Had Violet done this? She'd teased and taunted her, and now she landed the responsibility fully on Marian's shoulders, just as she'd insinuated.

It was Marian's fault! Another sob clawed at her chest. God was so far away at the moment. Hope was nonexistent.

You did this, didn't you?

Be careful, they're watching!

Don't go into the butterfly house. They're waiting for you!

Marian swiped at her eyes, the tears that burned trails down her face.

"Stop it!" she screamed at the voices that warned her and mocked her simultaneously.

The butterfly house loomed ahead, its form taking shape in the night, the moon reflecting off its glass. Marian was not shocked to see the door already open, but when she stepped into the butterfly house, she fell against the doorframe.

"No," she murmured. She looked wildly to the right, then to the left. Everything was dead. All of it.

The foliage that had bloomed so green and so full of life was withered and dry. Leafless, dead vines hung from the ceiling and the walls and curled along the walkway. The goddess statue she'd painted her message on earlier was now covered in moss, dead leaves and debris collected at its base. It was a shell of what it had been earlier today. A horrifying mockery of the beauty that was tended here by Marian's mother and then by Violet.

Concern urged Marian forward. Her feet slapped against the stone path that curved around the dead garden. If she hadn't been here just this afternoon, and if she hadn't witnessed Violet pruning the green plants, Marian would swear this place had been unattended for over a year. This was what the butterfly house *should* have looked like in the wake of her mother's death. In the absence of her tender care over each plant and each butterfly.

Now it was cold inside the butterfly house. Dry and lit only because the moon was laughing now. Marian looked up through the glass-paned roof to see the face of the moon—so full, so alive, so entertained by the tragedy unfolding beneath it.

Marian scanned the house for Mrs. Dale, but she saw nothing but dead things. Death everywhere, including her mother's sarcophagus, which was covered in dead leaves.

"It's time, Marian."

The voice chilled her. It traveled through the butterfly house from somewhere to her right.

"Who's there?" Marian cried.

"You know it's time. This has to end." It was a male voice. Not Violet's, but not Felix's either. The voice was familiar and yet it wasn't. "None of this is real anyway, Marian. You can see that now, can't you? You can see what your mind is doing to you? Playing cruel and wicked tricks."

"What do you mean?" She spun, searching for whoever was speaking to her.

"You don't know?" The voice had circled around behind her now.

Marian whirled to face it. "I don't know what you're talking about."

"Your mother suffered too. She didn't know either."

"Who are you?" Marian cried. "How do you know my mother?"

A choked laugh enveloped the butterfly house, a mix between irony and grief. "Your father tried so hard to keep her safe and away from everyone else. There are places for people like her—like you—but no. Died of a heart malady, your father claimed."

"She did!" Marian insisted.

"No." The word was spoken with brokenness. "No, no, she didn't. Your father refused to do what needed to be done for your mother. Refused to get her help. She needed *help*!"

Yes, her mother was odd. Yes, she collected butterflies. But that didn't constitute her needing help. It meant she was . . . imaginative, creative, and—

"I had to make sure she slept." Footsteps crunched over the dead plants. Marian twisted in that direction but saw no one there. "She would likely hurt you. Or someone else. It was only a matter of time."

"Make sure she slept?" Marian echoed.

"What better place than the room? *The* room. The butterfly room."

Marian's mind raced, trying to piece together what the voice was saying and who it belonged to. The butterfly room? Where her mother painted butterflies? The hidden room with her brushes and easels and paints? Or her bedroom where she'd hidden the box of butterflies, kept carefully as a memorial to those who'd gone before? Or—

Marian jerked her head around at the snap of a vine beneath a shoe. The butterfly room . . .

"Do you mean the room just off my bedroom? The one with the butterfly in a globe, my mother's favorite piece?"

"Ah, it is coming together for you. Yes, yes. She died there. I meant it to be quick, merciful—you know, painless. But your mother was, well, she was already paranoid and expecting something. I'm sorry." A sob now. The grief-stricken agonizing kind that sucked the breath from a person's being. "But it had to be done. For everyone's safety."

Marian choked back the bile that rose in her throat. "You killed my mother? You—" Marian scowled into the shadows, willing the demon to come forth so she could stab him with the hatpin she still clutched in her hand. But he remained hidden. And then . . .

"Mrs. Dale!" The memory of why she'd come to the butterfly house in the first place slammed into Marian. Mrs. Dale. The butterfly room. Had this angel of death already silenced Mrs. Dale there? Just feet away from where Marian had slept?

As she charged for the door of the butterfly house, the male voice called out from behind her. A hand grappled for her arm, but Marian shook it off, leaving the door open in her wake.

It didn't matter anyway.

The butterflies were already gone.

27

REMY

"Tate!" Remy cried against Tate's palm that pressed against her mouth.

He dropped it, but before she could react, Tate fell against her, leaning his forehead on the wardrobe.

Remy could feel his chest heaving against hers as he drew a shuddered breath. Her fear flipped to concern, then back to fear. "Tate, what is going on? What's wrong?"

His voice was muffled as he spoke into the wardrobe, not releasing her from the weight of his body.

"Remy, you have to leave it alone. Please. Just leave it all alone. Get Elton to write about the Butcher, but leave Marian out of it. *Please.*" The desperation in his voice squelched the fear she'd been accosted by.

Tate hadn't attacked her. He was acting out of some sort of desperation she had yet to understand.

"Then tell me!" Remy twisted her neck to try to look at him.

Tate still pressed against her, his face to the wardrobe. Remy pulled her arms from beneath his weight and, instead of resisting him, embraced him.

She thought back on those dark nights in foster homes when terror clawed at her as a little girl. Remy knew that fear intimately. That fear of the unknown. That fear of very real, very possible—even probable—danger. Something that all children should be protected from, only she had been left to do the protecting herself.

A flash of something burned in Remy's memory. Flames. The smile. She could make out a little bit of the face now, a thick smoke distorting it in her brain. Younger. Male. It was the first time Remy had realized that safety and security would come only from herself. They'd come from nowhere else. In her young mind, not even God was big enough.

If that was how Tate felt now, who was she to lash out in defiance against his reaction caused by fear? Who didn't strike out when threatened? Who just sat back and waited to be overtaken?

"Tate." Remy held him, nuzzling her face into his neck. "It's all right. I don't know what's going on, but I'm here. It's all right."

His head moved against hers as he rejected her words. "You don't get it. You really, *really* don't get it."

"Then help me understand." Remy splayed her hands on his back.

Anyone in their right mind would think *she* was stupid to embrace Tate Arnold. But she could feel it in his body. Feel the trembling. It wasn't anger or violence, and it wasn't all fear.

"You're trying to protect us, aren't you?" she whispered into the column of his neck.

When Tate didn't respond, she knew she had hit on some element of truth. "Do you know who killed Aimee?" she breathed, silently begging God that it wasn't him.

"I-I don't know." He turned his face just enough to bury it against her hair. "I *don't*. I just know this place is cursed, Remy.

Müllerian Manor is cursed, and the more you dig, the more you try to uncover . . . it's all meant to stay dead. To stay buried."

"Why do you have the globe with the butterfly?" She had to ask. It was glaringly obvious she'd seen it, and as awful as it sounded, Tate owed her some explanation.

He pulled away from her, his eyes finally connecting with hers. The wounds in him ran deep, and she could see apology and hurt and fear and protectiveness all wrapped into his expression.

"Because I didn't want the police to confiscate it."

"Why? What does it mean? What does it matter, Tate?"

He spun away from her, jabbing his fingers through his dark hair, his elbows sticking out on either side of his head. She could tell he battled within himself what to share, what to keep secret.

"Elton and I, we're just writing a book." Remy gave a little laugh. "But I think I can speak for Elton that if it's ending up killing people, it's not worth it."

Tate chewed his bottom lip as he turned toward her, then dropped onto a chair against the wall. "That's what I don't know. It wasn't supposed to be this . . . this volatile, this violent! I just came here to save you all from my family, you know?" He winced, his face begging Remy to understand. "That's all I care about. My family. No one was supposed to die."

She cautiously moved to the trunk his suitcase lay on. There was space beside it, so she leaned back against it. "You keep saying your family, but you're the last of the Arnolds, Tate. And even that doesn't make sense given what I know of your family tree."

He gave a short laugh, and even though his smile was troubled, his expression relaxed a little. "Yeah, well, that's a story in and of itself."

"I think I'd like to hear it." Remy matched his smile. "It beats spending hours at the library."

Tate groaned, "Ohhh, man." Then he heaved a huge sigh.

"Fine." It seemed his resolve to keep secrets was finally breaking down. "The butterfly globe belonged to Marian's mother, Verdine."

"Okay," Remy encouraged.

"Marian didn't know about the globe and what it meant until long after her mother was killed."

"Killed?" Remy inserted. "I don't understand."

Tate eyed her. "You didn't figure that out?"

"Well, I found an article in an old gossip magazine. It alluded to the fact that Verdine Arnold had been the one murdered and found in a pool of blood in the butterfly room. But I didn't know for sure. I'd heard it was Marian who'd been found there."

"It was Verdine," Tate confirmed. "Her husband, Mr. Arnold, tried to keep it from Marian. He wanted to protect her from the truth, and then I think the facts just got muddied over the decades."

"Ghost stories tend to do that."

"Yeah." Tate grew quiet, looking down at his feet for a long moment. "I . . ." he started again and then stopped almost immediately. He sniffed. His brow drew into a v between his eyes. "Do you smell smoke?"

It was such a sudden shift that it took Remy a few seconds to comprehend his question.

Tate stood, his frown deepening. "I smell smoke."

"I don't smell anything," Remy replied. She sniffed deeper. "Wait. Maybe I do."

Tate strode to the bedroom door and twisted the knob. It resisted. He tried again, then glanced at Remy. "Do the doors here have locks on the outside?" He sounded incredulous.

"I don't think so." Remy hurried to his side. "It won't open?"

"No. Something is wedged up against it. That or . . ." Tate stepped back. A thin ribbon of smoke curled under the door and around his feet. He swore under his breath and tugged on the doorknob with great force. "Something's on fire!"

Remy ran to the window and shoved the curtains back. Tate's room overlooked the back lawn, and all appeared normal. The trees in their blazing autumn colors mimicked a fire, but the other angles of the manor Remy could see looked fine.

"Stay back." Tate held out his hand toward her and then leveled a solid kick to the bedroom door. It gave a bit, but the door was made of solid wood and hung on strong brass hinges. More smoke filtered into the room. "Grab some towels in the bathroom!" Tate commanded. "Soak them in water. Now!"

Remy rounded the bed and rushed into the bathroom. She went to the sink and turned the water on. A small stream dribbled from the faucet and then nothing. "What the heck?" She spun to the bathtub and twisted the knob on its fixture. Her second of relief at the flow drained as quickly as the water did when it diminished to a drip and then nothing.

"The water's been turned off!" she called.

Tate slammed his shoulder into the door. It groaned but didn't give. "Look for a tool, something I can use to pry the hinges off." He dove for the dresser, pulling out the drawers and rummaging through the contents.

Remy coughed as smoke began to float upward. The bathroom had nothing. Nothing that could be used to break free the old hinges on the door.

"I found something!" Tate yelled.

Remy sprinted back into the room. Tate had a large knife and was working on one of the hinges. He coughed as smoke circled around him.

"Elton!" If this floor was on fire, Elton's rooms were directly above it. Remy reached for the landline phone on the bedside table. No dial tone. The phone was dead. Had someone cut the lines? In a last-ditch effort, Remy pulled her cellphone from the pocket of her jeans. If she could get even a smidgeon of a signal, hopefully Dean would answer Elton's extension when she rang it. Or Mrs. Flemming, who had to be around here somewhere.

Or Boggart. Surely the fire was visible to the rest of the manor's occupants.

The cellphone made no connection. "C'mon! C'mon!" Giving up on Elton's extension, Remy tried dialing 911, giving a squeal when she heard a ring. In seconds she was connected to an operator.

Remy recited the address of the emergency into the phone. "There's a fire. I'm locked in a bedroom in the south wing—"

"Hello?" The operator spoke over her. The signal broke up. "-llo?"

"Unbelievable!" Remy held the phone away from her ear. The call ended. Blast the signal! Remy scanned the bedroom. "Do you have your cell in here?" Remy didn't see one.

"No," Tate grunted. "I left it in the car." He'd managed to pry the top hinge off. He'd pulled his sweatshirt up over his nose and mouth as the room filled with smoke.

"I'll open a window." Remy hurried to the window.

Tate yelled after her.

"No! You'll feed the fire oxygen. Don't open the window!"

"But we *need* oxygen!" Remy argued.

"Just give me—" Tate coughed again.

Remy's eyes burned as the smoke grew thicker. She imitated Tate, pulling her shirt over her nose and mouth.

A few seconds later, Tate swore again. The door hung inward a bit at the top hinge where he'd been able to force it loose. But now he stood with his knife in hand, the blade having snapped. "Cheap piece of crap." He threw it across the room.

Their eyes met in mutual urgency.

Tate coughed again, squinting through the smoke. "How do you feel about climbing out a second-story window?"

He pushed past Remy and opened the window. Cold air rushed into the room, and Remy sucked in a breath mixed with smoke. It burned and chilled her throat at the same time. A roaring sound increased outside the bedroom door. Remy saw orange flames licking at the top of the door where it hung at a slant from its hinge.

"Tate!" she called, pointing.

Tate grabbed the sweatshirt at the end of his bed. "Put that on! You don't want bare arms. I don't know what we're going to have to climb over."

Remy made quick work of following his instruction. When finished she met him at the window. He was leaning out of it. Tate pulled back inside, his expression somber.

"There's a small gable about three yards down. If you lower yourself from the sill, you can pretty much drop onto it. From there we can make our way along the roof and maybe get into the house in another wing."

"If that wing isn't on fire, you mean," Remy half shouted as the flames crackled louder. Heat permeated the room, making her sweat.

"If it is, then we don't have a choice but to jump. But let's get out first."

"Get out just to go back in?" Remy muttered to herself. Yet it made sense. If the rest of the manor was still untouched by the fire, they could climb back in and hopefully call for help, then run outside without breaking a leg.

Remy hoisted herself onto the windowsill. She could feel the edges of the sill digging into her hips.

"Remy." Tate held on to her waist. "Turn around so you can lower yourself down."

Remy did as she was told, twisting her body.

"Be careful," said Tate. "Now, I'll help lower you as much as I can. Hold on to me, not the sill."

"How are you going to get out?"

"Just do it!" The urgency in Tate's voice prompted Remy not to argue. Tate gripped her wrists, and she gripped his. Lowering herself wasn't as easy as he'd made it sound. After struggling for a bit, finally Remy's feet collided with the gable roof, her knee slamming against the peak.

Rubbing her knee, Remy turned and looked up at the window

for Tate. He had disappeared into the room. "Tate!" Smoke billowed out the window now. "Tate!" she screamed again.

This time he returned to the window. He clutched something like a football, wrapped in cloth. Remy knew instantly it was the butterfly globe. Tate swung himself out the window, hung with one arm, and dropped the remaining distance to the gable roof. Steadying himself, he tipped his head toward the roofline. "Go!"

Remy edged along, nervous she'd lose her footing and catapult over the edge. The next set of windows was just ahead, but Remy could see the window glass was clouded with smoke. The fire must have reached that room.

"This whole wing is engulfed!" Tate shouted behind her. "Keep moving."

"What about Elton? And Dean?" Remy shot a panicked look at the attic level and the circular window in its peak.

"We can't help them until we get ourselves to safety," Tate yelled. "Maybe there's a trellis or a downspout we can grab on to. Keep going."

Remy maneuvered her way down the sloping roof to an overhang. She hoisted herself up onto the next gable, thankful the shingles didn't give beneath her frantic clawing. Once there, she noted there was a clear path to the wing where her room was located. "I left my window cracked open," she said, remembering.

"Head for it!" Tate shouted.

Remy didn't hesitate. Feeling surer on her feet, she ran along the rooftop, angling to the right and over another odd gable that made no sense, until she reached the line of windows on that wing. She spotted her room ahead and saw no smoke rising from the open window.

"I think we're good!" she cried over her shoulder.

On reaching the window, Remy pushed the screen inward until it broke free and fell to the floor. Seconds later, she and Tate were standing in her room with only the slightest hint of smoke in the air.

Tate shoved the globe into her arms. "Take this and get yourself out of the manor. Go down the stairs on the north side. Avoid the main entrance."

Remy nodded, clutching the globe to her chest like a baby.

Tate gripped her shoulders. "As soon as you're out, run to the groundskeeper's cottage and call 911. See if you can find Boggart or Mrs. Flemming. Hopefully both of them are outside."

"What are you going to do?" Remy grabbed at him as Tate readied to exit the room.

He touched her chin for a quick moment. "I'm going to look for Elton. There's no way he can survive the fire by himself."

"But Dean can—"

"Dean will need my help." Tate sprinted from the room, leaving Remy alone.

She held the globe close and wondered why she was protecting an ornament with a dead butterfly inside. Yet as she hurried to follow Tate's instructions, she knew what she was protecting was a piece of Tate, a part of the Arnold legacy. And it might be the only part left by the end of the day.

Sirens blared in the distance. Boggart stared at the manor as flames shot through the roof of the south wing and spread across the center of the building, smoke billowing from its windows. Mrs. Flemming had collapsed on an iron bench beneath a maple tree, rocking back and forth in a silent cry. Remy paced in front of the entrance, waiting. Tate had disappeared. Elton and Dean were nowhere to be seen.

With firefighters on their way, Remy made her decision and sprinted over to Boggart. "Hold this. Do *not* let it go!" She pushed the sweatshirt-wrapped butterfly globe into his knobby hands.

"Where are you—?" Boggart's words were cut off as Remy charged toward the manor's entrance. "Remy!" His shout bounced off her back.

"Remy!" Mrs. Flemming cried out.

Remy flew up the stairs to the large front door, opening it and falling back as smoke plunged through the doorway.

"Remy, come back!" Mrs. Flemming again.

Tate and Elton. They were all Remy could focus on now. She bullied her way into the smoke-filled entrance, squinting against the burning of her eyes as she raced toward the staircase. Remy coughed, sucking in air but only getting smoke. It burned her lungs, cutting off oxygen. She tried again, but it was like attempting to breathe something solid. It scorched her throat.

Tate.

Elton.

Remy grabbed for the banister, only to feel arms snake around her waist.

"Let's get you out of here."

It was a firefighter, decked out in his protective gear. The oxygen mask gave him the sound of Darth Vader in a blazing inferno. Remy fought against him, but she couldn't cry out. She couldn't breathe. She sagged backward as the man pulled her away from the thick smoke. Remy looked up the staircase, now engulfed in smoke, and saw flames licking at the books.

Müllerian Manor, including all its secrets, was going up in hellish flames.

Blackness invaded Remy's mind. She couldn't see any longer but could sense the firefighter lift her. She felt hot ash falling on her. Something collapsed in a monumental crash, and there were shouts.

Remy heard no more.

Her throat and chest hurt like the worst bout of bronchitis. Remy awoke in the hospital to the cadence of beeps from machines registering her oxygen, heart rate, and who knew what else? The room was remarkably bright, the sheets covering her crisp, and hanging on the wall was a small TV airing a cooking show, the volume on mute.

Remy moaned, trying to come to grips with where she was. A hand slid over hers.

"Shhh, Miss Crenshaw." It was Mrs. Flemming. Something about the older woman was endearing, familiar, even comforting. Remy grabbed at the housekeeper's hand.

"Elton?" she choked out.

Mrs. Flemming gave a delicate cough. "There, there. You must rest. No speaking. You inhaled a lot of smoke, young lady. You're lucky to be alive."

Remy knew then. Elton had not survived. "Tate?" she whispered hoarsely.

Mrs. Flemming averted her eyes and gave Remy's hand a firm pat. "I'll go get the doctor." The housekeeper hurried from the room.

Elton, Tate . . . If Mrs. Flemming's response was any clue—any horrible, awful clue—then they hadn't been saved. Probably Dean too. All of them perishing in a fire that made no sense, its origin so sudden, so unexpected. Was it because of the Butcher? Had Elton's silly ghost stories been proven to be real? Had the Butcher returned from the dead, not just for Aimee but for them all?

Remy turned her face to the side, letting the tears soak into her pillow. No family legacy or mystery or serial killer cold case was worth the lives it had stolen.

28

MARIAN

MARIAN SLIPPED on the polished hardwood as she ran across the foyer, her feet damp from the cold dew that had settled over the lawn. She lay sprawled on the floor of the manor. Pulling herself up, she grabbed hold of an umbrella stand for support and continued her panicked race to the butterfly room.

If Felix's mother was inside, if something had happened to her . . .

You won't be able to forgive yourself.

She tripped, hitting the wall with her shoulder. Violet breezed past her and through a doorway beyond. Marian's breaths came in quick gasps, and she debated for a brief moment whether to chase after Violet. But it wasn't Violet. It hadn't been her voice in the butterfly house.

Regaining her balance, Marian surged forward, passing the doorway Violet had disappeared through. She would come to terms with who or what Violet was later. But now? She knew each second that ticked by could mean life or death for Mrs. Dale. Marian plowed up the stairs, hitching her nightgown over knees as she ran. Her feet were bruised, but she didn't care.

Finally she reached her bedroom and burst inside. It was exactly as she'd left it. Bedclothes on the floor. Dead butterflies strewn across the sheets and the carpet. The message on the mirror. Mrs. Dale's scarf.

"Miss Arnold, are you all right?" Frederick whirled from his position across the room where he had obviously been searching for her. "I heard noises. I came to—" His voice broke as he took in her expression and the state of the bedroom. "What on earth has happened in here?"

"Frederick!" Marian motioned for him to follow her, and she launched herself toward the door that led into the room. The strange room. The room that served no purpose other than to house the table and her mother's butterfly globe. She yanked open the door, her breath catching in her chest as she prepared to see Mrs. Dale injured or perhaps already dead.

Frederick was quick to follow her, and Marian reached for his arm as she saw nothing, absolutely nothing out of the ordinary.

"Oh, thank God," Marian gasped, hanging on to Frederick for support. Mrs. Dale was all right. She had to be.

The older man patted her hand, but it was evident he was perplexed. "What has happened, Miss Arnold? I heard running, and I came to check on you. Your room, the butterflies . . ."

Marian glanced behind them at the open door to her bedroom. Then she eyed the glass dome that was sealed over the monarch butterfly. "Do you know why that is here? What is its significance?" She pointed to it, not answering Frederick's question.

He shook his head in bewilderment. "It was your mother's."

"Did she die here?" Marian jabbed her index finger toward the floor. She knew she was being harsh. Knew she was demanding of poor Frederick things he probably didn't know.

He paled a bit.

"Frederick, tell me. No more secrets, please!"

"Yes." He nodded, tears brimming in his eyes. "I found her. Your mother. She was . . . already gone. I think she was trying to save the butterfly."

"That one?" Marian pointed at the dome. "Why, Frederick? Why a brittle old butterfly that can do *nothing* for anyone!" Tears coursed down Marian's face. She feared the man from the butterfly house would arrive at any moment. And what could she do to protect Frederick, let alone herself?

Violet had been right.

She *was* going to die.

She had waited too long. Procrastinated and avoided the questions. Pretended that her father had told her the truth about her mother when all along she knew her mother was not like other mothers.

Frederick shook his head, a tear sliding down his wrinkled cheek. "Child, don't make me tell you."

"Is it that awful?" she breathed.

"No." Frederick shook his head and pushed back his white hair from his forehead. "It is that *sad*. That butterfly, to your mother it was . . ."

"It was what?" Marian insisted.

"It was your brother's second goodbye."

Marian froze, staring at Frederick in disbelief. Words were lost to her for a moment as she tried to understand what he'd just revealed.

"My brother? I don't have a brother!"

Frederick dipped his head and turned to face her, the sorrow in his eyes deep and raw. She could see that to Frederick, whatever had happened had been like yesterday to him.

"His second goodbye?" Marian frowned. "That means—"

"Your brother died shortly after his birth," Frederick said, and the truth ripped into Marian with a painful audacity. "Your mother claimed the monarch flew through the window as she held his infant body. She claimed it kissed her face with its wings before falling to her breast beside the babe."

Marian sucked in a grief-stricken sob. She covered her mouth with her hands as Frederick continued.

"She buried the boy in Milwaukee, but the butterfly she preserved. She mounted it, preserved it with some concoction to harden the wings, and sealed it under glass. That was when she started collecting the butterflies."

"Collecting them?" Marian whispered.

"Yes, saving the dead ones." Frederick swiped another tear from his face. "She stored them in boxes. Your brother's butterfly she kept under glass." He glanced at the dome on the table. "That is your brother"—Frederick rested his gaze on Marian—"at least that was what your mother believed. He was her first-born. Her son."

"I-I . . ." Marian fumbled for words.

Frederick walked slowly around the table, running his aged fingers along its edge while surveying the walls, the ceiling, the floor. "This was your brother's room. She had it built so that he would be near when you came. Her children. Together."

Marian shuddered. The idea that the butterfly was her brother —no. Yet she'd had a brother, and her brother—if Frederick was indeed telling the truth—was dead. Had been dead for years and years. But what was in this globe was just an insect, memorialized. Worshiped. Turned into something that solidified the fact that her mother would never release herself from grief.

"Your mother would sleep in here the nights you stayed," Frederick added.

"I never saw her come in here."

Frederick smiled. "You wouldn't have. Your room isn't the only way in." He went to a panel in the wall. He pressed against a knot in the wood, and the panel moved, sliding in and then over.

A dark void was behind it. A row of narrow, small steps.

Frederick turned to her, his eyes sad. "How else do you think I got here before you? From the glass house?"

His voice became frighteningly familiar.

"Your mother lost her mind, Marian. Her *mind*." A fervent resolve stretched across the older man's face. "She was hurting the ones around her. She was hurting *you*. And your father was being pressured to have her hospitalized—though he didn't want to do that. I'd heard the stories of those places. The torture . . ." Frederick ran his hand down the wall in a caress. "It was the right thing to do."

Marian's knees gave way, and she clutched at the table as she lost her footing. It toppled over, taking her with it. The domed glass tumbled after, and Frederick launched toward it, catching it in his hands. He tenderly set it down, eyeing the butterfly that had been frozen to its perch by a formula of the artist's craft. Assured it was in one piece, Frederick crouched beside Marian as she curled on the floor.

"You didn't know, child." Frederick's gnarled hands smoothed the tousled hair from her face. His gesture was gentle and meant to be reassuring. "You didn't know you'd be just like her. I saw signs of it when you were young, and so did your father. And the butterflies? There's healing to be found in them. One more chance to fly again, to be renewed."

Marian pulled away, cringing against Frederick's touch. No more was he the grandfatherly sort. He had known her since her childhood. He'd watched her grow up. He had kept a horrible secret along with her father and mother, and he'd watched it slowly overpower her mother's senses.

"You need to fly again, Marian." Frederick slipped a narrow cord from his coat pocket. "Let me free you, child. Free your mind and give you a new hope if even for a moment."

"I don't need you to free me of anything." Marian's protest was weak, and she heard the doubt in her own voice.

Movement behind Frederick made Marian lift her eyes. Through the hidden panel in the wall, she caught a glimpse of Violet. A dark look on an equally dark face.

Let it end. Violet mouthed the words with perfect lips. And then as Marian struggled to right herself, still reeling from shock, Violet dissipated into a shadow. Like a cloud of black smoke drifting away.

"This won't be difficult if you don't fight me." Frederick straddled Marian, his elderly frame remarkably wiry and strong.

Her mind struggled to make its way through the shock of what she'd learned. She bucked beneath Frederick, whimpering, trying to free herself from him. But she could see Violet in her mind's eye. Just end it. Let Frederick end it.

Lie still.

You should die.

A brother.

Her mother's hallowed butterfly.

Frederick.

He had killed her mother.

But why?

"Why Loretta?" Marian willed strength back into her limbs even as Frederick wrapped the cord around each of his hands.

"Loretta?" Frederick's matter-of-fact response frightened Marian. He met her confused look. "I've no idea why you think I would do anything to an innocent woman."

Marian resisted Frederick's attempts at pinning her down. He slammed her shoulder to the floor with the heel of his hand. The cord stretched between his hands, pressing against her throat.

"You k-killed Loretta." Marian whimpered, the cord cutting into her neck.

"I did no such thing." Frederick's eyes filled with hurt. "Why would you think that? This isn't about taking lives—it's about *saving* them. Saving your mother. Saving *you*!"

Marian struggled to comprehend. If this was about her mother, then what had happened to Loretta? Or Percy?

"And the milkman?" Marian coughed as the cord pressure against her throat increased.

Frederick leaned over her. "Percy did that to himself. The poor man was never the same after your father cut the majority of the staff here at the manor." Frederick clucked his tongue and shook his head. "When I realized Percy had returned and done that to himself, I left the butterflies for him in homage to his pain. He should never have done that to himself. He had so much to live for!"

"Then why *me*?" Marian choked. Her hands flew up to fight against Frederick's. She grasped his wrists as he pressed down, drawing the cord taut against her windpipe. She tried to raise her knees, her hips, anything to push the man off-balance.

Frederick grimaced, and a tear slipped free and landed on her cheek. "You have no idea what your mother suffered, but I saw it. And I see the devil in you, Marian. He will consume you. But I'm here to save you."

She dug her claws into Frederick's skin as he tightened the cord, cutting the air off to her lungs. Writhing beneath his weight, Marian instinctively fought for the ability to breathe.

But the ceiling of the butterfly room began to blur.

Her head lolled to the side, and as Marian's eyes lost their focus, she watched her brother's butterfly slowly fade to black.

29

REMY

THE POLICE ASKED HER a slew of questions, but the hard fact remained: Müllerian Manor sat there smoldering, a burnt-out shell of what it once was. Remy was unable to give the police—Detective Ambrose specifically—much at all to assist in the investigation. Initial findings had determined the fire to be the result of arson. Evidence of accelerants had been found. The water to the main pipes turned off. Landline cut.

Who had started the fire? Was it in any way tied to Aimee's death?

Ambrose seemed to hope that Remy would provide the answers to such questions, but she couldn't. Now she rode in the passenger side of Ambrose's unmarked car, staring out the window as the trees lining the road whizzed by. Orange. Yellow. Green. Brown. Autumn had lost its appeal for Remy. She no longer cared about cozy sweaters and coffee-inspired afternoons.

Instead, she saw flames. She saw smoke. She saw Tate running to Elton's rescue.

Tears trailed down Remy's face as the blackened husk of the manor came into view. The north wing still stood, the wing that included Remy's room—or rather Verdine Arnold's room, the room Aimee had died in, and Marian Arnold's bedroom. The rest of the manor had collapsed. The roof had fallen in, the frame was charred, and the bricks and stone were black and crumbling.

Ambrose cast a sideways glance at Remy. She could guess what Ambrose was thinking. She was concerned that Remy wouldn't cope well with returning to the manor. She'd expressed as much at the hospital just before being released.

"Are you all right?" Ambrose ventured, turning the car into the driveway.

Remy didn't know how to respond. This place, this evil place, had stolen from so many. Lives taken in the past and in the present. "I c-can't believe it" was all she could think to say, the words coming out as a raspy whisper.

The car pulled to a stop, and Ambrose shifted it into park. "We don't have to get out right away. There's no rush. Let's just sit here for a while."

Remy appreciated the detective's sensitivity. It wasn't long ago that she'd felt a bit jealous of the detective and the vibe between Ambrose and Tate. Now? Ambrose was her only friend left—if she could call the detective that. Unless she counted Mrs. Flemming, who was as cuddly as a weasel, and Boggart, who had no compulsions toward friendship whatsoever.

"Did they . . . ?" Remy swallowed, her throat still hurting from smoke inhalation. Flashes of memories flickered behind her eyes. A different fire. A body in a chair. That leering smile. She squeezed her eyes shut against the unwelcome images. Elton. Tate. Dean.

Ambrose remained silent behind the wheel, her eyes focused straight ahead, somewhere beyond the windshield.

Remy turned to her. "Do you know, have they found—?" But she couldn't finish asking it. Couldn't voice the question because by doing so, it made what had happened final, a horrible reality.

Ambrose shook her head and looked to the ruins. "We haven't found any evidence of bodies yet. There's a lot of debris to sort through. Three floors of stone and brick and beams and—"

"So they could still be alive." Remy cut off Ambrose's explanation.

Ambrose's brows came together, and she released a deep sigh. "We had our best team out here. There are ways to find people in ruins like this, from using dogs to high-tech equipment, and no matter the disaster—fires, earthquakes, hurricanes—I'm sorry, Remy, but they found no signs of life."

"They might have gotten away." Remy was desperate, and she knew she sounded like it. But she'd lost her mother in a fire. Her mother's boyfriend too, someone she didn't care much for but who was a human being all the same. Now? All these years later? A repeat? "They might have gotten away," she parroted herself.

Ambrose's expression hardly encouraged Remy to engage the theory further. "If they had, then they would have gotten help, don't you think? Elton couldn't have wandered far in his condition."

"I don't need you to argue that they're dead." Remy held up her hand. "Just let me hope, please. For a little while longer, let me hope." She locked gazes with Ambrose.

The detective's eyes softened, and she dipped her head. "Okay, Remy." The agreement was laced with a tone that implied she'd allow Remy a short period of delusion that the men had somehow made it out alive and were just unaccounted for.

Remy pulled the handle on the door and stepped from the car. The smell of burned timbers flooded her senses, hurting her throat and lungs. She covered her mouth. Had Müllerian Manor stood just yesterday, magnificent and ominous? Had it been only yesterday that she'd asked Tate about his ancestors? That she'd taken photos of his . . .

Remy stiffened, reaching into her pocket for her phone. She punched in her passcode, tapped the gallery app, and pulled up the photos of Tate's prescription bottles.

"What is it?" Ambrose rounded the car.

Remy looked up. "I took some pictures yesterday." She hesitated, not wanting to betray Tate. But what did it matter now? "Do you know what these medications are for?"

Remy turned her phone so that Ambrose could read the prescription labels. "They're for people with schizoaffective disorder." Ambrose tilted her head. "Where'd you take these pictures?"

Remy ignored the detective's question. "Is that schizophrenia?"

Ambrose's green eyes grew sharp, and she studied Remy for a moment. "It's a form of it. It shares some of the symptoms plus depression, maybe bipolar. I'm no expert. Whose prescriptions are they? I didn't see the name on the labels."

Remy bit her lip. That explained the night at the hotel. Tate had been experiencing an episode. Remy closed her eyes, trying to remember back to her earlier days when living with Lucas, her foster brother. Had that been his diagnosis too? She wasn't sure she ever knew or had been told.

"Remy?" Ambrose touched her arm.

Remy snapped out of her musing. She stuffed her phone back into her pocket. "Never mind."

"No, no. You don't show me that and then tell me *never mind*."

Remy squelched a sigh and leveled a frank stare at the detective. "I don't want you to draw the wrong conclusions about someone."

To Ambrose's credit, her expression grew sensitive, and she nodded. "I get that. And I won't. There are a lot of unfair stigmas attached to individuals who have that disorder. There are lots of variations and symptoms."

"The prescriptions were Tate's." Remy's admission relieved her at the same time she felt as though she'd wounded him by revealing his secret.

Ambrose pondered for a moment before responding. "You don't think he—"

"See?" Remy reared back, glaring at Ambrose. "That is why I didn't want to say anything. You're going to blame him for the fire."

"No." Ambrose lifted her palms toward Remy. "Not even close. I was going to ask if you thought he'd come here *because* of his condition."

"What do you mean?" Remy frowned.

"Well, if you were digging into his family history, what with all the weird stuff that's happened here over the decades"— Ambrose shrugged—"I just wondered if maybe he wanted some influence over the narrative of his family."

Remy eyed her. Ambrose was intuitive. "That's exactly what he came here for."

Ambrose nodded. "Listen, let me be straight with you." Remy crossed her arms over her chest, eyeing Ambrose. The petite detective smoothed back her blond hair and gave Remy a grave look. "I did some research on everyone here at the manor. After the nurse's death, it's standard protocol."

"You found out I was in foster care, didn't you?" Remy offered the info in resignation. She'd probably jumped to the top of Ambrose's list. Troubled past often meant negative behavior.

"Yes," Ambrose admitted. "And I applaud you. You've obviously worked really hard to get to where you are. I can't imagine that was easy."

Dang it if she didn't sort of like Ambrose now.

"Anyway, I looked into Tate's history. You know he was in the military?"

"The Marines. Yes. He told me so himself."

"He was discharged, Remy. For mental-health reasons. He couldn't stay in the military with his condition."

Tate hadn't told her that part. That must be the thing that haunted him. She saw it now. Nothing could be worse for a military man than to receive a diagnosis that ripped him from his purpose.

Remy's heart broke for him. Tate had battled for his nation and then battled for his mental health.

"I'm going to guess," Ambrose concluded, "that Tate thought his condition to be hereditary."

Remy stilled. She stared at Ambrose. "You mean . . ."

Ambrose shrugged again. "I'm only theorizing. I have no evidence. But what if Tate was here to keep this from getting discovered. That his family has a history of mental-health conditions, and that—"

"Marian Arnold was—"

Neither woman finished her sentence. They merely stared at each other. Though the issue of mental health was far more understood today, it still had far yet to go. Schizophrenia and its counterparts were often branded into roles where people assumed violence, or assumed they were wildly creative like Van Gogh, or that they were unhygienic reprobates who wandered the streets and weren't capable of living quality lives with successful careers and meaningful relationships.

Remy turned toward the manor's shell. "If this is true, then what from the Arnold history is real and what has been fabricated?"

Ambrose followed suit, and both women stared at the remains of a century's worth of cursed pain.

"I believe," Ambrose said, "Tate Arnold was here to ask those very questions."

Remy curled in the bed, wrapping the blankets around her body like a burrito. Willing sleep to come while wishing it away at the same time. All she could see when she closed her eyes was the fire. It taunted her, blazed through her subconscious as a wicked nightmare. Now she was here, in a hotel room, unable to sleep and unable to return to the Twin Cities or resume normal life.

The arson case was open, the investigation into the fire ongoing. Aimee's murder investigation was open as well. It would be days before the mounds of the manor ruins were cleared and sifted through as they searched for human remains. While a part of Remy held on to hope that maybe the men had somehow escaped the fire and just hadn't surfaced yet, she knew logically that wasn't the case. Elton Floyd, revered biographer, had been unable to make it out of the manor alive. Tate, the ex-Marine, had showed his bravery by leaving no man behind. And Dean had proven himself a faithful caregiver until the very end.

It had been three days since the fire. Three days. If they were alive by some miraculous twist of fate, they or someone with them would have contacted her by now.

Remy opened her eyes and stared at the hotel wall. There was no point in trying to piece together the story of Marian Arnold and the Butterfly Butcher. Not now. Not with Elton gone. She'd cried more tears in the last forty-eight hours than she had since she was a child. Of all the various emotions she'd had to work through, grief due to loss was not one of them. She'd never been close enough to anyone to feel loss. Not like this. She'd grown exceptionally fond of Elton, and she'd felt herself drawn to Tate, inexplicably so. Somehow it seemed as if all that had happened in the last month was orchestrated to bring each one of them to Müllerian Manor. An odd assortment of people bound together because of one person. Marian Arnold.

But the fire had stolen that from Remy. It had turned to ash what little hope she'd been welcoming into her heart.

"What's the point?" she whispered to the wall. To God. Life was stricken by legacies of broken families. Of families with dark secrets. Of families struggling with mental illness or other troubles. Were there none that left hope and a strong foundation? Was every family tree rotting from the inside until a powerful enough wind arrived to blow it over, roots and all?

Her own family tree was empty, branchless, like a dead trunk that stuck from the ground like an oversized toothpick. Remy didn't know or remember the names of her family. Her mother, a face without a name anymore. Oh, she had it somewhere, but Remy had made it a point early on to dissociate from her mother. From her mother's boyfriends—any of which could have been her father. Her grandparents should be on the tree, but their refusal to take part in raising Remy had given her due cause to erase them as well. And there was no one else . . .

Remy swallowed.

No one else.

The fire. The Dowell Street apartment complex fire. She'd been so little, yet flashes returned to her. Remy buried her face in her pillow, willing them away. She had experienced two tragic fires in her lifetime. How coincidental was that? Or maybe it wasn't. The bones in her car. The butterflies. The doll on the bed. Now the manor fire. The fire linked her present to her past. Was *she* linked to the manor?

Remy bolted upright in bed as she heard the mocking laughter from her memories. She fumbled for the switch to turn on the bed lamp. The room was empty, but she could still hear it. The laughing. Remy pulled the covers to her chin and stared at the blank television screen on the wall. In its reflection, a memory began to form. A memory that coincided with the laughter that rang in Remy's subconscious.

She could see the memory taking shape. The chair with her mother. The fire blazing out of control. It licked the bottom of the curtains until they erupted into mesmerizing and terrifying orange flames.

She was crying.

Mama! Mama!

Remy could hear her young self wailing. She reached for her mother, but her mother didn't respond. She had passed out long before the fire had started. Remy remembered that now. She'd eaten stale popcorn for supper.

Another laugh haunted her, and Remy watched the TV as though her memories continued to play on its screen.

He was there. The smiler. The one with the grin that stretched wide enough to show his teeth. He was the one laughing. He was by the door, preparing to open it. Remy turned toward him—he would help her. He had to help her. But he ignored the flames, the smoke that encircled them. He ignored the sparks that popped from the walls that were blackening under the fire's tongue. He crouched.

"Remy, come here." He crooked his fingers.

She had stumbled forward, her arms stretching out for him to pick her up and carry her to safety. But he didn't. Instead, he smiled again.

"You stay here."

It was an instruction. Remy had been taught through slaps and hard words to obey. Now she whimpered, protesting against the logic of the command that even at four, she could figure out made no sense.

The smoke wafted between them.

His face grew blurry as her eyes watered.

"You stay, Remy. You know what's coming if you don't." And then he had left. Opened the apartment door and left her behind.

Remy snapped back to the present and scrambled from the bed. Her feet tangled with the blankets, and she fell to the floor. Shoving off the carpet, she stumbled into the bathroom, grabbed the glass by the sink, and ripped off its paper top. She filled it with water and, without pausing, splashed it in her face.

You stay, Remy.

She heard the words again with such terrifying clarity. She wasn't supposed to have survived! He had started the fire—purposefully.

Remy snatched a towel and wiped her face, catching the drips of water as they trailed down her neck. She strained to remember who the man was. He wasn't old. He couldn't have been more than a teenager himself. His face was just out of reach of her memory. Only his smile. His teeth.

She hurried back into the room and picked up her phone. Ignoring the late hour, she dialed Detective Ambrose's number. The detective answered on the third ring.

"Remy?"

"What else did you find out about me when you did a background check?" Remy didn't even bother to say hello. She sat on the corner of the hotel bed, staring at her reflection in the mirror attached to the wall.

"Umm . . ." Ambrose's groggy response told Remy she needed to be patient and give the detective a chance to wake up.

"My foster families? Do you have records of them?"

"Uh, yeah," Ambrose affirmed. "Yeah, all of them."

"And my grandparents' names?"

"Sure. Of course." Ambrose cleared sleep from her voice with a cough. "Don't you have those?"

Remy studied herself in the mirror. Her straight, shoulder-length hair. The pink streaks that she'd given herself to form some sort of identity that was her own. Her brown eyes. She was average. She didn't look like anyone she knew. She had been careful to emotionally carve herself into a person without connections because that was simply easier to control. Just her. No family. No names. No history.

"My mother's information—you have that too," Remy assumed aloud.

Ambrose sounded more aware. "I have that, yes. Your birth father was listed as unknown. There are records of siblings and—"

"Siblings?" Remy interrupted sharply. "What siblings?"

Ambrose was quiet for a second. "Remy, you had a sister who

was sixteen when you were born. She passed away a few years ago from cancer."

"I don't remember her. I don't know if I ever knew her."

"Okay." Ambrose's tone gentled. "And you had a half brother."

Numbness washed over Remy. "And what happened to him?"

"You don't remember?"

"What happened to him?" Remy demanded.

Ambrose sighed into the phone. "Well, there was a fire—"

"I know about the fire," Remy snapped.

"Right. And your mother and your mother's boyfriend were both killed. You and your brother made it out okay."

"How old was my brother at the time?" The smile. The teeth. The face. It was all beginning to piece together in Remy's mind.

"He was fourteen. You were both put into the system and separated," Ambrose answered, apology in her voice.

"What was his name?" Remy demanded.

"Jacob. Jacob Thompson."

Remy didn't recognize the name. She didn't remember anything except the fire, the teenage boy's grin, and the command that she obey or else.

"I didn't obey," she breathed into the phone.

"What?" Ambrose sounded confused.

"I didn't obey." Remy stared into her own eyes, the mirror showing her what she needed to know. That at four years old, Remy had determined to take her life into her own hands and become something. Her own someone. Without the rest of them. "He tried to kill me, but I didn't obey."

30

MARIAN

OCTOBER 1921

S HE WAS FREE. Suddenly she was free. The weight was lifted from her chest. Her throat opened, and she gasped, sucking in air with a hoarse cry.

A guttural groan sounded, and something banged into the wall. Marian sucked in another breath, her throat throbbing from being constricted. Awareness began to flood her, and she opened her eyes, rolling onto her side, gagging. Saliva ran down her chin, and she coughed, choking on the blessed relief of sweet air rushing into her lungs.

Another collision and then a grunt.

Marian pushed herself up as Frederick stumbled past her, his aged body hunched as he made for the secret passage in the butterfly room's wall.

From just out of view, Marian heard a shout, and then a crutch was shoved between Frederick's legs, tripping him. The butler collapsed, rolling into the paneled wall. He reached into the passage, grasped the first stair, and tried to pull himself up.

Felix struggled toward him, his crutch supporting him as he hobbled after Frederick. The fury on his face was nothing Marian had ever seen. He dove for Frederick, flinging his crutch aside as he landed on the man. The impact caused Frederick to fall back into the room. His elbow bumped the secret panel, which slid back in place.

"Felix!" Marian screamed as his fist connected with Frederick's face. Something about seeing it jolted her into action. "You're going to kill him!" she cried while dragging herself across the floor toward the two battling men.

Frederick had already capitulated. His aged body gave in to the younger man. He held up his arms to protect his face, but Felix resorted to kneeing the man in the side. Frederick groaned in pain, gasping for air.

Marian reached out and grabbed hold of Felix's arm. "Stop it, Felix! I'm all right. You don't want to kill him."

"I *do* want to kill him!" Felix snapped. Fury was mixed with a need for justice, and Marian could read the resolve in his eyes.

Marian hugged Felix's arm as he tried to tug it free. "He's wicked, yes, but you can't . . . Felix, I need you!"

Felix ceased his struggling against her.

Frederick groaned again and pulled his knees up to his chest.

"This has to end," Marian heard herself say. Her throat was raw and tight, her words just above a whisper now. "But not that way."

Felix pushed off from the older man, shoving himself backward, his good leg bent at the knee to give him stability.

Frederick moved back toward them, all motivation gone from his eyes. What remained was a sad old man. Tears stained his cheeks as he cast a desperate plea toward Marian. "You're not well, Miss Arnold."

"Shut up!" Felix growled.

Frederick didn't seem to notice. "I know you hear the voices—"

"What voices?" Felix interrupted.

Marian stilled, staring at Frederick. Had he entered her mind? For somehow he knew.

"And you see shadows. Things that don't exist." Frederick locked eyes with her.

"What *voices*?" Felix repeated his question.

Frederick ignored him and continued, "You talk to people who aren't there."

Marian instantly pictured Violet. She shook her head emphatically. "No. She is real. Violet is real."

"Who is Violet?" Felix looked between them, confusion written across his face.

"Yes, Miss Arnold," Frederick echoed, "*who* is Violet?"

Marian looked desperately between her would-be killer and the childhood friend who had saved her life. "You know her. She tends the butterfly house. *Violet*."

And then Marian knew.

The look in Felix's eyes.

The expression on Frederick's face.

"Violet is real," Marian insisted in a whisper. "The voices are . . . they're people who have passed away. I see their spirits. I-I'm not making this up."

"I know." Frederick pulled himself closer to her. "It's all right." He shot a glare toward Felix. "I'm merely telling her what she needs to know."

"What do I need to know?" Marian asked, but she wished she hadn't. She didn't want to know.

Frederick's expression was one of pity. "You're not a spiritualist, Marian. You don't commune with the dead. You commune with the nonexistent. These voices, these visions, they do not exist."

"That's not true." Marian shook her head.

"Explain yourself." Felix glowered at Frederick, the resonance in his deep voice commanding the old man's compliance.

"You've seen it, haven't you, Felix? Her delusions. She believes there are butterflies. In the butterfly house. At this time of year, in this climate? All the plants are dead. There's nothing in there. There have never been more than a few butterflies that Marian's mother coaxed to life from cocoons, and her plants died when she did. No one tended them for over a year! The only butterflies left in the manor are in the boxes Verdine stashed away. The dead ones she preserved."

"That's not true!" Marian said vehemently. She turned to Felix, pleading, "Tell him that's not true. There are butterflies everywhere in the glass house. And the plants are . . ." Her words trailed off when she caught the broken expression on Felix's face.

"She's like her mother," Frederick went on. "And no one took care of them. This misery they suffer from—"

"I don't *suffer*!" Marian cried.

"But you *will*! Once your cousin Ivo discovers your condition, he'll have you institutionalized. They will experiment on your brain there. Torture you with electricity. Cut open your head to *fix* you. I spared your mother that—I wanted to spare you that."

"Father never would have sent Mother to a place like that!" Marian protested.

Frederick *tsk*ed. "He may have ended up with no choice. She was becoming worse. More delusional. As you will. And Ivo will be forced to take the same action in order to get you care."

"Ivo is in jail. He wouldn't do that to me." Marian's argument was weak, she knew. Ivo might be behind bars for Loretta's death, but that would not be for long once Frederick, the real perpetrator, was taken into custody.

Frederick's face fell in defeat. He turned to Felix and issued a mournful plea. "Please, Felix, don't let Marian suffer. End it now."

Felix leaned over Frederick, raised himself onto his knee, and glared down at the man. "The only one who needs to end is you, you butcher."

"I'm *not* a butcher," Frederick seethed. "I'm a savior. I protect them."

"No, you kill them," Felix snarled. "You claim their deaths with butterflies, and you memorialize them in your mind like some putrid act of grace. You're far more deluded than Marian and her mother. You've made yourself out to be God. But you're not God. You're a pathetic little man who can't see precious life for what it is. Protect it, yes. Cherish it, yes. But never—*never*—devalue a person's life as expendable!"

REMY

OCTOBER, PRESENT DAY

Her brother. Jacob Thompson. The name repeated itself over and over in Remy's mind as she drove back toward Coldwater Valley.

She had requested to stay outside the area, even though Ambrose didn't want her to stray too far in the event they needed her for the case. But Remy needed the distance. Now she returned, her plan to meet Ambrose at the station. There were connections to discuss. The Butterfly Butcher from the past appeared to have risen from the dead the last few weeks, but the fire had stolen the attention from him.

Remy saw the coffee shack on the corner and steered her car toward its drive-through. She waited as the vehicle in front of her was served. A few moments later, it was her turn and so she pulled up to the window.

"Remy." Abigail gave her a sympathetic and understanding smile. "How can I help?"

That was sweet. *How can I help?* Remy had found most people she'd run into, even strangers, had been saying "I'm so sorry" or "Are you okay?" But Abigail's question opened up a safe space Remy hadn't felt since the fire.

She blinked back tears and waved her hand in front of her eyes. "Sorry."

"Don't be sorry!" Abigail leaned forward, resting her arms on the windowsill. "It's been awful—I can't imagine! Do you want a triple today? It's on me."

"Quad?" Remy would regret it later if she got the shakes, but right now she wanted the caffeine.

"Quad it is. Almond milk? A shot of syrup?"

"Make it a full-on latte, no syrup, and yes to the almond milk." Remy leaned back against the headrest while Abigail set to work.

The espresso machine hissed, and the milk steamed. Soon Abigail was mixing the milk and espresso together. "Do you have a place to stay?" she asked through the window.

Remy nodded. "A hotel." She didn't add that she didn't know how long she'd be staying there. That when Ambrose said it was okay to leave, she'd probably return to the Twin Cities. What she would do then, she didn't know. She had no ties, and what had never bothered Remy before now pained her more than she wanted to admit.

"Oh." Abigail scrunched her face as she handed Remy her latte. "Hotels are awful. I have an extra room. You can stay with me."

Remy preferred her privacy. "I'm good. But thank you. That means a lot."

Abigail checked to see if anyone was waiting in line. No one there. She turned back to Remy. "And they haven't found . . ."

Remy shook her head and busied herself taking a sip of the brew.

"Gosh." Abigail sighed and looked to the sky. "Sometimes I wonder what God is thinking."

"Yeah," Remy laughed wryly.

"I mean it!" Abigail's eyes widened. "Heck, I was raised a

good Midwestern girl with values—church every Sunday, youth group every Wednesday—and I tell you it doesn't matter how much faith you have in God, when stuff like this happens, it shakes even the strongest. It's like, if God is so powerful and so big, then why does this stuff happen?"

Remy stared at Abigail. "I don't think you're supposed to say that out loud."

Abigail chuckled. "I figure if God already knows my thoughts, He knows what I'm going to say. Besides, I don't have anything super amazing to give you as an answer. I know people try to make you feel better, but the fact is, life just . . . *is*."

"You think God doesn't care?" Remy challenged.

"Oh no," Abigail said. "I think He *does* care. I think nothing is out of His control. I think this life is all a part of moving forward and that God has bigger plans we just don't understand at the moment."

"So blind faith then?" Remy didn't mean to sound cynical, but it came out that way nonetheless.

Abigail's smile was patient. "Not blind. No. Just belief. Belief in the evidence God has given us of His existence. Belief in the personal experiences I've already had—the blessings. Belief that, in the end, He will make all things good."

"That hasn't been my experience," Remy admitted before she could stop herself.

Abigail lifted her own coffee cup and took a sip. "You're here, aren't you?"

"What do you mean?"

"You're alive, Remy Crenshaw. And from what I can tell by looking into your eyes, life has bruised you, but it hasn't left you broken. That's God. Without Him, you'd be far worse off."

"You really believe that?"

"With all my heart, Remy." Abigail smiled, then pushed off the window, her eyes brightening. "Hey! You want to hear the weirdest thing?"

"Sure." Remy was still thinking about what Abigail had said.

"Remember when we first met, I asked you about Jack?"

Remy frowned. "Mr. Floyd's research assistant before me?"

"Yeah, him. So anyway, he showed up here this morning!"

"That's nice." Remy wasn't sure what the grinning barista expected her to say. If this Jack had returned in hopes of being Elton's research assistant again, he was in for a disappointment on multiple levels.

Abigail chuckled. "Funny thing. He grew a beard with a mustache." Remy readied to take her leave, but Abigail continued to chatter. "Have you ever seen those . . . oh, what are they called, the type of mustache the cowboys and bandits used to have back in the Wild West?"

"Handlebar mustache?" Remy offered.

"That's it. Jack had a handlebar mustache. I might have ruined my chances with him when I laughed. I laughed *at* him—I couldn't help myself, it was funny."

Remy shifted her car into drive. She was starting to say goodbye when something in her mind clicked. "Wait. Jack was here this morning?"

"Mm-hmm." Abigail nodded.

"And he's grown a handlebar mustache?"

Abigail's eyes shadowed. "Yeah. Is something wrong?"

Remy calculated the odds in her head. Dean had a beard—and a handlebar mustache. Was it possible that Jack and Dean the new nurse were one and the same? But when Dean arrived, Mrs. Flemming or Elton would have for sure recognized him. She was stretching now, stretching for hope that should have long been set aside. Still. She had to ask.

"You say you saw Jack just this morning?" Remy ventured.

"That's right," Abigail confirmed.

"This morning," Remy mused. "Did he mention anything about the manor fire?"

Abigail shrugged. "He seemed sad. I mean, he'd worked for Elton. So he was like 'that's tough' and all."

"Did he say why he came back to town?" Remy pressed.

"No. But I was surprised to see him. I thought he had moved on for good." Abigail tilted her head. "Why? What's wrong?"

"It's just . . . this Jack sounds a little bit like Dean, the nurse who was in the fire."

"Oh." Abigail paled. "Well, that'd be weird. Elton would recognize him as Jack. That wouldn't make any sense."

"I know," said Remy. "It doesn't, but, I just—"

"You know what was strange?" Abigail lifted her eyes in thought and rolled her lips together. "One of the dates we went on a while back, Jack made a comment about Elton, that he could get Elton to do anything he asked. That Elton trusted him and never questioned him like other folks did. I thought that was weird. Like Jack was implying he had some control over Elton. Which begs the question, if he had it so good, why'd he leave in the first place?"

It was a good question, but then Jack wasn't Dean, and Dean wasn't Jack. Unless he was. Remy made herself reconcile to reality. No. Dean was dead . . . unless he wasn't. Adrenaline surged through Remy. If Dean and Jack were one and the same person, that meant Dean had survived the fire. How he had survived was beside the point. "Did he pay cash or credit?" Remy demanded.

Abigail was taken aback by Remy's urgency. "I-I . . ."

"*Cash* or credit?"

"Cash."

"Did he say where he was going?"

"No. He drove off toward the east side of town. I know Jack enjoyed spending time at a cabin over there along the creek."

"Who owns the cabin?"

Abigail sucked in a breath, unrest written across her face. "I don't know. I think it's a rental situation. He needed to get away from the manor from time to time for a little R and R."

"Thanks, Abigail," Remy said. "Thanks for everything."

"Yeah. Sure." Abigail's worried expression trailed after Remy as she squealed away from the coffee shack.

31

MARIAN

OCTOBER 1921

IVO SWEPT INTO THE MANOR, freed after the police had arrested Frederick. "I'd say you're a sight for sore eyes, but we need to talk!"

Marian hadn't left her chair since early that morning, not since the police had hauled Frederick away. He continued to claim Percy Hahn had taken his own life, and they were prone to believe him, but Detective Fletcher stated he was certain Frederick had lied about Loretta's murder. The butterflies and bones were obvious signs of Frederick's work.

She'd never been so relieved to see Mrs. Dale serving tea. She had been safely ensconced in Dale Cottage as the events had unfolded, and her scarf had merely been used to draw Marian out. Felix was helping his mother now that the manor was down to just the two of them to keep it running, although Marian hadn't the slightest care about that now. Felix had hardly looked at her since the police had left with Frederick.

Mrs. Dale had busied herself making breakfast. "We all need a bit of food to perk us up," she'd said. That Felix had followed her and not remained behind with Marian frightened her.

All the accusations Frederick had leveled on her. The depths of Marian's soul felt them. Understood them. Hated them. Feared them. Now Felix was avoiding her like some pariah that she wasn't. She really wasn't!

The clearing of a throat tugged Marian's attention back to the present. Ivo eyed Marian with a frustration she'd not expected. His handsome face was covered in a short beard. He'd not shaved while in jail, that was evident, as were the dark circles under his eyes.

"You didn't call my lawyer!" Ivo slouched on the arm of a stuffed chair opposite the one Marian was curled in. "I thought you'd at least do that."

No. She hadn't. So much had happened since Loretta's death. It hardly seemed merciful to tell Ivo that calling his lawyer had slipped her mind. Marian didn't know how to respond, so she remained silent.

"Instead, I get hauled down to the clubhouse, and then they throw me behind bars with some sap who can't hold his liquor!" He raked his hand through his hair that was loose over his forehead, no longer slicked back with pomade. "You let them think I'd do something to Loretta."

"I'm sorry." Marian's weak voice was only because she was trying to hold back tears. She waited for Ivo to ask how she was doing. Frederick was gone. It was just her now, and Mrs. Dale and Felix. But Ivo had been wronged—at least in his eyes. He'd had time to dwell and muse on it, and he was not happy.

"Do you know they wanted to throw the book at me for the hooch too?"

Marian wasn't surprised. Ivo and most of his friends had been tipsy from their drinking and carousing. In retrospect, she regretted not putting an end to it the moment she'd witnessed Ivo pouring the first glass.

"They let me get on the horn, and I called my lawyer for my-self." Ivo shot her a sour look. He played with the rolled-up cuff of his shirtsleeve. "Helps to have friends in high places, if you know what I mean."

She didn't. Not at all.

Marian wished Felix would return. Even Mrs. Dale. It was all so overwhelming. Her insides shook from Frederick's betrayal, and her throat hurt from his efforts to, what had he said, put her out of her misery? As if she were an injured animal.

She felt sick to her stomach. Is that what she was? Injured? Beyond help? Were the things she heard and saw so extreme and awful that she was worth nothing, deserving of death?

"Yes, I know." Ivo was still yammering, his chest heaving with offense. "Don't think I haven't spent days behind bars thinking of Loretta. But I need to move on now. I need a distraction, Marian. I can't live in Loretta's memory."

Marian could understand that, she supposed. Distractions provided relief and were sometimes needed in times of trial.

Ivo slid off the arm of the chair onto its seat, his right leg hanging over the arm and his left braced against the floor. He crossed his arms and eyed her. "Loretta—" he gave a small snort—"heck, she was pretty swell, you know? But with your father gone, well, it left me in a bit of a bind."

Her father? Marian had no idea what he meant.

Ivo studied her for a moment, then smiled. "You have no idea, do you?" He rolled his eyes. "Of course you don't." He sprang from the chair, restless, and marched to the expansive window that overlooked the front lawn. He pushed his hands into his trouser pockets. "You know, it was your father who matched Loretta and me."

Dread settled on Marian's shoulders. It wasn't over. Freder-ick was gone, yet there remained an awful pall over Müllerian Manor. Like a poison that couldn't be eradicated no matter how desperately one tried.

Ivo continued, "Habington Brewery and Loretta's father were a bit of mud *your* father just couldn't clean off. This war against our industry—thanks to the Woman's Christian Temperance Union—has everyone trying to stay afloat. Those dames didn't think of that, did they, when they got on their high horses? They put all the common folk out of work when they shut down the breweries, as if we had the means to make soda or cheese!"

Marian shifted in her chair. Ivo shot her a crooked grin that felt patronizing. An invisible pat on her head that it was too bad she was so naive to everything that had taken place.

"Your father wanted to keep you out of it—especially after what went on with your mother. The last thing Arnold Brewery needed was scandal. Lotta good that did," Ivo scoffed.

"What do you mean?" She thought they'd been talking about Loretta's family brewery, Habington Brewery. What did that have to do with the Arnold Brewery? Marian curled up in the chair and hugged her knees. She was beginning to shiver. She wished Ivo would just leave. And yet his mention of her mother was enough to prompt her question.

Ivo's look of disbelief shamed her. "You really don't know, do you?" He returned to his chair, leaning forward, elbows on his knees. "Your father slipped Habington money under the table to keep Habington Brewery afloat. When he demanded it back, Habington was already on his way to bankruptcy and had to do something to get the heat off him. They knew your mother was unstable, mentally and emotionally. Everyone knew as much." He leveled a frank gaze on her. "That's right. Everyone knows, Marian."

Knows? His use of the present tense pierced her soul. She shrank back into her chair.

Ivo pressed on with an intensity that made Marian wonder if he thought he was helping her—acting out of some righteous, misplaced responsibility. "Loretta's family resorted to leaking information to the gossip rags about your mother's strange behavior—blackmail against your father. What had been a friendly loan he tried to collect payment on turned into Habington threatening to out your mother's mental instability to the press." Ivo leaned back and crossed his leg over his knee. "A lot of us thought your father should've done something far sooner—before Habington got it in his craw to out your family's private matters."

"Done what?" Marian pushed the word from her throat.

Ivo smiled patiently. "Make an effort to save the Arnold Brewery so he didn't go belly-up like Habington was about to. Your father got me involved, smart man that he was. I offered to hitch up with Loretta and form an alliance. Merge our families and merge the breweries against the government's amendment and the pearl-clutchers. It would silence Habington because he wouldn't want to ruin his daughter's reputation with the accusations against your mother. And you weren't going to be of any help. We all knew about you."

"Me?" Marian echoed.

Ivo gave her a pitying look. "Aw, c'mon, Marian. You know I think you're the bee's knees, but you got your mother's . . ." He paused to twirl his finger toward his head. "You really think you can live a normal life?"

All hope drained from Marian, along with her last ounce of confidence.

Ivo continued, oblivious to the hurt he was showering on her. "So I cozied up to Loretta." His expression grew wistful. "I actually did have feelings for her. And with Loretta and I being close, things were looking swell until your father's investors pulled out and the brewery went bankrupt anyway."

"You came here then?" Marian asked. She was trying to put the pieces together. It was becoming clear to her that Frederick— out of loyalty to her mother, to *her* even—had come to believe he was enacting mercy. Saving them. But he was just a small piece in a much larger puzzle.

Ivo nodded, his mouth set in a grim line. "I did. Fact is, cousin, Müllerian Manor can still serve a purpose. We need a place to move goods through, and the way your mother had this place built, with the dead-end hallways, the random rooms . . . well, it's perfect. It'll drive the coppers nuts."

It suddenly became obvious, and in an awful, horrible way. Ivo wasn't here for her, wasn't here because of any familial connection. No, he was here for the manor. His cronies who had come to the dinner party were probably all people working in his business of running liquor underground.

"But Loretta . . ." She bit her tongue and stared at Ivo, a sickening realization coming to her, another piece of the puzzle. Frederick hadn't lied. Percy Hahn had died by his own hand. Frederick was only responsible for her mother.

Ivo grimaced. "Yeah, that was a tough one."

"You killed her?" If Marian could have shrunk deeper into her chair, she would have. All this death. All this secrecy and covering up . . . and she was stuck in the middle of it. Unwittingly, unknowingly smack-dab in the middle.

Ivo shook his head. "No. I couldn't do that." He blinked away tears. An act or real, Marian didn't know. "Loretta, she just needed . . . well, heck, Marian, I needed to keep her in line. She was nosy. Not sweet and compliant like you are. She asked too many questions and got in the way. I knew there were rumors about your mother's death and her *health*. I thought maybe if I scared Loretta, she'd get sidetracked by the idea this place was haunted or something. She was the curious sort, thought she could solve mysteries like some private eye. By distracting her with that mess in her drawer, I thought maybe she'd stop poking her nose into the brewery's business. Leave that to the men. It was harmless really, the butterflies in her drawer."

"And the bones?" Marian whispered.

Ivo gave a short laugh. "That was for a little added effect, nothing more. I found a dead squirrel in the woods and thought why not?"

Marian didn't echo his humor. It was too terrible.

Ivo scooted to the edge of his chair, a beseeching look on his face. He reached for Marian's hands, but she pulled away from him. A hurt expression flickered in his eyes. "Gosh, Marian. Really. Cecil and I, we're in deep, and there's money to be had if we stay. People aren't going to give up their liquor no matter how many church ladies have the ear of the government. As for Loretta, she loved the nightlife and all, but she wanted to know everything Cecil and I were doing. Who we were talking to. She wanted *in*, and Cecil wasn't going to have a woman in on the take. I was planning to end things with her, but then she had to go and tell me she was gonna have my kid. So I tried to sidetrack her with the butterflies and the bones."

Shocked, Marian bolted upright. "Loretta was expecting?"

Ivo winced. "Don't make me feel like such a cad! I already feel sick enough as it is. I don't know! She might've been giving me a line. Either way, I just wanted to scare her. It was Cecil who decided to take care of her. What was I supposed to do? It's not my fault Cecil knocked her off!" Ivo's words ended in a little wail, his eyes begging Marian to understand.

But she didn't understand. No. Not at all. "So it was Cecil who killed Loretta." Marian remembered passing the man on the stairs the morning Loretta's body had been found. He had looked frightened. But now she knew it was fear of being caught, not fear of Loretta's killer. "But her body . . ." Marian squeezed her eyes shut against the memory of Loretta lying so still on the bed, butterflies spread around her like a memorial.

Ivo winced again, biting at his thumbnail.

"*You* helped cover it up for Cecil, didn't you, Ivo," Marian accused, "out of loyalty to your partner?"

Ivo cleared his throat. "With the story about your mother's death—the fact she was so enamored with butterflies—then you said that milkman had been found in the glass house? There was already a killer out there, making his mark. Why not push Loretta off on him?" A tear escaped Ivo's eye. "You've gotta believe me, Marian. I didn't know Cecil was going to do it, but when he did . . . well, we had to protect ourselves."

Marian tried to rise from her chair, but Ivo jumped to his feet, the action sending her huddling back in her seat.

He bent over her. "Listen to me! We're just trying to survive here! The ban on liquor isn't a small thing. It's the entire economy of Milwaukee—of our *lives*. Yet it doesn't have to stop us. There's an entire network, and we can make a go of it. Here. I'll even include you, Marian."

Ivo straightened and paced the room, then returned to stand over her. His eyes drilled into her with an urgency her spirit immediately responded to. It was instinct to care for one's family. To be there. Loyalty was part of the fabric of who Marian was.

"I need Müllerian Manor, Marian."

She met Ivo's stare and shook her head.

Ivo crouched in front of her, resting his hand on her leg. "Listen to me," he pleaded. "There are pieces of your father's brewery—of *your* brewery—we can still salvage. But I need a place where we can work from. This is it. Here. The manor."

Marian sighed. "No, Ivo. I can't do it. It's not right."

He scowled. "What do you mean, not right? It's not right to try to stay afloat? It's not right to make a living?"

"A living or a killing?" Marian's pointed question hit its mark.

Ivo fell back onto his heels. He stared at her in disbelief. "You think I'm the bad guy, don't you? I'm just trying to take care of you."

"I don't need to be taken care of, Ivo." Marian leaned forward, finding her voice. The question in Ivo's eyes gave her a tiny bit of hope. "I never asked to be taken care of."

Ivo's laugh was cutting. "You need to be taken care of. Your *mother* needed to be taken care of. I didn't *want* it to come to this, but I'll make sure you're taken care of."

Coldness swept through her. "You'd . . . you'd kill me?" Hearing the words spoken aloud sounded preposterous.

Ivo patted her knee. "Oh no. Never. You're family after all. I'll be square with you. It's a great place, Marian, it is. I've got a room reserved for you. There are nurses and doctors close by—they can help you so you don't get worse. Like your mother. There are new things they can do to figure out what's wrong with your head."

"Nothing's wrong with my—"

"Sure there is. You know it. I know it. Let's get you help."

Terror immobilized her. He was manipulating her. She wasn't sure what to believe of his story or if he'd ever had feelings for Loretta to begin with. But it was more than evident that he'd been planning to get her out of his way if he'd already made arrangements for her care at an institution.

He had known what Frederick had known, which meant her father had known too—that Marian was following in her mother's footsteps. Only Father had tried to care for them both at the manor. Ivo wanted to get her out of his way entirely.

32

REMY

S HE SHOULD HAVE CALLED Detective Ambrose, but Remy hoped a text would suffice. There was no way she was going to wait around for the police. She knew they would demand that she "stay back"—if they even took her seriously to begin with. Foolish? Probably. Remy didn't care. She increased the pressure on the gas pedal as she wound her way onto Highway 69. Cabin by the creek. She didn't have an address, but it couldn't be that hard to find.

Turned out she was wrong. That much was clear. Driveways all along the highway led to wooded lots with cabins and mobile homes. Okay, so the creek was more than just a trickle. Apparently it was waterfront real estate but without the hefty price tag. Everyone and their mother seemed to live here.

Remy had pictured a remote cabin. A hideout. A place like in the movies where Tate and Elton were tied up in a back room with the evil Dean/Jack pacing in front of them, waving a gun, as he slowly lost his mind.

She really needed to stop watching so many movies. But as someone once told her, *"Why read a book when you can watch it on the screen?"*

This was why. Books didn't mess with a person's head like movies tended to.

Remy wrestled her frenetic thoughts back to the task at hand. She yanked the steering wheel to the right and pulled off the road. She needed to think, to figure this out. She wasn't going to just find some random cabin. She'd have to go knocking door to door on the off chance the supposedly dead Dean was really Jack who'd escaped the fire with Elton and Tate and they were now hiding away for . . . what reason? Why? Was she completely losing it?

She leaned her head on the steering wheel.

Think, think, think . . .

Remy took inventory of the events that had occurred since her arrival at Müllerian Manor.

Tate had come to the manor to protect his family name.

Someone left a newspaper clipping on the table with the story of the fire from her childhood.

Someone had left dead butterflies and animal bones in her car, on her bed with a doll.

Aimee had been murdered.

Tate had experienced some kind of manic episode.

Dean had arrived.

Müllerian Manor had burned down, with arson probably being the cause.

Tate, Elton, and Dean had all perished in the fire—maybe.

Amid all of that, she had been deep into researching Marian Arnold and the Butterfly Butcher. Verdine Arnold. Butterflies. The family legacy. The butterfly globe that Tate had risked his life to save, which was still in the care of Boggart—she hoped.

What if . . .

Remy lifted her head from the steering wheel and grabbed her notebook. She started writing down her racing thoughts.

What if Percy Hahn truly died by suicide and the Butterfly Butcher never killed Marian Arnold?

What if the story of the woman found in the room with the butterfly globe was really about Marian's mother, Verdine?

What if the Butterfly Butcher killed only two people—Verdine Arnold and Loretta Habington? If so, that meant Marian Arnold hadn't been killed . . .

Remy wrote her final thought, underlining it three times in her notebook: *MARIAN ARNOLD LIVED.*

And Tate knew this! He had to have known it, which was why he'd come to Müllerian Manor in the first place—not just to protect the reputation of the Arnold name but to protect his great-grandmother, Marian Arnold.

"Protect her from what?" Remy spoke into her empty car. Understanding began to dawn. "You weren't protecting Marian; you were protecting *yourself.*" She remembered the prescription bottles. Ambrose's brief biography of Tate's stint in the military. "You were protecting your entire family line from being made a show of. From a spotlight being turned on to you—especially if this form of mental illness is inherited and you share it with Marian Arnold and Verdine Arnold."

These types of stories caused sensations. Not only did true-crime junkies love to read about murder mysteries and cold cases, they loved a good glamorization of mental-health problems. On one hand, the world fought to validate those with mental illness. On the other hand, those mental-health conditions were billed as a source of entertainment.

It was a vicious circle, and one Remy understood, despised, and was intrigued by all at the same time.

"You knew." Remy leaned back against the headrest. Her questions, her research, and her gut told her Tate could have answered it all. But he hadn't. It was to protect Marian. To protect the family. To preserve their legacy from becoming cheap entertainment.

Boggart probably knew the family's secrets too. It was why he was the crotchety old groundskeeper. It was why he defended Marian. He had known her. Remy *knew* he had! At some point, Boggart and Marian had crossed paths.

Remy's phone pealed. She glanced at it. Ambrose.

"Hello?"

"Where are you?" Ambrose demanded.

Remy looked around her. "Somewhere on Highway 69."

"You're sure Abigail saw Dean?"

"She said she saw Jack. Whose description is an awful lot like Dean's." Remy peered out her windshield at the highway as a few cars and trucks zipped by. "It's a long shot. I'm making assumptions, I know, but—"

"They're worth following up on."

Remy heard the dinging of keys in a car ignition. Ambrose was getting into a vehicle.

Ambrose continued, "I ran a check on Dean—the nurse? The agency Mr. Floyd supposedly got assistance from said the medical aide they sent to assist Mr. Floyd just showed up in Florida. Long story. But it seems he was paid off by someone to ditch out, and that *someone*—Dean—took his place. I ran a check on Aimee too."

Remy stilled.

"Aimee never worked as a nurse for that agency. She *was* registered as a CNA with the state, but that's it. So I checked into her even more." A car engine came to life in the background. "Are you driving?"

The abrupt shift in the revelation from Ambrose startled Remy. "No." Remy frowned, waiting.

"Okay, good. Don't drive. I'll come meet you," Ambrose instructed.

"What else did you find?" Remy didn't care what Ambrose was doing now. She just wanted information.

Ambrose released a heavy breath into the phone. Remy could picture the detective manhandling her steering wheel as tires squealed in the background.

"Aimee had a marriage license registered. She was married to . . ." A few seconds' hesitation and then Ambrose said, "Jake Thompson."

Remy slammed her hand against the dash. "My half brother!"

"Who bears a striking resemblance to Dean, Jack—whoever the guy is," Ambrose concluded. "I looked into your half brother last night after we talked. He was sent from home to home over the course of two years, and then he ended up in juvie."

"For what?" Remy thought she already knew.

"Attempted arson." Ambrose's blunt statement brought it all back.

The fire.

Her brother telling her to stay put.

His smile.

His laughter.

Ambrose was still speaking. "If Jake Thompson actually committed arson, he was never caught."

"He started the fire that killed my mother and her boyfriend." Remy heard herself say it, but her voice sounded as though far away.

"Tell me what happened." Remy's deduction didn't seem to surprise Ambrose.

Remy closed her eyes. "He told me to stay behind, to obey, but I didn't listen. After he left, the smoke was so thick I couldn't breathe." Remy's voice wavered. An onslaught of memories washed over her. "I had to get out of there."

"And you did," Ambrose reassured over the phone.

Remy remembered now. All of it. "I crawled to the door and opened it. The neighbors—they were there trying to get out of the building too. I remember they grabbed me and helped me. Then a firefighter picked me up, and when we got outside, I looked for Jake. He was gone. That's when my entire life changed."

"And you've done good, Remy," Ambrose said. "You're strong and capable, and Jake wasn't able to stop you."

Remy's eyes flew open. "But he's trying. For some reason he's trying. Why now? After all these years? Why me? And wouldn't Elton know if my half brother Jake first posed as his research assistant *Jack* and then came back as his nurse *Dean*?" Remy sucked in a breath, willing herself to think logically. "Not to mention, why Elton? Why here?"

"There's something else you should know," Ambrose said.

Somewhere deep in Remy, she knew what it was.

"As I was digging, I looked into your mother's records too. When your half brother, Jake, was born, his father was killed in a drug-related incident. The records show that after that, your mother and her dead husband's brother got really close. The time sequence lines up, and . . . my guess is he's your father."

"My father was also Jake's uncle?"

"Yeah. Your mom was married, had Jake, her husband died, she hooked up with his brother, and they had you."

"And then my father flaked out on us all," Remy concluded.

Ambrose was quiet on the other end of the line.

"So my mom raised me along with Jake, who probably knew his dad's brother—*my* dad—had stiffed us all."

"That sounds about right," Ambrose confirmed.

Remy's insides were churning. "Well, that brings family drama to a whole new level. But why would Jake hate *me* so much? I'm as much a victim of our mother sleeping with brothers. Why go to all this trouble, and why pull Elton into the drama?" She still struggled to piece it all together.

Ambrose's response was solemn, but it sliced through Remy like a well-sharpened blade. "I don't know what Jake's motives are, Remy, but I can tell you this. Jake's father and your father were brothers, and their father was Elton Floyd. Elton is your grandfather, Remy. And he's Jake's grandfather too. You're all tied together, and you all ended up at Müllerian Manor."

Ambrose pulled behind Remy's car and got out, slamming her door shut. As the detective approached, Remy opened her door very much aware that her face was streaked with tears.

"This is gutting, I know," Ambrose said. "I can't explain the motive, and I've no idea why your brother wants to wipe all traces of the family from history. That said, I *do* have hope now that Elton and Tate are still alive. I don't know how, but it could be that they escaped the fire."

Remy clung to Ambrose's words. "And Dean-slash-Jack the old research assistant is really my half brother, Jake?"

Ambrose held up her hands. "I don't have conclusive proof yet, but that's what it looks like. We don't know why he left as Jack and came back as Dean, or why Elton didn't say anything. He had to have known who Jake was."

"Mrs. Flemming too." Remy recalled how Mrs. Flemming had acted as though Dean was a bona fide nurse, not the prior research assistant.

"Yeah. There has to be a good reason for why they tolerated your brother's reappearance." Ambrose straightened, her petite frame appearing far stronger than Remy felt at the moment. "I've called for backup. I have a good idea which cabin Jake is holed up in." Ambrose rested a hand on Remy's shoulder. "We're going to find them, Remy."

"But Elton . . ." Remy reflected back on how she'd found this job in the first place, how she became connected with Elton Floyd, the well-known biographer. "I answered an email," Remy began. "I'd submitted applications to various job sites. I got an email from what I assumed was one of the sites, but maybe it wasn't. Maybe it was Jake."

Ambrose nodded. "Could be."

"He lured me here under the pretense of the job as Elton's research assistant. But first *Jack the research assistant* had to leave. When he did, he left Aimee behind—his wife."

"Was Elton in on it, do you think?"

Ambrose frowned. She held up her hand for Remy to stay silent as dispatch communicated over her radio. Ambrose responded and then added for Remy's benefit, "We've got maybe five minutes before all this breaks loose. Backup is almost here."

Remy squeezed the bridge of her nose. "I don't think Elton was part of it." With everything inside her, Remy wanted to believe that Elton was somehow a victim too.

"But did Elton kill Aimee?" Ambrose wondered aloud. "Maybe he found out who she was. That she was his grandson's wife. That—"

"No." Remy shook her head. "I know it sounds like I'm trying to protect him, but Elton could hardly walk. There's no way he'd have been able to get down to the second level and kill Aimee. It had to be Jake."

"Why would Jake kill his wife?"

Remy met Ambrose's stark gaze. "I dunno. But he'd gone on dates with Abigail. Maybe his and Aimee's marriage was falling apart."

Ambrose spoke on the radio again, then nodded toward Remy's car door. "It's go time. You can stay here for now, or you can drive back to the station, but you can't come to the cabin."

"I'm coming," Remy argued.

"No, you're not."

Though Ambrose's command was clear, Remy fully intended to ignore it. Just like she hadn't obeyed Jake when she was four and told to stay behind.

33

MARIAN

OCTOBER 1921

IVO HAD LEFT HER BEHIND in the sitting room. His intentions were clear, and he'd made sure Marian knew he meant it for her benefit. But the truth was, with her incapacitated at the hospital, Ivo would slide into her place at Müllerian Manor. He would do whatever he wanted, and she would be gone, a figment of his memory. His promises, his assurances that he would visit, that he would oversee her care—none of it was true. They were all lies, and Marian knew it.

With a burst of panicked energy, she leapt from her chair and hurried through the manor. She needed to see it for herself. The glass house. In her mind she saw the foliage, felt the misty warmth, envisioned the butterflies dipping and circling in the air. But was any of it real? Or had her mind created a world she could feel safe in, while the actual world around her closed in on her? Was Violet part of the world creeping into her safe place, reminding Marian of her faults and weaknesses and giving voice to the subconscious thoughts she had never dared to speak aloud, but did dare to feel?

Is my family better off if I weren't here? If I died, would it be a relief to them? To me?

As Marian followed the path that ran across the back lawn, she noted how her gray dress matched the sky. Everything seemed gray now at Müllerian Manor. Even the brilliance of the autumn foliage was fading as the trees had, almost overnight it seemed, lost most of their leaves. Left behind were gray-and-brown scraggly branches, reaching toward the sky in a desperate plea for the former days of warm breezes and vibrant color.

The glass house loomed ahead, and Marian became instantly aware of how muted the glass appeared. It wasn't clear and reflective as she remembered it to be. Instead, the glass was mottled and dirty. She pulled at the door, and when it opened, Marian gave a little cry.

Frederick had been right. And Felix had to have known that day she'd told him they needed to close the butterfly house door quickly so as not to let the butterflies out.

There were no butterflies.

There was no green.

Even the air inside, though musty and smelling of mold, was cool.

Violet was nowhere to be seen or heard.

Marian knew this because Violet was inside of her. Violet was the part of Marian that knew she heard voices, *felt* things others did not, and the reality that Marian slipped into that *was real*—to her.

She sank to the floor of the butterfly house, the walkway cold on her stocking-covered legs. Ivo was right. She belonged in an institution. She was not like the others. She was—

"Marian?"

Felix's voice caused her to lurch, and she held out her hand. "Go away. Please."

Felix moved to a portion of the garden wall and eased himself onto it. He leaned forward. "I heard everything Ivo said."

She met his eyes. Felix knew. He knew what her mother's condition had been. He knew *her* condition. There was no hiding from it. It was part of her. It was going to ruin lives just as Mother's had, and in the end—real or not—Violet was right. She was better off dead. For everyone's sake. To relieve them of her—of the burden she was to become.

"We need to get you out of here." Felix's words broke through her psyche, and Marian stared blankly at him. He said it again but rephrased it in a way that was obvious he hoped she could grab hold of. "I can't protect you from Ivo. From his plans. He's your remaining male relative. They will let him commit you."

"Nothing I said to the police would matter. Ivo would claim I was ill. It's probably for the best," Marian mumbled.

"No!" Felix pushed himself off the wall to the ground beside her. He took her hands in his. "Marian, listen to me. I won't let that happen. It's *not* for the best. Not for you, not for me, not for *us*."

"Us?" Marian asked, empty of hope.

"Yes, us. It's *always* been us to me, Marian. Always." Felix looked away as if summoning strength from somewhere beyond him. He turned back. "I grew up with you. I saw you when you were younger, and you found beauty in places where beauty didn't exist. When you were afraid and there was no reason to be. I saw you in my mind when I fought in the trenches. You *live*, Marian. You live with all the beauty God created in you. Anything else is just a part of this broken and busted world. The same way the explosion took my leg, *life* takes from us. But God gives back. He brought me *home*. Because I prayed for it. I prayed for *you*. It's *always* been *us*, Marian."

Marian was at a loss for words. Felix released her hands and drew close, reaching up to cup her face. His breath was soft on her lips when he said, "You are worth fighting for, and I will do so every day of my life."

She crumpled. The tears she had been holding back broke forth. "I'll only hurt you. I won't be what you need."

"I need you," Felix reassured.

"But what if I get worse?" Marian cried.

"So?" Felix issued a watery laugh and slapped his thigh. "What if *I* get worse? Legs don't grow back, you know? I'm going to need you too."

A tiny spark of hope entered her. She swept her gaze around the butterfly house with its abandoned remains, her mother's legacy forgotten and decaying. Marian recalled the words she had painted: *He will haunt you.* Then she remembered the other words she'd painted, a moment inspired by Felix. Inspired by the warmth and faithfulness of a mother and son who stood by her . . . *You are wanted.*

If she couldn't believe that for herself, how then could she leave it behind for future generations to believe?

"Come with me," Felix urged. "Let's run away from here. From Ivo. From Müllerian Manor. Do it for us. Do it for you."

Marian shook her head. "No. I'll do it for them." The faceless visions of future Arnolds fluttered through her mind like butterflies in a soft breeze. "I'll do it for them."

REMY

It was nothing at all like the movies. The police took custody of the cabin within seconds. No bullets flying, no smoke bombs or tear gas. Just a full-on, well-coordinated approach and the cabin was under their control.

Remy hung back, listening to that frustrated command from Ambrose to do so. She stood by her car, which was parked well away behind the squad cars and a SWAT truck. It was difficult to see what was happening from here. She heard shouts, a few exclamations. The raid was, for the most part, uneventful.

A pair of police officers motioned for her to stay put, but Remy abandoned her place behind the driver's door and stepped forward. "What's going on?" She craned her neck to see.

"Please, ma'am, get back." An officer held up his hands, air-pushing her away. "It's not safe. Stay behind your car door."

Remy tried again to get a better look at the cabin. "I need to know what's going on. Was anyone in the cabin? Was anyone hurt?"

"No one was hurt," the officer reassured. "Now, please, back up."

There was rustling behind him. Ambrose broke through the line of cars, her flak jacket fit tightly around her upper torso. "It's okay, Officer. I've got this."

He gave Ambrose a nod and walked away.

Remy met Ambrose, who stopped her with hands to her upper arms. Remy was taller, larger, and she could force her way past Ambrose's tiny form if need be. But she didn't.

"It's over." Ambrose's words chilled Remy, and she froze, shifting her attention from the cabin to Ambrose.

"It's over? They weren't there?"

Ambrose's smile begged Remy to be patient. "We found Elton."

"Oh my gosh." Remy's knees threatened to buckle. Ambrose's grip on her arms tightened.

"He's dehydrated, but he's okay. We got Jake, Remy. It *was* him."

Remy's chin quivered. "And Tate?"

Ambrose's face scrunched, and she glanced over her shoulder. "Yeah, he's here too, and we're working with him now."

"I thought no one was hurt!"

"That's right, Remy," said Ambrose, "no one was hurt. But Tate's been off his medication for a few days, and the stress of all that's happened has been a lot for him to bear. He kept Elton alive. He gave Elton all the water, all the food that Jake had the minuscule bit of decency to leave them. But Tate is really shaken up."

"Let me help." Remy tried to push past Ambrose.

Ambrose pushed back. "Remy, we have trained officers— we've got this."

"Is he threatening anyone?" Remy asked.

Ambrose shook her head. "No, not at all. He's just scared mostly. He's experiencing an episode, and we've got to work through it with him. He'll be fine, though. We just need to build some rapport with him. Help him to trust us."

"He trusts me." Remy leveled a frank gaze on Ambrose. "Let me go to him. Please."

Ambrose hesitated, looked to the sky, then gave a sigh. She looked Remy in the eye. "All right. I guess it can't hurt."

A few moments passed as Ambrose led Remy around the officers and vehicles. She saw Dean—no, *Jake*—sitting on the ground in cuffs, officers standing over him. Their eyes met in a brief moment of stark awareness. She looked away. Not now. She couldn't face him. Couldn't face the reality of what he'd done to her—and to Elton and the people in their lives.

An ambulance was parked off to the right. EMTs were hefting a stretcher up into it.

"Elton!"

"Stay focused, Remy." Ambrose's blunt command brought Remy back to the situation at hand.

She was escorted into the cabin, and an officer approached, eyeing her. Ambrose held up a hand. "It's okay. Let her through. Tate isn't armed. He's not a threat, and she may be able to help him."

The officer stepped aside.

Remy was taken to the doorway of a small room with two beds and an open window. A cop was crouched in front of Tate, who'd pressed himself into a corner. The cop rose when Remy entered the room. Ambrose motioned, and he stepped past Remy and exited.

Without asking, Remy moved to the window first, closing the curtains. "I'm here, Tate." She willed herself to be calm. "I closed the curtains. I know you don't like them open."

He glanced at her, his expression blank. His face was covered in stubble, and his hair was sticking up every which way. But he looked so good. So very good. It took everything in her not to launch herself at him, to hold him, to convince herself he really and truly was alive.

Remy approached him slowly, then moved to sit down in front of him. "You all right if I sit here?"

He nodded.

"Okay, thanks." She prayed for the first time in ages, prayed that everything Abigail had said was true. That God somehow brought good from the bad. That there was a reason for it all. That she would know how to help Tate because his heroism meant everything to her. Everything.

"Tate?" She tipped her head, trying to catch his gaze. "Elton is fine. You kept him safe. I don't know how you all got out of the fire, but you kept Elton safe."

Tate lifted his eyes.

"Yeah." Remy smiled. "Tate, we're all safe now. All of us. Including you. The police are here to help. Okay?"

He nodded.

There was so much to say. So much to do. Tate needed medical care, she needed to check on Elton, and she wanted to pummel Jake Thompson until he bled. The range of emotions within her was vast.

"You know," Remy said with a small chuckle, "I'm going to need you, Tate."

Tate frowned, awareness beginning to seep into his eyes. "What do you mean?"

"I have a messed-up family tree." Remy felt a tear trickle down her face. "It's really messed up, Tate." A sob caught in her throat.

Tate reached out, his finger lifting a tear from her cheek. "I got you."

And she had him.

That's what family did.

34

A FEW DAYS HAD PASSEd since Tate and Elton were rescued. Remy had taken Abigail up on the offer of the spare room and crashed there while Tate and Elton received medical care.

Then there was Jake Thompson. Remy didn't want to see him—didn't want to face her half brother—but there were questions still in need of answers, and Ambrose was hopeful Jake would break and talk to Remy. Up until now, he'd maintained his silence. He hadn't even lawyered up.

Ambrose hesitated outside the interrogation room. "I'll be right on the other side. You're not alone."

"I'm not scared," Remy assured her. Not of Jake anyway. She was scared of what he might say. His motives. His reasoning. What he knew of their family that she didn't.

Ambrose opened the door, and Remy stepped inside.

Jake sat at a table, his hands cuffed and hooked to a ring welded to the steel tabletop. His stereotypical orange jumpsuit stuck out, a strange contradiction to the drab, gray room.

"Have a seat." He nodded toward the empty chair across from him as if he were welcoming her into his home.

Remy did so, never taking her eyes off him.

"Why?" She wasn't interested in making small talk.

Jake rolled his lips together and shrugged.

Remy leveled her gaze on him. "You started the fire all those years ago. You started the one at Müllerian Manor too, didn't you?"

Something sparked in his eyes, but he didn't respond.

Remy wanted to dive forward and grab both sides of his handlebar mustache and yank until his face bled. She restrained herself.

"Why would you do that? Why would you do that to Elton, our *grandfather*? What is it that makes you hate our family so much? And Aimee—she was your *wife*! Did you kill her too?"

Remy paused, letting the questions soak into Jake.

He eyed her for a long minute and then leaned forward, his cuffs clanking against the table. "Nothing like a family reunion to bring us all together."

It wasn't what Remy wanted to hear. She bit her tongue and waited.

Jake leaned back in his chair, his arms stretched out in front him and folded on the table. "Did you know when I was kid, I used to fly out to Elton's house in New York and play. But then your dad decided that he had a thing for my mom. That went over well in the family, especially since my dad was dead and *Grandpa Elton* blamed our mother for it. She was messed up and took my dad down with her. Then you were born, and your mom was barely out of jail and rehab. Your father—my uncle— skipped town. Grandpa Elton washed his hands of all of us. Nice guy that he is and all."

Remy waited. Everything in her wanted to reply, but she knew from experience how that could shut a person up. So she bit her tongue harder and waited.

Jake offered a dry laugh. "So then it became me, you, and our mom—and it was a string of one guy after another. Your dad? God knows where he ended up. My sister from my dad's first marriage hightailed it out of there as soon as she was old enough. So there I was. All alone. The forgotten kid with a wailing toddler and a strung-out mom. And Elton didn't do a thing. He had the money to help. I think he just wanted to wash his hands of the whole soap opera."

Remy swallowed back tears. She wasn't sure she could blame Elton for being done with them all. It still stung, though, that Elton hadn't fought for her or for Jake—*if* what Jake said was even true.

"I'd had it by the time I was fourteen," Jake went on. "Wasn't until years later that I found out you'd made it out of the fire."

"You set the fire?" Remy had a feeling Ambrose needed more of a confession.

Jake gave her a look but didn't say any more about it.

"And now?" Remy led.

Jake shrugged. "I figured out Elton had moved from New York to this old estate. The man is worth a lot of money, did you know that? Not many writers have the kind of bank account Elton Floyd has. Anyway, here he was looking for a new research assistant, and there were all these stories about a serial killer and a weird lady who once lived at the manor. I sent my own grandfather a résumé, and before long I became 'Jack the research assistant.' And Aimee became his nurse."

"So you told him who you were?" Remy asked.

"Of course. Once I was here." Jake's smile was thin. "Poor old man felt bad for letting us go. He even tried to apologize and say he'd lost track of us. But he was pleased to be reunited, and just as I'd figured, he needed heirs. You know, for his fortune?"

"Why did he accept you after all these years? And Aimee?" Remy didn't understand Elton's motivation to overlook the past, let alone tolerate Jake.

"Actually, he and Aimee got along well. I think he felt guilty for not fighting for us years ago. Then I told him about how I'd figured out you were alive, that I'd tracked you down in the Twin Cities. Granted, he ordered me to get out when he started putting the pieces together about the fire. He did exactly what I thought he'd do. He had Aimee send a message via that site and hired you so you'd come to the manor. Then he could finally do for the family what he'd been such a spineless fool not to do before."

The look in Jake's eyes turned bitter then, and Remy could read the intent behind his words. He'd *wanted* Elton to reach out to her. To bring her to the manor. She would be in Jake's way of inheriting Elton's estate. She had always been in Jake's way, for everything.

Jake leaned forward and folded his hands, the handcuffs clanging against the metal table. "Aimee stayed behind. Our marriage was on its way out anyway. She got all stupid and sappy over the old man." Jake uttered a disbelieving chuckle. "She got caught up in the story of the manor too. Got excited about figuring it out. She decided my grandfather was a nice guy, told me to back off and leave him be. She got in the way."

"So you killed her," Remy concluded. "Your own wife."

Jake's chest heaved in a sickening display of pride. He was enraptured by his own demented story now, and his tongue had loosened. "I mean, the Butterfly Butcher was bound to rise again, right?" His grin was the twisted one from Remy's memories. "You didn't take the hint either. How much more obvious could I get when I staged Aimee to look like the Butcher had killed her? Gosh, Remy, you're dense. I just wanted to get you out of the way, but it was getting fun, messing with your head. So I took bits of the manor's story and messed with you. I always liked messin' with you. Sneaking in and out of the manor was stupid fun. Leaving the old newspaper clippings to freak you out? Isn't that what brothers are for?"

His words were so chilling, they made Remy inadvertently shiver.

"I never set out to kill Grandpa Elton," Jake added. "I just wanted him to watch everything unravel. Because that's what happens you when don't treat family right. They unravel." Jake stuck his tongue between his teeth and bit down, wagging his head back and forth. "And so here we are."

"How'd you get out of the fire?" Remy asked, sitting on her hands so she didn't do something that would get her arrested.

"You know the room off your bedroom, the one with that stupid globe? Aimee went in there all the time and had so much fun freaking you out. Making you think it was the ghost of Marian Arnold with that dumb poem." Jake's voice was singsongy as he said it. "There's a secret panel in there." He sneered. "Probably put there during Prohibition. Or maybe it was added by Marian Arnold's wackadoo mom!" Jake's eyes widened, and he made a face.

Remy glanced at the camera in the corner of the room. She could feel Ambrose's eyes burning into her back through the two-way mirror. Okay. Much as she was tempted to, she wouldn't strangle the life out of her brother. She wouldn't.

"Anyway!" Jake splayed his hands on the table. "Your hero Tate was the biggest hitch in the plan. He was never supposed to show up at the manor in the first place. Then I found him hauling Elton down the stairs on his back during the fire. You were supposed to die with Elton, and then everything goes to me. But you climbed out the window and, *poof*, there goes the plan. All because of Tate Arnold's stupid heroism."

"But you helped him get Elton out of the house?" Remy didn't understand.

Jake snarled, "I had to improvise when Tate decided to play hero. I helped them both get out of the house. I took them out the back. That's when Elton passed out. Tate was frantic. I duped him into thinking I was helping by getting them both into my car. And away we went."

Remy shook her head. "I was in the front yard. Right next to the driveway. I would have seen you."

"There's a back entrance to the property. An old road. It's hardly used anymore, but still passable. That's where I parked."

"But why help Elton and Tate survive?"

Jake shrugged and leaned back in his chair. "Self-preservation. I wasn't going to end up burning with both of them. Then Elton had a big mouth when he came to in the car, and from there I had to figure out something else."

He blew out a breath and looked past Remy to the two-way mirror, raising his voice for Ambrose to hear. "That's that! Now you know! I was an emotionally stunted, fatherless kid who harbored a bitter hatred for the baby girl that shouldn't exist, except his mom slept with his dead dad's brother. I've a rich grandpa who was easy to manipulate and played along with my coming back as his nurse when I told him if he didn't, I'd kill his only granddaughter. The man may be a good writer, but not very smart when it comes to family relations." Jake leveled his eyes on Remy, the darkness in them burning through her. "I was always, *always* going to get you out of my way."

Remy leaned forward, skewering her half brother with a glare. "All this because of a dysfunctional family and the inheritance of the estate?"

Jake attempted to clap despite the cuffs. "Look at you, shortening the story to make it simple." He dropped his hands onto the tabletop, glaring right back at her. "My aim was to prune the family tree one branch at a time. It was already rotten. And dead trees deserve to be cut down."

Remy left the interrogation room. The minute she was in the hallway and out of sight of Jake, she fell against the wall. She slid down to sit on the floor just as Ambrose exited the adjoining room.

She hurried to Remy's side. "You did good, Remy."

"It's all such a mess." Remy shook her head in disbelief. She met Ambrose's eyes. "My family. We're a mess." Somewhere out there was her birth father, Elton's other son. "How do I come back from this? What am I supposed to do now?"

Ambrose glanced up at a fellow officer and tipped her head. He kept walking while Ambrose took a seat next to Remy on the floor. They leaned against the wall for a long moment.

"Maybe it's none of my business," Ambrose said, breaking the silence, "but I think when we uncover the legacy our families leave for us, it's on us to break old curses and start to heal, you know?"

Remy gave a short laugh. "Sounds nice, but how do you do that?"

Ambrose smiled. "It takes a lot of work. A lot of self-awareness. A lot of *therapy*."

They both laughed.

Ambrose continued, "Sometimes we shortchange the fact that the original concept of family and legacy and passing on to our children is biblical."

Remy side-eyed Ambrose.

Ambrose smiled again. "Something about how the sins of the fathers are passed on to the children and so on. But it stands to reason that if the bad passes to the next generation, so does the good." Ambrose tapped Remy's shoulder just over her heart. "And there's a lot of good in there. I think it's been protected. I think God has something bigger for you in mind."

Remy looked down at her hands in her lap. "I don't know how to find it."

Ambrose was quiet for a moment, and then she answered, "He finds you, Remy. In the chaos, He finds you."

35

S HE SAT BY ELTON'S SIDE as he recovered in the assisted-living home.

"State of the art!" He slapped the arms of his wheel-chair. "And have you seen my nurse?" He winked. "Good-lookin' dame if ever I saw one."

"Elton! She's barely in her twenties," Remy retorted.

"And you'd steal my hopes and dreams just because of an age discrepancy?"

"Yes," Remy laughed, feeling so very thankful she could laugh with Elton again.

He grew serious and tapped his finger on the tray in front of him. "I'm sorry, Remy. For everything. I shouldn't have allowed Jake to bully me at your expense."

Remy grasped her grandfather's hand. "You did it to protect me."

"Lot of good that did." Elton's smile was sad. "Once I let Jake into the manor, I knew I'd let in a whole lot of bad. I even bribed Mrs. Flemming when Jake showed up as Dean the nurse. Poor Mrs. Flemming. I told her to look the other way and not say a word."

"She's been faithful to you," Remy said.

"No. She's been faithful to Müllerian Manor. Just like Boggart has. Neither of them would ever say a word against the wishes of their employer."

Remy nodded. "Do you think they knew Marian Arnold?"

Elton sighed heavily. "I'm almost sure of it. From what I've uncovered in doing my own research—in *books*, mind you—the manor was used during Prohibition as a place for running rum, this after the drama of the Butterfly Butcher waned. It was in the fifties, a couple took over the manor and stayed there for quite a few years. I suspect they weren't new to the manor."

Remy's mouth dropped open. "Noooo waaay." She drew out the words as she stared at Elton. "You think they were Marian and her husband?"

Elton's eyes were thoughtful. "I wouldn't put it past her. I have a feeling she was a fighter. Like her great-grandson, Tate."

Remy leaned in closer. "Go on."

Elton nodded. "Well, the place was still in the Arnold trust— Ivo Lott had long since died. I believe Marian returned to live there without letting on she was the original owner. She probably hired Boggart and Mrs. Flemming in her later years, who eventually pieced it all together. Knowing what we know now, I believe that if we asked them and they would stop clamming up about it, we'd learn they took care of Marian and her husband. The husband had lost his leg in World War I. I'm not sure who he was, but if my deductions are right, he and Marian married and together they had a family. They lived and died there. One of the books said an occupant of Müllerian Manor in the 1960s signed up to help with experimental medications that were being introduced to the medical world."

"Medications?" Remy eyed him.

Elton seemed pleased to have found information Remy hadn't. "Yes, medications. For mental health. That's all it said. I don't know what her diagnosis was, but apparently this occupant of the manor wanted to make sure she did her part to help others in the future."

Remy blew out a breath of air. "Marian Arnold was a warrior."

"Yes, she was." Elton reached over and grasped Remy's hand.

"But the story of the Butterfly Butcher is still unresolved. I would have thought that if they'd caught the killer, it would've been in the newspapers. We haven't been able to pinpoint the details no matter how hard we try." Remy debated over whether it was worth researching further or better to let the Butcher just fade away into the past.

"I don't know," Elton admitted. "Perhaps the answer lies in why Marian Arnold disappeared from history. If my theory is correct, she returned years later but never made a showing of it. Prohibition maybe? It wouldn't surprise me at all if, after she disappeared, that Ivo Lott used the manor for his own purposes. Maybe even paid people off to have the story die in a cover-up of some sort—take the attention off the manor. There's enough unknown yet that I'm led to believe there are more threads we simply will never know."

"I may research it some more," Remy said.

"Well, I for one am going to let the book rest," Elton said with a determined look on his face. "It's time to let Marian Arnold lie in peace and give Tate Arnold his privacy." He squeezed Remy's hand. "I've got a lot to make up for with my own family legacy. A man could learn a thing or two from Marian Arnold's story."

Remy squeezed his hand in return. Words were one thing. Time would solidify them. But she had a feeling, deep down inside, that Elton meant what he'd said. That it was time to notice the tiny sprig of life at the base of their family tree.

It wasn't over yet.

New life was coming.

Remy's feet crunched on pea gravel that was spread across the walkway in the butterfly house.

Tate had come back to Müllerian Manor, the place of his ancestors. His home really. Only now it was a shell of what had once been.

He turned from his position with a garden rake. He leaned against it and gave Remy a welcoming but small smile. "Hey."

"Hey yourself." Remy had seen him since the day at the cabin, but never alone. Now she knew it was time. She surveyed the glass house. The garbage was gone. A lot of the dead branches had been clipped and discarded. "You've been working hard in here."

Tate looked around him. "Yeah. A little easier to focus here in the butterfly house. It sort of feels . . . right."

"That makes sense." Remy moved past him to the grave with the ominous painted words at its base. "We could get rid of those words there." She pointed to them.

"That's my plan. I want to fix this place up." Tate lifted his eyes toward the roof. "I want to get the glass fixed. Turn it into a greenhouse."

"With butterflies?" Remy smiled teasingly.

"Uh, probably not." Tate matched her smile. It evaporated quickly, though. "I found something you may want to see."

"Oh?" Remy followed him around the walk. In the middle of where gardens had once been stood an old statue of a goddess, reaching toward the sky.

"Check that out." Tate gestured toward its base.

Remy bent to look, and then she shot Tate a surprised glance. "Another message!"

"Read it."

"'You are wanted,'" Remy read aloud. "'M. A.'"

"Marian Arnold."

"Marian Arnold," Remy breathed.

Tate gripped the handle of the rake he still held and leaned hard against it. "You know why I came here to begin with, don't you." It was an observation more than a question, but Remy answered it anyway.

"I do." She ran her fingers over the words. "I don't begrudge you that either. I mean, it's obvious Marian Arnold went through a lot, and she spent her life trying to make the world a better place for *you*."

Tate nodded, relief in his eyes.

She pushed back to her feet. "Do you know if she had . . ." Remy let her words hang, unsure of how to finish the delicate question.

Tate spared her. "We know there's a history of mental illness in our family. It's bypassed most of us, but . . . well . . ."

"Not you," Remy acknowledged gently.

"Not me." Tate nodded. "People think I can't have a life or a relationship, but I can. I'm not defined by the disorder, and there's a lot of support that didn't exist in the past for Marian."

Remy took a few hesitant steps toward Tate. "She was a trail-blazer."

Tate pondered Remy's words. A light stretched across his face. "Yeah. You're right. She really was a trailblazer."

"Elton said he's no longer writing the book." Remy's statement made Tate still. "It's too precious a story really. And the Butterfly Butcher—well, there are other old cases to sensationalize."

"I appreciate that." Tate let the rake handle drop to the ground. As he straightened, he addressed her cautiously. "And you? What are you going to do?"

"Me?" Remy looked around the butterfly house. "I don't know what I'm supposed to do with all of this. My family. Your family. The stuff that's happened. It's pretty unreal."

"No kidding." Tate took a hesitant step toward her.

Remy lifted her face.

He reached out and grasped her hand. "You wouldn't be interested in helping me restore this place, would you?"

"The butterfly house?" She'd not expected this.

Tate nodded. "And maybe the manor after that. It's time to take it back from the past. Rebuild. Start again fresh."

She saw his gaze flicker to the right, and she followed it. A gasp escaped her, and Remy beamed at Tate. "The butterfly globe!"

"Yeah." Tate's grin was lopsided. "Boggart brought it to me a few days ago. Said it belonged here."

Remy closed her hand around Tate's. It was the only signal he needed. He pulled her toward him, wrapping his arms around her. Remy buried her face in his shoulder, breathing in his signature scent, relishing the truth that he was here. He was alive.

"I have just one question." Remy laughed. "No, that's not true. I have a *ton* of questions because I'm still trying to figure everything out."

"Go for it," Tate invited.

"So Marian essentially *left* the manor after the Butcher killed Loretta Habington. What happened to the manor after that?"

"It went into the Arnold trust. Her cousin used the place for years."

Remy drew a deep breath. "Did you know Elton thinks one of the occupants who lived here in the fifties and sixties was actually Marian?"

Tate pulled back from her and studied her face as if measuring whether she was serious. A small laugh escaped him. "I guess that wouldn't surprise me."

Remy nodded. "And if Marian Arnold married, and her male sibling on the family tree isn't the line you come from, then why do you still carry the name Arnold? Wouldn't Marian have taken her married name?"

"Maybe she did." Tate's brows shot up and held as though he had one more secret to share.

Remy gently slugged his arm. "Spill it, Tate."

"Well, my grandfather had done a lot of the research of our

family history, mostly because of mental-health concerns. He felt it would honor Marian Arnold not to have the family name die with her—and his own father had passed away by then, plus he had brothers who could carry on his surname. So he had our name legally changed to Arnold. My dad was born an Arnold, and I was later born an Arnold."

"What was your surname before your grandfather changed it?" Curious, Remy had to ask.

"Dale," Tate replied. "It's my middle name. We always tried to preserve it. My great-grandfather was a war hero—World War One."

"Wow." Remy breathed in deep and let it out as she surveyed the glass house. "Family history is so intricate, so . . . fragile."

"It's worth being remembered," Tate concluded. "These stories need to be told, the good and the bad, so we can learn from them. So we can grow."

Remy wrapped her arms around Tate's waist. "Can I stay here and help you restore this place?" Her gaze landed on the butterfly in the glass globe. A butterfly that symbolized the manor and who knew what other secrets hidden in its ruins. "We can restore the manor for Grandpa Elton too."

"I don't know if you want to be stuck with me—"

"Stop." Remy put her hands on his chest and pulled back. She caught his eyes with her own and prayed that what she meant would be reflected. "You know what Marian would say."

"What?" He tucked a strand of hair behind her ear.

"You, Tate Arnold." Remy placed her hand on the side of his face. "You are wanted."

His eyes slid shut.

She pushed up on her toes and kissed him. It was a promise. A promise that there was so much good still to come because there was so much life still to live.

36

MARIAN

OCTOBER 1921

MARIAN FINISHED packing her bag. A small one. A few dresses, a few trinkets. Nothing here at Müllerian Manor really mattered. Not anymore. At least not now.

It was nighttime. Ivo was supposedly—hopefully—asleep in his room in the other wing. Marian closed her suitcase.

"Are you ready?" Felix ducked into the bedroom from his place at the door. Guarding.

Marian nodded.

Felix backed into the bedroom, closed the door, and locked it. He made his way with his crutch to the bed, pausing to caress Marian's face with his eyes. "It's going to be okay. I'm not going to let anything happen to you."

"Do you think I'll ever come back here?" she whispered.

"Do you want to?" Felix asked.

"I don't know," she admitted. And she truly didn't. Yet in

leaving the manor behind, she felt that in a way she was abandoning the future too.

"We can someday—if you need to."

It was enough. Marian followed Felix into the butterfly room. Mrs. Dale was there, her own bag in hand. Marian was so grateful the woman was willing to go away with her and Felix. The future was uncertain—where they would go, where they would stay, how they would make ends meet. But at least they would be together. They would be family.

Marian's eyes fell on the butterfly globe on the table in the middle of the room.

"Do you want to take it with us?" Mrs. Dale asked.

Marian shook her head. "No. I don't want to live with second goodbyes. I don't think we were ever meant to have them. Our time is our time, and when it's up, we are meant to fly. But not here."

"Not here," Mrs. Dale echoed. She touched Marian's face in a motherly gesture.

"All these years," Marian mused, still fixing her eyes on the preserved butterfly. "I didn't know I had a brother."

"I'm sorry." Felix came up beside her.

"In a way," Marian said, reaching out and touching the glass dome, "I'm thankful. I can imagine he's waiting and I'll see him again someday."

Mrs. Dale nodded, then looked to Felix. "I'm going to go ahead. The driver I arranged to meet us will be at the road waiting."

"We'll be right behind you. Be careful." Felix and his mother exchanged looks, and then Mrs. Dale slipped through the open panel and passage in the wall.

"We need to go," Felix said gently. "We should hurry."

Marian looked up at Felix. He was so kind. So faithful. So willing to give everything for her—in spite of everything. "Why? Why me?" she asked.

Felix leaned forward, his lips brushing her forehead. "Because."

"Because?" She drew back, questioning his reply.

"That's all I need." Felix's smile was gentle, promising. "Because. We don't need any other reason. Providence intended this, so let's finish it. Together."

Felix led the way to the panel, his crutch softly thudding on the floor, his trouser leg pinned at the knee. He looked over his shoulder. "You coming?"

Marian pressed a kiss to her fingers, then touched the butterfly globe. "Goodbye, Müllerian Manor. Today my family begins again."

She left it behind. The memory of her baby brother, of her mother who died below his memorial butterfly. She left Frederick behind as well as his intention to correct what he felt was broken. She left Ivo behind. He would do as he wished here, and she wouldn't stop him. That was the sad part about lost family. The parts you couldn't get back, and the parts you couldn't heal.

Now Marian looked forward as she ducked into the passage and quietly closed the panel behind her. The future was frightening, yes, but Marian remembered the butterfly garden. Remembered it as she had seen it in her mind. Green, fresh, beautiful, filled with life and butterflies, faith and hope.

Perhaps that had been a mirage.

But it was real. In her soul. It was a promise to her from the Creator of families. Beauty was to be found. It was to be fought for. Braved through. Preserved. But she would preserve it the right way. She would cloak it in faith, in hope, and above all in loyalty and strength.

She would secure the future for her descendants so that they too could live.

AUTHOR'S NOTE

It was a journey to write this novel. It took five months of dwelling on the story, a couple of weeks reaching out to specific individuals who could help bring clarity and sensitivity to its pages, and then a wild few weeks putting it into words. But once they began to come, they couldn't be stopped.

It is my prayer that I have done a service to those ones who must manage their mental health on a daily basis. There is such a broad spectrum. I wanted to be careful not to sensationalize one over the other, and I wanted to make sure that accuracy was portrayed while telling a story through figurative scenes and circumstances.

Please know my intentions are to honor and respect those who navigate the world through different eyes. It is not my intention to be ableist, insensitive, or ignorant, and yet I know my own mental health experiences pale in comparison to many. Please forgive any unintentional insensitivities or misrepresentations.

So as we navigate life from a myriad of perspectives, may we always come back to one truth: You are made in the image of God. Of a God who loves you. Who seeks you. Who jealously fights for you.

Why? Because you are wanted.

ACKNOWLEDGMENTS

When my friend Sue Poll and I first walked into the Frederik Meijer Gardens & Sculpture Park in Grand Rapids, MI, we couldn't have imagined finding death and murder among the beauty of the place's butterflies! I knew then that not only were we both equally disturbed but we were equally matched in friendship and fiction, and this story needed to be written. So thanks to the Poll family, whose friendship has been a blessing the last few years.

A ginormous thank-you to my friend and proofreader, Elizabeth Olmedo. I gave you no time to proofread the ugly out of this story, and yet you did it with all your grace and enthusiasm. Thank you so much for all you do and have done to bring this story to life!

Special thanks to my Mastermind Group & Crits—Kimberley Woodhouse, Becca Whitham, Darcie Gudger, Tracie Peterson, Jocelyn Green, Jayna Breigh, Kayla Whitham, and Bethany Cox. Your insights and assistance in helping me with this story and the importance of the characters' experiences were genuinely game-changing!

Deep thanks to Liz Mason for taking the time to assist me with educating, clarifying, researching, and helping provide sensitivity to the subjects of mental health and specifically schizophrenia. And also to Lauren at @LivingWellwithSchizophrenia and her insights and vulnerability that she has brought to her own personal and rich daily life.

To my writing sisters, how I love you all! Kara Isaac, Anne Love, Laurie Tomlinson, and Sarah Varland. You have stuck by me through thick and thin, and while our journeys and roads veer off into the most un-writing of writing-related ventures, we are still bound together. Thank you.

Other thanks go to the tribe that keeps it all rollin'. Cap'n Hook, CoCo (Tinkerbell), and Peter Pan. Especially to CoCo, my own personal barista. I have raised you well, and now books are written fully caffeinated.

Finally, it takes an army to get a manuscript from my laptop to your bookshelf. So massive thanks to my Bethany House team and Baker Publishing as a whole! Also to Janet Grant, my agent, who helps me manage the day-to-day!

READING GROUP
DISCUSSION GUIDE

1. The story opens with Marian's life being affected by the current laws forbidding the sale of alcohol. Prohibition, while often glamorized in fiction as the era of gangsters and rum-running, had a significant impact on the economy. In what ways might Prohibition have affected your own family's history, or how do you think this time period would have been different (good or bad) had Prohibition never occurred?

2. Conservatories were popular forms of architecture in the days of grand estates and manors. If you were to design your own conservatory, which plants and other elements of nature would you want to include in it?

3. Butterflies carry great significance for many cultures, religions, and belief systems. For some, butterflies represent renewal and rebirth. For others, they carry an element of spiritual influence and superstition. When you think about butterflies, how do you perceive their significance?

4. In this story, there is a thread woven through the lives of the Arnold family that is both pivotal and life-changing in the area of mental health. This thread also affects future generations in profound ways. When you consider mental illness, what are some ways you see individuals with various diagnoses impacting our communities and lives for the better?

5. In what ways do you see Remy's and Marian's lives parallel each other, and in what ways do they differ?

6. If you could sit down and have tea or coffee with one of the characters, which one would you choose and why?

7. If you come from the position of faith, how do you believe God can work through individuals who experience life through a lens that views the world differently than you do?

8. The novel delved into a fictional serial killer from the 1920s. However, there have been serial killers throughout history, some well-known and others far less popular. Which ones have fascinated you in your studies and why? Or if you're not intrigued by true crime, why do you prefer historical cases in fiction but not in real life?

Read on
for a *sneak peek* at
the next book from Jaime Jo Wright

TEMPEST
AT ANNABEL'S
LIGHTHOUSE

AVAILABLE IN THE SPRING OF 2025

Keep up to date with all of Jaime's releases
at JAIMEWRIGHTBOOKS.COM
and on Facebook, Instagram, and X.

ANNABEL

THIS GREAT WATER will be my sepulcher. I will not be the first to find eternal slumber in its depths. I will not be the last. It is a peaceful monster that when awakened becomes a ravenous beast, with icicles as its teeth, fathoms of deep blue that freeze one's soul. A spirit that divides you from the inside and takes you on a journey—a quest.

At least this is what my father taught me. His interpretation of what was taught to him by those who inhabited this place long before the white man's arrival. Waters surrounded by the mountains of the Porcupine. A world of wilderness, of copper and iron. A great sea that claims and devours, and in its moments of serenity, slumbers. It becomes a mirror clearer than the scarred one whose blackness peers through as it reflects my face in the mornings. This mirror made of water shines back the light from the sun and pretends to be gentle and kind.

This is the *Anishinaabewi-gichigami*.

This is where I will die.

REBECCA

SILVERTOWN
UPPER PENINSULA OF MICHIGAN
1874

The violent water raged with waves that swallowed everything in its path. A vicious foe, it drove any living creature on the shore inward to the shelter of the woods. The trees took the brutalizing abuse of the wind that blew its frigid gales and turned otherwise peaceful blue-green water into a chilling, gray killer.

She clawed her way through the forest, rain pelting her face, assaulting the bare skin of her shoulders and neck. Her chemise stuck to her chest, the darkness cloaking her slight form. A branch raked across her face. She wrestled with it, her breath tearing at her lungs. The pain of needing air not sodden with moisture left her gasping and whimpering in the night.

Beneath her feet, the pine needles and ferns warred between spearing and cushioning her. She stumbled, her knee colliding with a rotting log lying on the forest floor. She tried to gulp deep breaths of air but came short of anything adequate to give her calm or comfort. She heard nothing over the sounds of the wind and the waves, but she knew. They were coming.

A glance over her shoulder revealed only darkness, outlined by shadows of trees, boulders and crevices, the lake beyond. The storm had come tonight. Then *they* came. A formidable offense captured her, then released her. For mockery? Sadistic pleasure? She didn't know. Only that they were not finished. They were hunters, storm hunters, those who answered the call of the demons that rose to claim their victims.

And now they were coming for her. Again. Relentless, like the waves of *gichigami*.

A songbird awakened her. That and the warmth she felt as the morning sun filtered through the treetops. The earth beneath her was wet, mud caked between her toes and her fingers. A gentle breeze lifted her hair, once soft like corn silk but now matted with dead leaves and clumps of dirt. She ran her tongue across her lips, tasted blood from a split lip, and winced.

Confusion cluttered her mind. She pushed herself from the ground, her hip sinking into the half-drowned earth. Her left hand braced her, mud oozing between her fingers. Blinking furiously, she tried to clear her thoughts, but her head throbbed with a pulsing ferocity. Looking around, she tried to assess where she was.

She sat up straighter, hugging her torso as if to hide herself from the trees that glowered at her. The sun flickered and twinkled, not unlike a star might, and for a moment she thought perhaps it was the only friendly thing here. She stretched her leg and startled as her toes scraped across something cold and hard. The realization horrified her, and in spite of the pain in her joints and the bruises on her legs, she shoved herself backward with a cry.

The gravestone sunk deeper on the left, the four-sided monument lying flat on the ground and covered with leaves, sticks, undergrowth—the refuse of time.

Bewildered, she moved to her knees, her breath catching as a sharp pain reminded her the injuries included more than just her legs and torso. Leaning toward the gravestone, she reached out and tugged away vines, revealing the etching hidden there. Her fingers traced the engraved name on the stone, *Annabel*, and a date, *1845*.

So many years ago. It was, wasn't it? She fell back onto her heels, sitting before the marker as if kneeling in prayer. Today was . . . well, it was . . . Her breaths came quicker now. She couldn't recall the year. Not the month. Not even yesterday. Nor why she was here now, bruised and battered, alone, and barely clothed.

A quick assessment of her body told her something terrible had happened, something she would never put into words, never tell a soul about. Part of her took solace in that she couldn't remember, but another part found it all the more frightful that she didn't know her own name.

The feel of something trailing the skin of her neck awakened her dulled senses. She cried out, batting at its feathery touch.

Even a spider or a beetle felt ominous to her now. Her hand connected with a chain. It was delicate and yet had somehow remained clasped around her neck. A locket was attached to the chain.

She pulled it away from her neck. The locket was open. Whatever had been inside it was now missing, replaced with dried mud as though it had been pressed into the earth. Looking down, an oval-shaped bruise on her upper chest confirmed her assumption. The locket had been viciously squashed between her and the ground at some point in her not-so-distant past.

Then her breath caught. Sitting there at the base of Annabel's grave, she read her own name as if for the first time: *Rebecca*.

That was all. *Rebecca*.

SHEA RADCLYFFE

SILVERTOWN
U.P. OF MICHIGAN
PRESENT DAY

A brown curl bounced in front of her right eye. Shea Radclyffe blew it away with an irritated puff. Lightning streaked across the sky, illuminating the ocean between her and Canada. Only it wasn't the ocean; it was Lake Superior. Or "Gitche Gumee" as Longfellow called it in his poem. The wipers swept back and forth across her windshield as rain pelted the glass. She squinted through the darkness of the night and the sheets of rain.

More lightning revealed the stretch of highway ahead, bordered to the left by endless miles of forest and to the right by the lake whose waves were . . . well, she certainly couldn't measure them, but she'd read online that they were capable of reaching thirty feet high.

Thunder rolled and thrummed, the lightning acting as a beacon, as the silhouetted lighthouse had been dark since the late 1930s. Another mile and Shea saw the gravel drive. She didn't bother with her indicator but instead turned onto the path, stuffing down the trepidation as she approached the abandoned site. Her car pointed toward the lake with its roiling waves, terrifying in their rage. White-capped waters, blackness beneath, tsunami-like emotion . . . all of this for research and a little self-care?

Shea doubted her sense of reason. But that wasn't new. She'd been doubting it since she left Wisconsin in her rearview window. And Pete.

She pulled the car to a halt and shifted into park. A lone light shone in the window on the arched door of the lighthouse. This wasn't like the ones she'd toured in Oregon on the Pacific Coast. She'd seen pictures of the historic building in Silvertown in the U.P. of Michigan. The lighthouse was perched on a vast cliff overlooking the lake. Cream-colored brick construction that included a two-story house, the tower abutting the north end and rising above the house's triple-flue chimney. At least that was what the pictures indicated. She could hardly see anything now.

Shea grimaced as she pulled a water-resistant parka from the passenger seat behind her and flung it over her head. Exiting the car, her shoes vanished into puddles. She kicked the door shut behind her. She ran through the driving rain onto a wooden platform and reached for the knob of the one-story structure added to the front of the lighthouse in, what, 1892? Was that right? Her mind was a jumble of random facts gathered from her research into the place.

Shea burst into the entry. The smells of woodsmoke and

age met her nostrils, plus a whiff of cinnamon and citrus. The warmth inside warred against her soaking wet blouse.

Two hands reached out and swung her parka off her head. The accumulated water slid down the side, avoiding giving her another shower.

"Welcome to Annabel's Lighthouse!"

Shea ran her hands across her unruly, sopping-wet curls, sweeping them back so she could see clearly.

The man hung her parka on an antique hall tree. Light filtered from the room beyond, which looked to be the kitchen. Small, cozy, with a woodstove casting an orange glow across the room.

He turned to her, a sideways grin mixing with a wince. "Not the greatest weather, but that's life in the U.P."

"Guess I'll get used to it!" Shea managed a laugh, her stomach curling oddly beneath the blue-eyed kindness of the man of obvious Viking descent.

He stuck out a hand. "Holt. Holt Nelson."

The lighthouse's private owner. Yes. She had exchanged emails with him when she'd booked the place as a rental for the next month.

Self-care, Shea, self-care. It was her new mantra. One drilled into her by a few concerned friends. A mantra she'd finally agreed to adopt.

She accepted Holt's handshake. "Shea Radclyffe."

"I know." His eyes twinkled as he held out his other arm to gesture her into the old kitchen. "The bestselling author extraordinaire."

"Hardly." Shea really wasn't that famous. Her novels had only just hit the bestseller list, and while her agent had sent her a dozen roses from her office in New York City, Shea tended to be more pragmatic.

"Either way, glad to have you!" Holt's shoes echoed on the scarred hardwood floor. A teapot sat in the center of a round wooden table with chipped white paint. A yellow ceramic teacup beckoned her. Holt gave it a casual nod. "I figured you'd like something to warm you up. I'd recommend sticking inside tonight and getting your bags out of the car in the morning. This storm isn't going to let up anytime soon."

Shea shot a nervous look over her shoulder toward the doorway she'd just entered. "Is there any reason to be concerned?"

Holt's chuckle was reassuring. "Nah. The lake can't get you at this elevation. Hence the lighthouse being built here."

"Oh. Yes. That makes sense."

Holt wasn't mocking her or even acting as though she was the outsider that she was. "I'll head out and leave you to it. Some of the light switches are dimmers, so just be aware you may need to turn the knob. A bit old-fashioned, but I like 'em."

"Charming," Shea acknowledged.

"I left some things in the icebox for you since I knew the storm was moving in—milk, eggs, bread and butter, that sort of thing. If you need anything, there's the phone." Holt pointed to a yellow rotary phone that hung on the wall. "You won't get a cell signal this far out—at least not much of one."

"Is there Wi-Fi?" Shea needed it to write.

"Yeah. It's slow, though, not gonna lie. It's not like we run fiber optics out here." He waited, and Shea thought she was supposed to laugh or something. So she did.

Holt nodded, apparently happy at her reaction. "It's satellite Wi-Fi, so it'll be sketchy at times. Best we can do in the Porkies."

The Porcupine Mountains. Yes. She was going to need to explore those too.

Holt bid her farewell, but Shea dogged his heels as he retreated into the little alcove and shrugged into his jacket.

"Are you going to be okay out in this storm?" she asked. Not that she wanted to room overnight with a complete *male* stranger.

Holt winked. "Born and raised, Radclyffe. This is nothin'."

His cavalier way of launching himself into the storm gave her an Aquaman sort of vibe, even though he more resembled Thor.

Shea shut the door and flicked the lock—not that she'd need it. She leaned against the door and stared into the kitchen, which led to the darkened rooms beyond.

She was here. At Annabel's Lighthouse. The infamous, haunted lighthouse of Silvertown. Shea glanced at her smartwatch. No text or missed call from Pete.

The silence from the man she'd married was the exclamation point at the end of her decision to come here. A ghostly lighthouse shrouded in mystery and lore was much preferred to a disinterested husband whose most exciting contribution to their marriage of late was changing the oil in her car before she left.

Thirty-five years old and she was finished. Finished being an afterthought.

Shea moved to the kitchen, lifting her eyes to the ceiling. Markings of old coal fires and days gone by scarred it.

Maybe Annabel had once drank tea here.

Maybe Annabel had once mourned the loss of a man who was supposed to love her.

The twisted part was that Annabel was dead. As for Shea? She didn't feel much different inside. Still, a spirit slumbered here that begged to be awakened. She just didn't know if either her spirit or Annabel's was going to be friendly or be something more sinister than what she'd bargained for.

Jaime Jo Wright is the author of twelve novels, including the Christy Award- and Daphne du Maurier Award-winner *The House on Foster Hill*, and the Carol Award-winner *The Reckoning at Gossamer Pond*. She's also a two-time Christy Award finalist, as well as the ECPA bestselling author of *The Vanishing at Castle Moreau* and two *Publishers Weekly* bestselling novellas. Jaime lives in Wisconsin with her family and felines.

Learn more at JaimeWrightBooks.com.

Sign Up for Jaime's Newsletter

Keep up to date with Jaime's latest news on book releases and events by signing up for her email list at the link below.

JaimeWrightBooks.com

Jaime Jo Wright   @JaimeJoWright   @JaimeJoWright

More from Jaime Jo Wright

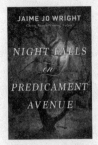

In 1910, Effie joins forces with an English newcomer to discover what lies behind the doors of the abandoned house on Predicament Avenue. In the present day, Norah reluctantly inherits the house turned bed and breakfast, where her first guest, a crime historian and podcaster, is set on uncovering the truth about what haunts this place.

Night Falls on Predicament Avenue

When Greta Mercy's brothers disappear from the Barlowe Theater in 1915, she will do anything to uncover what threat lurks beneath the stage. Decades later, revealing what happened to the boys falls on Kit Boyd, who must determine whether she's willing to pay the price to end the pattern of evil that has marked their hometown for a century.

The Lost Boys of Barlowe Theater

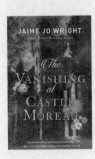

In 1865, orphaned Daisy Francois takes a housemaid position and finds that the eccentric Gothic authoress inside hides a story more harrowing than those in her novels. Centuries later, Cleo Clemmons uncovers an age-old mystery, and the dust of the old castle's curse threatens to rise again, this time leaving no one alive to tell its sordid tale.

The Vanishing at Castle Moreau

BETHANYHOUSE